PEARLS

Chris Johnson

For Sarah —
Hope you like it!

Chris Johnson

ISBN-13: 9780578673042

Cover design by: Jacob Johnson
Author photo by: Hayes Johnson
Library of Congress Control Number: 2018675309
Printed in the United States of America

For Jacob and Kray

Chapter 1

Attorney John Hart ripped open a large courier envelope and dumped out a gilded business card, and a hundred thousand dollars in cash. Ten wrapped bundles of hundreds, ten grand each. The front of the card read "Antonin Vacarro, Jr.," and underneath, "Financial Consultant." There was no contact information. On the back was handwritten, "Gabriella's. Sunday, noon." He poured a cup of coffee, and stirred in raw sugar and half-and-half. He creaked open an ancient set of French doors, and stepped onto the second floor balcony of a renovated nineteenth century townhouse, a condo overlooking Frenchman Street in the Fauberg Marigny area of New Orleans.

A few people shuffled along the sidewalk below. Leaning on the cool iron rail, he watched a drunk tourist sway along, gripping a white go-cup with a big stalk of celery sticking out of it. Down the street, a couple of bar workers with a water hose shouted, spraying garbage cans, sidewalks, each other. A taxi raced by. Soft Reggae music and a girl's laugh echoed from around the corner. Air currents slid by, alternately smelling like bacon and garbage. It was the first weekend of Spring.

Hart took a deep breath, blew it out. For the last few years, he had been working on a couple of wrongful death cases in federal court at Gulfport, Mississippi, an hour and a half from New Orleans on the Gulf Coast. A car had been rear-ended by an eighteen wheeler on Interstate 10. The car's driver was eight months pregnant, and her mother in law was a passenger. They died in a horrible, fiery cataclysm. Their estates were his clients. He had filed the joint cases just under the statute of limitations. After he filed, the defendant's insurance company had made a settlement offer: two million dollars, take it or leave it. He sipped his coffee and thought about that number. Small firm attorneys pass their careers dreaming of such a case, where liability and the money source are clear. But what are three human lives worth?

That was always the question. In the South, after insurance sponsored "tort reform" laws were recently passed, the dollar value of a person's life had been so severely limited that settlement offers of over a million dollars were unheard of, even in death cases. News, entertainment and social media had been saturated with the notion that paying large insurance claims makes everyone's rates go up, regardless of legitimacy. So self interested juries were routinely denying adequate relief to the most obvious negligence victims. Under normal circumstances, he would have happily taken the two million. But nothing had been normal. The whole matter had been a nightmare.

In each case, he was both the Plaintiff and

the Plaintiff's attorney. The pregnant driver had been his wife, the passenger his mother. His whole family was gone. Their car had been literally run over by a semi truck, then caught on fire. They were trapped, but had not immediately died. Several witnesses had cried through deposition testimony of the ladies' screams and pleas for help. Two million dollars was not enough. He had turned it down.

It was a stupid decision, and he knew it now. At the time he believed that taking the money would somehow silence his dead family, that they needed to have a final say. It was another reason lawyers should never represent themselves. Afterward, the insurance defense attorneys had effectively declared war. They had filed a dozen pretrial motions, challenging every aspect of the case, including whether the car manufacturer's poor design caused the fire, and should mitigate their client's exposure. They had hired several expert witnesses and a squad of investigators, had conducted exhaustive written and live deposition discovery, and filed dozens of documents, some of which were thirty pages or more long. All had to be answered in kind, with legal briefs.

They had done their best to demonstrate that the crash was actually his dead wife's fault, that she somehow had caused her car to be run over from behind on an exit off an interstate highway. They tried to prove that the unborn child might not actually be his, and even explored the possibility of exhuming the bodies, which the federal judge had quickly quashed. They painted his wife as unfaithful, his marriage as a sham, his mother as a drunk, and him as a lazy, clueless fool.

He had been forced to counter these outrages with his own expensive experts, responding to all the defense's assertions, no matter how arcane. He even had to hire a doctor to state definitively that the automobile accident was the medical cause of their deaths, a fact that could have easily been conceded by the defense. But they had strictly adhered to the insurance stratagem of never admitting liability, of trying to break the victim's will by attrition. And as usual, it worked. John Hart was exhausted, physically, emotionally, and financially.

The defense had gotten several continuances. When the case had finally been delayed as long as the judge would allow, they dropped a potentially fatal bomb imbedded in their initial pleadings. At the final pretrial hearing this past week, they argued that the case could not be fairly pursued without the presence of the truck driver, their client's employee, who had disappeared from the wreck scene, and from the planet as far as anyone knew. The judge had heard their arguments, and granted their motion. It had been six years since the wreck. She had given John Hart ninety days to find the driver. Otherwise, the case would be dismissed, and he would receive nothing from his family's killers.

In the growing morning clatter of New Orleans, he wondered if he could ever feel good again. He imagined this must be what people suffer when they know they are about to die, and realize they had never accomplished anything. Not just the fear of the end, but the additional weight of so many failed expectations. All the work, all the optimism and excitement that had driven him through the mental exhaustion of law school, all the dreams and plans he once had for an idyllic future were gone, replaced by dread, and depression, and the sickening acceptance that nothing good was ever going to happen again.

Hart was a sole practitioner in his home town of Bay Saint Louis, Mississippi, a small, busy tourist town perched on the edge of the Gulf of Mexico right up the road from New Orleans, and its closest real beach. He had one part time legal assistant. In addition to the overwhelming costs of the wrongful death case, over thirty thousand dollars in expert fees alone, it had taken hundreds of hours to manage. In the long process, he had gone broke. His savings, his house, and his wife's and mother's life insurance were all gone. The handful of criminal defense and family law cases he was handling in court were dwindling, in part since he had spent so much time pursuing this one.

He had been an attorney in a big New Orleans law firm when the wreck happened, but that seemed like another life. He'd gone feral for a couple of years, lost his job and house in New Orleans in fairly brisk order. He'd discarded decorum, and civility, and all the silly niceties he'd been raised to believe and tried to honor. He got drunk and broke things, and got in fights, and won most of them, as far as he knew. But some little corner in his brain had survived the outrage and resentful hatred, and the whiskey, and bothered him just enough to keep him sane. So he eventually went back home and opened up a little office in Bay Saint Louis. He rented a one bedroom house out on Cedar Point, close to the bay. He got back to work.

That was four years ago. He had now maxed out all his credit cards and his business line of credit, had borrowed the limit on the equity in his condo, and was surely headed to bankruptcy. He and his wife bought and renovated the condo as an investment, and it was the final thing of any value he still owned, sort of. The hundred grand, while definitely intriguing, was still probably not enough to save him and his small practice from complete financial insolvency. If he ever got any money he didn't already owe someone, he was going to take it and move away. And if he didn't, which was increasingly likely, he was just going to give up and move anywhere he could make some kind of a normal living. Either way, he was planning on quitting the thankless street level practice of law as soon as he could. In the meantime, the wrongful death case was no longer about the law, or justice, or even money. It was about vengeance.

Come Monday morning, he had to go back to the Mississippi Gulf Coast, back to war, representing anyone who had a little bit of money to help keep his one-lawyer operation open. Finishing the coffee, he went back in. There on his marble breakfast bar lay the card and the money. Vacarro surely knew how to get someone's attention. And Gabriella's. If Vacarro didn't mind meeting in the public eye, he found a good place to do it. The old Bourbon Street restaurant was still at the top of the New Orleans social circuit after a hundred years.

But how had Vacarro known where to have a courier deliver the envelope, or that he was even in town? That was definitely disconcerting. He'd rather not take the invitation, but manners still matter in New Orleans, and he had been invited in the most polite way possible. He had to go meet Antonin Vacarro, if only to return the cash. Any other course would be rude, and possibly fatal. Not that he was afraid to die, because he'd already done it. But seriously, how often do you get invited to Sunday brunch by the boss of the New Orleans Mafia?

Sunday it was warm. By the time he got to Gabriella's, he was sweating in his blazer, a requirement for the venue. He was glad he had decided to ditch the tie. The quiet walk across shady Esplanade and through the east part of the lower French Quarter had turned loud when he cut through from Royal to Bourbon Street. Late Sunday morning in the Quarter might be midnight on Saturday anywhere else in the United States. Some of last night's drunks were still spastically dancing in a few blaring techno clubs that never close, or even shut their wide front doors. Others were just getting out and re-primed, and a new crop were periodically hooting from creaky second and third floor hotel and condo balconies.

Everywhere, people stumbled along the ancient, uneven flagstones, even the sober ones. There was a rusty smell in the air. A couple drinking something red through straws were pushing a double stroller loaded with twin babies down the middle of Bourbon Street. The stroller towed aloft two large helium balloons labeled JUST and MARRIED. A line of well dressed patrons trailed from the front door of Gabriella's down the sidewalk. For a century, New Orleans society, tourists with money, visiting celebrities and dignitaries had patiently waited in line there for a table. Big shots had to wait just like everybody else. As Hart arrived, he crept toward the head of the queue, drawing some disapproving attention. A huge sweaty doorman glared at him, and he showed the business card. The doorman said, "Follow me." He was escorted into the restaurant to a few jeers.

A creature known in New Orleans as "The Raven" observed this from a third floor balcony across Bourbon Street and down a few buildings from Gabriella's. He wore a black felt fedora, and his skinny frame was draped in a black three piece suit, shirt, and tie, black shoes and hose. His skeletal face looked as if bone colored latex had been stretched over it. He wore black sunglasses, and black gloves. The balcony was hung on all sides with huge ferns, and entangled with thick brown vines that grew like wooden hair from somewhere on the roof, cascading over the side of the faded red brick building. The atrium effectively concealed his ghoulish presence from the tourists streaming three levels below.

Inside Gabriella's, it was loud and mercifully cool. It smelled faintly like boiled crab and baked bread. Hart shivered a little from sweat. The high ceiling was covered by hanging, spinning hardwood fans, and the opposing side walls were mirrored, making the relatively small space seem much larger. All tables were occupied, with big groups in the center, and two-seaters along the walls, under the mirrors. An army of waistcoated waiters and food runners scooted around the black and white parquet floor through the tight array of tables, delivering heavy porcelain plates of steamy grilled Snapper, and steaks, and hollandaise and crabmeat covered eggs, and wide bowls of gumbo.

Vacarro was oddly sitting alone at a four top in the center of the room, sort of shout-talking to a group at the next table, who simultaneously burst into nervous laughter. The din of conversation and clanging silverware made communication at any distance impossible. Vacarro waived the attorney over, standing up when he approached. They looked about the same age. "I see you got my card, John," Vacarro said, winking, extending his hand. They shook. Vacarro glanced at his gold watch, and said, "You're exactly on time. I'm impressed." They sat.

Vacarro was drinking what appeared to be a Manhattan. He was dressed in a light blue two piece suit, an open collared white cotton buttoned down shirt, and brown leather loafers with no socks.

John Hart said, "What do I call you?"

"Tony. Call me Tony. What are you drinking?"

"Nothing this time of day. I can't stay. I just didn't want to be rude."

"Well if you *were* drinking, what would it be?"

"Light beer."

14

Vacarro waived a finger at his waiter, made the order. He said, "You got the rest of the package, I assume?"

"I did, but I'm not here to take the money. You should have somebody swing back by and pick it up. It makes me nervous."

"An attorney nervous around money? That's kind of out of character isn't it? Besides, I understand you can use it right now." He smiled. John Hart didn't.

John said, "I guess I should be flattered, but really, how the hell would a person like you know anything about me? In fact, how did you know where to find me?"

Vacarro leaned a little closer and said, "Look, I don't know any details. I need an attorney over on the coast, and it was suggested to me by a mutual friend that I should meet with you. I heard you might be having some money issues, but no details. Sorry if that was offensive."

The attorney looked around the restaurant, and back at Vacarro. He said, "Mr. Vacarro, I'm not trying to be offensive either, but to be honest, I can't imagine that we have any mutual friends. You must have me confused with someone else. Obviously, I know who you are, or who people say you are. That's why I'm here to tell you personally that I'm returning your money. I just didn't want to be rude. Whether I need it or not is irrelevant. I run a small, clean law practice. I'd appreciate it if you would have someone come by and pick it up right away."

Vacarro snorted. He said, "I'll assure you, you *don't* know who I am. Most people don't know anything about the actual me. I'm the boss of an investment firm, not anything illegal. The New Orleans Mafia doesn't even exist anymore, so whatever you've seen or heard is wrong. What passes for TV news these days is just a bunch of bathroom rumors and gossip."

John said, "That, we can certainly agree on. You ever see any good news about attorneys on TV? Anyway, we don't know each other, and I would rather just keep it that way." He started to get up.

"Wait," said Vacarro. "Before you leave, let me say something. I really do need your help, and I'm obviously willing to pay for it." He leaned in and said, "And I swear, no matter what happened in the past, there is no longer any organization called the Bardino Crime Family, or the New Orleans Mafia, or whatever. That's all history."

John slowly held up both hands, said, "Mr. Vacarro, that seems..."

"Call me Tony," interjected Vacarro, "let me finish."

"I can't, Tony. I don't want to know about..."

"Please," said Vacarro, "just hear me out. You can keep the money either way. Call it a consulting fee."

The attorney stared at him, looked around, took a long breath. He picked up his beer, took a drink.

Vacarro said, "Good. Very simply, that old organization, the Bardino family, The New Orleans Mafia, or whatever was left of it, divested itself of all... tainted business connections after certain legal events a while back."

"Of course, I heard about all that."

"I bet you did. There was quite a bit of coverage. Some of it was even true."

John nodded, a faint tingle starting at the base of his neck.

Vacarro said, "You've had a lot of experience in criminal defense cases, haven't you?"

"I handle them all the time, along with injury cases, divorces, wills, estates, whatever I can eke out a living with. But I started out as a public defender. I have handled hundreds of felonies, I would guess."

"Jesus. You've tried that many?"

"No. You try some of them, but the vast majority are pleas."

"Because you don't want to have to deal with that many trials?"

"Because most of them are guilty."

"Interesting. How can you be sure which ones are guilty, and which ones are innocent?"

"Most of them, you can't be sure. You look at the evidence, and tell the clients what their options are. They decide what to do."

Vacarro said, "You get to see all their evidence, right? But you still don't know for sure?"

"A lot of the time, the evidence is irrefutable. But sometimes, nothing's perfectly clear before trial."

"Why is that?"

Hart sighed. He said, "Listen, on TV crime shows, you have state of the art forensics, and a concerned squad of detectives and lab technicians working overtime, trying to find the bad guy, which they eventually do. The evidence is clear, and the good guys always win. But in real life, some pissed off, underpaid cops roll up on, say, the scene of a shooting. They interview anyone who will talk to them, which is often nobody. Detectives show up and gather shell casings and a few samples of whatever evidence might be usable, and then everybody heads off to the next crime scene. Eventually, somebody gets arrested, and indicted. The prosecution may have some usable forensics, maybe not. A lot of defendants get charged based on circumstances, and maybe eyewitness or confidential informant statements which they, of course, deny. Basically, the trial is a lying contest among the witnesses, and the jury decides who to believe, and votes accordingly."

"How can you ever know if your client is telling you the truth?"

"You can't. Why does that matter?"

"Well, it seems like it should. To you, at least."

Hart nodded, looked around the restaurant. He said, "See these people? Most of them have money, went to private schools, then college, then got a good job. Maybe along the line they got divorced, but besides that, they've never been in any kind of legal trouble. So their principles and character have never been tested."

"Principles and character?"

"Principles and character. The kinds of things that preachers and politicians always talk about. Morals or whatever." The waiter dropped off another round. "See Tony, most of these people have good intentions to some degree, and maintain them all through their lives. They go to church, give some money to the Salvation Army ringer at Christmas, and show up at each other's weddings, and eventually their funerals. But all along, they are never really tested. Their principles aren't ever challenged, so they stay intact. Character-wise, they might have done some illegal things in college, or on vacation, but they never got caught. And though they may have committed a few crimes, they have never been charged with one.

"Now, you take that same person, stick him in a case where someone is accusing him or her of a felony, and they are faced with the possibility of going to prison. All of a sudden, their 'principles' go out the window. Maybe they did it, maybe not. If they did it, they've justified it in their minds somehow. So even if they aren't innocent, it was excusable, because they have convinced themselves they had no choice, or it's somebody else's fault they did what they did. If they didn't do it, they didn't. But either way, self interest kicks in, and they will throw the first person they can under the bus, as the saying goes. Felony defendants are always willing to implicate their friends, or neighbors, or anybody else, to get the attention and blame off themselves."

Vacarro said, "So people's principles, or character, or morals, mean nothing under pressure."

"Nothing. You can't believe a damn thing a person charged with a felony says. For the sake of argument, say that five percent of all the people indicted for felonies are stone cold innocent. Didn't do it, weren't there, don't know who did it, or anything about the case at all. You know what those people tell their attorneys?"

"What?"

"Well, they're actually innocent, so they say, 'I'm innocent.' What else *would* they say? Now, the other ninety-five percent are either guilty of what they were indicted for, or of something close to it. You know what *they* tell their attorneys?"

"'I'm innocent'?"

"That's right. And they are just as earnest,

and scared, and believable as the innocent ones. You know how you can tell the difference?"

"How?"

"You can't. That's why I don't waste my time trying to practice psychology, and concentrate on practicing law. My concern is due process, not so-called principles, or morals, which are just things people say. I'm only interested in whether the prosecutor can prove his case beyond a reasonable doubt to a jury."

"That sounds like *you* have no principles."

"Maybe. That's what people who don't do what I do, or see what I see, or hear what I hear always say. They base their opinions on the crap about lawyers they see on TV." He took a sip of beer. "But maybe I have the greatest principles, because I am required to. I swore an oath to protect my clients, good or bad. That's my job. Whether or not my clients are actually guilty of anything is not my decision or my responsibility, and my personal opinion is irrelevant. And believe me, if somebody I'm representing gets convicted in a criminal case, they stay convicted, because I've done my job correctly."

Vacarro said, "Interesting. So attorneys can have their own personal principles, or morals, but are relieved by their professional oaths from abiding by them. That sounds like a lawyer's argument."

"Not at all. It would be immoral, or more precisely, unethical, to violate my oath. I may occasionally personally disagree with what my duty requires, but I have to do it anyway. It's why most non-attorneys can never understand what we do. You have to accept that legal and personal opinions sometimes diverge, and still do your job." He looked around again, relieved that none of the other patrons were paying attention to their table. He said, "Now that we've covered legal philosophy, why don't you tell me why we're here?"

"Interesting." Vacarro leaned in and said, "Apparently, a guy I met in Bay Saint Louis last weekend is missing, and I'm the last one he was seen with. A Bay detective named LaRue called me."

"I know LaRue. What did you tell him?"

"That I didn't know anything about it, which is the truth. If this guy turns up dead, I guess they are going to want to blame me for it."

"Why would the guy turn up dead?"

"Well, he's missing, so he either got lost, or took a powder, or he's dead. That's how these things normally work, right?"

"It's important not to jump to conclusions in any case. Let's say he turns up dead, and you were the last one to see him, is there anything that would implicate you?"

"Yes, my name. The whole Mafia thing."

Hart closed his eyes, rubbed them with both hands. He thought of a woman he had passed a little while ago, walking down the sidewalk on Bourbon Street, spray painted from head to toe, clothes and all, like a red, white, and blue barber pole. He thought about his empty business account, and chasing down his few clients for tiny payments. He downed the rest of his beer, and waived at the waiter. He thought about the ridiculous concept of principles. He had discovered in the most brutal fashion that high minded standards had never done a damn thing to protect good people from evil. Without looking at Vacarro, he said, "OK, I suppose we're consulting. So tell me about this meeting."

At five o'clock, The Raven adjusted his black fedora and removed his sunglasses. A light rain had begun, and the tourists below were darting between the protection of balconies and hotel porticoes. Out of Gabriella's emerged his great-nephew Antonin Vacarro and the mark. The Raven's unblinking dark eyes peered through binoculars. His nephew started to walk away. As if in afterthought, he turned back and formed the "peace" sign, like a hippie, holding it up toward no one particularly.

The Raven noiselessly skittered off the balcony, emerging from an alley half a block away on Royal Street. He deployed a wide black umbrella, which mostly hid his fearsome countenance. Striding a block to Chartres Street, he made an end run on most of the eastern French Quarter foot traffic. He crept across Esplanade

Avenue, a short distance from the Mississippi River, and headed into the Marigny. Two blocks away, the wide river roiled past the teeming French Market, held out of it by levees.

A young Creole man, no more than seventeen, was sitting on a bench under an awning in front of a catfish restaurant on Frenchman Street, looking at a weekly entertainment newspaper. He slid a picture out of his shirt pocket, looked at it, looked around, and went back to reading. The picture was of John Hart. The young man had been hired to kill the man in the picture. His homeless life had been interrupted when a stranger gave him five hundred dollars, a loaded .32 revolver, and the picture. He was instructed that the man in the picture would be walking down Frenchman sometime on Sunday afternoon, maybe even Sunday night, headed back to his condo. If he killed the man, and managed to get away, he would receive ten thousand dollars cash, and a ticket out of town. If he got caught, and told the police anything, he would be killed in jail.

The Raven glided down the sidewalk. Not breaking stride, he flashed a wad of cash at the young man and waived for him to follow. They entered a small brick courtyard around the corner. The Raven stopped, his umbrella blocking an overhead security camera, and waived the young man toward a closed door.

As he passed, The Raven pulled out a

small pistol with a silencer, and shot the kid in the back of his head. He fell, and The Raven leaned over and popped two more muffled shots into his head, and quietly laid the gun beside the body. Picking up the newspaper and the picture, he re-emerged on Frenchman, strolling casually toward the Quarter, reading the folded newspaper under his umbrella.

On the way back to his condo, John Hart had stopped in a dark joint to let the rain pass. He slouched in a rickety cane-backed stool, his elbows cooled by the old hammered copper bar top. The place had featured live blues music on Bourbon Street since before World War II. He'd had enough beer for a Sunday afternoon, and ordered a soda. A blues guitarist plucked away in the front corner. There were maybe five people in the whole place, counting the guitar player. Hart stared at himself in the mirror behind the bar. How had he gotten here? Broke, lonely. Well, maybe the broke part was temporarily over, since there was a hundred grand back at the condo, if he wanted it. If he was willing to take on representing the boss of the New Orleans Mafia.

He thought about the last few years. He had been suicidal, he guessed, at times. Maybe. He had been down a long dark hall in his head, one that he had not known existed prior to the, what? Disaster? Calamity? What is the correct term for it? Is there one?

He remembered the exact moment he first saw his wife. He had been one of several appointed felony public defenders in Gulfport, Mississippi for his first two years of practice. In those days public defenders and Assistant District Attorneys gathered at a dank little downtown bar every Friday, telling war stories and trading barbs, mostly friendly. Attorneys who made any real money drank at better places.

At one of these gatherings appeared a long, lean, auburn haired stranger in a bone colored, skirted suit. She marched to the bar, squeezed into a standing space next to his barstool, and ordered a dry vodka martini with olives. She pulled a compact out of her small leather clutch, and mirror-faced her lipstick. He realized he was staring at her at the same time she did. The bartender placed her drink in front of her. She looked over the compact at him, snapped it closed, and said, "Mister, didn't your mother teach you not to stare? That just cost you one martini. Pay the man." She grabbed the drink, and strutted across the dim room to an open booth. He was stricken.

Even half drunk, it physically hurt to remember. The blues player took a break, and sauntered up to the bar, seating himself two stools down, towards the back. A barely audible recording looped Jelly Roll Morton overhead, which had been playing the whole time. People streamed by on the sidewalk, headed both directions, like they all had something important to do. One of them howled, and another way down the street answered, like a whiskey mating call.

Hart realized his head was in his hands, and sat upright. The only other couple of patrons left. He turned to the guitar player, said, "That was good playing, mister. What's your name?"

"Robert Johnson," he said, standing up, offering his hand.

Hart said, "Seriously? Like the blues man who sold his soul to the devil?"

Johnson chuckled, said, "Yeah, just like him. I guess my mother didn't know that story." He sat back down, and studied John Hart in the mirror for a few seconds. He said, "I don't mean to be stirring around in your business, mister, but you look like your dog just died."

Hart thought about that, smiled crookedly. "Nothing that simple," he said. "But thanks for asking. Let me buy you a drink."

"I don't drink," said Johnson, "and I got to go back on, anyway."

"No drinking? Isn't that kind of odd for a blues player?"

"Yeah, well, there are better ways to deal with your troubles, my friend."

John Hart grunted. He said, "Not around here, there aren't. Maybe you're in the wrong business."

Robert Johnson chuckled. He said,

"Maybe so, my friend, maybe we all are. All I know is, I used to drink 'til I passed out, and every time I woke up, I still had the same problems, plus a hangover. Drinking doesn't help, it just helps you hide. At some point, you just have to stop running, and turn around and fight." Robert Johnson got up, patted Hart on the shoulder, and walked back to the small stage. He swung his guitar strap around his neck, and said to the bartender, "Hey Jack, how about giving Jelly Roll a rest?" He started playing Robert Johnson's "Cross Road Blues."

Hart took a sip of his soda. He had followed her to that booth that afternoon. In eight months, they were married. Not long after, he had finished a couple of years as a public defender, and felt that he had his courtroom bona fides. So he contacted Signago and Sims, the big New Orleans firm who had offered him a job out of law school, to see if it was still good. It was. In terms of age and influence, the firm was the apex of legal prestige in the deep South. With his job came membership in a country club, invitations to join Mardi Gras Krewes, and eventual entry into the quirky upper social circles in New Orleans.

When they all died, he had just made full partner. Ten years of grinding out insurance defense trials, depositions upon depositions, endless motion hearings, stroking the right egos up the chain in the firm, supporting the right judicial and political candidates. With his promotion came his own group of young trial attorneys, a good book of business, the clerical and paralegal staff to support it, and profit sharing. He had incentives to bring in new business that could up his base pay considerably, and increase his bonuses by multiples. He had finally started producing to his and his wife's expectations, and the fading nightmare of law school and abiding poverty seemed like it was all worth it.

Then they found out she was pregnant. At first he had been, to be honest with himself, pissed off. He had been accumulating vacation time for several years, which was maxed out. He had never been out of the South, had never had time. He had been looking forward to a long trip to Europe, or some remote island. Then, boom. *You're going to be a daddy, mister, and things are about to be different.*

Now, he was ashamed of himself. He really had been, what? Angry, upset with her, disappointed? Selfish beyond belief? His mom had been so incredibly happy, had treated him like he'd just achieved some great feat. She was a widow living in Bay Saint Louis, where he grew up. She and their priest went off like Roman candles, and he was immediately ashamed about his initial selfishness. They said that God had willed the whole thing, that He had been paying attention to all of Lawyer Johnny Hart's hard work, devotion to family, and church-going piety, and this was the payoff.

He damn sure hadn't always been in the favor of God, and his mother, and The Church. He had quit his first tour of college and moved to Austin, Texas, quickly settling into the life of a bartender. He had spent five years out there, working, partying, playing guitar, writing a few songs, dreaming of being a rock star. Bartending around the trendy Austin music scene, he made enough money to get by, and even occasionally met some of the real rock stars who frequently popped in and out of the clubs. Those days were now idyllic. He wasn't expected to accomplish anything, and he didn't.

His father, who he barely remembered, had died when he was very young. His previous military service had accorded him an impressive funeral in the Bay Saint Louis City Cemetery. John Hart's primary memory of his father was the startling grave side military rifle salute. There was a little story about him in the small local newspaper, which his mother had framed. His sister was two years older, his only sibling. She had been valedictorian of the tiny Catholic girl's school in Bay Saint Louis. She was the Golden Child, had gotten a scholarship to Yale, did everything perfectly. In college, she studied international diplomacy, and while he was partying in Texas, she was doing a tour in the Peace Corps, well on her way to being the first female president.

One day, when he was lounging around Lake Travis outside Austin, he found out she had died in a helicopter crash. Just like that. Then he was the only child, and his mother was alone back in Bay Saint Louis, and she needed him. So he cut his hair, and went back home. From then on, he had done practical things - school, work, church, family. According to his mom and the priest, God himself had actually intervened to cause his wife to become pregnant.

But God was not present that day on Interstate 10, in Gulfport. Hart's wife, mother, and coming child, whose gender they had decided to discover at birth, were not in a state of grace. They were roasted in the hell of a car crash, underneath a big truck. He had been shocked out of a dream world where he had walked the path of the saved, and the principled. He had buried the roasted remnants of his small family, and had come to know the rotten side of his character. He had discovered the same low sentiments in new characters all around him. He had left one dream, an idyllic, paint-by-numbers scripted one, an easy passage along a well lighted trail to paradise, and entered a nightmare where every trail looped to the same dark realization that joy itself was a cruel lie, and the only possible end was rot and decay.

The rain stopped, and the light outside started dimming a little. He paid his tab. Before he strolled out of the darkness of the bar, into the smelly late afternoon of Bourbon Street, Robert Johnson chin nodded his way. Hart pointed back. He eventually crossed Esplanade. On Frenchman, he walked right by the dead Creole kid, lying a few feet out of sight.

Back home, he dug the envelope out of the bottom of his bedroom closet, and took out the money. He stared at it, and thought about the day, and what the money represented. He had told Vacarro he needed a little time to think about taking him on as a client. There had been no charges filed yet, but there would be. Mafia bosses don't hire strange lawyers for no reason. A man had gone missing for over a week. There would be charges.

What should he do? His life had been ruined. He was slowly descending into insolvency, and could only expect more of the same. The past could not be changed, but what about the future? Maybe this is it, he thought. Maybe everyone has a crossroads moment when all they want or need, and all they used to believe, and everything they still have head inevitably toward confluence, and collision. Whether the real Robert Johnson had made his bargain with the devil was a question that men had debated for decades. But one thing was undebatable: John Hart was standing at his own crossroads, and the devil had just offered him a deal.

Chapter 2

Sixty miles northeast of the French Quarter, Bay Saint Louis, Mississippi sits on one of the few high spots along the edge of the Gulf of Mexico. In between the two cities, the Pearl River snakes into the gulf, and marks the coastal boundary between Mississippi and Louisiana. Over time, the Pearl River and its tangle of swamps and sweaty brackish marshes produced a species of amphibious human beings owing its genetics to some combination of the French, Spanish, Anglo, African, Acadian, Native American, and Pirate bloodlines that traversed and occupied its country, and its survival to consumption of alligators, sharks, turtles, snakes, catfish, ducks, dove, turkeys, quail, oysters, a kaleidoscope of saltwater fish, and any other edible creature unlucky enough to draw its hungry attention, and come within range of its guns, arrows, traps, lines, knives, or sheer barehanded determination. From this species emerged a singular entity and adopted resident of Bay Saint Louis known about town as "Captain Fleming."

One of his many odd characteristics was the utter lack of any reliable indicator of age. He may have been fifty years old when Hurricane Katrina flushed him out of the lower Pearl River delta, but he may have been seventy. He had long since quit aging, having attained a living mummified state, the result of saltwater, sunlight, and rum. He knew two languages: English, and some type of rummy Captainese that he had developed on his own, a combination of English, French, cussing, grunts, gestures, threats, and scowls. He looked liked a skinny, tanned leather Santa Claus in a fishing shirt and shorts, flip-flops, and a wide brimmed straw hat that was as well weathered as him.

He had a little rented shack in the back of town, across the tracks from the Depot District. He had no job, or car, or any official way to identify himself, but he did have an old three wheeled gas powered golf cart, which he used to ride each morning from his shady lair to the beach, to look for treasures. There at dawn, under Easter egg colored skies, he patrolled. For hours he would walk, looking for little pieces of dried cypress, sanded and buffeted by the beach and wind into ornamental size, which he later would drill and string, along with seashells he found, into hanging ornamental mobiles, which he sold to tourists.

Every weekend in the Bay was a street festival, official or not, with bands, sidewalk retail booths, and roving hordes of tipsy tourists. And every other Saturday or so, Captain Fleming appeared in town and sold his hand made ornaments, and spent the money getting drunk. "They ain't killed me yet!," he always declared, as he slurped down rum all day.

Before he got too drunk, he'd amble

around to a few bars, giving hurricanes a good cussing, then steering into palaver about long lining and tuna fishing, and shrimp trawling, and the gawddam oil business, and oyster dredging, and blue crabs, and all the ways a good man willing to work could make a living off the gulf, if he's willing to get off his ass and work, and how he always was, and did. Somebody would inevitably call him an old pirate, which would set him off cussing the sorry pirates that had sailed and skulked and hid around from here to New Orleans for three hundred years, making a living off of stealing other people's honest work, and still do. He hated them all, he always said, from back when the sorry bastards used big wooden skiffs to sneak up on merchant sailing ships headed to New Orleans, to the bushwhacker Jean Lafitte himself, to the candy-assed fish pirates still running around out there today, robbing a man's traps and lines, and sometimes his fishing boats and crews.

Before he inevitably got cut off and ejected, Captain Fleming would entertain his temporary audience by a roving performance of an ongoing melodrama of his devise, which, though not officially named, could properly be called The Last Great Drunk. In this tragedy, he was alternately the hero of all manner of hellfire adventures and heroics, or of sweet loves lost, or the capturing of all types of violent, delicious sea creatures, or of when he was a young man,

and the conquering of battalions of torrid har-
lots in dangerous ports. He had an impressive
number of tattoos, most of them inscrutable,
and stories attached to each, which changed
over time. He was happy to perform The Last
Great Drunk for rum, and was even sought out,
mostly by tourists. But sought or not, when he
was on the rum, he performed for anyone not
nimble enough to disengage his attention, or too
polite to ignore him out of respect for his age.
Beachfront bar managers would tolerate him for
a little while, then herd him out the door to the
next place.

The Captain would eventually turn mor-
ose. For a few moments, the tapestry of his ancient memories, real or not, would overcome
him as he gurgled down a final glass of rum or
two, secret regrets sometimes filling the deep
crevasses of his face with tears. He would quit
talking altogether, and stare at the floor, or way
out into the gulf, and ruminate. But soon he
would rally, now unfriendly, announcing a general violent disdain for everybody in the world,
and especially in his immediate vicinity, which
would have undoubtedly meant, at one time in
his life, danger.

The transition was always abrupt, and
usually triggered by some perceived slight, either by Fate, or the government, or some gawking tourist who didn't realize just how important of a drunk he really was around this town,

dammit. This final phase of The Last Great Drunk was the signal for bartenders citywide to initiate ejection, which involved coaxing him toward the door, enduring invocations of multiple ancestral curses, and gale force cussings in full rum Captainese.

These matters were usually perfunctory. Somewhere in his addled mind he always understood the value of the right of re-entry, and had never, as far as anyone could remember, actually gotten violent or tried to hurt anyone. On the rare occasions he wouldn't leave, or couldn't make it outside himself, the cops were called, but only out of respect for the Captain's safety. They never took him in, and nobody on the force, or at the jail, or down at city court wanted to unravel the potential nightmare of fooling with him, unidentifiable and obviously broke and harmless as he was. So they would get him calmed down, and he would sleep it off in the back seat of a patrol car, or on his golf cart.

The Captain's drinking schedule was unfixed, but when he did make an appearance downtown, it was always on a Saturday afternoon. So when he shuffled into a rustic restaurant and bar by the city marina named Canecutter's at ten o'clock on a Friday morning, blathering about a human head, it wasn't because of rum. The bartender was getting set up for lunch, and the handful of wait staff didn't have time to deal with him, so nobody listened. The Captain, not being sure what to do in a bar that time of day, or week, stuck with the familiar, grabbed a seat at the bar, and started in on the rum.

John Hart's office was in an upper corner of a two story bank building that had stood on the lofty corner of Main Street and Beach Boulevard in Bay Saint Louis since 1900, overlooking the Saint Louis Bay and the Gulf of Mexico. It was a brick and concrete sentinel that had resisted many brutal hurricanes. In an era where old bank buildings had long since given way to wrecking balls or condo developers, it still housed a bank branch, and had become a symbol of the city's stubbornly polite determination. Through the last century, several attorneys and accountants had maintained offices upstairs; these days, only Hart and his ornery part time assistant conducted business there.

Entering from the Main Street side, Hart plodded up the old stairs. Passing down the heart pine hallway, he entered his office, which faced the gulf. He leaned his creaking office chair back, feet on his desk, looking out over the water. Today had been one of those reminders of the drastic difference between how he once imagined his life as an attorney would be, and how it had all turned out. All day, he had been in a divorce hearing, a mundane affair that had trundled through the normal accusations, threats and embarrassments, and predictable stories of rudeness, and insults, and rampant credit card spending.

After a long lunch break, the trial had resumed with his client's estranged wife telling about how his client had spent years being threatening and ugly to her and the teenagers, and increasingly inattentive to normal husbandly marital duties. That is, until Memorial Day weekend last year, when she decided, at their friend's fish camp down in Delacroix, to let him have a go at it with her old high school best friend, who was in from Baton Rouge for the holiday. "I thought it would, you know, spice things up some," she said from the witness stand. This caused the reclining judge, in post lunch meditation, to involuntarily snort, and nearly dethrone herself, knocking over her go-cup of half and half tea. Luckily, it had a tight lid on it.

The witness' attorney, who had obviously never before heard this part of her story, said, "Whoa! I mean, Miss Herold, are you sure you don't want to rephrase that? Haven't you stated to this court, and in your *sworn* pleadings, that your legal basis for seeking a divorce is your husband's *adultery*?" John Hart, who had never heard this before either, was studying his client, who looked proud.

"He did it, alright," she said, "He committed adultery. Several times in that one weekend. I saw him." As echos of her revelations bounced around inside the big old courtroom, her attorney quietly accepted their fatal case implications. He decided not to invite further damage, tendered the witness, and took his seat with affected dignity.

Hart rose and after a savory pause, said, "Mrs. Herold, you just testified that your husband had permission to have sex outside your marriage, is that correct?"

"Yes it is."

"You gave him permission. In fact, it was your idea."

"Yes, you heard me. That's what I said."

Hart shot a glance at the opposing counsel, who put his hand on his face.

"So your legal claim that he committed adultery is specious, isn't it?"

"Objection!," said her attorney, struggling up. "Judge, she can't be expected to know what 'specious' means."

The witness said, "Sit down, you old fool. I do know what 'specious' means. Maybe it was specious." Pointing at Hart's smirking client, she said, "But I didn't give him permission to like it that much. And besides, there was some other adultery, too, that I didn't tell you about before, and the marriage ought to be over without us having to go through all this here in court. We shouldn't have to sit up here and tell about our personal lives, and be embarrassed like this in front of strangers." Turning to the judge, she said, "Ma'am, why can't we just say we're divorced, and you sign it?"

The judge said, "Actually, young lady, you both can agree at any time on an Irreconcilable Differences divorce, which I am sure your attorney has explained."

John Hart said, "We will be happy to stipulate to the no fault basis, judge, and focus strictly on the equitable distribution of assets, since we now know that the fault basis claim has no merit."

Her attorney, wary of any new courtroom revelations, but seeing an obvious chance to save his client some face, said, "Judge, if Mr. Hart is through, I believe I am entitled to redirect?"

The judge said, "Aren't we going to have a stipulation to no fault? What is the point?"

The attorney said, "We probably will, judge. I have to confer with my client first, in private. Meanwhile, for purposes of completing the record, I have a single question on redirect." Turning to his client, he said, "Mrs. Herold, you just testified that there was more adultery. Why don't you tell the judge what you mean?"

"Well," she said, "after all that business at the fish camp, for a few months, all he wanted to talk about was him and her doing it. Even when we were, you know, *alone*, and, you know... doing it ourselves, that's all he could talk about. And I just got sick of it. Look at him right now. He's happy about it. Look at him grinning."

"Just move along, finish answering the

question," said the judge.

She continued, "So, right before I hired you, and we filed this case, I decided, well, 'I know how to fix his wagon.' I checked around and found *his* old best friend from high school. He lives right down there in Lakeshore, and has a cabinet shop. He ain't bad looking, either."

Hart's client stopped grinning and sat up in his seat, staring.

"Anyway, I went down there on a Friday afternoon, around closing time, like I was looking for new cabinets. I stayed in there after they closed, him showing me his different types of doors and handles, and whatnot, until everybody else was gone. And, well, more adultery got committed, right there in the shop. Twice."

Hart's client launched over the table like a bullfrog and charged the witness stand. He tackled his wife, and was trying to throttle her when the Bailiff got a clear opening and whopped him over the head with an old hickory police stick he had bought a couple of years back at a flea market up in Picayune. So that ended the trial for the day. They had stitched up his client at the emergency room, then took him to jail. He had a list of criminal charges now, including aggravated assault, if the D.A. didn't decide to bump it up to attempted murder. He would have to stay in jail until he could make bond, which would be no time soon, so he would lose his job. Hart couldn't represent him on the criminal charges, even if the client could afford it, because he had been a witness. Of course, there would be no more payments on the divorce case, which would now effectively go into limbo.

He thought about college. When he had gotten accepted to Ole Miss Law School all those years ago, it was like getting an invitation to the good life. It really made his mother proud, maybe for the first time. He went there filled with history and ambition, ready to grapple with great legal concepts and philosophies, and contribute to the venerable legacy of American law. And he was a natural litigator: convincing, commanding, sometimes even funny. It was a struggle, financially and mentally, but he made it. He graduated well enough, and received several offers, including a rare bid from Signago and Sims, which was one of the best available legal jobs in the South. They had been in New Orleans since the 1880's, representing shippers and oil refiners, and the great two headed beast of commerce, banking and insurance. They had offices all over the coastal United States, and one in London. For John Hart, it was a second invitation to the good life.

But he had turned them down. He wanted to live on the Gulf, in Bay Saint Louis, where he grew up. Mostly, he wanted to get in courtrooms and try cases, which was the only thing that really appealed to him about being an attorney.

At the big firm, he would have been in the litigation division, but he would first have to spend several years grinding out discovery and writing motion briefs before he would be allowed on his own in court. It's just the way things work in the hive of a huge, old law firm.

So he set up a small office over in Gulfport, the biggest city on Mississippi's short span of coast, a half hour east of Bay Saint Louis. He got on the rotating public defender list and took appointed felony cases by the box load from the senior judge in the circuit. The rest of his time he filled with representing anyone who could help him pay the rent. Compared to his other options, it was at least a fifty percent pay cut, probably more. But he figured Signago and Sims had been around for almost a hundred and fifty years, so they would still be around in a couple more. Maybe their offer would still be good then.

He had rented a small apartment in Bay Saint Louis, got a cheap truck and a good used bay boat, with low gunnels, a center console, and a big, fast outboard. He drove along the beach to work in Gulfport every day. During the week, he defended car thieves, burglars, and drug dealers, whoever rotated up on his list. He was co-counsel on a couple of murder cases. In his private practice, he tried divorces, and contract disputes, and misdemeanors. On Saturdays, he ran out in his boat to Cat and Ship Islands, and the Chandeleur chain, and Freemason Island, and the vast coastal grassy marshes along the Mississippi and Louisiana coasts, sometimes with friends, sometimes alone. He caught speckled trout, Redfish, flounder, and every once in a while, a big old Blackfish. On Sundays, he took his mom to Ruby's, a seafood place by the water across the bay. Long before interstate highways, it had been a roadhouse on U.S. Highway 90, the only practical route from New Orleans to the Coast. It had evolved into a trend-proof steak and seafood joint, where his mom always got the broiled stuffed flounder with crab-meat Hollandaise.

Gazing at Cat Island, way out on the horizon, he slowly shook his head. That was at the tail end of the good days of practicing law, back before the internet made everybody think they were lawyers. He chuckled. People have always thought they understood how courts work, and what attorneys do, from watching TV, or movies, where abundant evidence always leads to a clear answer. Sometimes a witness leaps up and admits he or she's guilty, or the real culprit has an attack of conscience, and turns himself in, and the good guy gets out of jail. On TV, there's always a clear right and wrong, good and evil.

In real life, almost none of that happens, because human beings are consummate liars. Sometimes, there is a clear right and wrong, but usually not. Most people would never try to explain engineering to an engineer, or plumbing to a plumber, but they always try to explain law practice to lawyers, based on some ridiculous oversimplification they saw on TV, or read on the internet, or heard on social media. As he had said many times, it's like focusing on one piece of a puzzle, and thinking you see the whole puzzle. Or like walking down to the beach, seeing the surface of the water, and thinking you understand the Gulf of Mexico.

Many more people were representing themselves, mimicking their favorite fictional legal characters in open court, making speeches, flouting the rules of evidence and procedure, and the law. Trial judges for the most part showed them bemused patience. Work for small firm lawyers had dropped off significantly. Making a living as a traditional sole practitioner had gotten much, much harder as a result of the internet.

Hart preferred criminal defense cases to any others. For one thing, the matter is usually either settled or tried within a reasonable amount of time. For another, the clients usually instinctively understood the need to pay the attorney. The problem was, most people charged with serious crimes also qualify for public defenders, who were no longer appointed by judges, but supplied by the elected Public Defender. Given the choice between paying a private attorney or paying a Bail Bondsman and getting a free attorney, most chose the latter. It was an economic fact that kept the vast majority of felony criminal cases outside the practical reach of private practice.

He had a few injury cases. He would accept them if the injury was serious enough, and there was clear liability, and an adequate money source. Those were his rules. But even stridently following his rules, injury cases often take years, because insurance companies prefer defaming injured people to paying any significant money to cover their insured clients' screw-ups. This is especially true in big cases where the negligence is obvious, because their only effective defense is trying to starve out the injured person, and drive down the settlement amount. It made him sick to think he had defended liability insurance during his time in New Orleans. Then there were his divorce cases. They were the worst kind, simply because of the nature of the legal conflict. Divorce may be the only time a regular person comes in contact with the legal system, and under the most adverse of circumstances, the breakup of a marriage. John Hart had discovered the hard way that most people who claim to hate lawyers do so because of divorces. It was always the same thing: legal pleadings, the papers filed in a lawsuit. Divorce lawyers have to write their client's versions of what happened to the marriage in those pleadings. Inevitably, the estranged spouse considers the pleadings to be a personal attack by the attorney who wrote them. They imagine the attorney to be an evil enemy whose mission is to destroy their lives and take all their money. In reality, that attorney probably has no actual knowledge or opinion of the other person whatsoever, and could have been the attorney for either party. They are just happy to have a paying client.

John Hart mulled all this. When he was a law student, and everybody stilled called him "Johnny," like in high school, he had wanted to do something important with his life, mainly for his mom. So this is why he busted his butt back then? So he could barely scrape by, knowing that a lot of people think just being a lawyer inherently made him a bad person? He thought about what he had heard from the old attorneys when he first started. *Stay away from divorce cases if you possibly can. It's a different kind of law practice. In divorce court, everybody is unhappy. When lawyers get to the point they hate practicing, it is usually because of handling divorces.*

He thought about Vacarro's money. He had put it in a bank bag, which was in his desk. After their meeting, he had told Vacarro he had to think about it. He knew the hundred grand was no consulting fee. He either had to take the money and represent the guy, or give it back. A hundred grand was enough to help him stave off eviction and foreclosure, keep him alive for a little while. Which would be awesome, except for the whole Mafia thing. And it surely still existed, no matter what Vacarro said about it. Denial of its own existence was always the essence of the organization, wasn't it?

Not that he was opposed to representing criminals, he had done it his whole career. But none of those clients had posed a serious threat to him like Tony Vacarro could. Still, it was hard to imagine that Vacarro was really the head of some dangerous criminal enterprise. He came across more like an ex-president of a college fraternity than the head of anything ominous. And he was apparently legit, as well.

According to its bio, his company, the closely held Puglisi and Vacarro, Ltd. was a highly successful asset investment, investment banking, and specialty insurance concern, and Tony Vacarro was some kind of a securities and equities guru. He had made a lot of money over the last few years, and had loaned a lot out, at credit card interest rates. In addition to traditional investments, the company loaned money to a variety of entrepreneurs who normally couldn't get money from the staid brick and mortar banking system, and had decent security for the loans. At least in part, Vacarro was a legalized loan shark. But charging Mafia *vig* does not make one a Mafioso. He was undeniably a nephew of the Bardinos, the Mafia crime family that had practically run the city for most of the twentieth century. So he was either in the Mafia, or it just didn't effectively exist anymore. Hart wondered if he even still cared.

He was shocked back into reality by someone pounding on the locked door downstairs. By the time he got there, the pounding had resumed a second time. He swung open the door, which had his name and phone number lettered on its glass panel, just above the phrase "By Appointment Only." Hart said, "Well, hello, Mrs. Abercrombie. I don't believe you made an appointment for today..."

` "I certainly did not," she said, indignant. "I called, but I got some surly woman who refused to tell me where you were." She brushed past him, and started clomping up the stairs. He followed, slowly. "She wouldn't tell me her name, either. So rude and unprofessional. You should fire her right away. Besides, considering your fees, I should be able to show up any time I want."

As Hart arrived back in his office, she was perched on the edge of an interview chair. He said, "It's an answering service, Mrs. Abercrombie. I don't know who answered the phone, or her name, and I doubt if she knows mine either. I only have a part time assistant, and that's also why I only see clients by appointment, like it says on the front door." He smiled, which had no effect on her. She cocked her head, and did not move. He sat down and slid open a wooden file drawer in his desk, where he kept current litigation matters. The drawer smelled like his grandmother's house when he was a little kid.

Looking at her file, he said, "Since you mentioned my fees, you haven't made any payments after your initial deposit of... it looks like two hundred dollars. I believe our arrangement was for you o pay me two hundred a month, and I haven't been paid anything. Can I get the rest now?"

"Now? Of course not. I need you to get *me* more money. Obviously, you haven't been properly monitoring my case. I'm the victim here. I have a mortgage, and bills, and a child to raise, with private school tuition. And besides, two hundred dollars is a lot of money for working people. You lawyers are all the same. It's all about the money for you. What about justice?"

"Mrs. Abercrombie, as I have said to you before, the world is full of attorneys. You can certainly go to another one at any time. Besides, I thought you didn't work. And I got the judge to award you temporary alimony, remember?"

"Work? Who has time? Besides, I'm psychologically damaged from years of abuse, and most likely disabled."

"Ma'am, I have no doubt what you are telling me is true. We can have you examined by a psychiatrist I know and have her testify, if you like, at the trial. Of course, psychiatrists are expensive, and may not be covered by your insurance."

"Here we go again. Money, money, money. That's all you people think about. What about me? Have you been listening? Like I said, I have a child to raise. My ex caused me more stress just this past weekend. He was supposed to have my son back home at 5:00 p.m. sharp, and he wasn't there until ten minutes after. I was worried to death. I thought my baby had been killed in a car wreck, or his father had kidnaped him. We should sue him for ... for mental anguish. That's it, mental anguish, and it's worth at least a million dollars. I just saw one on TV, cases like that get a million dollars all the time, and that's how you can get the rest of your fee, since you are so obsessed with money, after taking your ungodly percentage of it. That's what you people do, right? I'm just saying, since that initial two hundred dollars, which is hard to come by for a disabled person, obviously isn't good enough for you."

Hart said, "Ma'am, that two hundred dollars was split between the court clerk, for filing fees, and the Sheriff, for service of process. That left me exactly fifteen dollars, as I explained to you in our first meeting, when you signed a contract to pay me ..."

"Well that's not my concern," she interrupted. "The whole legal system is so corrupt. Why can't you just do your job? A poor victim like me can only..."

"Excuse me," he said, "please let me finish. You made a couple of points, and I want to clarify them. First, your baby son is, I believe, seventeen now? And that private school tuition and your mortgage is being paid by your ex, over the objections of his attorney, according to the temporary order I got the judge to issue. The same order that makes him pay your temporary alimony and child support. The only person involved not getting paid is me. And by the way, suing someone for emotional distress is a different legal action from a divorce matter, and certainly not something I have been hired to do. Nor would I, for that matter."

"And why not?"

"Because I was hired to do a divorce. I would never represent someone on a second case to get paid what I am already owed on the first one."

"But you don't have any choice. Once I hire you, you have to do what I say," she said, leaning back in her chair, and crossing her arms.

"Mrs. Abercrombie," Hart said, "I will assure you that is not the case. In fact, I think it's time for me to..."

"Are you sure?," she cut in, "because I think you're wrong about that. My friend Myrt's cousin is a lawyer down in New Orleans. We just had lunch the other day in the city, the three of us, and this other lawyer, she's a woman, and at least acts like she gives a damn, and anyway, *she* said..."

She launched into an exposition on the lawyer's responsibility to zealously represent the client's interests, which she knows for sure is true, because she looked it up ten minutes ago on the internet, and how that meant, at least to her, and she swears-to-God to that other attorney, the one who actually cares, and probably doesn't have to be told to do her job, unlike present company, that he had to do exactly what she said, because, after all, who understands what her interests are better than her? She was soon plowing through another iteration of accusations against her soon-to-be ex husband, at crescendoing volume; something having to do with her Shih Tzu dog's outrageous vet bills, and two teakwood deck chairs that used to be on the flybridge of their cabin cruiser, and...

"I'm sorry, Mrs. Abercrombie," interrupted Hart, "but you're fired."

Startled, she said, "Wh- what? Fired? You can't fire me, I'm the *client*, you idiot. Haven't you been listening? You have to do what I say!"

"Actually ma'am, I don't. I am in private practice, and I represent whomever I choose. We have a signed fee agreement, and you have not abided by its terms, so now I am withdrawing representation, and you may seek other counsel. Please take your file and leave, I'm done." He got up, started down the hall.

Blustering around him down the stairs,

she yelled, "I've never been so mistreated in my life! I'll file charges! I'll report you to the Bar Association! I'll ruin you on social media! When I hire another lawyer, a *good* lawyer this time, I'll sue you for everything you own! And I want that two hundred dollars back too!"

"Good luck on that one," Hart chuckled. "Because I don't have anything to take. Maybe you should hire your friend Myrt's cousin in New Orleans, the good lawyer who gives a damn." She slammed the front door. It had been the same thing in court today. These divorce cases were sucking the life out of him. The clients gripe and lie, and they demand their attorneys believe their lies. They accuse their exes, the person they once swore to God to honor and defend for the rest of their lives, of all manner of crimes and perversions, real or not, all over money, or pride. Or just hatefulness. Anything to win.

Most of them had to finance their attorney fees, so he let them pay over time. And they were all broke, just like him. He spent a huge portion of his time chasing down payments. Getting fully paid on any case was like a snipe hunt. This is not why he went to law school, he thought. His soul, or what little was left of it, was tired. In any case, he was done for the day, and the week. He retrieved his keys off the desk. Out the side window, he could see some kind of commotion going on up Beach Boulevard at

Canecutter's. He was curious to see what was going on, and wanted a beer anyway. He thought about hiding the bag, but realized no one would ever suspect him of having any money in his office. It was just as safe in his desk as anywhere else.

Canecutter's was a rambling wooden structure, with decks all around, and a Jamaican color scheme, spread along the edge of the hill next to the city harbor. It had patio bars on both ends, and a grill that wafted smoke from fresh fish, shrimp, burgers, and pork ribs down Beach Boulevard every weekend. Bands played outside on Saturdays. Between the local and tourist foot traffic, and a steady stream of boaters coming up the seawall stairs from the harbor, it was usually pretty lively.

There were a couple of empty Bay Saint Louis cop cars with their lights rolling out in front. A news van from the TV station in Biloxi was just pulling up. Inside, the place was full, with waiters and food runners weaving in and out of the crowd. Two uniform cops and a detective had the slobbering and gesticulating Captain Fleming surrounded at the end of the main bar. The detective noticed the attorney and waived him over.

Oddly, John Hart was the only person in town who the Captain seemed to trust, and who could sometimes interpret his Captainese drunk language. The Captain took a swipe at putting his arm on Hart's shoulder, but missed badly, nearly listing out of his barstool before the cops caught him. Hart leaned as close as he would to the old man, who was mumbling something. After what sounded like a run through the consonant alphabet, Hart asked, "There's a human head in his golf cart?"

"We got that part, Counselor," intoned Detective Larue, "hence the heavy police presence. See if you can translate where it *came* from."

After more blathering, Hart announced, "Down the beach. On the other side of the Washington street pier and boat launch. There a stick in the beach, marking the spot."

"Tell him he has to show us where it is, exactly."

Hart said, "What am I, your interpreter? He's drunk, not deaf. He can hear you, you know."

"Whumptingrattle!," blurted the Captain.

"Look," said the attorney, "He's obviously a little tight right now. You think you can talk to him later?"

Looking around, lowering his voice, the detective leaned a little closer and said, "Look, Counselor, this ain't just a public intoxication. This is a homicide case, and this old drunk is, as we now say, a 'Person of Interest.' I need some kind of reason to not haul his ass downtown."

Hart said, "What condition is the head in?"

Larue said, "Well, I'm no doctor, but I would say extremely dead."

"I *mean*, how long has it been out there? Does it look like a recent kill? Like maybe the Captain could have done it, and not just found it, as he claims?"

"Well, normally we don't discuss details of ongoing investigations. But I am at liberty to say there is no reason to believe this man is connected to the death. At least at this time. This head fits the general description of a gentleman who has been missing for several days, last seen in this area weekend before last. We've been keeping it quiet, but I guess that's over. Now, if you're telling me you are Captain Rummy here's lawyer, I might be inclined to bend the rules a little and save us all the headache of having to process him. So what's it gonna be?"

Hart looked at the Captain, who tried to focus his eyes somewhere in the middle of the attorney's forehead. This was just what he needed, another client with no money. "Yeah," he said. "I'll vouch for him, for now. I'll try to have him over at the station tomorrow. Which is Saturday, by the way."

The detective leaned close, and said, "Don't try, John. Have him there. I come on at five." He winked, and slapped the lawyer on the shoulder.

"Ok, Larue," he said, "we'll be there."

The Captain tried to hug John Hart, but this time he fell off the stool, and nobody tried to catch him.

Around sunset, Tony Vacarro was sitting at a rooftop bar in the Central Business District of New Orleans, enjoying the warm weather, flirting with the bartender, watching the local news on a small TV. Apparently, a human head had washed up on the beach in Bay Saint Louis, Mississippi. The reporter was able to say, based on anonymous sources, that the head was of a male. They weren't officially saying who it was, but Vacarro was pretty sure he knew.

Now the cops would be wanting to speak. It was enough to take the fun out of happy hour. He downed the last of his third vodka martini, and signaled for another one. He was pissed at himself for having listened to the old man, his great uncle The Raven, who had made him meet with the missing guy. Vacarro had just done what he was told, and now he was in trouble.

But he hadn't really had any choice. He'd been terrified of his great uncle his whole life. When he and his cousins were kids, going to private schools and running around New Orleans with the other rich kids, they all called the old man "Uncle Dracula" and claimed he was a real vampire, and survived off the blood of little children. They used him to scare the other kids, threatening to send him over to their houses at night. It was intimidating enough that Vacarro's family ran the local Mafia. His own great grandfather had been a first cousin of Nofio Bardino, who had started the whole New Orleans Mafia. But having someone in the family who supposedly cannibalized kids was something extra, and usually the final word on the playground. Plus, The Raven looked the part, like a pasty living corpse. And that was decades ago.

What Vacarro had told John Hart about the Mafia was mostly true, as far as he knew. The old organization, the one known as the Bardino Crime Family, which had been around for most of the twentieth century, was indeed over. The feds had busted some clown associated with the family in a case over on the Mississippi Coast like ten or twelve years ago. He was running a casino they controlled, and he had gotten greedy, and stupid. He was charged with a list of bank and mail frauds related to some harebrained scheme involving the trade of illegal gemstones and tree frogs, and the funding of international terrorism.

Apparently, he was allowed to plead to a single count of money laundering. That's what Vacarro had heard, anyway. The guy, Bonacelli was his name, had gone to prison and surprisingly kept his mouth shut. But the publicity was too much for the family. Whatever was left of it decided to get off the boat before it sank. They had actually met out in the gulf on a floating oil rig, boating and helicoptering in. They had voted to dissolve operations, and split up what money or assets were left over.

It was where most of the original money in his company came from. Not long after all Bardino financial matters had been settled, and the old guard dispersed, Tony Vacarro's father, Tony Sr., died. He had been the oldest member of the Bardino crime family, other than The Raven. Tony had been working for several years in New York, on Wall Street, and came back to New Orleans to take over the company, which his father had intended to run.

For a couple of years after that, The Raven had disappeared. He was just gone, and Tony had free reign to run the company. He owned a third of it, with his sister and of all people, The Raven. All their shares were in an irrevocable trust. So basically, he couldn't get his money out, but he could use it to make more money he could get out.

When his uncle reappeared and resumed lurking in the late night French Quarter, Vacarro had heard about it from his half sister Lisette, who he rarely talked to. She had apparently kept up with The Raven out of some macabre sense of family loyalty. Vacarro couldn't imagine any feelings for such a thing, who was at best a serial murderer, and still dangerous at any age. His sister had told him that she was passing along a message: if their uncle had any requests of Tony, or the company, he would send them in writing, since phone calls or electronic communications can be monitored. Any written requests he received had to be destroyed immediately.

Tony had told her he didn't want to have anything to do with The Raven, or the Mafia, or anything illegal, but otherwise would do as he was told, as long as he didn't have to commit any crimes. Lisette had told him that she didn't know anything about it, was only delivering a message, and she certainly didn't want to be around anything illegal, either. Vacarro had gotten a few requests over the years, all having to do with the company funding different businesses. It was all legitimate, as far as he knew.

His mood was ruined now, and he ordered another drink. He had been hoping that all this would somehow blow over, but since the damned head had been found, he needed to think it through. He thought about Lisette, about how little he knew about his only sister. Well, half sister. She was nice enough, and sociable, and almost freakishly good looking, but just weird. There were several things about her he could never quite figure out. Like how she could be so smart, but never really accomplish anything. That exchange about The Raven was the last time they had actually had a conversation, as far as he could remember, and that was more than ten years ago. In the meantime, he had turned Puglisi and Vacarro, Ltd. into a regional power that was worth tens of millions. Like the Kennedys, he had taken illegitimate money and turned it into a legit empire.

Vacarro knew all about the old conspiracy theories linking the Bardinos with the CIA, and Bay of Pigs, and the Kennedy assassination, mostly from TV shows. He also had a vague notion of more recent family involvement in government spook operations in and around Central America and the Carribean, including the whole Iran Contra thing, and others less known to the TV myth makers, but no less notorious. He had heard about these things mostly from schoolmates, and friends, and brave strangers in bars. How The Raven had escaped prosecution all these decades was a mystery. Maybe he really had parlayed whatever he knew into a deal. Maybe he was just lucky, or charmed. That made as much sense as anything else.

Vacarro had gotten the note to meet the dead guy in his box at the office. It was very specific. He was to meet someone named Rilo Marshall at Tracy's, a restaurant, at noon on Sunday in Bay Saint Louis. The guy was supposed to have some kind of information for him, something about the business. That's it. So he did it, not out of loyalty, but out of fear.

Rilo Marshall had shown up as scheduled, but was fidgety and agitated. He didn't want to talk in the restaurant, he said. So after lunch they got on Vacarro's boat in the harbor, and went out to Ship Island, where they spent the day. At one point, Marshall had been bitching about something having to do with his uncle, but Tony couldn't really hear everything over the music, and he figured the guy was just drunk, anyway. They had come back in later, and as far as Tony knew, the other guy left. A few days days later, he had gotten a call from Detective Larue. He had told the detective he could go on the boat if he wanted, it was usually unlocked. He figured that would be the end of it, or at least his involvement.

Then he had gotten another note. This one explained the details of meeting with Attorney John Hart, and the hundred grand payment, and the fact that Hart really needed the money, so to insist that the attorney keep it. It instructed him to make the "peace" sign out in front of Gabriella's if Hart agreed to the representation, or needed time to think. If he refused the representation, make no gesture. Though every instinct screamed at him to refuse taking any more orders from his crazy uncle, he was still afraid not to. So he had met Hart as instructed.

Most of what he had told the attorney was true. As far as he knew, there was no actual Mafia any more, and he certainly hadn't killed anyone. This whole scenario had just turned into a real pain in the ass. He had to be in Baton

Rouge for a meeting Monday. After that, if he hadn't heard from Hart, he'd call him. For now, he was just getting drunk. He knocked over his martini glass, then ordered another. The bartender, aware of who he was, was not about to refuse to serve him.

They had gotten Captain Fleming's golf cart pulled around the back of Canecutter's, by the city harbor, and had him piled up in it, passed out. Hart left a business card stuck under the old man's hat, with instructions on the back to meet at five Saturday afternoon at the police station. Who knew if he would be there.

After a while, Hart hadn't seen anyone else he really wanted to talk to, and slipped up the stairs to a relatively quiet corner table. He could have gone back to his rent house, but being alone here was somehow better than being alone there. From here, he could see deep into the waning afternoon light of the northern Gulf of Mexico. He remembered the first time he had met Captain Fleming. It wasn't long after Hurricane Katrina had put over thirty feet of water in the area, and way before what was left had been rebuilt. The whole waterfront had been washed away, and all the businesses there, and anything in low areas. But a lot of Bay Saint Louis had largely survived, due to its elevation. Everything else on the Mississippi Gulf Coast was just gone.

His mom's house had made it, but was heavily water damaged. He and his wife were fine in uptown New Orleans, where the water surge from Katrina had devastated much of the rest of city. His mom came to stay in New Orleans, and he would spend a lot of free time over the next several months getting her house back in order. The power and water were out in the Bay for weeks. After a while, there was one functional bar in town, by the old railroad depot in the back of town. It ran lights and beer coolers off diesel generators.

John Hart first met Captain Fleming there. The Captain was telling anybody listening some long story about being up a Pearl River cypress tree for a couple of days, and had everybody laughing. Afterward, he and Hart had talked about all kinds of things. Hart had told him about growing up around the Bay, about wade fishing, and chasing girls, and hunting for the pirate treasure that was supposed to be buried on a property down the beach. The locals believed it was once the site of an actual pirate house. Supposedly, the pirates had stolen a bunch of gold from the French or the Spanish, and buried it there, and then somehow lost it. He and the other kids had dug enough holes around that area to make it look like the surface of the moon. Hart said the whole thing was probably a ruse for the tourists, but who knows?

He sighed. The aftermath of that disaster

actually seemed like good times now, because his wife and mom were still around then. Over the last few years, he had gotten a little better, except for the damned money situation. He had gone from being psychologically damaged, maybe crazy, certainly suicidal at times, to just plain mad at life. That was progress.

After everybody died, when he still had a house in uptown New Orleans, he couldn't stand to be in it alone. He had taken off work at the firm, an indefinite leave which ultimately became a permanent one. At the time he couldn't sit still, or imagine what he should be doing. After the funerals, all he could do was walk around the house, or the back yard. Constant motion is all that kept him sane. He had put in miles along paths he made in that yard, like an animal at the zoo who realizes he's trapped, but whose nature won't let him stop trying to escape. He could barely sleep. When he could, he only had one dream: walking down a dark hallway in some old hotel building that smelled like pigshit, where every room door was open, and the rooms filled with dead people. Fear made him keep moving, trying to find a way out, but he always came to the end, and a door he could not open.

In those days, the future no longer existed. He could remember the idea of it, but he could no longer see it. In his dreams he kept going down that same hall, in that hellish building he maybe saw once when he was a kid at the drive-in movies, when his parents thought he and his older sister were asleep in the back seat, but he wasn't. That was back when the air smelled new, like the grass in grade school on the first day of baseball.

Before the disaster, John Hart didn't really believe clinical depression actually existed. He had always been suspicious that some people were basically not mentally tough enough to handle adversity, and were just prone to weakness. Then they all died, and he had tumbled into depression himself, and was immersed in it, and lost his ability to imagine a better future condition. He learned that when you are in pain, nobody cares. Everybody has pain. Your pain is not special, or a different quality from other people's pain, whether yours is caused by losing your entire family at one time, or theirs is caused by a bad back, or hitting their funny bone too hard. Pain is pain. It's really just a question of scope and duration.

Another quality of depression, he had learned, is the realization that time itself is a manmade idea. "Now" is not a bridge between past and future, but a singularity that never changes, composed of breathing, and heartbeat, and pain. The old imaginary future, the one with exciting possibilities, was destroyed. He realized that hope was childish, and that life was not precious, or delicate, or joyful, but merely the obstinate ability to endure.

He had decided the accident was just a perpetuation of a family curse. First, his dad died young, then his older sister. It was the reason he became an attorney. When he went back to college, his mother had given him his father's leather bound journal. As a college student, his father had written literary quotes, and plans, and passages of prose. It was the only way John Hart ever really knew him, and it became something of a one-way conversation through which his dad explained life in written instructions.

One entry in particular contained five rules that had become guideposts for Hart's transition from the slacker world to the so-called legitimate one: 1. Don't hold other people to a higher standard than you hold yourself to. 2. Believe what you actually see, not just what you want to see. 3. Facts are not philosophical, they don't need defending or explaining. 4. Don't be lazy; there are only two kinds of people: those who *talk* shit, and those who *do* shit. 5. God loves bravery.

It was interesting that his father had juxtaposed cussing and the almighty, just as life itself was a mixture of the vile and the divine. John Hart had ingested these precepts, and believed them, and had tried to live by them. He had shed his lazy ways, and dedicated himself to making his mother proud. She had lost her patriotic, idealistic husband, and over-achieving, brilliant daughter. His mother did not deserve to be left with only a second rate child, and he was determined to give her some gratification after the injustices in her life.

But none of it had mattered. Adherence to those rules had done Johnny Hart no more good than they had done their author, who never even lived long enough to explain their meaning to his only son. He'd died on the job, in another fire. A freak accident, his mother had said. Smoke inhalation. That John Hart had once believed a causal connection existed between goodness and happiness now seemed idiotically naive.

As the sun went down, the nearly full moon loomed. He thought again about his options. A human head, probably connected to Vacarro, had just washed up, practically in sight of Hart's office. He had rashly agreed to intervene for the person who found it, maybe creating an issue conflict with Vacarro that could result in him being unable to represent either one. But probably not. So he was likely looking at a murder case. He hadn't been in one for years. Was he actually going to take on a client who was probably in the Mafia? That's how lawyers get arrested, or killed. Sure, Tony Vacarro had said the Mafia no longer existed, but isn't that what they always say? Maybe he had no choice, he needed the money. His finances had gotten that bad.

He closed his eyes, tried to focus. One night, in that terrible recurring dream, he was finally able to get the door at the end of the hall to open. And inside that stinking dark room was a dirty window. And outside that window was some light, but just barely. And it wasn't cloudy or gloomy, but new light. So the next time he went down the hall, he peaked in that room again, and the window was open a little. Not much, but just a little. And this happened over and over. Eventually, he went into the room, ignoring the stinking dead people down the hall, and forced open the window, and he jumped... .

He thought about his dad, and about his dad's rules, about how naive they both had been. He thought especially about rule number five: God loves bravery. That was maybe the biggest hoot of all. If there was a God, he was at best indifferent to bravery, or thievery, or goodness. Good people got killed every day, and bad people got rich, and real bravery got lost in the constant facile rantings of loudmouths on TV and social media. There was no divine reward system here on Earth, at least none that John Hart had ever seen. God didn't mind sitting back and letting his innocent family die in a horrible immolation, and the guilty son of a bitch that did it get away.

It didn't really matter to anyone in heaven or on Earth whether Attorney John Hart was truthful, or brave, or a talker, or doer, or just a broke small town lawyer with a dead family and a new, dangerous chance stay in business for a while longer. A decision had to be made.

Chapter 3

Monday morning, John Hart was shocked awake by the thought. After everything else, had he seriously been considering defending the boss of the New Orleans Mafia in a murder case? Even attorneys can't walk that tightrope long. He had called Tony Vacarro's office just after eight, told the receptionist who he was, and said he wanted to come in right away. He was put on hold, and another lady had come on the line. She told him to come in at eleven. With the hundred grand in his leather mail bag, he headed to New Orleans to give it back.

Saturday's questioning of Captain Fleming down at the police station had been uneventful. The old man had shown up on time, and composed. In his swampy accent, he told Hart and Detective Larue the story. It was pretty simple. He had been going down the beach, saw the head, marked the spot, and picked it up. The only remarkable thing about the whole meeting was his condition. He was perfectly sober, with no apparent hangover. Neither Hart nor Larue had spoken to him before when he was sober. By the time Hart ever saw him he was drunk, and the police only ever saw him as a result of being that way. He made his statement, one of the assistants typed it up, and he signed it. The Captain couldn't remember everything, so Larue explained to him that his lawyer had saved him from getting arrested by vouching for him to show up.

Outside, Captain Fleming thanked Hart for all the trouble. He said, "I guess they're gonna want me to testify one of these days, when they find out who did this."

Hart said, "That's a pretty good bet."

Captain Fleming said, "Well I'll be around, hunting for my little treasures." He started walking away, then he stopped, and said, "Lawyer, I know you're busy, and I do thank you. And I know I owe you some money, I just ain't got it with me right now."

Hart said, "You don't owe me anything, Captain. One of these days, maybe you'll help me out. We'll see."

"I will for sure if you ever need it, Lawyer."

Tony Vacarro's offices were impressive. Twenty stories up, the reception area's floor to ceiling windows overlooked much of the New Orleans Central Business District. The Superdome and the Mississippi River loomed in the distance. An elderly receptionist with a heavy New Orleans accent directed him to sit down, and went away to announce his presence. After a while, the receptionist re-appeared, and he followed her. They went through a side door, down a hall past several closed office doors, and a huge, unoccupied conference room, to a large, bright corner office with floor to ceiling windows on both sides. At a wide desk, centered in a corner of converging windows cantered a tall leather chair, silhouetted with its back to the door. Hart entered, his escort slammed the tall door, and he strode across the large space.

"Mr. Vacarro," he said, "I am sorry to have wasted your time, but I obviously had a little too much to drink the other day when we met. I should have told you then that I can't take you on as a client. I am a small, one attorney firm, and just not equipped to properly handle your, uh, concerns. I have brought your money back, and I want to make it clear that we have no..."

The chair slowly spun around. Hart was silenced, temporarily, by the shocking beauty of the woman in it. He said, "Excuse me, I thought this was Tony Vacarro's office? Maybe the lady out front misunderstood."

"She understood," said the chairwoman, standing, leaning across the desk, presenting her hand. "My name is Lisette. I am Tony Vacarro's half sister. He will be back soon, I'm told. It seems we're both waiting."

Hart stood, holding her outstretched hand a little too long, gawking. "I'm John Hart," he said. She had perfect blue eyes, and almost luminescent amber colored long hair. For a moment, he was struck as immobile as if he had seen the Medusa.

"Why don't we sit?," she said, reclaiming her hand. "Tell me what brings you here. Or is it a terrible secret?," she smiled.

Hart pondered this a second or two. He said, "Well, I am an attorney, so I suppose everything I do is a secret. Not all of them are terrible, though." He chuckled. "May I ask, why are you half siblings?"

"Oh, that *is* a terrible secret," she said, "a family secret, you might say. Tony and I have the same mother, but different fathers."

"That doesn't seem to be that unusual of a..."

"But our mother and his father were still married when I was born, Counselor, so as you can see, it's all very scandalous."

"It certainly has potential," he said.

"But you're here to disengage from family business, not talk about it, aren't you? You said something about returning money? That's not a normal activity for an attorney, is it?"

"It's probably not normal for anyone in any profession, Lisette. People tend to want to be paid for their work, it's just lawyers who always get berated for it."

"Berated? That sounds defensive."

"Maybe I am. Maybe I am. But tell me, what is it that you do?"

Forty-five minutes later, the receptionist reappeared and apologetically announced the unavoidable detainment of Mr. Vacarro by some important matter, so might he possibly reschedule the meeting? Hart made his arrangements, and swinging his bag strap over his shoulder, regretfully left the beguiling Lisette.

Driving away, passing over Canal Street, taking Royal through the French Quarter toward the Fauberg Marigny to check on the condo, all he could think of was her. He thought about what she had said. She was a part owner of the company Tony Vacarro ran, but she mainly entertained the clients. She was also an interior designer, having served many of New Orleans' richest families, and many others across the Gulf South. She had grown up in New Orleans, attended a private Catholic school for girls in Bay Saint Louis, Saint Mary's, and had gone to college in Europe. John Hart was older than her, and hadn't ever seen her in the Bay. He certainly would have remembered.

That day, she had dropped by to see her half brother about some business, she said. Hart was in a kind of daze. Talking to her, looking at her, and smelling her faint perfume had caused a blast of feelings he had not experienced in a long time. He had a difficult time remembering all the details of the conversation. She was well read and funny. Her favorite book was *A Confederacy of Dunces*, which meant she was smart.

On top of it, she was the prettiest woman he had talked to in, he couldn't remember. Hell, forever. And she was unaccountably single. He had been completely alone for six years, and was so used to it that he had become resistant to any type of intimate conversation or contact with women. He certainly was not opposed to the idea, but he felt hopelessly damaged, and did not ever want to share his injuries with anybody else. He had gradually grown to believe, when he thought about it at all, that he would simply be alone for the rest of his life.

He could not even remember the last time he had asked a woman to go out, if he ever had. Meeting Lisette had caused him to act completely out of his new sheltered character, and he had even asked if she would meet him for lunch soon. To his astonishment, she agreed. He was giddy. Not that one conversation meant he was cured, but this morning was the first time in a long while that he had briefly forgotten about the abiding sorrow that had long defined his life.

The condo was fine. He locked it up, and was retrieving some mail from the box on the wall downstairs by the front door when a neighbor emerged. He was a retired guy from Minnesota who had recently moved in. Apparently, someone had been creeping around Hart's condo recently. "It was late, late Saturday night, a couple of weeks ago," the neighbor said. "He was checking your front door, looked under the mat. Like he was looking for a key or something. I had just gotten in, and had not gone up the stairs inside. I saw him out the peephole. He didn't see me, thank God."

"You think he was a burglar? A lot of

out of town condo owners leave keys around for their friends."

"This guy was no burglar, he was too dressed up. And he wasn't checking anyone's place but yours. The thing is, he looked weird, even for New Orleans. This dude was wearing all black, from head to toe. And I mean dressed up. Coat, vest, tie, the works. Even a hat, like those kind they wore a long time ago, a fedora, maybe. Yep, and all black, creepy. But on top of it, he was pure white. I couldn't see him that well, but he looked like a ghost. Like a dead person who, you know, came back to life, a zombie, like you see in all those silly movies."

Driving back to the Bay, Hart thought about the day, about Lisette, about the creepy visitor. He thought about Tony Vacarro, and the head on the beach, and how all these things were probably connected. What could be the result of all this but more trouble? But he mainly thought of Lisette. That morning, he had intended to return the money. Now, he was actually considering keeping it. After all, wasn't he an attorney? What did he expect? Life is hard, and had been, and still would be. So why not just take the money, and get on with it? He laughed at his own rationalizations, because he knew this was all of a sudden related to Lisette. One conversation with her, and he was considering ignoring his own common sense.

And there was another thing. He had occasionally wondered at his own lack of interest in any kind of amorous relationship. His wife had been gone for six years. How much mourning was enough? It seemed that certain traumas have no time limit on periods of grief. He sometimes suspected that his own comfort level with depression meant he had grown to accommodate it. That maybe he had gotten so used to being relieved of expectations, he had accepted his role as a has-been. Less than halfway through life, and he was washed up?

He snorted in derision at himself. Was he really done? Did he need to be relieved of the responsibility of success forever? Half his cases these days were divorce related. The one consistency of divorce court is, no one is ever the clear winner. Everyone gets less than they expect. Is that a comfort to the attorneys who practice there as well? Always accepting mediocrity? Is that what he had become?

Back in the Bay, his assistant Miss Filomena was waiting to pounce. He was only halfway up the stairs when she started, loudly reminding him, in her Welsh brogue, of all the indiscretions that occurred in the week that had intervened since her last workday. Miss Filomena was technically retired, but three years earlier had agreed to become his assistant. She worked one day a week of her choosing, usually Monday.

She had spent most of her seventy-something years on Earth working for various law firms along the Mississippi Gulf Coast. Years ago, her American husband had been stationed at Keesler Air Force base in Biloxi. They were a young married couple then. She had gone to school to become a paralegal, and had been bossing Gulf Coast attorneys around ever since.

A widow with no children, she was determined to not only straighten out his meager case files, but his personal life as well. She had decided that he required a certain amount of female guidance, and had appointed herself. She was a devout Christian Protestant, as she emphatically reminded anyone in her vicinity, even though she was forced to adopt the Episcopalian religion, since her beloved Church in Wales was not present locally.

Filomena was her first name. He knew her last one, since he wrote her checks, but she wouldn't answer to it, being beneath her Welsh heritage, so he never used it. She had long since given up drinking alcohol, owing to some pernicious endocrine issue her doctor had discovered. Hart secretly suspected this was a red herring, that her doctor was simply protecting the rest of the world from an occasionally imbibed Welsh lady who was a decent threat cold sober. Giving up drinking had caused her to give up tobacco as well, since they were inseparable in her taste. Her predilection for cigars over cigarettes had made her somewhat legendary down the coastline in old Biloxi, in the joints and dives and illegal casinos that peppered the resort area long before legal ones wiped them out.

Her last remaining vice was cursing. She was Christian in every way, including charity, which many of her creed had long since abandoned. But she could not help her mouth, trained as it had been in the Welsh tavern her family ran in her youth, honed around the officer's clubs of her and her late husband's social lives, and tested among the cantankerous lot of whiskey swilling trial lawyers who employed her a generation ago. Consequently, she was always looking for some damned file, or lamenting some fookin' thing or another.

She was sitting in his office chair, with several files pertly stacked on the desk which almost hid her, being just a shade over five feet tall. She was busily rifling through his unopened mail. He quietly slipped into one of the interview chairs in front of his desk, placed his mailbag in the other.

Disgustedly ripping open envelopes, without looking up, she said, "Do ya ever listen to me sonny? One more week like this past one, and you can just plan on shutting down, mister. Did you know you haven't paid the fookin' rent, or the power bill yet? And do you see this?," she snatched up and waived an opened envelope, "this is the bill for your Bar dues. No Bar dues, no license. No license, no fookin' law office, and we can all go home, except for you, who will be working at being a greeter in a store, because you're too soft and worthless to be of any use as a common laborer..."

"Alright, Miss Filomena," Hart interrupted, "I get it. So how have you been this past week. Did you hear from your cousin, who was visiting the states, I believe?"

"Don't change the subject, you. I've been around your lot since before you were an angel's dream in heaven, so don't try your devious lawyer ways on me. Besides, that cousin of mine is out traveling around the colonies somewhere, probably visiting our so-called relatives in New York. They are all a bunch of Catholics, you know. Now what the hell are you going to do about money? And don't try to change the subject again."

Hart knew better than to respond at all, so he snatched something off the desk and pretended to read it. She was about halfway through her stack of bills, each delivered with editorial commentary and an apocalyptic warning, when he figured he might have to seriously consider taking Tony Vacarro's money. Maybe.

Besides, who the hell was he holding out for? Where was *his* family? Why did he always try to do the right thing, and follow the rules his father wrote, when everything in his life was a disaster? What good had the rules done him, or any of them? *Rule 1: Don't hold other people to a higher standard than you hold yourself to.* It sounds good, and he had tried to live by it. But in real life, if you're trying to be fair, you're the only one doing so. In real life, holding other people to higher standards than oneself is a human compulsion. The rules were designed to convince him to be better than human, and how to act when the shit hits the fan, right? But what about when the shit breaks the fan, and tears down the whole house in the process?

Except for a handful of dramatic, whiskey-fueled exceptions, he had even tried to follow the Christian rules of his youth. But for what? So he could lose everyone he ever loved, all at once? What is the point of trying to do right? He hadn't made a conscious decision to abandon religion, his life had simply come to an indefinite pause one day, and his religion had moved on without him.

She was now slapping phone messages she had written out from the answering service like dealing cards in a hostile game of Blackjack. "Why don't you return your calls when I'm not here? This one," she said, popping it down like it was a bust card, "is probably someone who has some money. See?, " she stabbed at it with a faded red fingernail, "it's it says 'Urgent.'

"Everybody thinks everything is urgent." He said, "Listen, I might have some good news. I have a possible new client who has promised to pay us a decent retainer. At least for a while, we could survive financially. So quit wearing me out about the money, ok? Now, you want to take a break? Why don't we knock off early today, and I'll deal with..."

"Ach-a-bloody-fi! We will not do any such thing! You got calls to make, Sonny, and promises don't pay the bills. Don't believe a damn thing 'til it's in your hands."

Hart thought, *What if its in your bag, sitting on the seat next to you*?

She continued, "Now, this last message is from the police, that gentleman, Detective Larue. Such a nice man, and a hard worker. He's of mostly French blood but has learned to overcome his deficiencies, I've observed. You could learn a thing or two from that man. Anyways, he is going to be here, in this office, at five o'clock sharp, to meet you. I will be gone by then. One of my neighbors has a garden party for some fookin' church fundraiser, which she does each year, and I cannot get out of it."

"Did he say what it was about?"

"No, he didn't, but he said he needed to speak. Now when are you going to replace this damned chair? If you do get any money, after you pay these bills, I insist that you go and buy a new chair. This broken one is unbecoming for an attorney, even a common scrabbler like you, representing all these people who don't pay you. You'd think one of them could at least fix your chair, or buy you a new one."

By five, Hart had returned all his calls, and

written as many checks as he thought he could cover. In the process, he had to reset his broken chair a few times. Whatever mechanism allowed the seat to be lifted or lowered and set in place was worn out. Consequently, his seat was always slowly lowering under his body weight. Eventually, it would lower to the point that he appeared to be sitting on a box behind his desk, and he would have to get up and readjust it.

Miss Filomena had mercifully left at 4:30, and Hart was just wondering what the detective had to say when he heard him stomping up the stairs. He got up and raised his seat. He and Larue shook hands and sat.

Larue said, "John, we know each other pretty well, right? I think we both moved to town about the same time, what, four or five years ago?"

"Yes, I think so. Actually, I was moving back to town. I grew up in Bay Saint Louis, and practiced law here a couple of years before I got married and moved to New Orleans. Why?"

"We've had a few beers after work. And you came to my house last year, to that shrimp boil. I mean, I consider us to be friends."

"Me too, but I'm a little confused. What are we talking about?"

"Well, I'm just wondering why the hell you didn't tell me the other day that you might have some connection to that head your drunk client found."

Hart started to say something, but the Detective held up his hand. "Before you say anything, let me finish. Let me tell you what happened this morning. Normally, it takes at least a few days to get a fix on a body part, even if it is a head. Not this time. Turns out, this is a missing person we have been aware of for several days, who was last seen with a gentleman named Tony Vacarro, right here in Bay Saint Louis."

He stopped, cocked his head, looking at Hart. "You may have heard of him, he is supposed to be the current boss of the New Orleans Mafia. Well, I talked to him right after we heard about the missing man, and Vacarro even let me look in his boat, which turned up nothing. Anyway, rest assured, we now know that our head is that of the missing gentleman from Gulfport, and this Tony Vacarro is the primary Person of Interest. So I called him again this morning, and do you have any idea what he told me? Calm as an oyster, he tells me, 'Talk to my attorney in the Bay,' and he names you. Well?"

During this time, Hart's seat has been slowly descending. He said, "That's not exactly true. I..."

"Is he your client, or isn't he? I'm having a hard time understanding why you told me you would represent that old drunk that found the severed head, if you already represent the guy who probably severed it. That's what you lawyers call a 'conflict,' isn't it?"

Hart said, "Well, in the first place, no charges have been filed, and I haven't been formally retained by anyone. So there isn't any conflict. And second, nobody knew who the head belonged to at the time. Did you?"

"No, I didn't. I'll grant you that. But it's awful coincidental, don't you think? Anyway, charges will be filed, John, I guarantee that. Your client Vacarro, or your friend or whatever, is probably going to be charged with murder. Are you getting shorter, or am I just seeing things?"

Hart got up and adjusted his chair. He sat back down, taller. "Is Captain Fleming getting charged with anything?"

"Vagrancy maybe, if I ever get around to it, but not anything related to the head."

"Then there will be no conflict, but thanks for talking to me in private. The fact is, and I don't have to tell you this, but Tony Vacarro didn't kill anybody."

Larue said, "OK, counsel, we may have to disagree on that. But just to make sure we're clear, this is murder. This isn't a misdemeanor drunk driving charge or some divorce case. The District Attorney is young, and wants to be in Congress some day. Your guy is a high profile target, and going to generate lots of free air time. This is a godsend to a politician."

"Believe me, I get the difference between a drunk driving and murder charges. I am quite capable of handling both. Is that what you mean?"

"Look, John, everybody heard about what you went through. Or at least what the rumors say you went through. I heard you were an attorney in New Orleans, in one of those big shot law firms and all, before the... well, before. We obviously didn't know each other then. But I'm guessing your New Orleans gig was all tailored suits and shiny shoes civil stuff, right? A bank suing an oil company, that kind of thing?"

Hart stared, sinking.

"Because this won't be that. I guarantee you the D.A. will not plea bargain this one. I know him. This is what he has been looking for, a case that will put him on national news. And prosecuting the boss of the New Orleans Mafia for murder? This is manna from heaven. The Mafia has been out of the news for quite a while around here. He will want to take this to the top of the mountain."

"So, are you asking me a question, or warning me, or what?"

"Just telling you that this is gonna be tough on everybody involved."

"Thanks. I didn't always work at the tailored suit place. I was a public defender at first, and have been in the arena a few times, and I'm not scared. Tough on everybody? I don't know what the rumors about me are, nor do I care, but I'm still here, still living and breathing, and that's all the 'tough' I need to prove to anyone." He was a little red faced, and his pulse was up, but his seat just then bottomed out, and he felt like a little kid looking over the desk, and he had to get up and fix it while swallowing the instant urge to laugh at his own nervous indignance.

Larue said, "OK, Counselor, I'm glad we straightened out that your daddy is as big as mine. But from now on, while this case is going on, me and you don't speak in public."

"I understand the routine, Detective."

"I don't know how much you know about the New Orleans Mafia thing around here."

"I grew up here. I've heard all the stories."

"Well, they're true. At least people believe they are, which is just as good. People are going to think this killing is a Mafia hit."

Hart said, "They always say that. Every low level felon I've ever represented around here eventually claims he's connected."

"Yeah, well, some of them probably are. Anyway," he said, standing up, "I said what I came to say. Watch your back. People are going to act crazy about this case. There's all kinds of taboos in their minds. And once they associate you with all that, that's the way they will think of you, from now on. As a Mafia Lawyer."

Hart said, "I appreciate the advice." They shook hands. After Larue left, Hart knew he had a matter of hours, maybe minutes, to get this scenario out of his life, if that's what he wanted to do. The money was right there. It was time for serious decisions.

He closed his eyes, and tried to picture the movie trailer version of his life: here he was, a street level lawyer in a small tourist town who made a sustenance living dealing with the legal issues of everyday people. When a person got arrested for driving drunk, or after a loud domestic argument the neighbors called in, or when somebody found out their spouse was cheating, or a person got t-boned by some fool running a red light, they called him. Small businesses needing contracts, or getting threatened by a customer, or needing to collect a bill called him. Basic, boring, cheap. Of course, there was his own never-ending family death case, which was likely to be dismissed soon. Since the disaster, his life had settled into a simple, predictable, slow decline.

It had not always been that way. When his family was still living, he was on upward track. Not that he had personally been all that important, or even particularly noticed, but he worked as part of a legal machine that had a hand in running everything in New Orleans, and across the Gulf South. His firm was one of bunches like it, dozens of attorneys and support staff handling insurance and banking litigation, but also maritime cases for shipping concerns in one of America's busiest old ports, as it had for a century.

Most of his work had been in defense of maritime and longshoreman claims. Workers in the shipping industry, either seamen on merchant vessels or on the docks, when injured, have their claims processed through a different set of rules than regular workers. Injuries to seamen on vessels or workers on the docks are processed through the federal courts, and firms like Hart's represented employers primarily in the shipping industry.

His long days had been spent generating and responding to "discovery," a legal practice originally intended to reveal relevant facts, but mostly utilized by defense attorneys to delay litigation. He took a lot of depositions, and answered a mountain of written interrogatories. It was lucrative work for the firm, each case providing a significant number of billable hours from the insurance company paying for the defense of the claim. So Hart was understandably shocked when a new longshoreman death case he was working on was ordered settled by his boss, the managing partner.

The case occurred at the commercial harbor of Gulfport, Mississippi. The deceased had been part of a crew unloading banana shipping containers when he was killed. The case had just been sent over, and had been assigned to Hart as lead counsel. This was a major development in his career, being his first lead on a case of this magnitude, and he was anxious to get into the details. Almost immediately, however, his managing partner told him to settle the matter, without delay, and at maximum terms for the dead man's family. Disappointed, Hart managed to convince his boss that he needed to visit the scene of the accident to properly understand it, and be able to draft an adequate release, and finalize the paperwork.

So he went to Gulfport, and investigated the scene. The dead guy had been crushed by a shipping container. It was a simple matter of malfunctioning crane equipment, and a tragic accident. He was satisfied that the case was clear, and needed to be settled. He went by to speak to the shift manager on duty at the time of the accident, but he was out with the flu. So he returned to New Orleans, and recorded his findings, and was again told to settle the case, which he initiated. But he was intent upon closing all loose ends, so the next week he scheduled a trip to go back to Gulfport, and called ahead to make sure he could catch the manager this time, and the meeting was set. His very pregnant wife wanted to come along and do some shopping, and they had picked up his mom in Bay Saint Louis. Those two had dropped him off at the industrial harbor in Gulfport and took off, forever.

Then he wound up here. What is the point of anything? All the dreams he once had were gone. He spent every holiday looking for an open bar. He engaged in all these imaginary conversations with his dead wife and the kids he never had. No first days of school. No birthday parties or Little League. No anniversaries, or Christmases, or Easter baskets. Nothing. His life story's imaginary movie trailer ended with no exciting conclusion, or even any reason to be curious. The main character once had a good life that he had worked very hard to achieve. Then he lost it all in a tragic event outside his control, and basically gave up. The End.

He thought about that for a moment. He had been dead now for a long time, mentally and emotionally. When he finally physically died, who would ever know he had been alive? He opened his desk drawer, looked at the money bag. He thought about his dead wife and mother. Would they approve of him now? He thought about the child he never had. They had decided not to find out its gender, so he never knew. He or she would be a first grader now. He thought about his own father's rules. Had he somehow let them all down? He thought about Lisette. It had been a long time since he had been taken with a woman in that way. Was that betraying his dead wife? Could he get on with his life? Then there was Tony Vacarro. Was he a murderer? There's just no way to know.

But a couple of things had bothered him all along, and the first one was obvious. If Vacarro had planned to kill the victim, why the hell would he meet him out in public like that?

And if he killed him on the boat, why go back to the Bay Saint Louis Harbor at all? And if he killed him on the boat after they got in the harbor, why let Larue search it without a warrant? It just didn't make sense.

And it didn't make sense, Hart decided, because he really didn't do it. Vacarro actually was innocent, as he'd been repeating. John Hart had represented hundreds of people charged with crimes they *had* committed. He knew it, and they knew it. He long ago understood that attorneys who decide they won't represent guilty people can't practice criminal law. But every once in a while, he got to defend somebody he believed was actually innocent. This was it. It was the reason he started practicing in the first place. The man was innocent.

So he made the decision. Whatever happened up until now, things were about to be different. No more anonymous suffering. No more anonymity, period. He called Tony Vacarro's cell phone. Vacarro answered. Hart said, "Sorry I missed you today."

Vacarro said, "What? I was in..."

Hart said, "Never mind. I talked to Detective Larue and he told me he called you again."

"Yes, he did. But is it ok for you and me to talk on cell phones?"

"Yes. Nobody's sitting around somewhere listening to phone calls. In the real world, that requires warrants. And they haven't had time, anyway."

Tony Vacarro said, "Ok. Listen, I don't know anything about the head. I swear, the last time I saw the guy, he was all in one piece."

Hart said, "Funny. I'm glad you still have a sense of humor, you're going to need it. Here's the deal, and my terms are not negotiable. First, what you paid me is a fifty percent deposit. I need the rest up front, right away, and it's non-refundable. In other words, if I get this all thrown out before trial, which probably won't happen, you don't get a refund just because we didn't have a trial."

Tony Vacarro said, "Done. I'm happy to hear it. I don't want an attorney who under-values himself. Besides, who would want money back after that?"

"Are you kidding? Everybody. Second, why the hell did you come to me in the first place, since I know you can find a far more prominent attorney?"

"It wasn't by chance. I was more or less instructed to hire you, by my uncle. Well, great uncle, I suppose, the one everyone thinks still runs the New Orleans Mafia. His real name is Marco Puglisi, but they call him "The Raven.""

"Obviously, I've heard of him, like everybody else. That's the 'mutual friend' who somehow knows about me? I find that hard to believe."

"All I know is what I was told."

"What, exactly, did he say?"

"Well, to be honest, we didn't actually talk. I got a note from him, sort of instructions."

"He wrote you a note?"

"It was typed. What difference does it make?"

"Everything makes a difference. Did he sign it?"

"No."

"So how do you know he sent it?"

"He sent it."

Hart said, "OK. But from now on, all communications with your uncle cease. And another thing: I do the lawyering. I don't care what your best friend, or cousin Bob, or some guy you met on the golf course says he knows about the law. I make the legal decisions, and I do all the talking. Agreed?"

"That's fine with me, Counselor. Do your job."

"Good. Now, you are their only suspect. They don't have anything to tie you directly to the crime right now, but believe me, the minute they think they have enough evidence for a warrant, they will be arresting you. As soon as I know for sure you are going to be charged, we aren't going to wait for the D.A.'s office to make an event out of this. Normally, you would be arrested, and paraded in front of the media, and have to bond out. I'll arrange for all that to occur away from the press. And after that, as soon as I know for sure you are going to get indicted, if it gets that far, I am going to waive it, and get you processed without any extra drama."

"What's the actual likelihood they are going to charge me with murder?"

"High."

"When is all this happening?"

"Any time, so be on standby."

"I will have the extra cash delivered to your office by Friday."

"No cash. I know your checks are good."

Tony Vacarro said, "Fine. There's one more thing."

Hart said, "OK, I'm all ears."

"Well, you haven't asked me if I really did it."

"I know."

"Why not?"

Hart paused, then said, "Like I told you when we met. Because it doesn't matter."

Tony Vacarro said "But I didn't do it. I swear on my mother's soul."

Hart said, "That's a pretty serious oath. But whether you did it or not isn't up to me to prove. My concern is whether *they* can prove you did, beyond a reasonable doubt."

"They can't, because I really didn't do it. It is... important to me that you believe I am innocent."

"OK, I believe you're innocent."

"Because I am. I did not kill that guy."

"In all honesty, I actually do believe you. But the jury is going to want to hear who did. It's not good enough to just say 'I'm innocent.' The so-called "presumption of innocence" is, in the real world, bullshit. Jurors tend to go into a case believing that a person who has been arrested and indicted is guilty of something, no matter what they say during jury selection. They want to know who did it, if you didn't. So who did it?"

Vacarro said, "It's obviously The Raven."

"Why would he set you up like that?"

"The company. It's actually owned by a trust. Terms of the trust are, if anybody gets convicted of a felony, they're out. The other members get his share. My dad set it up that way, to make sure the company was always legit, I guess. Me getting convicted of murder makes him millions."

"OK, but let's see what the evidence says."

After they hung up, Tony Vacarro sighed. He didn't give a damn about his dead mother's soul, which was already in Hell as far as he was concerned. But he really didn't do it. He had never killed anyone, or even thought about it. The whole New Orleans Mafia thing was amusing to talk about, especially the way it made people act around him. He automatically got the best tables in restaurants, and didn't pay cover charges, or even for his drinks half the time. There was a never ending supply of women. But as far as he knew, it was over. The New Orleans Mafia, also called the Bardino Crime Family no longer existed, other than whatever shenanigans his crazy uncle was up to. It was all over, and had been for a long time.

Hoyt McGinnis couldn't believe his luck. He had won an online lottery, something he had signed up for, a free tuna fishing trip out of Venice, Louisiana, with airfare, hotels, and everything paid for.

A former wise guy, McGinnis had become embarrassingly soft and domesticated. For many years he had lived in Cincinnati, Ohio, working for a huge sausage company that made Bratwurst and Knockwurst, and all of the German wursts and weiners the city is famous for, and he had gotten fat on his own product. He had even made Floor Manager in the process. He had been forced to discard his former street ways and become a domesticated everyman, in order to survive. And it had worked. He was living a completely boring life.

Hoyt McGinnis was supposedly from a little town in Utah, had gone to community college, gotten a two year degree in food management, landed a good paying job at the sausage plant in Cincinnati. He had met a pretty waiter at a pub up on Vine Street, and married her, and had two cute twin seven year old girls, and was still hoping for a son. But his real name was

Simons, and he was from nowhere near Utah. He was from Tampa, Florida, and had spent the last several years freezing his ass off in Cincinnati because he had ratted on organized crime.

He had been working as an apprentice stevedore down on the docks in Tampa, unloading containers and cargo from ships arriving from all over the world. He just turned twenty-one, and was out in Ybor City, having beers with some of his co-workers, when one of them, some older guy who was up in management, and never around the heavy equipment, pulled him aside and asked him if he wanted to make some extra money. It might be a little dangerous, he said, maybe a little illegal. If he did a good job, he might have a chance to move up, and make some serious extra money.

Simons had heard all the stories about the old Mafia, and how they relocated a lot of their tobacco and gambling operations to Tampa after Castro took over Cuba. He didn't know any details, but he knew with certainty that the older fellow with the offer was probably either in the Mafia, or working for it. And if he was, they were not likely to leave any loose ends, especially poor young ones, who nobody would ever miss. So he instinctively understood that to decline the old guy's offer would probably be deadly. Besides, he didn't give a shit about the law, and wanted the extra money. So he accepted, on the spot.

He kept his regular job, with regular pay. But soon he was asked to take what looked like a couple of boxes of bananas to a guy at an old gas station over in Clearwater, by the airport. He had sense enough not to look in the boxes. When he got there, he didn't see the vehicle he was supposed to be meeting, so he parked and walked around the side to the men's room. Another guy followed him in. After he peed, he was cornered by the other guy, who had a gun, and a laminated card that said he was from the FBI.

The special agent asked him if he knew what was in the banana boxes in the back of his truck. Simons pulled out a cigarette, lit it, and said, "I'm going to take a guess, here. Bananas?" The agent told him the boxes indeed contained a few bananas each, but the rest of their spaces were filled with enough Chinese fentanyl pills to make sure he spent the rest of his sorry life in federal prison, unless he agreed to do what he was told.

Simons had no idea what fentanyl was, and only a vague idea where China was, but he had a perfectly clear picture of what life in prison meant, so the choice was simple. The agent had duct taped a small digital voice recorder in between his shoulder blades, and said he'd be in touch, and left. The whole thing had taken no longer than a legitimate trip to the can. The other vehicle showed up, and the boxes were picked up. For the next couple of years,

Simons had worked his way up in Tampa organized crime. With the aid of the FBI, he became almost legendary for what he was able to get away with. He made ever increasing deliveries, in bigger volumes, always efficient, always without issues.

Fentanyl was the fastest growing illegal drug money maker. It was processed into pills identical to legitimate, highly expensive U.S. pharmaceutical pain killers. It was sent in shipping containers to Panama, and wound up in the U.S. ports of Tampa and New Orleans. From there, they went to the street dealers, but also to shopping malls, and dinner parties, and soccer games. Illegal painkillers were the first U.S. drug trend to be just as dependent on middle class parents as street gangs. It was the first truly democratic high.

His bosses could give Simons any load of pills, and he would get them out of the docks and all across Florida, either by driving or by boat, a 36 foot custom made cigarette with big twin outboards on the back. While other delivery guys were occasionally caught, requiring that they be bailed out of jail and immediately killed, he seemed to be invisible to the cops. He was by far the most successful drug delivery man in Tampa.

So successful, in fact, that someone way up the chain of command had noticed him, and he got told to go to New Orleans for a meeting. But he never made it. His FBI handlers, who by that time had almost complete access to all of the Bardino family movements and communications, knew he would not survive a visit to New Orleans. They yanked him out of Confidential Informant service, put him in witness protection, gave him a new name, and sent him to live in Cincinnati.

Hoyt McGinnis had never actually been to New Orleans, and by God, he was finally going. He didn't care if it was crazy hot, and mosquito infested. According to the videos and web sites he looked up, Venice, Louisiana is one of the most popular tuna fishing destinations in the country. Battling big yellowfin tuna out in the Gulf of Mexico was supposed to be an exhausting and fairly dangerous adventure. His wife couldn't understand why he wanted to do something that crazy, and out of the ordinary routine of their lives. Besides, the twins were having a dance recital that weekend, and he couldn't miss that, could he?

But he had gotten tired of being good, and normal. He was a former Mafia associate, dammit, and an outlaw badass, not the pudgy, middled-aged, middle-class sausage maker from some square state out west everyone, including his own wife, believed. So he had signed up, and won, and accepted the prize. When he got his airline ticket, the rules were clear. Only the prize winner could attend, not wives, or girlfriends, or dates. Winners only.

The Raven watched live video of McGinnis being delivered by a van limo. He and five other prize winners were driven from the New Orleans airport to Venice, the last stop on the last paved road in the swamps and sugar cane fields south of the city, a couple of hours in traffic. They all got drinks from the little bar, go cups full of whiskey, or vodka, or cans of beer. They gawked at the Superdome, then crossed over the giant Mississippi River, and traveled down the edge of it, blocked from its view by levees.

The Raven had a big, fifty-five foot fishing vessel, an old Sportfisher design named *Tit for Tat* that he mostly kept down in Venice, at a private dock, or up on Lake Pontchartrain. She was old, but still luxurious. She had a full time crew of three, and when in port, or in bright daylight, or in sight of any other boats or people, The Raven never, ever emerged. He monitored the outside world from his dark berth underneath its foredeck.

Finally arriving, all six winners jumped on the boat, grabbed beers out of the cooler on the back deck, or more drinks out of the bar in the salon. One of them said he hoped "Tit For Tat" had something to do with titty dancers, and they all laughed. The boat captain explained they were headed out right now, to catch the afternoon bite, and it was a couple hours' run, so everyone should get comfortable. There was a small staircase down from the interior parlor, which ended before a teakwood door in the galley. He told them to stay out of that area, for safety.

Behind the teakwood door, in the loud, dark bowels of the big vessel, on a cold aluminum bench bolted to the floor sat The Raven. Big twin diesels in the engine room underneath caused a constant vibrating racket. Where he sat had once been a big bedroom, a couple of open bunks and a head. The Raven had converted it to an office of death. The bedrooms and bunks had been removed, everything but the head. There was just enough room for one prize winner at a time, plus the guy who brought him in, plus the other one in there waiting, and some torture equipment, and a couple of buckets, and the seated Raven.

Back when the Bardino Family had the spook end of the U.S. government by the balls, his reputation as a killer had been well earned. He was the last of the old family, and his job had always been enforcement, and he still did his job. One event in particular had established him as legendary in the underworld. Because of their historic ties to the CIA, recently renewed in the Bay of Pigs disaster, the Bardinos knew President Kennedy was going to visit Dallas before everybody else did. They also knew well in advance all the potential motorcade routes. It was The

Raven's job to round up a few riflemen to stake out all those routes.

The idea was not to actually kill the president, but to take a shot at him, and scare him, to remind all the Kennedys who was actually in charge. Whoever actually shot was supposed to be killed in the process. That part was up to the government spooks. The Raven had known of the crackpot Oswald from kicking his little communist ass a couple of times when Oswald had been running around New Orleans trying to stir up support for Fidel Castro. He was a nut, and a good choice as one of the four or five necessary. The Raven found him, and put him in place. But Oswald had gone off script, and miraculously pulled it off.

Over the years, so many connections had been made between the Mafia and the assassination of John F. Kennedy, it had become a common assumption they did it. Congress even declared the whole thing a conspiracy in 1978. And Marco Puglisi, nephew of Nofio Bardino, now known to the public as "The Raven," was the man who had inadvertently arranged the murder of the President of the United States.

The Bardino family influence with the U.S. government should have eventually disappeared, but it didn't. There were always new covert operations in and around the Caribbean and Central America which required secret assistance. New Orleans was still one of the last places in the United States where boats and planes were so common, and marshes and swamps so vast, that thorough police monitoring of any kind of surface or low level air traffic was impossible. So even though the government could probably destroy The Raven and whatever crew he still had, it was still advantageous to keep him around. The Bardinos and U.S. clandestine services had been an open marriage for a long time, and The Raven was the last of their unholy progeny.

So the mutual secrets continued. After all, the Raven couldn't live forever. The prize winners up on the back deck of the boat were part of the latest arrangement. They were all informants in the federal witness protection program. And not just Mob informants. All of these people, as far as the government was concerned, were guilty lowlifes to begin with, then became more contemptible by becoming rats. They had to be relocated and housed for life, which was a logistic and expense nightmare.

So this new arrangement had been made. The Raven was paid out of unallocated black ops funding to exterminate the worst rats the federal government had adopted. It was a perfect arrangement for both parties. Because of the secrecy surrounding the government's witness relocation formula, it only took a couple of people on their end to make some idiot in the protection program believe they had won something in New Orleans, book a ticket, and send them to The Raven.

The selected rats were not always fishing trip winners. Some of them thought they were going to Mardi Gras, or attending a music festival, or judging some kind of ridiculous contest. No matter what the ruse, it always ended with a one way trip down the river. The practice was to drug them, then restrain them, then as they came back to consciousness, torture and dismantle them until The Raven was satisfied they had confessed everything they had told the feds. Then they were strangled by garotte, The Raven's favorite, because it took a few minutes. He didn't actually do the killing, but he was in charge, so these six-pack fishing trips actually made him possibly the first serial mass murderer in history.

Traditionally, the family had disposed of bodies in ones and twos, because it is difficult to dispose of a human body without leaving evidence. The Raven had resolved the issue by purchasing the *Tit for Tat*, and shipping them all out to the gulf. With its legitimate charter license, he could disappear batches of rats six at a time. He was well paid for this service, but he was already rich and mainly did it for the pleasure of their suffering.

As they headed down the river, Hoyt McGinnis and the other winners stood on the back deck, or sat on the wide transom. The diesels were loud and smoky. They were all amazed at the ships and shipping industry facilities along the banks of that stretch of river, which tourists usually never saw. After they had been out a while, a deck hand passed around motion sickness medicine, little adhesive patches tourist fishermen stick behind their ears, hopefully to avoid the terrible consequences of getting seasick. McGinnis said he didn't want one, but the captain said it was a requirement of the trip, so he took one. Screw it, he thought, it was a cheap buzz. All the winners stuck them behind their ears.

A while later, as they passed the last marina on the Mississippi River at Port Eads, McGinnis was feeling funny. He thought it might be the diesel exhaust from the engines. Some of it always back drafted to the passengers. Or maybe it was the movement, but he had grown up in boats in Tampa and never got seasick. He was sitting on the transom. The rest were in deck chairs, drinking.

The guy closest to him had been loudly blathering about his old lady back in Texas, not his wife, of course, 'wink-wink' he said, and winked, and laughed, and jabbed the air with his elbow a couple of times. He had slowed down, and was slurring his third iteration of the size of her tits and prowess in bed, har har. Two of the others were actually asleep, and the rest were nodding. McGinnis realized what was happening. He had been drugged. Just before passing out, he ripped the patch behind his ear off, and let himself fall in the river, hoping he missed the boat's propellers.

None of The Raven's deadly crew had seen McGinnis go in the river. The Raven was not happy, being strident about cleaning up messes, which was his job. When the remaining five woke up a while later, he derived less pleasure than usual from the process. They all argued there was a mistake, then made threats, then apologized, then confessed, then begged and screamed, and struggled and kicked, and choked and spit, then passed out, and eventually died. One at a time, they all did.

At dark, the Raven emerged in the moonlight. The *Tit for Tat* was well out in the gulf now. He climbed up the narrow aluminum ladder on the outside of the tuna tower to the flybridge. Below, the crew opened hold doors on the back deck, and hauled up a custom made machine that looked like a big sausage grinder. It had been inspired by the operations of "pogey" boats, big fishing vessels that net up tons of fish and grind them up alive on board for the oils and feed meal they provide. Louisiana was one of the few places left in the country that still permitted it.

The Raven's grinder was designed with a powerful electric engine, and had rows of rotating, razor sharp stainless steel teeth, which easily cut through the large pieces of flesh and bone fed into the vertical chute sticking up on one end of it. Standing in the upper station, observing the bloody proceedings below, The Raven made a swaying black spot in the starry sky. The crew cut the winners up and fed their disjointed parts in the chute. At the other end, a swarm of small sharks fed on rat chum.

The shock of the cold river had kept Hoyt McGinnis from passing out. He somehow missed the boat's twin screws and bobbed up in the roiling, muddy, fishy current. He had spent the next half hour battling the drug, whatever it was, the river, and sausage fat fatigue while struggling toward the west bank. He mercifully crawled out of the water, up the muddy bank, immediately covered in stinking rotten black tar, and gnats, and mosquitos, and everything else that had wings and could bite.

With his last energy, he crawled as far as he could through a stand of cutting marsh grass, and rolled over on his back. He berated himself for being so stupid, and weak. He knew he could never see his wife or kids again, and involuntarily howled. He cried, blubbering, and swore revenge. Right before he lost consciousness, he realized he'd never make it out of the Mississippi River swamps alive. Alligators were bound to eat him before he ever woke up again.

Chapter 4

The first Monday of each month, in the airy old county courthouse on Main Street in Bay Saint Louis, the Circuit Court, which handles state criminal cases and big money civil ones, calls its docket. It is a great clamoring gathering of prosecutors, public defenders, defendants, cops, bailiffs, private attorneys, and court clerks, of bail bondsmen, parents, spouses, girlfriends and siblings of defendants, and a few members of the curious, gossipy, general public. There are far more criminal matters than civil ones, and docket call is where trial schedules are made, motion hearings set, scheduling orders handed down, and the general business of the county's biggest trial court conducted.

John Hart had a civil matter on the docket, a contract dispute between two local business owners, a motion he had filed to compel further discovery from his client's opponent. The other side apparently didn't receive the clerk's notice in time, so the hearing was reset. Hart hung around, because he wanted to catch Assistant District Attorney Laura Jones at the break. In the couple of hours it took to make it through the criminal docket, a handful of private attorneys announced readiness to try or plead their cases. John Hart was pleased to see that Thaddeus Ros was one of them.

Tad Ros had been in private practice for

decades. He was possibly the last of his era of courtroom characters, and most likely known or heard of by every adult in the county who had lived there for any amount of time. He was the oldest attorney in town, and charged his clients the most, based largely on the popular myth among street criminals that he somehow held sway over the local judiciary, either by reputation or graft. A lot of people actually believed he had bought off or blackmailed all the judges. It was a street myth widely believed among the segment of the county population most likely to appear before the court as criminal defendants.

This irritated other attorneys, and all the judges, since it tended to validate the popular perception that the whole court business was somehow part of some grand conspiracy. John Hart chuckled at the absurdity of it all. People actually believed that modern elected judges were all willing to risk prison and their careers over a little bit of money? It was ridiculous, and would require the knowledge and participation of all the judges, and dozens, if not hundreds of people, which would turn into thousands over time.

Ros was at most five feet, four inches tall. He always wore a tailored three-piece suit with matching tie, pocket square, and coordinated socks. His thick white hair was brushed straight back, pompadoured for extra height. His shiny custom made shoes were exceptionally high heeled, nineteen-seventies style. Even in his high heels, he only slightly cleared the attorney's podium when addressing the court. His small stature was counterbalanced by an impossibly huge voice, which was by nature full and baritone, and made courtrooms fairly resonate.

Thaddeus Ros had a little docket call act, a show he liked to put on, which the judges mostly tolerated. Judge Hal Donahue was presiding. He had come up through the system as Ros' slightly younger contemporary. With maybe five years separating them, this was in a time when trial attorneys were not allowed to advertise for business, and drew attention and clients by flamboyance. Consequently, Judge Donahue, who as a young attorney was himself a fairly well known courtroom character, was inclined toward enduring a certain amount of traditional grandstanding. But not much.

When his client's case was called, Ros took his time clumping to the podium in his heels. He placed a worn legal sized leather portfolio on the podium, and said, "Judge, my name is Thaddeus Ros," which caused a church chuckle to roll through the gallery crowd, front to back.

The judge said, "I'm sure everybody knows who you are, Counselor." Initially welcoming a little entertainment in the complicated business of the day, he picked up his coffee cup and leaned his heavy chair back.

Ros dug out his reading glasses, mounted them on his sharp nose, and picked up the old leather case. Holding it up for the judge to see, he said, "Judge, I carry with me at all times a copy of our great country's Constitution." The case looked old enough to have contained the original one.

"We've all heard about your copy of the Constitution, Mr. Ros," intoned the judge. "Now, what is your announcement? Are you and your client ready for trial, or is he going to enter a plea?"

Ros rocked back on his heels a little, and said, "Judge, I have been addressing you and your contemporaries and predecessors in this very courtroom for over fifty years now." The judge took a sip of coffee, and looked at the news headlines on his computer screen. Ros said, "And in all those years at the legal bar, I rarely recall, no, I will say that I can *not* recall a matter as egregiously violative of my client's Fourth and Fourteenth Amendment protections against unreasonable search and seizure, and the very precepts of due process which undergird this institution..."

The judge sat up and said, "Did you just say 'violative' and 'undergird' in the same sentence?" Everybody else laughed, but the judge only half smiled. He said, "Look, Counselor, I have a docket to get through. So is it go or no-go on the trial?"

"Well, your honor, that is the dilemma. This reminds me of a similar matter back in the sixties. That's the nineteen sixties for the benefit of the people in this room who weren't even born then," the crowd laughed, "and I believe a few years before you yourself, Your Honor, were admitted into the practice of law..."

"We all know how old you are, Counselor. Now let's hear an announcement before we all get any older," said the judge. Everyone laughed again, but the judge didn't smile this time.

Ros actually held his hand up for quiet, and said, "But that is a story for another occasion. I see you are strident in your request for a definitive statement. Still, I feel I have a sacred duty to my client, and not only my client, but to the good people of this community," he swept his hand toward the gallery, "whom are supposed to be under the protection of a law enforcement authority whose credo used to be 'Protect and Serve,' owing fealty to this very Constitution itself," he held up the portfolio, "the meaning of which has been enshrined in American jurisprudence since the early days of our August republic..."

The judge sat his empty coffee cup down too hard, and up popped the Assistant District Attorney Jones, and said, "Judge, can we move that to the heel of the docket, and speak to Mr. Ros at the break, in chambers?"

"That's fine," said the judge. "Counselor,

be ready to meet in chambers at the 11 o'clock break, with your mind made up. Next case."

At the break, the judge said he wanted to talk to Ros alone. John Hart found Laura Jones standing in the side hall outside the judge's chamber door. The judge's chamber was an office accessible directly from the courtroom, and also from the side hall. The old courthouse had high, hard ceilings and tall doors, with transom windows overhead, and gaps underneath. The building's floors were made of the steely wood of Live Oak trees that stood all over Hancock County when the French came ashore there three centuries earlier. Consequently, the hallways and courtroom itself were echo chambers, and there was no real noise privacy anywhere in the building.

Laura Jones was the most tenured attorney on the new District Attorney's staff, having worked for his predecessor, and his. She had been the first African-American Assistant District Attorney in the district, and was prosecuting felony cases when the current D.A. was still a schoolboy. Hart said, "I heard that the head old Fleming found was ID'd. I expect there will be an arrest warrant soon, so let's talk about surrendering my client Tony Vacarro to avoid a circus."

Laura Jones said, "That information hasn't been made public, so I couldn't comment. Tony Vacarro? Is there some reason that's a person I should be aware of?"

John Hart said, "Only if you read, or watch any TV. He's supposed to be the last of the Bardinos in New Orleans. Come on Laura, have a lot of human heads been washing up on the beach lately, or just that one? You know exactly who and what I'm talking about."

Jones said, "Maybe, but even if what you say is true, you know the investigation is ongoing, and..."

"And its focused on one person, Tony Vacarro, my client. Which is what I'm trying to talk to you about."

From inside the judge's office, they heard the judge say, "Dammit, Tad, I'm tired of all the grandstanding. I've been doing this a long time too, and you come across out there like you're disrespecting the Court."

Ros said, "Hal, I'm just trying to make an honest living, and giving my clients their money's worth."

"*Honest*? Is that what you call charging some country fool a minor fortune because his grandson's a screwup and he thinks you have all the judges on your payroll? That's *me* those rumors are about, and you got these people believing that I'm a crook. I don't appreciate it one bit."

Ros said, "Well now, Hal, I've never said any such of a thing, and I certainly can't help whatever crazy rumors the public chooses to believe. You know they've always believed the worst about lawyers, no matter what the actual truth of the matter is. Hell, I remember in grade school, or high school, first reading about how ..."

The judge said, "Oh shut up, before you start quoting Shakespeare to me. You've never tried to discourage that kind of talk either, have you?"

Outside, John Hart and Laura Jones could hear the conversation like they were in the same room. Hart motioned her across the hall, and across a stairway landing, to the jury room. They stepped inside and closed the heavy door. It smelled like an attic in there.

Hart said, "Look, I know the only suspect is Vacarro."

Jones said, "All we have is a head. We might not ever find all of him."

Hart said, "What the hell do you need all of him for? You've got his head, and I doubt if the Bull sharks passed up the rest. Let's talk. If you confirm to me that Tony Vacarro is going to be charged, I'll surrender him. I'd like to spare him a perp walk."

"And ultimately plead him, I assume. We've got plenty of evidence already. Half the county apparently saw your client and the victim together at a restaurant downtown and at Ship Island the day he went missing. Your client and the victim left the island together, his wife reports him missing the next day. A dozen days later, his head floats up, and that old drunk finds it. Maybe I can get the boss to approve Manslaughter and twenty, no parole."

"Don't fool yourself. Your boss wants to be in Congress one day. He won't even make an offer on this one, he's gonna want the publicity. Besides, there won't be any plea. My guy didn't do it."

"What? Come on John, you don't really believe that. Of course he did it. He's the boss of the friggin' New Orleans Mafia. We think the dead guy was a member, too. In fact, you'd better go get some extra life insurance, yourself." She immediately remembered John Hart's dead family, and smacked her head. "She said, "I'm sorry, Counselor, I wasn't thinking..."

John Hart said, "It's OK, Laura. Anyway, let me know something ASAP. And there will not be a plea. He didn't do it."

Jones laughed and said, "That's fine with me, John, I don't mind being remembered as the prosecutor who brought down the boss of the New Orleans Mafia. I'll see about letting him surrender, but you know I can't make a move without approval."

Hart said, "I know. Oh yeah, another thing. There is no New Orleans Mafia any more."

John Hart spent part of every day that week dealing with what was rapidly becoming a futile quest to get justice for his dead family.

His wrongful death suits were themselves dying. In the last round, the judge said he had to produce the missing driver, who was last seen running away from the crash site, and never found. Hart had sued the trucking company for, among other things, negligent hiring and training of the employee, who they should have to locate and produce as a witness, and he couldn't find. Of course, they had no motivation to do so, and were now being allowed by the court to hide behind and benefit from their own deadly stupidity.

He had argued these points last time in court, dwelling on the obvious injustice of the defense's position. The judge seemed sympathetic to Hart's one man show, and his lamentations about justice, but she had no real discretion, and had given him ninety days to produce the driver. Otherwise, she had said, the case would be altogether dismissed, and he could take it up on appeal.

As far as anybody knew, the driver was dead, and Hart looked like he had been a fool to turn down the pretrial settlement offer. The cops never had any leads on the guy, and neither had a progression of investigators John Hart had blown a small fortune on, until now. He had been told that a guy who might possibly fit the six-years-later profile, sketchy as the original was, may have been spotted around the fishing docks down in Venice. It wasn't much, but it was something, at least.

But he would have to deal with that next week. Mercifully, it was Friday, and he had a date with Lisette that night in New Orleans. He shivered a little. He hadn't been on a real, night-time date in several years, and was nervous. He decided to get one beer before he made the drive. Perfectly legal, and he needed to calm down.

As he headed through the main room of Canecutter's toward the patio, one of the bar-tenders said, "Mr. Hart, we're glad you're here, because your buddy Sid staked out the patio bar, and he's probably about to start some shit, from what I hear."

"Great." said John Hart, "Barley or corn?"

"Oh, definitely corn," said the bartender.

"Perfect," John Hart thought. Just what he needed after another long week.

Everything about Sid was big. He was six foot four, about 300 pounds, and loud. He was usually friendly while drinking, even overly so, as long as it was beer. Or as he called it, "Bar-ley." Occasionally, things got sideways when he drank whiskey, which he referred to as "Corn."

Sid had been born rich. His grandfather had been a big oil man, and used to invite the Louisiana governor down to New Orleans for fish fries at his house. Sid grew up thinking that sort of thing was normal.

His proper name was Sidney Hightower

Fortenberry, Jr., D.D.S. He was a dentist from New Orleans, and relatively famous on a wide arc from about Morgan City, Louisiana, to about Panama City, Florida, along the central Gulf Coast. This resulted from years of heavy TV commercial saturation. Sid's dad, also a dentist, had figured out the TV advertising market a long time ago, realizing it was the fuel that made the money machine run best.

Sid's dad had been a tall man too, in good shape, and photogenic. He had borrowed some money from Sid's grandfather, the oil tycoon, and had started running TV commercials when his colleagues, comfortable with making decent money out of single offices, thought he was crazy. Way before everyone else, he understood the concepts of product packaging, and messaging, and redundancy. He had made a fortune opening slick, efficient, and affordable dental clinics all along coastal Louisiana, Mississippi, Alabama, and Florida.

His clinics were all colorful, bright and clean. He was the first to have televisions in the reception areas, and a playroom for the kids. His slogan, "Smile With the World!" was a simple variation of the old saying "When you smile, the whole world smiles with you," and it had worked. He had set up offices, trained dentists and staffs, and stayed involved until a series of strokes forced him to retire a few years back.

Sid, who couldn't stand fooling with

other people's teeth, was now the commercial face of the operation. He was also barred by the family-run trust's Board of Directors from physically attending any of the company's dental offices. There had been some nasty business a while back, some embarrassing news articles about the excessive amount of nitrous oxide the company was using, especially in one of the offices close to Sid's main house in New Orleans.

It was a PR nightmare that had cost the company a fortune in campaign contributions and heavy rotation ads to hush. In the end, Sid had to agree with the state medical board to stay out of his own clinics, in order to keep his licenses. Which was fine with Sid, because he hated dentistry. Fortunately, the company had an army of young dentists, and a new batch graduated from school every year.

Before he ever became a famous TV dentist, Sid had his own legend. When he was in high school in New Orleans, he was a hellacious first team all state defensive end on the football team, blasting through blockers, destroying quarterbacks and running backs like a madman. LSU had won the Southeastern Conference recruiting battle for him, and he had arrived on campus a local celebrity.

Unfortunately, during a physical exam, a heart murmur was discovered, which ultimately disqualified him from playing. So before he had a chance, the path he had always assumed he would follow, college, then pro football, was unalterably blocked. Suddenly relieved from the burden of expectations but still an adored, somewhat tragic figure at LSU, Sid literally dove into the life of a regular college student.

Like many big athletic men, he was surprisingly agile. While prone to pratfalls, he was also quick to recover. Sid was often observed in college tumbling down some staircase, then rolling it out at the bottom, springing in fanfare to his feet and the crowd's applause. As a freshman, since he was out of sports, he went through fraternity rush. He awoke one morning on the couch of a stranger, and discovered someone had written "SID VISHUS" across his forehead in thick black permanent marker. After initially trying to scrub it off, he realized it was going to be there for a while. So he shadow boxed the phrase on his forehead with hunter orange paint, and continued through rush that way.

Normally, such a thing would doom a prospect's chances with the traditionally snotty LSU fraternities. But Sid was a bona fide rich kid, with family political connections, and naturally fun as hell, and was therefore considered a valuable asset for any fraternity. Somehow, his neon face art only made him more attractive to the frats. He got bids to join every one he visited, and the rest sent him one anyway. In the end, he decided not to pledge any of them, for fear of picking favorites, and cutting off future parties. Consequently, he spent his lengthy undergrad career wooed by fraternities and private party throwers, attending as sort of a guest celebrity.

He eventually graduated, and got accepted to dental school. He did not have to endure the ribbing dental students usually get about not being able to get in medical school, since by then his father's practice was worth a fortune. Despite his disgust for other people's mouths, the lure of family money drove him through. He had graduated, barely.

John Hart made his way outside to the packed patio at Canecutter's. Sid was sitting at the horseshoe bar, talking to a woman who was standing a few feet away. John Hart walked up behind him. Sid was spread across enough space for three or more people, having empty stools on either side of him, which were wisely ignored by several standing patrons. Otherwise, there were no empty seats anywhere. Reggae music pulsed through the overhead speakers, and the breeze smelled like the spicy shrimp cooking on the open air grill by the fence.

The lady Sid was talking to was wearing gym clothes and athletic shoes, and had two new beers in her hands. She was apparently waiting on the bartender to bring her tab, or change. She looked like she had just come from a workout. She stood outside Sid's massive arm span, but could hear him clearly over the music and din of the crowd.

Sid was saying, "... so ever since we met, you know, I thought that maybe we could join a health club *together*," he slapped the teak-wood bar for emphasis on 'together,' and she flinched. "And get on a health kick, you know, and start getting back in SHAPE," he thrust his right fist in the air for emphasis on 'shape,' attracting the attention of most of the patio, "and looking GOOD," thrust his left up on 'good,' which attracted the rest, "...and, before you start SCREWING THE SPINNING CLASS INSTRUCTOR BEHIND MY BACK, and BREAK MY HEART, but then...," he looked up and squinted at a spinning ceiling fan, like he was divining some great credo, and slapping the bar again, which made the whole patio jump, said, "IT PISSES ME OFF, of course, that you would do something like that to the Sid Man, because I don't deserve it." He shouted, "YOU KNOW I'M A LOVER!," thrusting both hands up on 'lover,' which startled a tourist group that had just wandered up, and actually drew some scattered applause.

Somebody yelled, "SMILE WITH THE WORLD, BABY!" and Sid yelled back, "SMILE WITH THE WORLD, MOTHERFUCKERS!" and everybody laughed.

Turning back to the workout lady, who was still waiting for her tab, he said, "And so we have to have MAKE-UP SEX out back behind the gym on the hood of that spinning class bastard's old Jaguar convertible."

He stopped long enough to grab and drain his drink glass. John Hart figured it was something expensive, but when Sid was on the corn, he would drink any available whiskey. He said, "Then, of course, I got to kick you to the curb, you know, for appearances sake, but we will still secretly love each other. Can't you SEE IT?" He nodded, grinning, air toasting her with his rattling go-cup of ice cubes.

The bartender slid her tab across the bar. Warily eyeing Sid, she sat her beers down, and signed her credit card receipt. She picked the beers back up and stared at him. He was still grinning. She started to say something, had it right on the edge of her tongue. It looked to John Hart like it was going to start with a "d." But she stopped, turned, and walked away. The crowd lost interest and went back to its general business.

Hart tapped Sid's shoulder, and said, "Hey. Who was that?"

Sid said, "Hell, I don't know." He turned around, and focusing, said, "Well, gaw-DAMN it's my favorite counselor!" He flung open his arms, whacking a couple of customers, splattering their drinks.

Amid the cacophony of scraping bars stools and scrambling wet people, Sid remained fixed and calm, holding his smile and outstretched arms for a hug, like a great whiskey

Buddha. Which he was, in effect, because like the Buddha, he had no enmity or fear, but truly believed, on the base level of his heart, that everybody loved Sid. Except, for some reason, cops.

John Hart ignored the hug, looking to see where the lady Sid had just accosted was going. He said, "When exactly did you meet that lady?"

Sid let his arms down slowly, disappointed. He said, "Just now, I think. Well, we never actually *officially* met." He looked around for his drink. "And believe me, she is no lady. By the way, quit being so serious and get us another drink. Some asshole keeps spilling mine." He looked around, noticing the stares, giving little knowing smiles and waves and winks. "Hell, get us all one," he said, "everybody around here looks like they're out."

John Hart said, "Sid, if you never met her before, how do you know she's no lady?"

"Because of the language she was just using, apparently before you got here. She called me some stuff I never even heard of before. Ha!" Then he hooted loud enough that it made him cough and quickly sneeze back-to-back, like thunder. It made everybody on the patio, already sensitive to his danger, jump again.

John Hart sighed. He said, "And why did she do that?"

Sid said, "Because I paid her a gentleman's compliment on her awesome tits. Both of them." He grinned. "OK, two compliments."

Sid had a well known and wildly socially inappropriate affinity for women's breasts. John Hart said, "Sid, just because titty bars are called 'gentlemen's clubs' doesn't mean that actual gentlemen ever compliment strange women's ... ." He noticed some abrupt movement in the crowd, and out of it popped a pissed off man, a workout dude in a way-too-small, stretched out t-shirt, and with big, veiny arms. He was marching in front of the lady that Sid just insulted, and headed his way. At the same time, Detective Larue showed up, with a new female colleague in tow. The veiny guy, who had a couple of ecstacy pills wrapped up in the tin foil from a cigarette pack in his wallet, and knowing plainclothes cops when he saw them, veered and headed out to the sidewalk, followed by his offended girlfriend. Sid hadn't noticed any of it.

Detective Larue was out of Sid's sight line. He said, "Angel Williams, meet one of our local counsel, John Hart, and his friend Dr. Sidney Fortenberry, the famous TV dentist, and as you may soon notice, a clumsy fool of a drunk on certain occasions. The counselor seems to know most of our local problem drinkers."

Sid recognized the detective's voice and, scowling, didn't turn around. He wasn't interested in meeting any new cops, either.

John Hart said, "I prefer the term "clients," but it's part of being a working class lawyer." He shook her hand, trying not to glance at her chest, which, to a normal human field of vision, largely dominated it. She was from the area, she said, had once been a lifeguard down the beach at the state water park. She had done a few years in the Mississippi Bureau of Investigation before she just joined the Bay police as an investigator.

During the couple of minutes she was chatting, John Hart was seriously hoping that Sid would not turn around. Investigator Williams had obviously had breast enhancement surgery at some point, and had made the common decision that one should, while getting enhanced, go for it. So when Sid finally got bored and spun around in his barstool, her robustly enhanced chest and his wide green eyes were on exact latitudes, and not far apart. This time he truly froze like a plaster figurine Buddha. Glaring, silent, he instantly started turning a little pink.

John Hart, on the other side of Sid from the two investigators, gave him a sharp kick in the leg, saying, "Sid, shake hands with Investigator Williams."

She held out her hand, but he didn't move.

Hart kicked him harder, and said, "Shake her hand, Sid." Which he did, slowly.

Detective Larue said, "Looks like Dr. Fortenberry here might have had a little too much to drink this afternoon. What do you think, Hart?"

Hart said, "Not at all, LaRue. He's a tourist in a tourist town, just having fun." He laughed a little.

Williams was trying to pull her hand back, but Sid still had it. Hart kicked him again, this time good and square on an ankle bone. Sid squeaked a little, like a kid letting the air out of a balloon, and turned her loose.

Detective Larue, seeing a potential police issue developing, and not wanting to get involved, said, "Alright Counselor, looks like you've got a handle on things here, we'll see you soon." They both turned started walking out.

Sid, meanwhile, had turned deep red, like he had forgotten how to breathe. The cops were almost out the gate to the sidewalk when he suddenly remembered, and gasped, and squawked "THOSE FUCKERS ARE AWESOME!" loud enough to be heard down the street.

The investigators stopped and turned. LaRue started back, but Williams held her hand in front of him, and walked back to the bar, slowly, until her chest was maybe six inches from Sid's gawking face. She said, "What fuckers are you speaking of, Dr. Fortenberry?"

He jawed silently, like a fish on a dock.

She pulled out her handcuffs, insinuating them into the narrow space in front of his nose, dangling. She said, "Because, let's get one thing straight. We all know who you are, and we definitely want you to spend your big money in our little city. But if you get out of line," she stuck the index finger of her other hand in the middle of his forehead, tilting it up until he was staring into her eyes, "You get to wear these. Are we clear?"

"Yes ma'am," he said, and hiccupped.

As they left, the crowd applauded. Sid unironically waved to them, then stood up, intending to take a bow, but lost it, and executed what looked like it could have been a planned belly flop onto a nearby table full of steaming crawfish flats and a large order of smoked tuna dip with extra crackers.

That evening, John Hart and Lisette were talking in the candlelight of Sofia's on Chartres Street in the French Quarter. The small Italian restaurant clamored with conversation and activity. Headwaiters, waiters, food runners, water glass fillers, table bussers and a Sommelier tended the two dozen or so white linen covered tables. Conversations echoed off the twelve foot, ochre-colored painted brick walls. Ancient cherry wood ceiling fans stirred the aromas of fresh Italian bread and impossibly sweet Jasmine blooms in vases around the room.

Lisette wore a light yellow cotton dress, and a simple, medium length pearl necklace. It was luminescent and the low, moving candle light made her look like a Renaissance painting. Hart said, "I don't think I've seen anyone wear pearls like that since I was very young. They are very pretty on you." He was a little embarrassed, and blushed.

She laughed, and said, "So you're saying I'm out of fashion?"

He said, "No, not at all. I realized that was stupid even as it was coming out of my mouth."

She said, "Don't sweat it, Counselor. I don't care about trends. Actually, pearls are the perfect jewelry, because they are above trends. They're among the oldest, if not the oldest jewelry ever worn. Each pearl is unique, there are no two exactly alike. And each one is born from pain. Think about it. The oyster gets a piece of hard, sharp sand inside its shell, and can't get rid of it, and it causes an irritation, which the oyster isolates by making a pearl around it. It's the prettiest thing on the outside, but it has a heart of pain."

Hart said, "Wow, I never thought of pearls that way. Should I be scared?"

She said, "Probably," and laughed.

He asked her if she had read any interesting books lately. She explained one, a philosophy based on the horrible fate of terrestrially abandoned souls. She said, "The story goes, our planet was, for bad spirits, a holding place, or a sort of jail for the cosmos. Think of it like England exiling their criminals in Australia. Or the

French, dumping theirs in New Orleans. Earth was used as a jail for all these undesirable spiritual characters spread across the galaxy. Aliens came here, thousands of years ago, and genetically engineered our human forebears to be receptacles of rejected bad spirits. Over time, they evolved along different humanoid lines. Eventually, our line killed off the rest. Voila."

Hart said, "Are you telling me you believe these things?"

Lisette took a sip of wine, her eyes casually mesmerizing. She said, "Do you go to church?"

"I was raised Catholic. When I was a kid, we went all the time. When I got older, I went sometimes." He picked up his glass and took a sip himself.

She said, "Because, if you believe Moses parted the Red Sea with a stick, I guess you can pretty much believe anything, right?"

"I think they call it 'suspension of disbelief,'" he said.

"Which is vital for all religions, right? In all other important matters, people generally demand some sort of proof, right Counselor?"

"I agree. Plus, your alien spirit story would certainly account for all the lowlifes our species tends to produce. But there's a math issue."

"Please, cross examine."

"Reproduction. As the population expanded, did they keep dropping off souls?"

"Good point. The philosophy states that all living creatures have souls that are unique. Part new, and part inherited from their parents, like DNA. So there are some mostly good ones, and some mostly bad, and some just mixed. But even the best ones are still descended from the evil originals, and therefore always in exile. It's why we can never contact our cousins, out in space. We are pariahs, and they don't want to talk to us."

"So they don't visit anymore?"

"We became too dangerous. There are many Earths in the universe."

"So basically, trying to be good is futile."

"Right," she said, as their Bouillabaisse arrived, "and against our very nature, so the pursuit of personal pleasure is the only natural state."

Hart said, "I have to ask, what was it like growing up in your family? You know, the scrutiny?"

She said, "You mean the whole Mafia thing?"

"Well, yes. What did the other kids say?"

"They were too scared to say anything. That's the whole purpose of the myth."

"What myth?"

"The myth of the New Orleans Mafia. There never was one."

"Seriously? What about the Commission

and all that stuff back in the ..."

"I didn't say there wasn't a Mafia any-where. Just not here, not really. There was never a seat on the so-called "Commission" for anyone from New Orleans. My great grandfather played along with the La Cosa Nostra image because it scared his business competitors, and made it easier for him in the ports and harbors, where the real money around here is."

"Sounds like you have been studying the subject."

"As you said, I grew up surrounded with it."

"So I don't have to worry about getting whacked for representing your brother?"

"My half brother. He and I are very differ-ent. But no, you have no worries from any fic-tional New Orleans Mafia characters. Whatever organization that may have existed back then is long gone. By the way, how does his case look?"

"Well, he hasn't actually been charged, so technically there is no case yet. I can't really talk about the details, but it is going to be a fight."

"What's the charge going to be?"

"Murder."

"Goodness. Surely not capital?"

"Doubtful. Those are almost always cases where there is good forensic evidence and eye witnesses, which is very doubtful here. Besides, either way, if you get convicted, you never get out of prison."

"If you get convicted."

"*If* you get convicted. I don't think that's going to happen."

She said, "Do you mind me asking, how is your case going in federal court? You mentioned it the other day at lunch."

"Oddly enough, I got a call today. The guy that caused the accident may have been spotted, down around Venice. But probably not, it would be a miracle to find that dude after all this time."

Saturday afternoon, John Hart arrived back in Bay Saint Louis right after Sid got up. He was drinking coffee and reading the local paper. Hart had paid a couple of tabs to clear Sid's damages, and had gotten him out of there before the cops or the veiny dude decided to come back. Sid had immediately gone to sleep on his couch, and Hart had gone to see Lisette. Sid said, "So what happened? How much do I owe?"

Hart said, "You don't remember anything?"

Sid said, "Nada."

Hart said, "Well, nothing major got broken, so I covered it. We'll worry about all that later. You feel ok?"

"Yeah, I'm a little dinged up, but nothing serious. How bad was it?"

"Well, not horrible, considering. You might want to call a certain new police officer in town, a detective, and apologize to her."

"*Her*? Oh crap, tell me she doesn't have big..."

"Huge. And after you made a characteristically subtle comment about them, she actually whipped out her handcuffs and threatened you. Although, I have to say, I don't think you took it as a threat. Come to think of it, the whole scene was sort of odd, like maybe she was flirting or something."

"Sure. Me and a cop, that would work out perfectly. What else?"

"That's about it. I thought you had sworn off the corn. What happened?"

"Hell, I don't know. Boredom, I guess. Plus, I just saw Number Four couple nights ago at the Renaissance Club. You know, the one that takes up the whole top floor of..."

"No, Sid. Only rich people know about that place. The rest of us hear about it from them."

"Well I should take you up there sometime. Anyway, you know, she was always my favorite. If I had ever had any kids...," he mulled that, sipping his coffee. Sid had a legion of ex-wives, and had taken to referring to them by their order of marriage, and divorce. Oddly, at least one of them was a two-timer, with two different numbers, and she wasn't even number four. He never had any kids, or even an acrimonious divorce. In fact, he loved them all, and they all apparently still loved him. Or tolerated him, because he had been impossible to live with. In each case, they lasted a year or two, and simply had to retreat to normal life for self preservation.

Number Four, huh?," said Hart, "how many were there, anyway?

Hart and Sid were good friends, but had only been hanging around since he moved back to Bay Saint Louis after the accident. Back then, Sid had just gotten divorced again, and they had met each other out at bars. Sid had been a crucial diversion in the bleakness of John Hart's life, and had even made him laugh occasionally.

"Eight, I think. One of them was twice. She was a titty dancer."

"Nice. In the French Quarter?"

"Nah, those are tourist traps. In a real titty bar, up by Lake Pontchartrain. Those girls know how to party."

"So why marry? Seems like you aren't real serious about it."

"Well, at least half of them we flew to Vegas, sort of on a whim."

"While drinking? How the hell can you get flights booked, and manage to..."

"Well, you know, I told you before about the plane."

"Oh, yes. The private jet. I forgot about that."

"Yeah, I need to forget about it myself. But anyway, I've been clean since the last divorce, which was, what, four or five years ago?"

"That sounds about right."

Sid said, "By the way, where did you run off to last night?"

"Oddly enough, I had a date."

"What? The perennial single man?" Sid punched him on the shoulder, "Cold hearted, and immune to the wiles of women? What happened? Has the great seal been broken, or are you still a refurbished virgin?"

"Nah, didn't even try. I don't want to rush this. Her name is Lisette, and I have definitely never met anyone on her level."

"Lisette? Not Tony Vacarro's little sister?"

"Well actually, yes."

"Yeah? He and I used to run around some at LSU. Well, a lot. She was in Europe or somewhere then. She was kind of screwed up, I remember him saying. Their mom killed herself, I think."

"I don't know. Maybe she will tell me next time."

"Next time? Holy crap, this *is* serious. When is next time?"

"Next weekend, I think. We've already been to lunch a couple times, and on one real date. But I'll worry about that later. This week is going to be interesting."

"How so?"

"I'll be surrendering Tony Vacarro, as

soon as I know they are going to arrest him. Oh, and meanwhile, I suggest you call our new detective, and do some apologizing." He flipped the detective's business card out of the breakfast bar. "Wait until you see her again. I may just start calling her Number Nine."

Chapter 5

Monday morning, the courthouse was inundated with people. The gallery was overflowing, and the stairs leading up to the court room were clogged. Someone had propped the cavernous courtroom's double doors open, and an assistant Bailiff, who was rarely ever needed, was busy scooting people out of the way as he closed them. Three TV stations had set up on the lawn outside, including one national channel, and more were on the way.

Somebody at the courthouse the previous Monday had overheard at least part of the conversation between John Hart and Assistant District Attorney Laura Jones, and repeated it. The rumor that Tony Vacarro was going to be charged with murder made it downstairs to the clerk's office, then during the week it crept out to the coffee shops and lunch places in town, and by Saturday a social media posting about it had gone viral. Hart, not a participant in social media, had missed it. He had been out Saturday night at Canecutter's, wanting to break his normally dreary weekend routine. He went there to catch a local rock and reggae band of middle aged white guys named "The Saltines" and had slept in late Sunday morning in peace.

Tony Vacarro wasn't on social media either. He had not heard anything, or noticed the fact that he was the subject of everyone's whispering attention at Tracy's, where he had driven late Sunday morning for brunch. Under high cypress beams, seated by himself in a corner booth, he had already eaten all he wanted of his Eggs Benedict, and was halfway through a second spicy Bloody Mary when the Sheriff and the police chief crowded through the front door, looking like they were practicing a three legged picnic race as they hustled through the tables toward Tony Vacarro. A herd of deputies and city cops had instantly appeared outside.

The Sheriff snatched Vacarro up by one arm while the police chief wrestled with the other one, initiating a short tug-of-war over who was going to cuff him first. The Sheriff won. Each holding an elbow, they marched him toward the front door and the gathering crowd outside. They tried to cram him through the door at the same time, each wanting to be in full view of the flock of video recorders, but rebounded off both sides of the door frame, crunching Vacarro briefly between them. They quickly had to reorganize in single file, this maneuver being won by the Police Chief, who headed out first for the phone cameras. Loudly announcing the murder charge in tandem, they paraded him, dazed, to the Sheriff's truck, dramatically declining questions.

Monday at court, Hart stood by the prosecutor's table, waiting on Laura Jones to emerge. The Sheriff had not allowed him to see Vacarro on Sunday afternoon at the jail, or earlier that morning in the holding cell in the back of the courthouse, claiming security concerns. As a result, Hart had been unable to deliver the clothes he had hastily gathered that morning. The hall door going out past the judge's chamber burst open, and Vacarro was trundled in looking like he had just gotten caught trying to bomb something.

He had short chain shackles on his wrists and ankles, which were connected together by another one too short for the job. He was hunched over and frog hopping between two of the stouter deputies, who each gripped him under an elbow. They had him in a bullet proof vest, a ridiculously large one like a bomb squad uses, and orange and white striped prison scrubs. Some smartass had put a white baseball cap with black lettering on his head from the last Sheriff's election that said MACKENZIE FOR LAW AND ORDER.

Jones was following the procession, and Hart was headed toward her when the Bailiff barked "all rise!" louder than normal in all the excitement, and the courtroom crowd stood up and got quiet and still. Judge Donahue moseyed around the dais and plopped in his chair, spilling some of his coffee. "As you were!," he fairly shouted, and the bustle resumed.

Jones made it around the crowd, and to her seat at the prosecutor's table, alongside her boss, the young D.A., who had not been at a docket in this courtroom since he got elected. Hart glared at her as long as he could, but Laura Jones never looked back. Vacarro was hopped directly to the attorney's podium in between the jury box and the judge's dais. Hart squeezed in between one of the deputies and his client, snatched the hat off, and flipped it on the floor behind them.

The judge said, "OK, we're on the record. We are going to get to scheduled matters as usual, but first we are going to hold an Initial Appearance for the Defendant Tony Vacarro, who appears to be present. This is normally done at a lower court, what we call a de novo court, but for security purposes we are handling it here, at my direction. Mr. Hart, I understand you are this Defendant's attorney?"

John Hart, said, "I am, Judge, and I would like it clear in the record that I have not been allowed access to my client until this very moment, which is egregiously unconstitutional on a number of levels..."

Interrupting, the judge said, "Wait, what did you say? You haven't yet spoken to Mr., ah, Vacarro about this matter at all?"

Hart said, "Judge, my client was arrested yesterday, about noon. I was contacted and went to see him at the county jail, shortly after he was booked. The Sheriff denied me access to him all day. This morning, I went back to see him in the holding cell, as is our custom, and was denied visitation again. Whether we will file any substantive motions as a result of this blatant affront to my client's absolute Constitutional right to counsel, as well as other due process rights, has not been determined."

The judge said, "What the hell, state?," looking at the prosecutor's table. The young D.A. refused to look up, glaring sideways at Jones. She popped up, but before she said anything, the Sheriff's bass voice intoned, from a cluster of cops over near the judge's chamber. He said, "Judge, that was my decision. As you know, I am the chief law enforcement official in the county, and I have the authority, for safety purposes, to temporarily deny counsel here access to this dangerous murderer, for the safety and security of all concerned."

The judge said, "Sheriff Mackenzie, I know what your position is around here. I believe I swore you in all four times you got elected. You are in fact the chief law enforcement officer in this county. But you are not an officer of this court, and are not to address it unless you are first addressed by it. The extent of your legal authority outside the courtroom is pretty clear. The extent of your authority inside it is up to me." Looking back at the D.A.'s table, he said, "State, you were saying?"

Just loud enough to hear, Jones said, "Judge, it's the state's position that the Sheriff has, ah, the authority to temporarily keep counsel from seeing his dangerous client for public safety and security purposes." She quickly sat down, as a few people in the gallery snickered, like chirping crickets.

The judge stared at Laura Jones for a few seconds, then the D.A. for a few more, and then the Sheriff longest of all. The courtroom was as quiet as if it were empty. Eventually, he said, "Let's get this straight right now. I am fully aware of who this Defendant is, or who you think he might be, but there will be no further independent decisions made regarding any rights, or authority, or any other matters of the law, without formal presentation to, and ruling by this Court. Is that clear?" Everyone in the courtroom nodded, even the gallery. "Now," he said, "State, what's the actual charge?"

Jones said, "Murder, Judge."

The judge said, "This Defendant has no bond set yet, state, which is the primary purpose of this hearing. I assume you all don't want one?"

"That's correct, Judge," said the young D.A., rising, loudly clearing his throat, and adjusting his tie. "The state requests this Defendant be denied bond, for reasons which we will be prepared to..."

The judge said, "You can talk now?"

The D.A. said, "Uh, excuse me, Judge?"

"Sure, you're excused," the judge said, "I

guess you had a frog in your throat earlier, isn't that what we used to say? Or was that before your time?"

The gallery snickered again, and the Bailiff yelled, "Quiet in the courtroom!"

The D.A. said, "I'm not quite sure what you are asking, judge, but with regard to the bond, I..."

"I'm saying that you just about elbowed Ms. Jones there out of her seat earlier, but it seems you have now recovered your ability to speak. Congratulations. Please, go on." The judge, who thought the young D.A. was eminently unqualified to hold his office, fake grinned.

The D.A. said, "Thank you Judge. The charge here is murder. We believe this Defendant is part of a well known Mafia family based in New Orleans traditionally known as the 'Bardinos,' and may in fact be the leader of that criminal organization, and involved in numerous nefarious transactions there, and here on the coast. As such, he is not only a flight risk, but should be assumed to be a danger to the community, to witnesses, and officers, and possibly even to the Court itself."

The judge said, "Nefarious transactions, huh? Hmm. Well, Defense, your turn."

Hart said, "Judge, my client has a second home here in Bay Saint Louis, a compound actually, down the beach, and was having Sunday brunch downtown yesterday, which is his normal habit, when the whole local constabulary showed up to arrest him. He's no more of a flight risk than you or me. He has community ties here that go back generations, and he'd have to get a face transplant for people not to instantly recognize him anywhere between Texas and Florida. There's nowhere for him to run, and more importantly, no reason to, because he is innocent. I'm asking for him to be released on his own recognizance. I also have to say, the way this has been handled, the state may have critically damaged his rights to due process, by initially denying his right to counsel. I just don't know yet. I have to talk to my client to find out what other Constitutional rights of his they have blatantly violated. We will reserve filing dispositive motions until later."

The judge said, "So neither party wants a bond set. Not surprising." Looking at the D.A., he said, "State, are you asking me to deny bond based on the Defendant's reputation in the news and entertainment media? Does he have any prior convictions?"

Standing, the D.A. looked at Jones, who shook her head. The D.A. said, "No sir, but..."

"Has he been charged with anything related to his alleged membership in some criminal organization, as you previously alluded to?"

"Well, no sir, but..."

"Are there any pending federal charges

you are aware of?"

"No sir."

"Well, are you purposefully trying to prejudice this court, or possible jurors, by introducing irrelevant innuendo and rumors into the court record?"

The young D.A. said, "Judge, this is a bond hearing, so the rules of evidence do not apply. I am simply speaking on behalf of the community I serve when I say…"

The judge said, "Son, I know what kind of hearing this is, and what the damn rules say. I was probably holding a bond hearing the day you were born. Your position is noted, you can sit down." Looking out at the gallery, he said, "I've heard enough. I have concerns, to say the least, about this man's fundamental rights being violated. That said, the Sheriff does have some discretion in securing the safety of everyone, including the Defendant. I am sure counsel will file the appropriate motions, if need be. I believe the Defendant has sufficient community ties to be released on his own recognizance. He is instructed to check in with the Clerk of the Court every Friday morning until trial, assuming there is one."

The D.A. said, "Judge, the law requires you to impose a bond in a murder case."

Judge Donahue said, "Then appeal me. Anything else?"

At Hart's office, Tony Vacarro was in the little conference room, being simultaneously babied and harangued by Miss Filomena, who had gotten churned into a roiling Welsh cauldron of spittle and indignity over the rough treatment Vacarro had gotten down at the jail, and in court. In actual fact, his stay had not been terrible, given that it was jail, since the deputies on hand had been fairly star struck. He had been fed well, and slept comfortably in a single bed cell after politely and repeatedly declining to tell "real life" Mafia stories.

But she wouldn't hear that, and was invoking ancient curses in indiscernable brogue when Hart mercifully entered, giving Vacarro a break. She left the room, after giving him an unnecessary pat on the top of his head, which was at her chin level with him seated. Irritated, Vacarro said, "Well, I thought that went fucking well. What happened to your arrangement with the prosecutor for me to quietly surrender?"

"Evidently her boss cancelled it after that internet thing went crazy. Something like two million people had read about it by the time they arrested you."

Vacarro snorted angrily. "How the hell did anybody even know about what was going on?"

Hart said, "Who knows? Somebody heard something, and the rumor got out."

"I thought you were a big shot around here, and this kind of thing couldn't happen. "

Hart, controlling a flush of anger, said, "You did, huh? Well, that doesn't make sense, because when you hired me you said you were just following your uncle's orders. Let me tell you something, Sport, I never said I was a big-shot, or anything close to it. The world's full of lawyers, and if you don't like what I do, you are free to get the hell out of here and hire another one."

Vacarro said, "Well, I didn't necessarily mean..."

"Yes you did. I've been dealing with en-titled rich boys like you all my life. Ultimately, you think you can treat people like crap because you have the daddy's money to do it. Well, that doesn't apply to me. I'm an attorney, and I put myself through hell to earn that title. Whatever I have in this world, which isn't much, I *earned*. Right now, you're in serious trouble, and if you don't like what I'm doing, or the way I'm doing it, hit the road." He pointed toward the door.

Vacarro clasped both hands on his head, stared at the high cracked plaster ceiling, and said, "Maybe I said that the wrong way. I get that you can't control what other people do. I don't want another attorney, but I swear I did not kill that guy. Just how really serious is all this?"

"Deadly. They could still go for Capital Murder, the death penalty, but they probably won't. It's too much trouble in a circumstantial case, and besides, you get life anyway for plain old murder."

Tony Vacarro put his head down on his hands, on the table. Without looking up, he said, "Promise me that won't happen."

Hart said, "I promise I will do the best I can with the case I have. That should be more than enough."

Vacarro sat back up, and said, "OK, what do we need to do?"

Hart said, "First, I want to know everything. Is there still a New Orleans Mafia, and are you running it or not?"

"In short, no. The Bardino Family was officially dissolved over a decade ago, I don't know exactly when. It was after some fool named Bonacelli, who was connected to the Bardinos, got popped in what ultimately turned out to be a money laundering scheme in a casino they controlled over in Biloxi."

"I obviously heard about it. Everybody did."

"Yes, well Bonacelli went away, and the feds got a couple of the older Bardinos to plead, but they didn't rat out the whole operation, whatever was left of it. They're dead now, died in prison. After they went to prison, there was a gathering out in the gulf, on an oil rig somewhere. I wasn't there, I was working in New York then. Plus, I don't have any Mafia business connections, and never did. They had a vote, and dissolved the whole thing, just like a company. The Bardino crime organization ceased to exist. I think the idea was, everything that was dirty had been seized, which was very little, and everybody the feds could put away, they had put away. The rest of them and their properties were sort of cleansed, and they just couldn't win any more, so it was time to quit. Technology had gotten too good, surveillance, the internet and all. So they split up what was left among the members, and everybody went their own ways.

"This was not long before my dad died. He wound up co-owning Puglisi and Vacarro, Limited, which was set up back in the nineteen fifties, just a shell that owned a few properties. It was probably conceived to launder money, but it was also a legit business. When everything got split up, The Raven owned a third of it, and dad got two thirds. It was in decent shape, held some safe stocks, municipal bonds, utilities, a little cash here and there, some commercial real estate.

"So how did you end up running it?"

"When my dad died I was still in New York. My dad had a trust, which distributed everything to me and Lisette equally. What a crock, since she doesn't know anything about running a business. I was the Trustee, and the money in the trust was required to be invested in the company, with a lot of restrictions and conditions. As Trustee, I had the discretion to either hire a manager for the company, or do it myself. I chose the latter, and Lisette agreed, and we control two thirds of the company. Anyway, the Raven agreed to it too, according to Lisette.

"We made some good aggressive investments, and got lucky on a couple other issues, and the next thing you know, we were on a roll. I built it up to what it is today. We make our own investments, loan some money, and also manage other people's money. We accept limited partners on some projects, but the company remains private, closely held. It's just me, my sister, and The Raven. And we are one hundred percent legit. There is no more Bardino crime family, or any kind of Mafia in New Orleans that I know of. Except maybe whatever my crazy uncle is up to, if anything, but nothing that I or the company are involved in. That's the truth."

"The crazy uncle who told you to hire me."

"The same."

"What if I had refused your offer?"

"I don't know. Like I said, it was just a note I got, and it said somebody was sending you that money, and I needed to put you on retainer."

Hart said, "Why do people still think of you as the head of the New Orleans Mafia?"

"Back when they dissolved the family, the word got out in New Orleans, and of course, nobody believed it. The rumor was, it was all a ruse to get the heat off. I don't know for sure, I wasn't here then. My dad and The Raven were apparently seen by the public as the last two members of the old Bardino crime family standing. So when my dad died, everybody sort of assumed I became the boss, since The Raven is too old and crazy. It's all street rumors."

"So what happened to the note you got from your uncle?"

"I burned it, as instructed."

Hart said, "Am I in any danger that you know of?"

"Not that I know of."

Hart looked at the floor for a second. He said, "Okay, what's your relationship with Rilo Marshall?"

"I just met him that day. He was in operations on the shipping docks in Gulfport for a company that our insurance division underwrites. He has a pretty decent portfolio we manage, but it wasn't big enough that I had personally noticed it before. I thought I was going to talk to him about some private placement deals we have going. You know, investment banker issues that are only available to certain groups since they are not public offerings. That Saturday, I was going to be in Bay Saint Louis anyway, and I met him over at Tracy's for brunch, then we hopped on my boat and went to Ship Island for a while."

"Where did he work?"

"On the docks in Gulfport. He's some kind of boss, I don't remember if he said where exactly. You know, there's a ton of businesses over there."

John Hart winced a little, remembering his last trip to that harbor, six years ago. "Okay, what exactly happened?"

"Nothing, really. We ate, had a couple of Bloodies. I asked him if he had anything he wanted to tell me, or if he wanted to talk about his financial condition, and expectations, or whatever. It's sort of a routine, you know. I'm trying to get him talking, since I don't know why he's there."

"What did he say?"

"Nothing. He seemed agitated. He thought I had some kind of message for him, not the other way around. I think he was probably spooked, you know, because of the whole New Orleans Mafia thing. We never got to any real conversation."

"So what did you talk about?"

"Just normal stuff. Sports, a little politics."

"What else happened?"

"I was thinking about taking my boat out to Ship Island anyway, although it was still a little early in the year. So I asked him if he wanted to take a ride, and we did."

"What happened out there?"

"There were actually quite a few boats

out. We all anchored up and sort of tied together in a flotilla, and had a great time. We got back in about dark, and he got off the boat. I never saw him again."

"Where did he go?"

"I have no idea. I was busy with the lines, and he just left. Didn't say anything, just took off."

"Anything you're not telling me?"

"Nothing. The Raven set me up. Why he did it, I don't know."

"Does Lisette work at your company, too?"

"Not really, but she does have an office."

Hart said, "I thought she was some kind of interior decorator. Why would she need an office there?"

Vacarro said, "Because she wanted one, and I need her support in the company. She actually is a decorator, and a pretty damn good one. But when you talk to her, don't let her fool you with her trippy dippy hippie crap. She's smart as shit. She went to college in Europe, in Switzerland at a place you never heard of, I bet. I can't remember the name of it."

"Okay. Not that this is necessarily relevant to anything, but in the spirit of full disclosure, I have to tell you that your sister and I recently saw each other socially. We had a dinner date this past Friday, in New Orleans."

"I don't care, as long as it doesn't affect my

case. Like I said, I don't really keep up with her, but I think you're the first guy she's been on a regular date with in a long time. Maybe ever."

"How's that? I understand she's your sister, and you two don't hang around each other, but surely you have noticed that she's extremely good looking. Seems like lots of men would be chasing her."

"I have noticed. But I think they're all just scared."

"Of what?"

"What else? The Mafia."

Lisette stood on the Mississippi River levee next to Jackson Square in the French Quarter, looking out over the roiling water as it meandered its way to the gulf. The terrible river current had claimed many drunken derelicts on this part of the waterfront, vagabonds who had ended up in New Orleans, flushed down the river with all the rest of the country's refuse. New Orleans had partially started as a dumping spot for French miscreants, and along with all its beauty, had always been the country's main drain and catch basin.

Lisette's own mother died in that river, right out from where she stood. Locals said it was a freak accident, or robbery, or lunacy, or voodoo, or what would now be called postpartum depression. Because no person in their right mind, especially somebody from New Orleans, would get in the Mississippi River right there, at the top of a curve, where the current is fastest, and the undertow best. But she knew that most of the gossip was lies, as her whole life had been tainted by a lie, and a death. A suicide.

Lisette had always heard the rumors, whispers of her mother's scandalous presence in the family, and her death. There had been an investigation. It was all over the newspapers, taboo events for a Mafia family. Young Lisette heard all these things. Sometimes the other elementary school girls said she was a bastard, and her mother was a whore, right before she dragged them down by their hair and tried to strangle them with it. After three elementary schools, the word got around New Orleans to all the other mothers, then passed to their curious daughters: leave off talking about little Lisette and her mysterious dead mother.

The same thing happened at home. At Christmas and Easter, when her great Italian family gathered and made prayers for the dead, her mother always received the least mention. Like she was some embarrassing family secret. Like Lisette was some kind of freak.

She had been sent to high school in Bay Saint Louis, to Saint Mary's, an all girl Catholic school perched on the edge of the gulf. She spent week nights at the family beach house and compound, a fenced five acres on the beach just west of town, and weekends back and forth between New Orleans and the Bay. At St. Mary's, she found out what the big secret was. When she was a junior, another student, a second cousin whose father was also in the New Orleans Mafia, told Lisette what everyone else in the family seemed to already know. Her mother had been some kind of a Gypsy-Italian stripper down in the Quarter. Her father got her pregnant, and they had to get married. That had produced Tony Jr., her older brother. A couple of years later, her mother got pregnant again. Only this time, it was by another man. So after Lisette was born, the story went, her mother went down to the Mississippi River by Jackson Square, and drowned herself. She just walked out into the current, and was gone. Her natural father, whoever that was, had already been killed and dumped in the river before her mother joined him there. No one in the family knew if Lisette was a really illegitimate or not, and after that, no one talked about it. Her mother had killed herself to save Lisette.

Which also meant that Lisette was not a true Vacarro, or kin to the Bardinos, as everyone else in the family could claim. After that revelation, Lisette had confronted Tony about it. He was a bigshot senior in high school in New Orleans at the time, and told her to shut up, forget about the rumors, and keep her place. When she pressed, he called their mother a whore, said Lisette was probably one too. He threatened her with being disinherited from the family if she ever mentioned it again, and he probably could have done it. He was the oldest, and a boy, and therefore her superior, by ridiculous patriarchal tradition.

So she never spoke of her supposed half blood with anyone in the family again. But she knew, and later confirmed it medically. She knew that they knew, and she understood that she would always be considered an interloper, an illegitimate flourish in the family mosaic. She had been forced to realize, at a critical age, that no one could be counted on, that she could either retreat into the cocoon of loveless family fortune and victimhood, or harden herself to the anonymous indifferences of life, and learn self reliance. So she had quit going to New Orleans altogether.

In high school, she had been something of a phenomenon, academically. She placed highest in every class, had scored highest on every test. But there was always talk about special treatment and Mafia influence. These slanders burnished her determination to excel. Her father then sent her to college in Switzerland. There, she was away from the family business, and no longer the subject of daily gossip in New Orleans. At college, she continued to develop academically, studying philosophy and economics, and graduating with a degree in each.

Even then, many of her classmates assumed she was a Mafia princess and got special treatment. But not everyone fell under that delusion. She had made a handful of friends, mostly women, but also a few men, who were aware of her acumen, and didn't see her as merely a product of her rich upbringing, but as the strong, intelligent, independent woman she had become. But then their father died, and for the first time since high school, she made it back to New Orleans.

The funeral, in the great Saint Louis Cathedral on Jackson Square in the French Quarter, was a royal level event for New Orleans society. The Archbishop officiated, and in addition to the dozens of extended kin of the original Bardino family, every socialite in town showed up. It was a rapturous media event, with local and national gossip shows slathering over New Orleans Mafia history, an era which time and subsequent craziness in the American political environment had become nostalgic for a lot of the public. There was a lot of chatter about old killings, and new rumors about the modern existence of organized crime in New Orleans. This is when Tony Vacarro became the new crime boss of the Bardino Family as far as trash TV, social media, and street gossip were concerned. Other than the practically invisible character known as The Raven, Tony Vacarro, for many years a resident of New York, was widely believed to be the last in the line of the old true New Orleans Mafia.

After the funeral, there had been a meeting with her brother and the old man's lawyer at his firm's offices down on Poydras Street, next to the federal court building. She hadn't spoken to her brother since he called her a whore in high school. That had ended their association, as far as she was concerned. Surprisingly, Tony Senior had left her and Tony an equal stake in an irrevocable trust which funded the legitimate family business.

This had been a shock to her brother, who had spent several years on Wall Street, and was prepared to take over the company's management, but not to hand half of it to some stranger he barely knew. When he said so, the lawyer assured him that he had no choice. So for stability sake, he had told her he regretted calling their mother a whore, and her too. She told him that all was forgiven.

But it wasn't. Staring at the river, remembering, Lisette was mesmerized by its currents. It was a living, moving, three dimensional body of transportation and trade, life and death. All those years ago, Tony's cruelty was the first time in her life that she had been the object of the callous disregard all men seemed to possess toward women. It had injured her, young as she was, and festered inside. Eventually, the injury healed, and became scarred. It hardened deep inside her, an irritation so invasive and immutable that it had to be completely sealed, and cooled, and fortified, and isolated, like a pearl. She smoothed it, and polished it, and let her pain turn it into something beautiful, and peaceful, and cold. And it was nothing more or less than a pure and perfect hatred of her brother Tony Vacarro.

She had stayed in New Orleans. She had done all the traveling, and studying, and trying to understand the pernicious human race she cared to. She made Tony agree to her having an office, and started looking around for something useful to do. In the meantime, she had begun coming down to the waterfront, where her mother died. It was at first a sort of communal experience; she sat and gazed out at the endless passing of river water that drained most of North America, and was a literal highway to the rest of the world. The reason New Orleans existed. The reason she existed. The reason her mother did not.

She quickly became a missionary to the homeless who gathered there. She brought them food and water. The New Orleans police would inevitably come along and run her beneficiaries away, and she took care to never identify herself. She had been gone for so long, nobody recognized her as her father's daughter. Once, a young man on the waterfront had accosted her for money, and groped her body, threatening anyone in the area to stop him. He was not homeless, or desperate, or even particularly needy, just an aggressive young punk with enough jailhouse tats to indicate that he was genuinely dangerous. She had managed to slip away from him, and back toward the crowded Jackson Square, and safety. She had vowed to never again be unarmed at the waterfront. Or anywhere.

As for John Hart, she was... intrigued. He seemed to have a hell of a capacity for bad luck, maybe even an attraction for it. And he was obviously injured, a psychological study in trauma and durability, and maybe a little fatalism. But he also had a sort of nonchalant defiance of convention, as if he really just wasn't affected by the mundane concerns that occupy normal people. Like they were beneath his attention level. He didn't even know about all the latest celebrity news constantly spewed in between beer and insurance commercials on television. That made him interesting. And even though he had been traumatized, he had no apparent doubt that everything could be better, if he just wanted it. He just wasn't sure he wanted it. That made him somewhat intriguing.

She had never even been in a relationship. She had always treated men the same way single men normally treat women. She knew she was good looking, and kept her body in shape, and could have just about anyone she wanted, man or woman. When she had sexual urges, she went out, found one to satisfy her, then cast them aside before there was ever a chance for any kind of personal feelings.

John Hart was a danger to her in every way. She had lied to him about the old New Orleans Mafia. It certainly had existed, and had run the moving parts of the city for the better part of a century. Sure, the feds had helped kill off the old group, and the rest split up the chips and moved on. But it most definitely *had* existed. And there was so much more. One thing she hadn't lied to him about, though. She had been having a good time, and was looking forward to their next date.

John Hart sat in U.S. District Court in Gulfport, Mississippi, taking notes while opposing counsel made its arguments at a motion hearing in the wrongful death cases. The federal judge had made her previous ruling about locating the driver, and the defense had filed another motion, wanting to know what was going on. The defense lawyer had droned on for over an hour, deliberately running up his time which, in federal court civil litigation, was at its highest pay rate. His time included the junior counsel in court with him, and two paralegals back at the office. He had started around the same track for the third time when the judge cut him off.

She said, "Counsel, I get the gist of your argument. You feel like your client is getting damaged in some way by the Plaintiff's inability to locate your client's former employee, the one who allegedly caused these deaths. Is that pretty accurate?"

The attorney said, "Well, Judge, that's a stark way of saying it, when you put it in those terms, although I remind the Court, and state for the record, that we have never formally conceded that there is any legally cognizable employer- employee relationship which would cause an agency and therefore confer upon my client vicarious liability for the actions of an apparently -or suspected, I might say- intoxicated individual who we think clearly misrepresented his status and professional abilities to my client prior to what can only be described as an unfortunate accident..."

"The judge said, "I understand, counsel. Your client isn't responsible for anything. That about the size of it?" She didn't wait for his response. Looking to John Hart, she said, "Ok Counselor, your response?"

The insurance defense attorney interrupted, saying, "Excuse me Judge, I wasn't through. If I may say, with regard to the unforeseeable intervening superseding circumstances of the independent decisions made by the only truly culpable individual associated with this admittedly unfortunate matter, the driver of the truck, whom the Plaintiff has not been able to locate and produce, because of apparent lack of due diligence, which has correspondingly caused irreparable damage to our ability to properly defend what we consider to be, under the circumstances, an inherently flawed pair of Wrongful Death matters, we believe..."

"I understand what you believe, Counselor. You have now stated your position, as far as I can tell, three complete times in this hearing alone. I heard these same arguments the last time we convened, when I gave the Plaintiff ninety days to locate the driver, and communicate to the Court that he had been located, and subpoenaed, and was ready to testify. That was," she turned to the court clerk, and asked, "how long ago?"

"Forty-two days, Judge," said the clerk.

"Forty-two days ago, Counselor. That ruling was on your motion. You made, as I recall, the exact same arguments then as you make now. I granted your motion. The Plaintiff still has, I believe, Forty-eight days to complete this requisite, or not. That about sum it up?"

The defense attorney was, for the first time in this case, temporarily stumped. He finally said, "Judge, we must say, at the risk of sounding like we are contradicting the court, but strictly for the record, as is my duty to represent my client's interests, that we disagree with the Court's assessment of our position in the terms stated, and that we are simply trying to address a significant issue, in light of recent 5th Circuit precedent in furtherance of the oft stated public policy of discouraging civil cases of a frivolous nature, which has caused us, in this matter, undue expense..."

The judge cut him off again. She said, "Counselor, I've about heard enough from you today. Speaking of the record, you've peppered it with references to the deaths of the victims in this case as 'unfortunate,' and the combined suits filed in this court on behalf of their estates as 'frivolous.' Meanwhile, we have no further information from you or the Plaintiff, and you have managed to waste this Court's time, while increasing expenses for all involved, including not only your client, but the Plaintiff, and this Court."

The defense lawyer, red faced, said, "Judge, in light of what we can only consider to be prejudicial statements made by this Court today, I am going to have to move for your honor's recusal, and ask for time to brief the matter, without tolling the Court's previous time line for the Plaintiff to produce the responsible Party."

"Denied," said the judge.

"But Ma'am, I wasn't through with my argument, for the record."

"Yes you were. And do not refer to me as anything but 'Your Honor' or 'Judge' or some other honorific that does not refer to gender."

"What? I don't understand, Judge. You seem to be overly sensitive to, and therefore inclined to misinterpret and mischaracterize our statements regarding these and other matters associated with this case, resulting in...:

"I've heard enough from you today Counselor. Your recusal motion is denied."

"Then we move for an order allowing interlocutory appeal on the question of recusal, Judge, since it appears that you are biased, and in any normal, rational analysis, we believe it would appear so to any reasonable person."

"I'm aware of the legal standard for recusal. Denied."

"But Judge I don't think you're seeing this clearly."

"Counselor, you are getting, as my father used to say, dangerously close to the end of the pier with this. You have now stated in the court record that I am 'overly sensitive' and not rational. Is it possible that your own personal biases lead you to these inaccurate conclusions?"

"But Judge I have to object, and ask for your immediate recusal, and if you deny my motion, I have to warn the Court, I intend to file a petition for review of Your Honor's actions here today."

"Noted. Denied. File your petition. Sit down, you're done for the day." Turning to Hart, she said, "Counselor?"

Hart stood up, and said, "Your Honor, I am diligently seeking the Defendant's employee, who I think my investigators may have located, but are in the process of identifying. We will report to the Court our progress in due course."

"Fine. Do you have any motions?"

Hart was temporarily stumped, but he realized the judge's meaning.

"Judge, we move for an Order requiring the Defense to pay our expenses and attorney fees for the necessity of having to prepare for and attend this hearing, which we believe was at best cumulative and repetitious, if not outright frivolous."

"Motion granted." She turned to the defense and said, "Counselor, how much are you charging your client for being here today?"

He said, "Judge, you are not entitled to examine what is fundamentally an attorney-client relationship privilege..."

"Which you opened the door to by complaining to this Court earlier about your client's expenses related to what you apparently consider to be a frivolous case presided over by a biased judge. Let me remind you, Counselor, that I was an insurance defense attorney myself for twenty years before I first became a state judge, and eventually a federal judge. So I have some idea what your firm's invoices look like. How much are you being paid?"

"I think this is entirely improper, Judge. I am charging four fifty an hour for litigation, and preparation for litigation, which is the cap limit our client will pay for this region of the country."

"Your client the insurance company, or the named Defendant?"

"Judge, I'm not sure what you mean, because the existence or non-existence of available insurance is deliberately concealed to prevent bias..."

"I know what the rule says, Counselor. Who do you send your bills to?"

"The insurance company, Judge."

"Fine. How about your assistant there, what is she being paid, and the paralegals and other assistants?"

He said, "Judge, I actually do not know what the staff makes."

She said, "Well, have the staff figure it out, and send it to me by, let's say, this time tomorrow. The Court will examine it *in camera*, and it will not be filed, or otherwise made available in the record."

She turned to Hart, said, "Counselor, prepare your time, and your staff's time, and submit it to the court's staff in the morning. You'll be reimbursed by the Defense at the same rate they are paid. We will calculate what you are owed."

John Hart said, "Thank you, Judge."

The judge said, "Don't thank me, Counselor. This is a matter of judicial efficiency, not bias, as the Defense has suggested. I remind you that, no matter how unfair this Court's rulings may appear to either side of this case, it is following the rules, not making them. You must produce your witness in the time prescribed, or I will dismiss your cases. That's it."

Tony Vacarro had come to his station in life not just by family connections, but also by talent. He had been an average student at LSU, and was often seen roaring around in some off-road vehicle piloted by his good friend Sid Fortenberry, who was known around the Baton Rouge campus as "Sid Vishus." They were usually headed to raid a sorority house, or vandalize a historic campus monument, or to beat the all time beer run record, leaving a trail of empty cans and dented cars across campus. The wayward sons of New Orleans' rich and powerful just didn't give a damn about regular laws, which they regarded as mere recommendations to be heeded by the peasantry.

But bad behavior aside, Vacarro had actually been something of an ace at things like statistics, and reinsurance, and equities, and the arcane currents of macroeconomics. When he finally graduated LSU, the Bardinos were still running things in New Orleans. His father was one of the top three guys, and was ambivalent about whether Tony Jr. joined the family business or not. The younger Tony, however, didn't want anything to do with it, and got himself a job in New York.

The traditional New Orleans Mafia was doomed back when Tony's distant step-cousin Nicholas Bonacelli, a genuine street asshole from Chicago, was brought down to run one of the family's properties, the Cronus Casino over in Biloxi, Mississippi. True to his nature, he had gotten himself arrested in some stupid scheme ultimately connected to funding international terrorism. The dominoes fell quickly. Petrino Mallini, the Bardino Family boss at the time, just disappeared and was never found. A couple of the older Bardino guys had gone away to prison forever. A couple more died during the legal process.

The feds had taken most of the casino holdings, and cash, and some properties on the Mississippi Gulf Coast and in New Orleans. Somehow, his crazy great uncle The Raven didn't get convicted of anything, or indicted, or even arrested. Apparently, even the immunity he was offered was not enough for cousin Bonacelli to rat on the Raven. What was left of the Bardino family officially dispersed. They had one final meeting and called it quits, as he had told Hart.

He hadn't told his attorney the part about flashing the peace sign after they first met. "If the attorney is hired, or wants time to consider the offer," the note read, "when you leave Gabriella's, hold up two fingers. If he declines, do nothing."

Tony Vacarro wasn't sure exactly what that meant, but he had a pretty good idea. He was going to have to keep that part to himself.

Chapter 6

John Hart walked out the front door of his elevated house, stretching, twisting his back, ready for an early morning bicycle ride along the waterfront of the Saint Louis Bay. He was headed down the stairs when he saw the raccoons had gotten into his garbage again.

The raccoons had first been engaged four years earlier when he moved into the little rental house on Cedar Point, a block from the edge of the bay, north of downtown. He had just moved out of the big house in New Orleans, and had to downsize his stuff. This had resulted in a bunch of garden sized trash bags full of, among other things, hundreds of pages of outdated documents and papers of different types. The garbage pickup was Monday, and that Sunday he had lined the street with bags. He figured out later that some leftover jambalaya had made it into one of the bags. It was late in the year during a cool weather snap, and the northwest wind was ripping.

The next morning, the marshy land southeast of his house was white. Not completely, since several breaks in the papered surface were rent by prickly palm trees, and needle covered rockachaws, and a bunch of razor sharp stands of saw briars. The raccoons, driven into a frenzy by their first encounter with jambalaya, had shredded all the garbage bags, and the wind had scattered the thousands of white papers over an area the size of a football field. He had spent most of the next two days picking it up, getting scraped and poked, and cut up, and gnawed by fire ants, and plotting revenge. That was the first skirmish in The Raccoon War.

He had gone to the hardware store, and gotten two brand new heavy aluminum, lidded garbage cans. The night before the next garbage day, he had strapped down the lids with heavy duty bungee cords, and had placed the shiny, heavily loaded, tightly secured receptacles down by the mailbox. He had scanned around the area, scoffing at the unseen, outgunned little burglars. He had even put some extra food in the cans, just to be irritating, and gone off to bed.

The next morning, the bungee cords were where the cans used to be, rolled up neatly in a smartassed way and laid side by side near the mailbox. The dinged and scratched up, sticky and stinking garbage cans and lids were scattered across the road and in the ditch on the other side. Whatever was left of their former contents was across his front yard and down the road in both directions. Angry but impressed, he had gone back to the hardware store.

This time, he mounted galvanized hooks high on the vertical wooden piers that elevated his house. There he hung his garbage bags. This was well beyond anything the raccoons should be able to reach, and he would only be required to remember to put out the bags, in the cans, on the morning of garbage pickup. No big deal. As it turned out, it was the easiest garbage conundrum the raccoons ever solved, being expert climbers under any conditions. The unfortunate scheme also resulted in relocation of the stinking offal pile from out on the street to under his house.

At that point, he had gotten serious. The Raccoon War had turned into a real thing, and control of a vital residential function was officially at issue. For a long while, he was forced to keep his damn garbage inside the house until the morning the garbage truck ran. Of course, he often forgot garbage day as he raced out of his driveway, late for court or some vital meeting. Consequently, for most of the early part of the war they were winning, and his house stunk.

Time passed, and his bunker conditions became intolerable. Hart went back to the hardware store. It took a while, but he had installed stainless steel eyebolts this time, and strung heavy picture wire eight feet overhead between the wooden piers under his house. He made a bunch of "s" hooks out of chopped up coat hangers to hang garbage bags up on the wire. The bags dangled a good five feet off the ground, and when slid to between the posts, several feet away from either side, should have been the final shot in the last skirmish of the conflict.

Many times he chuckled upstairs as he

heard the whole local Raccoon herd scrambling around underneath, scratching and clawing up the wooden piers, and down them, and trying to figure out how to get at that delicious garbage. It was the only real humor in his life, other than the odd night out with Sid, who he had recently met. As long as he could see the garbage hanging there in the mornings, he could remember to put it out by the road. Even if he was running late and forgot, at least it didn't stink up the house.

This went on for a long while. So long, in fact, that John Hart came to consider the Raccoon War won, a thing of the past. He had actually started feeling sorry for the insidious little thieves, and even left some food out for them a night or two. This was completely unnecessary, since he lived in a low lying area that had stands of water year round, and was in effect an active swamp in the edge of the city. It was full of minnows and tadpoles, salamanders and grass snakes, and lizards of every type and color, and a constant supply of various amphibian eggs, and bird eggs, and babies of all these, and all the other things that Raccoons naturally eat. The Raccoons were never going to go hungry, they just preferred his cuisine to theirs.

Then, the impossible happened. He went down one garbage day, and the Raccoon War was back on. Somehow, they had figured out how to get to the overhanging garbage, and pull it down.

After his customary cursing cleanup, he popped out a canvas beach chair, and plopped down to ponder it. There was no way they could get there by the wood piers, it was just too far down the tiny wire. But there was nothing else to climb on, so they had to have accessed the bags from underneath. But unless they had a Goliath raccoon, they couldn't have possibly gotten to it. Yet, they had. He concluded that absent some human or supernatural assistance, they had to have climbed on top each other, forming something like a raccoon pyramid to get the garbage. It was the only rational explanation.

That's when he started to suspect a higher intelligence among the raccoons, some kind of wise raccoon who could problem solve, and innovate, and was once again winning the Raccoon War. He kept his garbage inside the house for another while, to regroup. Naturally, the smell became intolerable again, so he had taken to setting his cans out on the porch in the daytime, raccoons being night raiders. He put them in the washer/dryer room at night.

Soon enough, he forgot to bring the garbage in. Sleeping on the couch, the TV yammering sports news, he was awakened by a scramble of activity on the front porch. Simultaneously flipping the porch light on and jerking the door open, he set off a cavalcade of raccoons of all sizes, all gray and white and black, some red here and there, and all stripey, piling over each other to get down the stairs, cascading like a furry waterfall, dozens of them. In a few seconds, they were all gone, scattered in every dark direction from the bottom of the steps.

Except one, who sat up on her huge haunches at the top of the stairs, facing him, no more than four or five feet away. Her amazingly complex hands hung by her sides, palms up. Owing to her girth, they were plumped out on either side, like she was holding them out on purpose, and saying, "What?" He figured this big female was probably the smart one, the Raccoon Queen.

The Raccoon Queen gazed up at John Hart. Not that the Queen had ever known Hart's name, or even that it had a name, or wondered what it was. As far as she was concerned, all creatures that don't eat raccoons *are* raccoons. This was just an extra large, hairless one that lived in a big lighted hollow tree in the forest of her country. And just like all other raccoons, she was its master. She was checking out its teeth and claws. Other than sheer size, she saw no threat.

She was in no hurry to leave, since she was not in immediate danger, and had never seen the hairless one this close. For as long as she could remember, this big raccoon had been leaving delicious food out for her and her burgeoning tribe by the hard trail in front of its tree. When it first got there, the food was in flimsy cocoons, easily ripped open and scattered, and searched for food. Later on, it used cold, shiny shells, which it tried to secure with some kind of short, stretchy vine. She had observed this from a tree across the street, and had some idea of the diabolical design. By examining and pulling on the vines, she quickly discovered how to take them off, and get to the food. Many times she had watched it stomping around, barking loud noises in some exotic raccoon dialect, putting the inedibles back in the shiny shells, and them back by the hard trail.

The big hairless raccoon had tried to hide her tribe's food in many ways, but she had always been able to get it. It had taken to hanging the food cocoons under its tree on strong tiny vines, out of reach. Every night for a long time, maybe a season, she had visited and studied, and tested, and sent young raccoons on different missions, with different experiments, to try and get the hanging food from under the tree, without success. This went on, and her tribe nearly revolted, having been made fat and complacent by its easy food, and suddenly being driven back to slithery food conventions.

She got an idea from some ants across the street she sometimes watched for entertainment. She had noticed that they often scramble into interlocking formations, making themselves into bridges, or ladders, or whatever temporary structure was necessary to accomplish some job. She figured raccoons could be similarly assembled, and had arranged for several of her youngest and strongest to link up, in layers, and make themselves a raccoon pile, which eventually reached high enough to let one crawl on top and get to the food.

This innovation worked one time only. For a long time after that, the hairless raccoon kept their food inside its tree at night, only putting it out in daylight, just before a big loud monster carrying other hairless raccoons came down the hard trail and ate it all. Anyway, this time it was easy to get at, and she wasn't leaving. She ignored the hairless one, and started back eating.

The big female raccoon had just sat and eyeballed him for a good while, then sort of shrugged and went right back to eating, like he wasn't there. He wondered if Raccoons were prone to frontal assault. They had always been violent con artists, their vicious criminal nature disguised by an evolved camouflage of misleading cuteness. He had heard stories of them getting cornered by dogs or foolish humans, then morphing into Tasmanian Devils, a blur of vicious clawing and deadly teeth, mauling everything in the vicinity. Figuring he'd rather deal with the garbage cleanup tomorrow, he eased back in and closed the door.

The Raccoon War had gone on for a couple

of years with no decisive human victories, or any clear solution. The problem was, he had to be able to put the garbage out. He really couldn't always move it in and out of the house between garbage days, and he couldn't drive it way out to the county dump himself, and he couldn't cram all the food down the sink, since the sewer lines out there barely worked anyway. His position was thus far a sort of inverse siege where the only way to defeat the surrounding enemy force was to starve it away. There had to be a better plan.

Turned out, the solution had been available all along. He eventually realized that the picture wire scheme under the house had always been the answer, he had just given up too soon. Before, he had been spooked by the evident raccoon pyramid, and had missed the obvious. The higher the garbage is hung, the least effective the pyramid can be, based upon basic weight and gravity considerations. Six or seven feet of garbage elevation should be enough to finally end the Raccoon War permanently. So even though it was a pain to have to hang his garbage way up on the line, involving a short step ladder, anything beat keeping it in the house. He had worked out the logistics, and the scheme held. Quite a bit more time passed, and he again came to consider the Raccoon War won, and finished.

Yet, it had happened again. He had hung a bag, seven feet up or thereabout at the lowest point, in the middle of a ten foot span of stainless steel wire. The garbage was inaccessible from above. Somehow, it had been ripped open like a stinky pinata. He had paced, and thought, and actually scratched his head, without realizing it. A while later, he finally figured out how they did it. One of them, and it surely could not have been the hefty Queen, had to have hung upside down and hand walked down the wire to the garbage, like an acrobat. It was the only explanation.

The Queen had been watching as the hairless one eventually reemerged with the food. This time it hung so high that the greatest raccoon pile would never work. For a long time, every night the food was out, the Queen observed, and plotted, and tested. She constructed a series of young raccoon ladders and piles, to no good. She sent some of the more daring out on the tiny vine, trying to balance, but they always slipped, and dangled, and fell before they got anywhere near the food. The situation eventually seemed hopeless, and the Queen seriously considered abandoning this part of the forest to the hairless one.

But one night she got her greatest inspiration. There were overhead vines stretched between bare tree trunks down the side of the hard trail that lit up at night. She had seen small raccoons, chattery ones with long bushy tails, running on the tops of these tiny vines many times.

These types of raccoons were always flying around in the trees, and squabbling, and barking, and chasing each other, and playing, and generally burning up unnecessary energy.

They were, she had observed, an odd mixture of crafty long-term plan makers, and crazy short-term chance takers. They were the forest leaders in gathering and stashing dry food for the cold season, but had no plan at all for avoiding the big monsters that periodically roared up and down the hard trail. When one came they would try to ignore it, not wanting to be bothered in their revelries, then panic at the last possible second, running back and forth, unable to decide how to get out of the way. Panic and indecision left their dead dotting the hard trail everywhere in both directions. For this reason, the Queen had never trusted them.

That night, she saw one of these chattery little raccoons up on one of those long tiny vines. This time, it wasn't walking on top, which it could do, but was scooting along upside down, hanging by its hands, which weren't even as good as hers. So she got a couple of her best young raccoon climbers. After a lot of instruction, and a bunch of tries, her students had gone across the tiny vine under the big raccoon's tree while hanging upside down, just like the little chattery ones. They had gotten to the food cocoon, and gloriously tore it open.

Every time John Hart had thought the Raccoon War was over, the Raccoon Queen had come up with some innovation. He knew she was always out there watching him, although he had only seen her that one time. In his loneliness, he had formed a kind of begrudging respect for her. He couldn't leave the garbage inside, and every time he put it out, she and her tribe scattered it. So he eventually gave up, and conceded. The Raccoon Queen had won the Raccoon War, and John Hart had been forced to conclude that as long as he lived on Cedar Point, periodically cleaning up garbage was like cutting the grass, something that just had to be done.

So he smirked at the mess, and gave a wave to the old girl, who he figured was watching from somewhere, and hopped on his bike, and headed down toward the water.

It had gotten hot in Bay Saint Louis. Under the hill of the city, the marina was full of boats for the season. Tony Vacarro had brought his yacht *Negotiable* over to its slip on the bulkhead, which the locals called "Millionaire's Row." The Bay Saint Louis Harbor, and Bay Saint Louis itself, had always been his refuge, away from the bustle of New Orleans and the crowd of big boats on Lake Pontchartrain, and down the Mississippi River at Venice. Vacarro had always loved the festive atmosphere of summertime in Bay Saint Louis. Only now, it was tainted by the looming murder trial, and the real possibility of life in some dank cage at Parchman Penitentiary, the infamous hellhole up in the mosquito swamps of the Mississippi Delta.

It was late Sunday evening, and Vacarro and Hart were sitting in the open upper deck, having a beer in the peach colored sunset. This past week, prosecutor Laura Jones had called Hart and said they were definitely going to indict. They had a new witness, someone who could testify that Vacarro and Rilo Marshall were in a loud argument on his boat right before they left Ship Island. Also, forensics had fixed the time of death around that same weekend. It was more than enough probable cause for an indictment. By agreed order, and without a public pronouncement, he had waived indictment, and had set a quick trial date.

Vacarro said, "John, I understand our strategy, I guess, but didn't waiving the indictment make me look more guilty? I mean, why couldn't we tell the Grand Jury my side, and take advantage of that "presumption of innocence" that lawyers are always talking about?"

"Defense attorneys don't get any input in the grand jury process. We can't even appear. They only hear one side of the story, so the D.A. can basically get anybody indicted. I didn't want the grand jurors to run all over the county poisoning the jury pool with whatever dramatic story they've heard from the D.A."

"Aren't they sworn to secrecy?"

Hart looked at him for a few seconds, and said, "That's interesting. How the hell can you come from a whole line of professional criminals, and still be so naive about how the real world works? People don't keep secrets, Tony. It's contrary to human nature. You really don't seem that naive about everything else."

There was another pause, and then they both laughed. "OK, Counselor," said Vacarro. "It's only my life we're talking about, so let's laugh it up, what the hell."

Hart said, "Believe me, it's better this way. Besides, like I told you before, they're already going to think you're guilty, so at this stage we don't have much to lose. No jury pool is going to think you're sitting up there as a defendant in a murder case because you didn't do anything. They're all going to assume you're guilty from the outset. It's up to us to turn that notion around."

"If they all think I'm in the Mafia, why are we not trying to get the trial moved?"

"To where, Tupelo? You have to be tried in Mississippi, and there's no county in this state where people haven't heard of the New Orleans Mafia, or seen you or something about the Bardino Family on TV or some kind of media. Besides, we're going to have to use that assumption to our advantage."

"How could that possibly be an advantage?"

"Like I've always said, everybody's a lawyer, but some of us have licenses."

Vacarro said, "I still can't believe they are trying me for a murder. Hell, I've never killed anybody. I wouldn't even know how to go about it."

John Hart said, "That's good. That's exactly the kind of testimony we need to hear when you take the stand, if it ever gets that far."

"I don't know. How come everyone else says the defendant never testifies? Isn't that sort of a rule of thumb?"

"We've been over this. When you say 'everyone else' you mean your friends, right? Everybody has some inner lawyer who thinks they know how to do the job better than the real ones."

"Yeah, I guess so, but why do so many people say that? It has to have some truth if everybody believes it, right?"

Hart sighed, said, "It's what I call "Flock Logic." "Flogic," if you like. He sipped his beer, looked around, pointed northeast, toward the long beach down the waterfront by the bay bridge. A flock of terns were circling, about to land on the sand. He said, "See those birds? You ever wonder why they don't all just run into each other, and crash? I mean, who's steering? Is there some lead bird that decides for everybody when to take off, and where to go, when to land?"

"I never thought about it."

"All we know is, they have figured out how to stay in the flock, in their own space, to move with the crowd, with no disruptions. No one individual has to make decisions about where to go. It keeps them safe to stay in their own flock. Humans are the same way. There's a tendency to come to general conclusions, and rally around other people who think the same way. That way, you don't have to think things out, or make your own decisions. An individual can be totally wrong about something, but not notice, because he's surrounded on all sides by people who are just as deluded as he is. That's the gravity that holds political parties together, and also the reason some people are so easy to fool with conspiracy theories. Lack of intellectual curiosity makes people cede their decision making responsibilities to a group. Flogic."

"Flogic. You make that up?"

"Far as I know, that's a John Hart original."

"OK, so what's the flogic behind the general belief that it's a bad idea for defendants to testify?"

"The simple fact that most criminal defendants are guilty as hell, and also not smart enough to survive any basic cross examination by a halfway competent prosecutor. But when people are actually innocent, and have a little intelligence, I think the jury should hear from them."

"So you actually believe me? That I didn't do it?"

"Yes, I actually believe you didn't do it. You just don't seem that stupid. I mean, about most things." He smiled.

"Well, I didn't do it. I was set up, and now I'm getting persecuted for being a Bardino, for things that happened in the past, that I didn't have any part in."

Hart said, "It's pretty obvious to me that you were set up by your uncle. Either he did it, or somebody did it for him. But you need to get over this dangerous notion of 'fairness,' so let me explain something I learned the hard way. 'Fairness' in this life is a child's fantasy. Like they say, the Fair is where you can win a goldfish, and get some cotton candy. There is no 'fair' in real life."

"Hell, if everything's on their side, how can we win?"

"It's only been on their side up to now. The legal system makes up for the one-sided investigation and grand jury system by making the state prove their case beyond a reasonable doubt. That's where we win this one."

"They don't have any evidence I did anything."

"That's another popular legal myth. People think "evidence" just means forensics, DNA and such. Untrue. 'Evidence' includes anything that comes from the witness stand. The overwhelming amount of trial evidence is testimony. People's observations, impressions, and opinions. It's up to the jury how much weight or credibility to give it. In your case, first they are going to parade a dozen people out there to say they saw you and the victim together at that restaurant, and at Ship Island, before old Fleming found his head on the beach.

"Also, we now have their discovery, and all their investigative reports, and we know their case is all circumstantial. We know there are extensive business ties between the deceased and your company. He had personal funds invested, which your company Puglisi and Vacarro, Ltd. managed, and which he was apparently annoyed about. The company he worked for in Gulfport, which is, oddly enough, the same one I was defending in that accident down on the docks, was primarily insured by an underwriter which is owned by Puglisi. They have a forensic accounting expert, but I haven't seen the report, and we don't know if they are going to use him or not. They're going to try to conjure up some sinister inference that the deceased was trying to bail on your company, and you killed him. The state will just be asking the jury to put two and two and two together."

"Was the deceased guy working there when your, you know, situation occurred? I mean with your family?"

"No, this guy got promoted after all that. He wasn't ever a witness, or involved in any way.

It's a pretty small world around here."

"OK, so this guy works for a company we re-insure, and he has investments we manage. So what? We do business with every major shipper and port in the southeast, and manage and loan funds to tons of people associated with shipping and ports. That's part of what we do. Among our investors and business associates, this guy was a low level concern at best, not anyone I would even know existed. He just wasn't important. No offense, but if he was any trouble to my company, we could make a call and have his ass relocated to Baltimore or somewhere pronto. That's what I don't get. This guy wasn't important enough to kill. And I just don't see how those facts can ever be enough to convict anybody."

Hart said, "They shouldn't be, but that's not all. They're claiming that somebody working for you set it up by calling his office. They have Mr. Marshall's secretary testifying."

"That's obviously crazy. We have my office phone records, right?"

"Correct, and no such call was made. The phone number used was a burner, one of those prepay deals, not registered to anybody. That's why you got the note to meet Marshall, because The Raven did it."

"So I was obviously set up. That should seal the deal."

"Except that, we don't have the note. All the jury will hear is, they received a call from what Mr. Marshall's assistant assumed was your office. He showed up, and now he's dead."

"But I had never seen him before in my life. This is crazy."

"Which is why you probably have to testify. Like I said before, in murder cases, juries don't want to just hear "I didn't do it." They want to hear some explanation or theory of who *did* do it, since the best witness to the crime is unfortunately dead."

"My crazy uncle did it. How do we prove that?"

"We probably can't, but we have the right to present alternative theories, so they can't stop us from saying it."

"So we blame it on The Raven. Great, I can count on that monster chasing me for the rest of my life."

"We'll hold out actually saying it until we need to. We may not have to. Anyway, he can't live forever, and running from The Raven beats waking up in Parchman from now on."

Captain Fleming never made appointments with anyone. In the first place, he didn't have a phone, which is why he had not called anyone when he found the Rilo Marshall's head down on the beach. Plus, he considered his own stealthy movements too important to let just anybody be able to get in touch with him any time they wanted.

So when he showed up at John Hart's

office, it was unannounced, and serendipitous for Hart, who had been needing to talk to him anyway, since he was going to be a witness. Hart had been in court down Main Street that morning, and walking back to his office, found the Captain sitting in his old golf cart by the curb out front.

In his office, Hart said, "Captain, how's it been going?"

The Captain said, "Well, they ain't killed me yet."

Hart said, "I see that. What can I do for you?"

The Captain said, "Lawyer, you might think this is funny, me being a broke old fool, but I guess I ain't getting any younger, and maybe I should do something about getting a will done."

Hart said, "Captain Fleming, why don't you call me "John" or "Johnny" like everyone else does?"

"Then you'd be expecting me to remember your name every time I saw you, and I can't get committed to that. But I can damn sure always remember you're a lawyer."

Hart said, "That's fine, Captain. By the way, you found anything interesting down the beach recently?"

"Well," he said, and chuckled a little, "Not much lately. Leastways, no more dead people."

"I'm glad you're here, because I need to talk to you about that trial."

"OK. But I also wanted to tell you, Lawyer, thanks again for how you always have helped me out when, you know, I get a little hitched up on the rum. And especially that last time, you know, when they could've probably penned me up down at county, 'til they figured out where that head come from. I ain't that fond of getting regulated, so thank you."

"That's no problem Captain, and I'll be happy to help you with a will. Now, you rent a little cabin out back of town, don't you?"

"That's right, it's about what the Social Security pays, with a little for the power, and the water, you know. I mainly eat and drink off what I get stringing them shells and wood and such up off the beach. These crazy tourists, they pay good cash money for that kind of stuff."

"Do you have a bank account, where the Social Security check goes?"

"No, I cash it, and I pay the landlord the rent and the power and such with cash."

"What kind of personal property do you have, like vehicles, or guns, or fishing stuff? I know you have some kind of treasure somewhere, you old pirate." He grinned.

"Well, I know that's what people around here call me, like I was one of these movie pirates. And that's OK, because I can't do anything about it. But I ain't no real pirate. Them back stabbers never did anybody any good."

Hart said, "I understand. But whatever

you have, you need to make a list of it, so you can say who gets what."

"I don't have much, Lawyer, but you never do know. I'm expectin' to hit that lottery any time now."

"Me too. Now, there's two kinds of wills. One is "holographic," which means in your own handwriting. That kind people do on their own, and is pretty much bullet proof if challenged in court. The other kind, I draw up for you, and it has to be witnessed."

"Why does that matter?"

"Well, if a person dies, and his will is probated, anybody with standing can show up and challenge the will, claiming the deceased was forced, or unduly influenced, or drunk, or somehow duped into doing what he did. If he wrote it himself, in his own handwriting, it is very difficult to overturn in court."

"That's something. So this hollergraphic thing, a man just writes down what he wants done with his things, and signs it?"

"That's it. Dating it helps, too."

"What if a man dies, and nobody can find his will?"

"Then all his possessions go to the nearest kin, if they can be found, and if not, anything of value eventually goes to the state. Do you have any close family?"

The Captain sort of grunted, and swallowed, and looked at the floor for a moment. He said, "No, Lawyer, I don't have no family, none I know of. They was all killed in that goddamn Hurricane Camille, back in '69, when I was a regular Captain, a fisherman, with my own business, and a good boat over there in Pearlington. I had sent my wife and kids right over here to Pass Christian, to some of her relatives, to get away from the low spots, I thought, and I stayed in Pearlington to tend to my boat. They went over there, right across the bay. I thought I was doing the right thing, but I sent 'em right into the worst part of the damn thing, 'cause that's right where it hit, and they all got killed. My wife, and my three kids. All of 'em drowned. I ain't never told anybody that before. I guess that's when I got pretty hard on the rum."

"I'm sorry to hear that."

"Yeah, me too. And I heard around here some time ago that you had them kind of goings on too."

"That's right. But like you said, it's not something we like to talk about. So how did you end up in Bay Saint Louis? Did you retire from the fishing business in Pearlington?"

"Not on purpose. It was that damn Hurricane Katrina that done it. This time she did hit Pearlington, dead on, and got everything. Boats, docks, house, equipment, and o'course none of it insured. That water came in there twenty five to thirty feet deep, if I'm sitting here. She washed me a couple miles up the Pearl River and left me stuck way up a big old Cypress tree."

"Well maybe they haven't killed you yet because it can't be done. Do you still have your property over there?"

"No. After I finally got my ass down out of that tree, I got one of those government workers to ride me over here to the Bay, and got in one of the shelters the Army had set up. They told me I was eligible for this and that, and old enough for Social Security, and after a while got me one of those little trailers, and later on this little bitty house back of town to rent, that had been too high and behind the tracks for Katrina to get. That little spit of property I had in Pearlington, some sombitch bought it in one of them tax sales, I heard. I ain't ever going back to Pearlington."

"OK. So you have no immediate family, but heirs go out several layers, to your closest cousins, and so forth, if you don't have a will. You may actually win the lottery, so it's better to name somebody as your heir in case that happens. I'll be glad to draft you one, although we better wait until after this trial. The reason is, if you don't mind me saying, that you don't have any extra money to pay me, and I don't want to look like I'm helping you out for the benefit of my client, the defendant."

"That's OK, Lawyer, we can wait."

John Hart said, "OK, can we talk about the trial a minute?"

The Captain said, "Heave on."

Sid hadn't been to the Bay in a while, figuring he'd let the last visit fade a little first. Down at the city harbor, he jumped on his fishing boat, a thirty-nine foot open fisherman with a t-top, an upper station, and triple three hundred and fifty horsepower outboard engines. He fired her up, released his lines, climbed the short aluminum ladder on the outside of the center console, and enabled the steering on the upper station.

He backed her out of the slip, her name *Smile* coming into view from the growing weekend minions up the hill, out back of Canecutter's, or in the outside patio, or milling around the seawall and green areas overlooking the harbor. Decks and balconies of the other beachfront bar and restaurants were full, being close to lunch.

Sid's presence in the upper station was not necessary, or even practical. It was strictly to afford him a better view of the goings on up the hill, since he was about to take a ride, and he had no committed passengers. He putted around to the fuel dock. While the harbor fuel guy cleated his lines and started pumping gas, Sid scanned around the top of the seawall.

After a couple of passes, he thought he saw a seriously good looking woman up there, by herself, staring back at him. He reflexively tooted the *Smile*'s ridiculously loud fog horn, which startled the hell out of the fuel guy, who nearly sprung off the dock backwards. Sid waived at her, and by God, she waived back.

Sid was down the ladder, by the quietly cussing fuel guy, and across the harbor parking lot quickly. Looking up at her, he said, "You look like you need a boat ride."

She said, "And you look like you're about to take one. You got any extra room?"

He said, "Hell yes! It's just you and me, babe."

"Let's go," she said, and headed down the seawall.

Rilo Marshall had gotten tired of being told what to do by a bunch of damn New Orleans Italians. He had never actually seen them, but over the last six years, he had formed a perfectly clear picture of the whole bunch in his head. He'd seen all the movies, and knew how they dressed, and talked, and acted.

They first contacted him six years ago, right after those couple of accidents, one on the docks, and one out there on the highway. Some poor kid got crushed by a shipping container, then the lawyer handling it on behalf of the shipper he worked for, Brownco, Inc., lost his wife and mother in some kind of horrible accident. He had heard a rumor the wife was real pregnant.

They sent him a note, left it in his locker

at work. He was a shift boss then, had worked his way up on the docks from when he was the lowest worm, which is what they called him then, when he was eighteen. He had gotten picked on, and pushed around, and cussed at. He took it all, and got better, and harder, and became the best stevedore in the Gulfport harbor, and they all knew it. And he wasn't stupid. He knew what most people did around there, that it wasn't just bananas coming through the port. There were a lot of things in those containers floating in from the Caribbean, but nobody said anything about it, and he didn't either.

So after that kid got killed, the big boss on the docks got sick, and then disappeared completely. Then Rilo Marshall got a note. He didn't remember exactly what it said, after all this time, but told him to call a number if he wanted to make a lot more money, and burn the note. So he did. He got made the boss on the dock, and all the sudden had a big salary, and investment account, a house and a new truck, and a place to hunt up around Picayune whenever the hell he wanted, as long as he did whatever he was told. And he did. He got another note every once in a while, telling him to move this container here or there, or leave this or that off a lading, or an invoice, just little stuff. He never saw anybody on that end, but had always just assumed the New Orleans Mafia was behind it all.

Then one day in the mail, he got a list of

his assets and some papers for taxes and what-not, which were always done for him by an accountant, and sat down to actually read them. Turns out, all his investments, and there was about five million dollars in stocks and the like, were going to this New Orleans company Puglisi and Vacarro, Ltd., whoever the hell that was, when he died. They also apparently managed his money.

Up to that point, he had always done what he was told, for the money. But he had never signed anything authorizing those people to do such a thing. He might just be a country boy, but he wasn't stupid, and didn't appreciate being treated that way. He called up this Puglisi and whatever and said he wanted to speak to the man in charge. So when somebody called his secretary at Brownco and set up the meeting with Tony Vacarro over in Bay Saint Louis, he had headed over there to get shit straight.

At a rooftop bar in the New Orleans Central Business District, John Hart said to Lisette, "I never told you this. I never told anyone. After the... accident, I sort of went into a black hole." He looked at her, past her, letting the horror of the memory flow through him. For a second, it made him nauseous, like going over a hill too fast in a car. He looked around, to make sure no one else could hear. "Anyway, I'm not trying to relive it, and not going to. It's just, I didn't think there was such a thing as, I don't know, depression, or PTSD or anything like that before my family died. I just figured those were excuses weak minded people used." He paused, took a sip of beer. He said, "I don't know why I'm telling you this."

She said, "It's fine. It's good to enunciate things that bother you. It exposes dark things to light."

"I guess so. It's just, you know, I am always ..."

"Alone."

"Alone, exactly. Who do you tell these things to? I can't imagine lying on a couch, telling everything to old Dr. Freud." He laughed.

Lisette said, "No, you'd rather guzzle down half a bottle of whiskey and fight the bar."

"Who told you that?"

"Nobody, but thanks for confirming it." She laughed. "It's OK to admit you have normal human weaknesses."

"Yeah, I guess. But I have to tell you, I went full feral there for a while. There are a couple of years that I just don't really remember. It was bad."

"It's bad when people you love die. Especially when they all die at once. That would have killed most people, but it didn't kill you. You went on a drunk, didn't kill anybody else. Altogether, I'd say you handled it as well as you could."

"That's some fairly low expectations, but

I guess you're right.

Lisette ordered an iced coffee, and she excused herself. While she was gone, Hart thought of the evening, all the things they had discussed. They talked about everything. She was conversant in just about any subject, but not annoyingly so. She knew as much about the New Orleans Saints as she did about Descartes, or Thomas Jefferson. She did not have any particular political affiliations, which was fine with him, since he didn't either. He had discarded any such puny considerations after his family died. They just no longer seemed important.

Walking away, she cast a hard shadow in the bright moonlight. She glided like a lynx across the big space strung high overhead with crisscrossed church lights so dim they barely competed with the moon and stars. In those few seconds, he imagined he heard an old echo, and flashed back to the nightmares, all those trips down that damned dark, stinking death hall, until he finally could see some light. He had jumped, but there was nowhere to land.

He had been in pain for so long, it had become a part of his being. He had learned to live with it by figuring out its nature. Pain is durable, but it needs attention to live. When you get used to it, then learn to ignore it, it finally goes away. You still have it, but you learn to not feel it. But in the process, you kill your capacity to feel anything.

Lisette directly threatened that numb sanctity. She was just as luminescent as the moon overhead, and the string of pearls around her neck. And just as mysterious, and cool, and remote. She reappeared, and everyone in the place watched her cross the floor. When she was halfway there, his pulse galloped a little, and for a second he thought he might be having heart trouble. Then he realized it was just a dead part of it getting shocked back to life. For years now, he had been alone in every way, and had come to accept that he would simply stay alone, forever. Yet in the course of a few weeks, Lisette had shattered those dark perceptions. By the time she arrived at the table, John Hart knew that one day soon, he was going to be completely, ridiculously, foolishly in love.

Chapter 7

Some famous people get that way by having talent and big ideas, and working hard. Some
discover or invent something, or win championships. Some get famous by sheer luck, like winning the lottery. But some people get famous
for bravery. Or stupidity, depending on how you
look at it. Fear is a byproduct of common sense,
and bravery is the rare human capacity for ignoring it.

Sammy Ward never discovered or in-
vented anything, or won any championships, or
saved anybody. But in Bay Saint Louis, Mississippi he was, at one time in his life, famous. His
fame was not because of long preparation, or
ambition, or any ingenious idea. Greatness came
to Sammy when he was only eleven years old, on
a big hill outside Bay Saint Louis, the result of
a dare. Sammy was the kid who had made The
Jump.

There was a gigantic pile of prime clay
soil out past the edge of town, on county owned
land, the result of some boondoggle the county
Board of Supervisors created many years earlier.
They had made a deal to purchase and extract
the dirt from a few parcels of property owned
by a couple of well connected citizens in the
county. It was a particular type of clay favored
by the federal government for building roads
and levees, and was viewed at the time as a valu-

able asset for future public developments.

The county dug it out, lots of it, and trucked it to their property, and piled it up. They dug and piled, and dug and piled, and never used the clay for anything. They kept digging and piling, until it eventually covered a few acres, and looked at some distance like an unfinished Egyptian pyramid, a mini mountain plateau that had somehow sprouted out of the flat coastal plain.

And there it stood unused for years. It became a joke, known derisively as "Supervisor's Hill," and was easily the highest point in the area. It was grown up with weeds and briars and all types of little gum trees and pines, which were periodically chopped down. At the top, on a moonless night, the lights of New Orleans illuminated the Southwest horizon. You could drive a truck up on it, or a car if you didn't care about getting stuck. The hill was a hangout for teenagers, and lovers, and dirt bike riders. It was the scene of many a first high school party, and beer bust, and hickey.

In the first month of summer one year, at the base of Supervisor's Hill, close to a relatively new Little League baseball field, a bunch of school boys had built a long, high, steep, and surprisingly sturdy wooden ramp. They had hoed and raked, and dug and wheelbarrowed a clear enough path straight down the ramp side of the hill, just wide enough for a bicycle. The idea was to ride down the long slope of the hill, hit the ramp, and launch into glory.

Out past the end of the ramp, the boys had piled up a bunch of stuff from the county dump down the road: mattresses, pasteboard boxes filled with wadded up newspapers, carpet pad scraps, and anything soft or spongy they could find. The deep pile stretched several yards in every direction around the calculated landing area.

On this Saturday morning, all the builders of the ramp were there, seven or eight of them, with their bicycles. The word had been spread, and several other kids had shown up to watch. Inspections were made, and predictions. There was lots of bragging. When the builders and their bicycles eagerly ascended the hill, the young crowd scooted back toward the baseball field, and waited. And waited. And eventually started giving up, since it was apparent that all the big talk was not translating into action, and probably never would. Fingers were pointed, and accusations made. There were sudden concerns about design, and materials, and safety. At least one ramp builder rode off to tell his mother, crying.

At this moment Sammy, who was not one of the builders, or a big talker, or even a particularly good bicycle rider, but just an anonymous kid in the small crowd, snorted. He said, more or less to himself, "You mean they're *all* chicken?"

This was loud enough for some of the disappointed crowd to hear, and several of them simultaneously dared him, if he wasn't chicken too, to do the jump himself.

Sammy had not accomplished much in his eleven years. In fact, he had just barely made it through fifth grade, and was generally regarded, if noticed at all, as a future dropout headed for an early life of physical labor. He had never played sports, and was not big, or mean, or daring. But he *was* from way out in the county where a particular brand of tough country boys were raised. His kind instinctively knew that any stunt that would probably end in major injury or death, but *might* be pulled off, was a rare opportunity for greatness, and impossible to deny.

He also knew that if he turned down a dare of this magnitude, his older brothers, all five of them, would kick his butt good for shaming the family name. So he marched up the long hill, borrowed some scared kid's bike, rode to the edge, and gazed down at the small crowd far below. He immediately understood why the builders had all chickened out. The hill was too high, the trail too narrow, the ramp too steep, the distant landing pile way too small. Making the jump would be suicide. For the first time in his young life, Sammy Ward knew real, cold fear.

But the decision had been made, the family name was at risk, and his own butt was in physical jeopardy no matter what he did. So before he could think about it any more, he shoved off. It was not just the fear of his older brothers that made him start down that hill. It was the certain knowledge that no matter how this turned out, his life was about to change.

Or end, which occurred to him right when he blazed up the ramp and launched. Boy and bike quickly separated, tumbling, rising, orbiting each other. A feral bonzai howl ripped the air. The young crowd gasped. Sammy and the bike were still as high as a flag pole when they cleared the landing pile. They eventually struck, bouncing, rolling, merging into a boy and bicycle tumbleweed that bent and cracked and grunted another fifteen or twenty yards before coming to an abrupt rest against the back of the visitor's dugout.

An ambulance came, and a bunch of parents and cops. He was dismantled from most of the bicycle, and loaded up, and roared off, sirens blaring. Surgeons dug most of the rest of the bicycle out of him, set bones, added rods and plates, plugged up holes, rearranged guts, and eventually stitched him all back together. The rumor was, his broken bones and other injuries set a record in the county hospital for an accident survivor. He stayed in the hospital for the rest of the summer.

When he hobbled into sixth grade that fall, The Jump had become lore, and he was a school legend. They said he had flown a hundred yards and gone as high as the old Mason building downtown, and was Banzai yelling at death the whole way, and fifty people were there and saw the whole thing. All the same cool kids who had ignored him for the first five years of school now wanted to talk in the hallway between classes, or sit by him at lunch, or pick him on their sports teams at recess, even though he was even worse than before.

So Sammy was famous for a time, a long time ago. The newspaper did a story about it, and published a picture of him all covered in plaster casts, strung up with weights and pulleys in the hospital. And he kept on being famous for a while. But whatever qualities drove Sammy to head down that hill were not enough to sustain him in school. Bravery, or stupidity, or craziness just doesn't translate into passing grades. As expected, he eventually dropped out of school and went to work.

When his former classmates graduated and went off to college, some of them, he was busy driving trucks and having kids. By the time he made his first appointment with John Hart, eight months ago, being famous for The Jump had long since worn off, and the rest of life had not been good to Sammy Ward. He had gotten old and bald, and divorced. His ex had actually left him on Christmas eve one year, with no warning, and took all five of his kids, along with the few presents under the tree.

He never recovered from the designed cruelty of it, and had long since given up on any idea of getting married again. Now he was disabled, down in the back from the millions of miles of trucking he had logged, and hurting everywhere else from old bicycle parts and scars. When he finally had to retire, one of his grown daughters, who was by law mentally disabled, had come to live with him. She was unmarried too.

"Mr. Johnny," Sammy had said, "There was something wrong with her when she was born. The doctor said, well, they thought she may have had her umbilical cord wrapped around her neck while she was still in her mother, and it made her brain lose oxygen, or something. But she never was right. She was always in the, you know, special classes in school."

Hart said, "I know, Sammy, I have seen her, seen the two of you at the grocery store several times. She seems very nice."

"She's kind of like a kid, sir. She doesn't really understand anything more than regular stuff like church, or cooking, or her TV shows, you know. And she doesn't have a mean bone in her body. If there's such a thing as heaven, she is the only person I ever met who is definitely, without a doubt, getting in."

Hart said, "Let's hope there is, and we all do. What can I do for you, Sammy?"

"Well, sir..."

"Call me John. Please."

"Okay, see... she's always been on disability, since she was a little kid, living with her mother, and now she's living with me, and they just cut her off for some reason, and we need that money to help us live on."

Hart said, "Well, we're going to see if we can do something about that. Let me worry about it. But first, I've heard most of my life about The Jump. They say half the county was out there, and you yelled 'Banzai' and flew a hundred yards. What actually happened?"

"Shoot, Mr. Hart, I've just about forgot what really happened, since I've heard other people talk about it for so long. But I can tell you, there wasn't any more than fifteen or twenty kids there, counting all the ones that built that ramp. And it was a good ramp. But none of them would, you know, go down it. It was too much."

"So why did you?"

"Well, I was dared. Back in those days, we weren't allowed to turn down a dare, I guess. It's hard to explain. And I didn't yell any 'Banzai.' I was, as my mama used to say, 'screaming bloody murder' the whole way because I figured I was about to die."

"How high, how far do you think you went?"

"In the air? To be honest, I don't know.

I had my eyes squinched closed the whole way, but I can tell you I was up there a while. All I definitely remember after being up on top of that hill is waking up and getting a bunch of ice cream. That part was pretty cool. The rest of it was stupid."

Now eight months later, Hart had been to three hearings for Sammy's daughter, and been denied all three times. He had filed his final request for review of the order, and was almost certainly going to be denied. The cold, rigid bureaucracy charged with deciding these things had determined that the two of them living together, though necessary for both of them, somehow relieved the government of the duty to provide her assistance, and the federal administrative law judge over in Gulfport rendering the decision even told Hart he was disgusted having to make the ruling.

Nevertheless, they had denied her claims, and John Hart's pleas, and he was out of options. Sammy was going to have to put her into a state facility, whose criteria she met. After years of loneliness, Sammy had finally gotten one of his kids back living in his home, after she was grown. And now she was going to have to move back out. On top of it, he had gotten caught short on his money, and was behind on everything, and his landlord had obtained a summary eviction order in court.

Unless Hart could do something about it,

Sammy had to be out of his house in three days, and he had nowhere to go. Sammy actually cried in his office, the tough little guy who as a kid had survived The Jump, who had suffered through getting backstabbed at Christmas, whose child-hood window of fame had narrowed, and faded, and then disappeared into history, finally broke down. It was the type of thing that only lawyers see.

Sammy had not paid him anything, be-cause he couldn't. Neither one mentioned it. It was another type of thing only lawyers see. Hart drew up a Notice of Appeal, told him how to file it, and gave him a check for the filing fee, and another for the five hundred dollar appeal bond, and sent him on his way. By doing so, John Hart had bought Sammy another several months of time in his house.

But the real matter on his mind was the trial of Vacarro, which started the next Mon-day. The state's whole case was meant to play on the unspoken assertion that this was a Mafia hit. Their expert was going to testify that the Vacarro's company was the beneficiary of a bunch of the deceased man's death benefits, and had a financial interest in him being dead. Also, it wouldn't require much of a push from the prosecution, because Mafia lore was part of the community fabric, going back to Al Capone. He had been a regular visitor to the Gulf Coast when

Prohibition had thrust the existence of organized crime into the public consciousness, Cuban rum came right through here on the way to Chicago. It got to the coast, the story went, on boats owned or controlled by the Bardinos, who were the real power behind the port of New Orleans, and had access to an unlimited supply of them, and the crews to run them.

And there was always the Kennedy assassination. Hart knew that most of the likely jury pool public believed, or just accepted, that the Bardinos had killed JFK in retaliation for the Bay of Pigs debacle, and his continuing refusal or inability to remove Castro. There were lots more stories. Hart knew that everyone would have heard the rumors, and probably believed them. It would be his primary job to prevent the state from convicting his client for his name. And he knew better than to crow too much about mere circumstantial evidence. Parchman was full of people whose attorneys had scoffed at the lack of forensic evidence.

So there was no need to oppose what he could not prevent. Let the state play on all their prejudices. He could play that game as well. After all, if Vacarro was a Mafia bigshot, how the hell did he let himself get so easily caught?

For the trial of The State of Mississippi versus Antonin Vacarro, a lot of registered voters had broken tradition and actually showed up for jury duty. The Circuit Court Clerk had sent out around a hundred summonses, and it looked like they all came. From this group, the final twelve jurors and a couple of alternates would be selected.

Once the crowd settled in, Judge Donahue said, "Most of you, this is the first time you have been in this courtroom, so let me tell you, everything in here makes a racket, and that makes it hard for me and these lawyers to hear each other, even though we have microphones and a sound system. Anyway, let's keep the shuffling around down to minimum, and no talking while we're in session.

"Turn your phones off. If I hear one, I'm going to have Bailiff Fitts over here hold on to it for you until court is over for the day. Just turn them off. Oh, and that also means nobody can record anything without my permission. It's up to me. That's the law in this state, and nobody is going to get that permission. Let's see, is that all?" He looked at the Circuit Court Clerk to his left, and she looked at her assistant. They both looked back at him and nodded. He said, "OK, that's all for now. We're going to take fifteen minutes of recess while these lawyers get ready to pick our jury. So anybody's got to go, or needs to make a call, or smoke your cigarette or whatever, now's the time."

Half an hour later, they began the long process of vetting the jury pool. The judge went first. He had to deal with any requests to be released for cause, whether for injury or disability, or hardship of any type. He could release anyone from the venire who he was satisfied had a physical reason they thought may inhibit their ability to sit through the trial, and pay attention. Then there were people who owned their own businesses, and single parents with small children, and a few legitimately sick people, and several he thought were just too old, and he didn't want to have to deal with them, but he couldn't say so. There were a bunch of people who he thought knew too much about the case, and couldn't be objective, so he let them leave. Surprisingly, there were quite a few who had not heard about the head on the beach, or Vacarro, or the case at all. After the judge got through with the venire, it was down to three panels of twelve, twelve of whom would decide the fate of Vacarro.

By tradition, the prosecution got to go next, asking general questions of each panel, and following up with individual questions. The D.A. was present, but Laura Jones was doing the talking. "Panel One," she said, "Do any of you feel you can not render a guilty verdict in this case, or any case, without a confession, or an eyewitness, or a video recording of the crime?"

A lady in the group raised her hand. Jones looked at her jury questionnaires, and said, "Mrs. Biggs, isn't it?"

"That's right," she said. "I just wanted to

know, why wouldn't *you* require some kind of eyewitnesses or confessions or something like that to charge a man with murder? I mean, what kind of evidence do you have?"

Jones said, "Mrs. Biggs, we are only required to prove each element of the crime charged, and how we go about doing that is not prescribed. For instance, we are going to prove..."

Hart popped up and sad, "Objection! Judge, she's about to try to argue her case."

"Sustained," said the judge. "All counsel approach." The judge flipped off his microphone, and the three lawyers crowded in front of the judge's elevated desk, where the court reporter could still hear. He said, "State, what the hell? You know better than to try that in this court."

The young D.A. said, "Judge, we believe that she was responding to a legitimate concern voiced by a registered voter concerning the efficacy of..."

"That's enough from you," the judge said, "I am talking to the actual attorneys in this case." He turned to Jones, said, "Well?"

Jones looked at the D.A. first, then said, "I just got carried away, Judge. It won't happen again."

The judge looked at Hart, said, "Defense?"
Hart said, "I'm OK, Judge."
The D.A. scowled at his elder assistant,

and the lawyers went back to their tables.

Vacarro leaned over to Hart, whispering, "Are we asking for a mistrial?"

"Hell no," said Hart, "Mrs. Biggs there couldn't have done us a better favor. That question she asked is going to be in the minds of everyone who that makes the final jury."

The state resumed it questions, Jones logging through standard issues regarding bias, and beliefs, and the difference between the religious philosophy of forgiveness and redemption and the statutory mandate of punishment and retribution. She overlapped quite a bit with the judge's previous questions, but the judge tolerated it.

The judge and the prosecutor had worked past noon. When Jones finished, the judge said, "Folks, this is the first lunch break we are going to take, and those of you who become jurors or alternates in this matter are going to hear me say this several times over the course of this case. While on lunch break, or any break, you are *not allowed* to discuss this case in any way, about anything, anywhere, with anybody. Period. You can talk about church, or fishing, or the Saints, or anything you want, but *not* this case. Is that clear?"

All of them nodded. "Okay," he said, "Be back here in one hour."

John Hart met Sid at an old family owned

steak and seafood place across the street from the harbor. They sat outside, on the patio. Sid was excited.

Downing the last half of his iced tea, he waived it at no one in particular, and said, "Brother, you're not gonna believe this. I think I finally met her. This could be the real deal."

Hart said, "Met who?"

Sid said, "Number Nine. The last one, ever. This time I'm serious. This is going to be my last wife, period."

Hart said, "Whoa, big man. You mean you asked another woman to marry you?"

"No, not exactly. But it's like, you just know."

"Like all eight other times?"

Sid said, "Well that's fair, but no. Way better than all the others."

"What happened?"

"I was fueling up my fishing boat the other day when I saw this lady at the top of the harbor walkway, and she was looking right at me. So I went over there and asked her if she wanted to jump on with me, and she did."

"Obviously someone who doesn't know you."

"Obviously. Anyway, we cruise out to Ship Island, down there on the point by the fort, where you can get right up to the beach, you know."

"Our favorite spot."

"Yes. So we've got the music going, and everybody else shows up, and we all get up in there close, and we're boat hopping, and set up with drinks, and food, and just jamming."

Hart said, "Nice. Something surely has to have happened to sabotage this perfect day at the island."

Sid said, "Actually, it could have. See, I was having a good old time when somebody said something about cops, and you know how I like that subject."

"I've heard some unflattering language from you."

"Normally, not my favorite. They always show up and ruin the party. Anyway, so I am explaining what I think, that the only reason anybody would want to even be a cop is because of being able to push around on people, blah, blah, blah, when she says, 'Sid, you know I'm a cop, right?"

Hart said, "Wait, you don't mean she's..."

Sid said, "Yes! Angel! The investigator you told me about! I was so fucked up that day I met her, I didn't remember!"

"So you didn't know it was her when she got on the boat?"

"Not at all."

"But she knew you, and thought that you remembered her, too?"

"Yes! Isn't that crazy? I didn't have a clue. She told me the whole story out there."

"Well, it's a good thing, because if you knew she was a cop, you never would have asked her on the boat, right?"

"Maybe. Hell, I don't know. You should see her in a bikini. Man, she is the one. This is going to be my best, and last marriage."

Hart said, "I guess it's good to go into marriage with the right attitude. How does that old saying go? The ninth time is the charm?"

"Right, jackass," said Sid. "We'll see. So how is your case going? You're picking the jury, right?"

"Yes. It's impossible to tell, really, until we get into the witnesses. The thing is, everybody in that jury pool is sitting there, thinking Tony's in the Mafia, and all this has something to do with that fact. So the question is, how do we deal with it?"

"So how do you?"

"My theory is, we go with it."

"You admit he's in the Mafia?"

"Not exactly. In fact, there actually isn't one anymore."

Sid said, "You really believe that?"

"Do you know any different? Now would be the time to tell me."

Sid said, "Hell, I have no idea, and don't want to know."

Hart said, "Weren't you guys big buddies at LSU?"

"Yeah, we were. But that was a long time

ago. He eventually went off to New York, and my old man made it perfectly clear that I was to have no further social connections with my good friend in the Mafia. It somehow had to do with the assholes who hand out dental licenses. He made it a condition of me being in the company. He didn't want me to make Tony mad, just to quit hanging around him. Like I said, he was out of state, so it was easy."

"You don't see each other now?"

"Well sure, every once in a while, and my old man is, God rest his soul, unfortunately no longer with us."

"So is Vacarro the boss of the New Orleans Mafia or what?"

Sid looked around and said, "Keep your voice down, babe. I really don't know. I've heard him say that the crime family no longer exists, that it was dissolved, like a company."

"You believe that's true?"

"If I had to say, I believe that he believes it's true. I think that the Mafia still exists in New Orleans, and always will. I think that old monster they call The Raven is still running it, and until he dies, he will. Of course, he may never die."

Hart said, "Well, that brings me back to my point. The jury is going to assume that the New Orleans Mafia still exists, and that Vacarro is in it, and that this killing is somehow associated with all that. If I try to deny all that, then I lose credibility, and hurt my client."

"You mean the prosecution is going to try to prove that?"

"No, the judge won't allow it. But it's the gorilla in the room, just like the saying. We just have to figure out how to deal with it."

Back in court, it was John Hart's turn to talk to the jury venire. Normally, by the time defense attorneys get to question the venire, all the obvious subjects have been already covered. The judge in particular had imbued the pool with the notions of due process, and duty, and the high concepts of presumption of innocence, and of proof beyond a reasonable doubt, and elements of the crime. In this case, he had already told them, the state had to prove the defendant had intent to commit a murder, and did it.

There was no point in re-plowing that ground, which can be very annoying to the jury pool. People can be very sensitive to insults of their intelligence. Over his career, Hart had crafted an approach to criminal defense that he felt was far more practical than preaching to people about civic duties. There was no point in trying to convince them to abide by legal ideals, without first recognizing their own tendencies.

Striding the podium with no notes, or even a writing pad, he stood beside it and said, "Panel one, in real life, none of you really believe in the presumption of innocence, do you?"

This caused a shuffle in the group, as the dozen all looked at him simultaneously. Laura Jones shot a glance at the judge, who had heard Hart's routine before, and didn't look up at all. Hart continued, "You heard me correctly. We all talk about the higher legal standards of our society, like the presumption of innocence and due process and so forth, but that's all just coffee house talk, right? I mean, a person doesn't get arrested, and booked, and have to put up a pile of bond money, and get indicted and forced to be in court to be judged by you people, his neighbors, because he's innocent, right? The twelve in panel one looked back and forth at each other. A lady on one end of the panel's group raised her hand. Hart pointed at her, said "Yes?"

She said, "I'm confused. Are you saying your client is guilty?"

"No ma'am. I'm asking you if you think so."

"Well, no, I don't know anything about him, or what the proof is."

"That's exactly what I want to hear, thank you. You see, to do this job, to be a juror in this case, you have to overcome your own natural tendency to assume things, and require that the state prove things to you. Can you do that?"

She said, "Yes, I can."

Hart said, "Do you also understand, as the judge told you earlier, that you are required to consider him innocent right now?"

She said, "You mean, in real life?"

"Yes, in real life. Should we ask the judge to cover it again? Judge?"

The judge tapped his mike, and said, "Prospective jurors, at this stage of this matter, you are required to presume and regard Mr. Antonin Vacarro here as an innocent person, legally and in real life. That presumption of innocence is, as we say, a fundamental cog in the machinery of the American legal system. You must continue to presume him to be actually and legally innocent until the state proves each of the elements of the crime charged beyond a reasonable doubt. Is that clear to everybody?"

The lady said, "Sir, what is reasonable? Does that mean any kind of doubt? It seems like everything can be doubted. Can you explain that more to me?"

The judge said, "That is an excellent question, and one we attorneys and courts have been wrestling with for a couple of centuries now. 'Reasonable doubt' means whatever it means to you. If the doubt is unreasonable, don't consider it. For instance, it's not reasonable to me to think that maybe a space alien caused something to happen. Even though that might be possible, it's not a reasonable possibility to me. On the other hand, if you have doubt about sufficiency of the proof that is reasonable, then you must continue to consider this Defendant innocent, and vote that way. It's that simple."

John Hart said, "How about the rest of you in panel one? Can you promise yourself, and this court, that you will put aside any secret assumptions of guilt you may have about Vacarro?" They all nodded. Turning to the rest of the pool, he said, "How about you, panels two and three? Can you make the state prove these things to you, beyond a reasonable doubt, and set aside your assumptions?" They all nodded, except one fellow in the back, one of the youngest people there. He raised his hand, and before being recognized, he said, "How come you keep saying they have to prove things? Don't you have to prove things too?"

Hart said, "I'm glad you brought that back up. The judge told you earlier that the state has to prove all these elements to you, and that the defense doesn't have to prove anything. What that means in real life is, Tony and I could sit here in silence, throughout the entire trial, and say nothing, not even cross examine their witnesses, or put on any witnesses or testimony at all. We could do that, and if the state was unable to prove its case beyond a reasonable doubt, you would still have to find him not guilty, because..."

Jones popped up, and said "Objection! Judge, he's trying to instruct the jury."

"Sustained," said the judge, "Let's move it along, Defense. They've heard enough about reasonable doubt for now. You'll get your standard instructions in."

Hart said, "Judge, I'd like to ask them one more question about it."

He said, "Fine, but that's it."

Hart said, "This is directed at the entire jury venire, all three panels of you. Does anybody think it's just fundamentally unfair that Tony doesn't have to prove anything, and the state has to prove everything *beyond a reasonable doubt*? I mean, do any of you think that's just too high a bar for the state to have to clear?"

Nobody said anything. Hart scanned through all thirty-six, and nobody spoke. He said, "Fine, for those of you who make the final jury, and alternates, you'll hear from all of us later on this subject. For now I thank you, and your neighbor Tony Vacarro thanks you for your time and attention."

After a break, the rest of the day was spent choosing the final panel. Outside the jury's presence, the attorneys had to consider each juror as they came up in order. For Hart, the process usually didn't take long, and the prosecution always operated under the assumption that they would win with any jury. By 4 p.m., they were done. The trial was set to start the next day.

For six years, the missing driver had been hiding out between New Orleans and Venice. New Orleans was still the last significant city in the United States where a person could disappear, lurking around the French Quarter, and the Marigny, and across Elysian Fields in the Bywater, blending into the anonymity of a transient street scene, and of loud, drunken tourists, and the homeless, and those trending one way or the other. Both the cops and the bad guys were looking for him, so there was no safety. But he had got a new name, and grown out his hair, and grew a beard, and was working pretty regularly as a deck hand at the fish camps in Venice, or anything he could get around the docks in New Orleans. Nobody looking for him really knew what he looked like now. He could still be found, but it wouldn't be easy.

The driver hadn't known, at the time of the wreck, anything about who owned the car he hit, or that there would be two women inside when he ran it over. The damned thing had a tinted back window, and he couldn't see in. Not that it might have made any difference, though. His orders had come on a note, and the language was clear. Find this car, run over it, wait on the cops. Keep your mouth shut, you'll be taken care of. Burn the note.

When he had climbed down out of the cab and heard the women screaming, he panicked, and ran. Some old guy had jumped out of a car and grabbed him, and accused him of being drunk. He had wrestled away, and took off into the nearby woods, and was gone. Running away was enough to get him killed, so he went into hiding. For a while, he'd heard about it incessantly on the TV news. The ladies had ridden to Gulfport with the dead driver's husband, a New Orleans attorney in town for the day on business. The driver had been pregnant, and the other dead lady, who lived in Bay Saint Louis, was her mother in law.

The plan, as near as the driver could figure later, was to take out this one lawyer, not his wife and mother. Those poor women were just in the wrong spot at the right time. In a way, it was the lawyer that got his wife and mother killed, so it wasn't his fault. That's what he told himself.

When it all happened, he had been trying to earn his way into the Mafia. He had initially gotten hired by answering a note someone had anonymously stuck to the door of an old apartment he shared in Kenner with a couple of other young hustlers. He called the number, was told where to be, and did it. He had to drive a truck to Gulfport, where he dropped off one trailer and hooked up another, and drove back to New Orleans. He was handed an envelope full of cash, and nobody talked to him.

Things went on that way for a good while, and he was able to get himself a better place to live, a little apartment on Magazine Street. He had a commercial driver's license, was working independently, and had picked up a gig running regular loads of bananas from the big port in

Gulfport, Mississippi, to New Orleans. He had heard that some of the loads were full of illegal drugs of some kind, but he wasn't sure. As far as anyone could tell, he was completely clean, and he was. He was dependable, would show up when he was supposed to, and never asked questions. He figured he was working for the Mafia, but nobody ever actually said so, or even talked about it. He always thought that was strange.

He eventually got recruited to take out the lawyer. It was all done in the same way, by printed notes in an envelope. The subject's car had a GPS tracker in it. The driver would be going to Bay Saint Louis on this day, at this time, in an eighteen wheeler cab, no trailer. Spend the night in a little motel out by the highway. In the morning, the target car would be heading in from New Orleans. Find it, and wreck it hard. Stay there, wait for the cops, do an accident report. The ten thousand dollars with the note was half his pay. He never got to collect the other half.

That night at the hotel, thinking about possibly killing someone had gotten tough, even for a tough guy. He had been an outlaw his whole life, stealing things, selling drugs, lying. Murder was a natural step up, and one he believed would be necessary to advance in the organized criminal world, if it still really existed. But imagining killing someone and actually doing it are two drastically different things, even for an outlaw. It wasn't going to be easy. But he had committed to it, and he couldn't back out. Plus, he had a whole bunch of cash, so he'd gotten a cab downtown, and found a little pool joint on Main Street in Bay Saint Louis that stayed open all night. He drank a bunch of whiskey, and shot pool until he couldn't see straight.

In the morning he overslept, and had let his damn phone battery die, and couldn't find his charger. He figured the target car would be parked somewhere by then, and it would be that afternoon before he could find it, and was hung over and pissed off at himself when he roared out of the motel parking lot. But the car wasn't downtown. Luckily, it was headed down I-10, east bound, away from Gulfport, and perfectly set up for attack.

It was a fairly easy maneuver. He caught up to the car in the far right lane. It was, as expected, a dark blue sedan, with darkened windows. He had just seen it when it exited the highway. He gritted his teeth and rammed it. The sedan slammed on the brakes, and got sideways, and the big truck cab just rolled right over it, and they both slid off the shoulder of the off ramp, and down an embankment, and into a treeline. Everything caught on fire. He got out of the truck, and ran.

He had later discovered several messages from that morning calling off the operation. His phone battery being dead, and him hung over, and no charger, and in a rush to make up time, he never got them. He heard later on the TV news that a lawyer's wife and mother had dropped him off at the port, and headed out to do some shopping at the outlet stores by the highway, then apparently over toward Biloxi, but never made it. So by a series of coincidental fuckups, he had committed murder, or maybe just manslaughter, but either way it was the wrong two people, and he knew he better get lost for good. He had hitched back to New Orleans, took what was left of his money, and a backpack of clothes, and hitched to Venice, and rented a little room, and disappeared.

And all this time, it had worked. As far as he knew, he had gotten away clean. The whole thing was so long ago, it seemed like another life, like it had all happened to another person. Along the waterfront, he occasionally heard rumors about the Mafia. Once, he heard some of longliners swear that the Bardino Family was no more, that they met out in the gulf one day and called it quits. So maybe it really wasn't the Mafia that hired him to take out the lawyer after all, and he really was off the hook.

The driver downed his last beer and walked along the first pier on the main marina in the Venice harbor. He hopped over the transom of the rented houseboat he now lived on, and froze. Taped at the bottom of the sliding back door was an envelope. He looked all around, and didn't see anything abnormal. He got the envelope, and eased inside. Satisfied that no one else was on the boat, he opened the envelope, which contained two thousand dollars and a note. It read, "We have always known where you are. Do not attempt to run again. If we need you, you will be contacted. If you are contacted, do as instructed. Burn this note."

Chapter 8

The atmosphere in Bay Saint Louis the first morning of the trial was more like Saturday than Tuesday. Early in the bright blue morning, several news crews had set up tables and staked out areas around the courthouse grounds. Every professional and amateur internet blogger from New Orleans to the Florida panhandle was there, posting ever escalating speculation about Vacarro, and the case, and the Bardinos, and the New Orleans Mafia in general.

John Hart and Tony Vacarro walked from his office down Main Street to the big courthouse like they were approaching a county fair. All parking spaces along the street, in the court area, and everywhere in Bay Saint Louis were filled. Some people had set up picnic areas, like they were tailgating, or were at a Mardi Gras parade. Here and there, men were dressed like movie wise guys. People had already chosen sides, and had made signs declaring the guilt or innocence of the dashing suspected Mafia boss before anyone had seen or heard any evidence at all.

People were shouting encouragement or insults. A couple of college students came up to Vacarro and tried to shake hands. He fist bumped them, and they both howled and whooped like they were at a football game. A vendor was pushing his four wheeled cart down the middle of the street, selling flags and balloons and t-shirts with Vacarro's face on them. Some of them said "Free Tony." Others said "Guilty," or "Head Hunter." The biggest seller had an excellent fake picture of Vacarro in period Mafia style clothes, and underneath it said "Godfather, Part IV." He also had prosecutor voodoo dolls, and some that were supposed to be Tony Vacarro in black and white striped clothes. If the vendor knew you, he'd sell you an ice cold beer from the cooler hidden in his cart.

Hart guided Vacarro in the back way up the elevator. They walked through the back hall to the rear courtroom door entrance, where Hart and Laura Jones had first discussed the case a while back. They paused, and Hart said, "Here we go. I understand you're nervous. That's normal. But let's be as calm as possible, and remember, don't say anything to anybody unless I specifically tell you to. And don't make eye contact with anybody in the gallery. Believe me, somebody snuck some kind of camera in here this morning, and we don't want to make it easy on them. Just keep your chin up, be calm, and look straight ahead. OK, let's go."

When they swung the door open and went through, three young men in the back row of the gallery, voluntarily in court for the first time in their lives, stood and cheered. Old Bailiff Fitts had throttled and marched them up front to the attorneys' podium by the time the judge's chamber door swung open.

The Bailiff yelled, "All rise!" a little louder than normal.

The judge clomped around the back of the dais, and plopped down in the big oak and leather chair which, but for its comfortable padding, could pass for the state's retired electric chair. He took an unnecessarily long sip of coffee, eyeballing the quiet, standing gallery, then the lawyers, and finally the three scoundrels standing shoulder to shoulder at the podium, and trying not to look back at him. "Be seated!" he yelled, and the whole room quickly did, except those three.

Leering at them, the judge said, "Let me explain something to you, and to everyone else here. We are going to have this trial, and it is going to be orderly, and dignified. This is not a sports event, this is a court of law. Now you on the left, how do I know you?"

The young man at the podium said, "Uh, you put me on paper last year. Uh, sir."

"You still on probation?"

He nodded.

"I can't hear your head rattle son, is that a yes or a no?"

"Yes. Uh, sir. Judge."

"What was the charge?"

"Burglary of a Dwelling, Judge, but it really should have just been..."

The judge said, "Shut up. I don't need to

hear the burglar theory of burglary law. I remember you, you're the one who broke into somebody's back yard pool house, drank up all their booze, then got naked in their hot tub with your girlfriend, right?"

"Uh, yes sir."

"And it was your parents' own next door neighbor, right?"

"Yes. Uh, sir." He faked a cough so he could cover up an uncontrollable grin with his hand.

"What about you other two geniuses? Either one of you on paper for anything?"

The one in the middle said, "Yes sir, but it's just a misdemeanor possession."

The judge said, "Just a misdemeanor, huh?"

"Yes sir. It was a felony at first, but they couldn't prove all those pills were mine, so my lawyer made them knock it down to a misdemeanor." He grinned.

The judge took his time glancing over at the Circuit Clerk to his left, who just shrugged. Turning back, he said, "Son, that might not be the stupidest thing I hear this week, but right now it's in first place." He looked at the third one. "What about you, son? You got any convictions?"

He said, "No sir."

"Well I suggest you start running with a better grade of idiot, because if you continue to hang around these two, it's just a matter of time." Standing up, he picked up his microphone, and said, "I'm speaking to everyone here. This is the last time I will say this. There will be no outbursts in this courtroom. If you can't control yourself, leave, it's that simple. Otherwise, you get to go hang around the holding cell with these three." He sat back down, and said, "Mr. Fitts, escort the Three Stooges to the holding cell. They are in contempt of this court, and are to be locked up until further orders are issued."

The Bailiff said, "The upstairs holding cell, judge, or the downstairs one?" The upstairs cell was were they kept actual detainees, criminal defendants who were still in custody and making court appearances. The downstairs one was the abandoned old county jail, a small brick structure on the grounds used mainly as a storage place for old files. It was full of tiny cells and heavy iron bars, formerly used to hold condemned murderers who were hung thirteen steps up a staircase in the back.

There was still a trap door on the second floor, and a big galvanized eye bolt in the plastered ceiling directly over it. Most locals, and pretty much everyone who worked in the courthouse, figured the place was haunted. Sometimes judges would stick low level criminals in it for a while to scare them straight, hopefully. The judge grinned, and said, "I believe the downstairs one will do today." The Bailiff led the three out the back door, where they were met by an unfriendly deputy and herded down the stairs. The Bailiff returned to his spot in the courtroom by the judge's chamber door.

The judge said, "We all set? Bring in the jury."

Bailiff Fitts stepped out to the jury room, and returned leading them in. They filed and shuffled their way in to the jury box, which was in the old style, facing the judge, placing the jurors' backs to the bar rail and long oak pews of the public gallery.

The judge said, "Ladies and gentlemen, today we start trial in the matter of, what is it?"

The Circuit Clerk popped up and said, "The State of Mississippi vs. Antonin Vacarro, Number CR-102367, Your Honor," and sat back down.

The judge said, "State, are you ready?"

Jones leaned forward in her seat, and said, "We're ready, Judge." The D.A. had left Bay Saint Louis after a few media interviews outside. Laura Jones was assisted by a young man who looked like he just got out of law school.

"Defense?" said the judge.

Hart stood and said, "Ready to proceed, Your Honor."

The judge said, "Members of the jury, the charge here is murder. Each side gets to make a *brief* opening statement," he looked right at the lawyers, then back at the jury. "Which is not to be considered evidence, but is just to familiarize you with what is expected to be shown, or not shown, by the evidence. State, you're first."

Jones strolled up to the podium and said, "Fellow citizens, this case is very simple. We are going to prove to you that Rilo Marshall, the deceased victim in this case, was in town from Gulfport, had come to Bay Saint Louis to meet the Defendant at a local restaurant. We're going to prove that the victim was an upper level operations manager on the docks in Gulfport, working for a blue water shipping company that had significant financial ties to the Defendant's family owned investment company in New Orleans, Puglisi and Vacarro, Limited. The Defendant is the president of that company, and runs its day to day operations.

"We're going to prove that the victim was himself an investor in that company whose considerable life savings were managed by it, and that the company was and is actual beneficiary of the deceased's estate." Half the gallery murmured. She paused, to let the noise die. "We're going to prove that they met in March of this year, right downtown at Tracy's restaurant, for lunch. They then got on the Defendant's boat, and left the harbor. They were seen by witnesses you will hear from arriving at Ship Island some time later. They spent the day out there, around several witnesses who then saw them leave. At some point, they got into an apparent disagreement. You are going to hear from a witness that will testify that she heard Rilo Marshall yelling at Vacarro on the boat, just before they left the island."

She walked to the front of the jury box. She said, "Nobody sees Defendant return to the harbor, apparently after dark. Thirteen days later, Mr. Marshall's head is found down on the beach, just west of the Washington Street boat launch. The coroner will testify that the deceased was killed by a blow to the back of the head, and that the man had been dead between ten days and two weeks. We believe there is only one person with the motive and opportunity to commit this crime, and that person is Tony Vacarro." She pointed at him. "We believe at the end of the case, you will find Tony Vacarro guilty of murder." She returned to her seat.

The judge said, "Defense, do you intend to make your statement now, or do you want to wait until the state rests its case?"

Hart said, "We'll go now, Judge. This will be brief." He laid a file on the podium, and walked around in front of it, not too close to the jury, and crossed his arms. He said, "This might surprise you, but most of what the state just told you is true." There was more mumbling in the gallery, that quickly abated. Hart said, "But they left a lot of information out. What they are not telling you is, those two never met each other before that day. Tony Vacarro had nothing to do with setting up the meeting. In fact, nobody can prove why the meeting even happened, because nobody knows. The state can't provide a single forensic connection between Tony Vacarro and the death of Mr. Marshall. Not one.

"The evidence they will show you is all circumstantial. They are going to want you to connect a bunch of dots by jumping over a lot of missing ones. And at the end of their case, they won't be able to prove he did it. And you know why? Because he didn't." Hart walked back to his table, and sat.

The judge said, "State, call your first witness."

The state's first witness was the deceased victim's executive assistant, who said someone called her from Vaccaro's office and set the meeting. She said her boss had been adamant about seeing Vacarro as soon as possible, and he never said why."

Laura Jones handed her a paper. She said, can you identify this a phone record from your office at that time?"

"Yes ma'am."

And is the call you reference indicated there?"

The witness pointed it out, and the record was introduced in evidence.

On cross examination, John Hart said, "Can you show us on this record where the call you receive originated?"

"No sir."

"Why not? Doesn't the record indicate the source and time of all calls received or made from your office?"

"Yes sir, but as you can see, this one says 'unknown."

"Do you know why?"

"No sir, I don't. I just took the message."

Hart said, "Was the caller male or female?"

She said, "To be honest, I couldn't tell. I just remember there being a poor connection, and the person saying they were calling for Mr. Vacarro there, and to tell Mr. Marshall, my boss, to meet him at that restaurant. That's all I know."

Next, the state called a waitress who had served Vacarro and the victim. Laura Jones tediously walked her through the day, including details of her preparation for work, and the other workers she saw, and what the specials were, and how she could be sure of what she remembered, and so on. In what would become a pattern of plodding, tedious testimony, the first two foundational eye witnesses, both employees of the restaurant, soon began boring the gallery. They were used to seeing dramatic confrontations and fast scenes of fictional trials in the movies, or the edited excerpts of real ones on TV, and were unprepared for the exhaustive details of real life litigation.

Toward the end of the day, the state only made it through five of the twenty eyewitnesses they had listed, and more than half the public gallery had left. After the judge released the jury, he met with the attorneys in his chambers. The actual D.A. had just shown back up. He had instructed Jones prior to trial to take as much time as possible putting on the case, for the publicity. The three prosecutors took all the available chairs. The judge said, "State, you seem pretty particular about all the minutiae with these witnesses. You think we really need to hear about what clothes everybody was wearing that day, or can we move along a little quicker?"

Standing, leaning against the wall, Hart said, "Judge, we're willing to stipulate to the fact that my client was at the meeting. If this is the pace we can expect, I may be out of business before the state rests."

The D.A. said, "Judge, they can concede whatever they want, but we are entitled to take as much time as we deem necessary to…"

The judge said, "Mister District Attorney, let me explain something to you. You aren't entitled to a damn thing. I control the courtroom, not you."

"And Judge, you continue to cut me off every time I try to go on record in this matter."

"What record?," the judge said, "do you see a court reporter in here? This is an informal discussion between a judge and some trial attorneys, who are officers of the court. These things occur all the time, which you would know if you were an actual courtroom attorney, instead of..."

"An elected official, just like you are, Sir. And since this is an informal discussion, let me say, I think your bias against the state in this case may be subject for review, if it continues."

The judge said, "Just so we're clear, I am not against the state, or even you personally. I understand you got elected, and how. Being kin to the right people around here goes a long way, and knowing the right ones goes the rest. The thing is, there are a dozen people in this district, several of them assistants in your office, who are better equipped to be the District Attorney than you are. I think you got where you are by something other than talent or experience, that's all. Now, you want to get me recused, or sanctioned? Take your best shot." The young D.A. wisely chose to remain silent.

After the attorneys left for the day, Bailiff Fitts walked in the chambers, and said, "Judge, I went ahead and turned those three goofballs loose from the old jail downstairs."

The judge said, "Good. Did you show them the gallows in back?"

"Yes sir, as always."

"Were they scared?"

"Well, no sir. They all wanted me to ask you if they could come up here one weekend and spend the night in there, and live broadcast the whole thing on the internet. I told them 'hell no' and next time they acted up, I'd make sure you put them in the real jail. That one, they're scared of."

The judge said, "This is the generation that'll be running things after we're gone, Fitts. The country's in trouble."

The Bailiff said, "I hear you, Judge. But I'm pretty sure that's what our grandparents said, too."

The next day, the Circuit Clerk announced the judge had a last second emergency that necessitated cancelling court for the day. Hart took it as an opportunity to catch up on some other matters, and for the most part dodged the crowd outside on the way back to the office. There were a few less people outside than the first day. Apparently, a few still had to go to work. After a while, somebody rapped on the door down the stairs. It was Captain Fleming, and they went back up to his office. Sitting at the desk, Hart said, "Captain, how have you been?"

He said, "They ain't killed me yet, Lawyer."

"Let's hope they don't any time soon. What can I do for you?"

"Well, it has to do with them eventually killing me, I guess. I wrote down one of those wills you told me about, in my own handwriting, if anybody can read it, and it's in this envelope, along with a couple things. First off, I want you to hang on to this for me, and wait until I die before you open it up."

Hart said, "Captain, I normally don't hold original wills, since if a fire or something happens..."

"But I need you to. I can't have this at my house, it might never get found. I don't have anybody else, you know."

"Yeah, I know, Captain. I know how you feel."

"I believe you do, Lawyer. You know, maybe it ain't my place to say this, but I saw you with that new gal recently, downtown at one of them fancy joints, you know. Anyway, besides her being real pretty and all, I hope you don't mind me saying, she's done a whole lot of good for your drag-assing, too."

Hart said, "I appreciate that, Captain, but I'm really not comfortable talking about..."

"I know, Lawyer. It's hard to let dead people go, and get on with it. I couldn't, but it would be good if somebody could. You usually mope around a lot, but I seen her change that some, is all."

Hart said, "I appreciate it. I really do."

The Captain said, "You remember the first time we met? It was after Hurricane Katrina. We were talking about that pirate treasure 'sposed to be buried somewhere down there by that Pirate House property, remember?"

"Yes I do. I've been hearing that story since I was a little boy, running around on the beach. We dug all over the place back then, looking for that treasure."

"That's right, we were downtown at the one joint that was still open at the time, by the old depot, back of town."

"That's how I remember it."

"And I was telling one of my yarns and you were the only one listening to me and laughing at my story, and not just me."

"It was a good story, if I'm remembering it right. Something about you rescuing a man up the mast of a sunken sailboat, sticking out of the water, and he was dressed up in a big yellow chicken suit, with feathers and everything. I forget, what was the explanation for that?"

"He didn't have one, and I didn't ask him. He was just damn glad to get off that sailboat mast. That really happened, too. All them yarns I tell are true. I might shine 'em up a little bit for story telling sake, but you wouldn't believe all the crazy stuff I've seen and done in the Gulf of Mexico. Anyway, I know you don't have time to listen to me. I just appreciate you always being nice, and taking care of me in a tight spot or two, and never griping at me about paying you. I wanted you to know that, and I am gonna square up with you one of these days."

Hart said, "Captain, you don't owe me a

thing. I look forward to hearing all your stories, and I know they're true. That's my payment, and I mean it."

"Well, we'll see," he said. "You take it easy, Lawyer."

Late in the day, the judge had finished his personal business, and had the clerk contact the attorneys for a conference call. He said, "I apologize, but I had an issue related to being old that had to be tended to, which is all I'm going to say about it. I want you to know that I will be here and ready in the morning, and there will be no more delays on my account. Anything else?"

Laura Jones said, "Judge, I need to announce that there's a potential problem with one of our listed witnesses, which I just found out about. We intended to call a young lady who heard the victim shouting at the Defendant out at Ship Island, on the boat. It appears she has absconded."

The Judge said, "She what?"

Jones said, "We can't find her, judge. She may have left the area."

The judge said, "I know what the hell 'absconded' means, State. It means you lost track of one of your most important witnesses, right? So just say so. 'Absconded' makes it sound like she's up to something. Alright, you told the jury in your opening that she was going to be here, and testify, didn't you?."

"Yes, sir. That may be a problem now."

The judge said, "No, it *is* a problem, or you wouldn't be telling me about it." He said, "Defense? What do you say if they can't produce this witness?"

Hart said, "Sounds like a mistrial to me, Judge."

Jones said, "Judge, she made the statement. We think we can get it in under at least two hearsay exceptions in the Rules of Evidence."

"Well, you can think again," said the judge. "You're not going to hang this Defendant's case on a witness that can't be cross examined in open court. And there won't be a mistrial. This case is going to proceed to a conclusion, as fast as possible. So here's what I'm going to do. State, if you can't find her, and if this case goes to jury deliberation, I'm going to instruct the jury that they are not allowed to consider having heard that statement made by you, and to draw whatever conclusions they desire about why you made it. The defense can address it in their closing, however they see fit."

Jones said, "But Judge, aren't you going to allow us to make our motion, and argue the evidence rules and law on that question?"

"You sure can. I have heard that same motion and argument a hundred times, at least. I argued it myself a few times, when I was sitting in your chair. The lesson here is, don't ever tell the jury something you can't back up. You've been practicing around here for quite a while, and should know that. You can proffer whatever you need to make your record, but that statement will not come in to this trial without that witness being present, and there will be no mistrials, or interlocutory appeals. This meeting is over."

That evening, John Hart drove over to Mandeville, on the northern edge of Lake Pontchartrain, to meet Lisette for dinner. In the waning sun, on the balcony of an old lakeside restaurant that was once some rich New Orleanian's weekend house, they ordered cucumber salads, shrimp and grits, and bread pudding. Hart said, "You know, I'm not counting, but we've seen each other several times now. Have you noticed?" He winked at her.

"I have. If it's more than two or three, it's my personal record."

Hart said, "Wow. What makes me so lucky?"

Lisette said, "It's not luck. Luck doesn't exist. That's a myth created by people who don't prepare or can't perform to describe people who do."

"So you like my performance?"

She slid her hand up his leg, and said, "I certainly do, so far."

Hart said, "How is it you've never dated

anyone?"

Lisette pulled her hand away, slowly. She said, "Is that what this is? Dating?"

Hart said, "That's not what I meant. It's just, you have to know how good looking you are. I mean, you must have always had men following you around. They would have no choice."

She said, "At the risk of sounding conceited, that's more true than you can ever know. The thing is, I know I look like my mother, who I never met. Because of her beauty, she got used by men all her life. I've always been careful not to get too personally entangled with people over what amounts to entertainment and sex. I think it's best for people to avoid labeling everything and just enjoy their time together while they can, don't you?"

He said, "Yes. Like I said, I wasn't trying to pin you down. Do you mind me asking, what actually happened to your mother?"

She said, "I'm not ready to talk to anyone about that. I'm sorry, but I may never be."

Hart said, "I'm sorry too. Maybe I just need to shut up. But I did want to tell you that this thing with you, whatever you call it, has been a complete surprise. I had sort of accepted being alone forever. I mean, this is embarrassing, but I haven't even, you know, been out with anyone since... since I was married." He looked out across the lake, realizing his face was a little warm.

She said, "I know you went through something terrible, John. But nobody really knows how to understand anyone else's pain, so I won't say I do. I think all we can really do is move forward, and remember the good things, and learn from the bad ones, and try to forget about the pain. I'm happy to be here with you tonight. That's all I know for now."

Oddly, after a half hour of salad and iced tea, neither one had yet mentioned the murder case. Lisette finally said, "So, how is my brother's trial going?"

Hart said, "Well, for one thing, it's going to be a long one. A couple of weeks, at least, at this pace. That's pretty long for our jurisdiction."

"Cases on TV seem to go on forever, don't they? Two weeks doesn't seem that long for a murder trial."

Hart said, "Those trials take so long *because* of television. District Attorneys and judges get plenty of face time, and they are both usually elected, so it's good publicity. For defense attorneys, it's also the best kind of advertising. That's why on TV, they take three days to cross examine a witness, when it can be done in an hour or two."

"Do you like the fact that cameras aren't allowed inside the court?"

"Not just cameras, but any recording. I

don't like them, because what goes on in court should not be subject to editing. Culling highlights for dramatic effect doesn't accurately reflect what goes on in there, and just bolsters the ridiculous myth that what we do is somehow staged for entertainment. People's whole lives are at stake. This is deadly serious, not entertainment."

"So what do you think about Tony's chances?"

Hart smiled, said, "What, are you kidding me? He's got John Hart at his side. How can he lose?" They laughed, and toasted tea glasses. Then he got quiet. "But seriously," he said, "the state has a dead person, so they have a case. A lot of the jury are going to think he's actually guilty. This is going to come down to me convincing them that the state just hasn't met their burden of proof."

"You mean the guy's head is not enough?"

Hart said, "That just means somebody killed that guy. It doesn't prove your brother did it. And the head's all they really have."

"How so?"

"Well, we just found out the prosecution lost one of their best witnesses. Some lady claimed she heard the victim yelling at Vacarro about something, but now they can't find her. The judge is not going to allow her statement in under hearsay rules. Without that witness, I don't think they can win."

"That's great. What happens if they don't?"

"I assume your brother takes us all on a long cruise."

"I mean, to the murder case?"

"In theory, they get back out there and try to find whoever did it. In reality, it would be over."

"Win or lose, it's good for your law practice?"

"Yeah, I guess it is. And frankly, I need a lot more business."

Lisette swirled her tea, looked at it, then at Hart and said, "Surely my half brother paid you a significant fee?"

Hart said, "He did. Thank God, because I didn't really realize how close I was to complete insolvency, according to my accountant. That money saved me. It paid off the money I had borrowed on the place in New Orleans, which is the only thing I actually own. It would have been lost in another month or two. All my credit cards were maxed out, and there were lots of them. By the time everything was caught up, and taxes paid, and we paid the office and house rent through the end of the year, I'm back above zero, and no debts, and some to spare. So yes, he saved my practice, but I need a lot more business, and this case should help."

Lisette said, "How is the civil case going, do you mind me asking?"

Hart sighed, said, "It's not good. We're never going to find that guy, even if somebody really saw him in Venice. Criminals slip in and out of Venice like catfish. Anyway, I can't believe these bastards are going to get away without paying for what they did. But that's the way it works, I'm probably going to lose. Think of the irony. The biggest civil case of my life, and the story of my life at the same time." He sat back, crossed his arms, and stared at nothing out in the lake.

She said, "I'm sorry I brought that up."

Hart said, "It's OK, I appreciate that somebody cares."

She said, "Let's talk about something fun. What's going on with your friend Sid and his new lady friend?"

Hart laughed. He said, "He's apparently back in love."

"It's that serious?"

"Oh yes. When I met him, he was just getting divorced for what I now know was the eighth time."

"Believe me, he is the gossip subject extra ordinaire in New Orleans. I've heard all the stories. But these aren't hostile divorces, are they?"

"Not according to Sid. He just likes to be married, I guess, although he swears she's the one."

Lisette said, "Maybe it's just the sex," and pinched his thigh.

Hart said, "Maybe so. You want to get the main course to go?"

She said, "No objection, Counselor."

The next morning, the young District Attorney did not attend. Laura Jones went back into her exhaustive examination of eyewitnesses from the restaurant. Midway through the third witness, close to lunch, a soft spoken lady was recalling her excellent ahi tuna from that day when Investigator Larue came in the courtroom. He signaled for Jones' assistant, who met him at the rail. The assistant then approached Jones at the lectern, and whispered to her. Jones said, "Judge, may we approach?"

All three attorneys went to the judge's elevated dais. He turned off his microphone and leaned forward. Jones said, "Judge, apparently there has been an investigative surprise in this case, and there may be new evidence. I'm afraid I have to request a short continuance, so we can ask for a search warrant."

The Judge said, "What the hell for?"

"I'm not exactly sure, Judge, there's been an anonymous tip. I need to talk to the investigator."

"Well, let's quit right here. You report back to me by five o'clock. I swear, between me having to miss yesterday and you moving through these witnesses like a cold snail, we're liable to be here until Thanksgiving."

At five o'clock, the report was murky.

With all the attorneys in the judge's chambers, including the actual District Attorney and the court reporter, Jones told the judge that somebody had called the anonymous tip line at the Bay P.D. and reported that blood was on Vacarro's boat, which was in the city harbor.

Hart said, "Judge, this is ridiculous. That boat's been searched already, what, twice? How could they have missed blood? And he's been using it. I was on it the other day. And we're entitled to know who the informant is."

Jones said, "Judge, that's not possible. The tip line is set up to be anonymous. There's no way to know who called it in. Besides, the defense is not entitled to see any evidence in an ongoing investigation."

Hart said, "What? We're only barred from viewing the evidence in a felony investigation until a preliminary hearing is held. We're in the middle of a trial here, and the procedure rules entitle us to see whatever this is, right now."

Jones said, "Judge, we don't believe we have to reveal anything until we get a warrant, collect samples, if any exist, and get labs back."

The judge said, "Sounds like you don't really have anything to reveal. How long does the lab take, if anything is found?"

"Not long, judge. A couple of days."

"OK, I'm going to give you your warrant. That doesn't mean you get any new evidence in. We'll ride that horse when we get to it. Tell your lab to rush any necessary tests. Defense, you can proffer all your arguments against the warrant, for the record. Like I said, there won't be any mistrials or interlocutories."

Hart said, "Yes sir."

The judge said, "I'm going to briefly continue this case, just long enough for the state to find out if there's anything there. If there is, we're not waiting on lab results, so State, you'd better plan ahead. You ought to have your investigators out there this evening."

The judge had to tell the jury members and alternates that the trial would be delayed for a short time. He gave them a number to call at the Clerk's office each afternoon to find out if they had to be in court the next morning. He told them they couldn't go out of town without permission, which caused some eye rolling and grumbling. He said, "I'm sorry, on behalf of the court system, that you-all have got to put up with this. It's temporary, and I'm just going to ask you to bear with us. Also, as a reminder, you can't discuss this case with anyone." Then he adjourned.

Filomena made a rare Thursday appearance at the office. She waddled in to Hart's office, and plopped down in one of the interview chairs. She said, "Ach. Mr. Hart, I have some bad news. Or maybe it's good news for you, depending on how you feel, I guess."

"What is it, Miss Filomena?"

She said, "I'm afraid I'm going to have to leave you, Sonny. I've only just found out, I've got to go back to Wales, to my old stomping grounds, as they say, back when I was just a girl, and before I knew the evil ways of men, and especially American lawyers. You see, I have a sister there, as I told you, and she's going to need me to help her now, and we're all we have left, as it happens."

Hart said, "I'm sorry to hear that, but I guess I have to be happy for you, getting to be with your sister, and some more family too?"

"Aye, there's nieces and nephews, and babies, and all that crap."

Hart chuckled. He said, "Well, surely they'll all benefit from your gentle charm, and loving touch."

She said, "You make fun, boy. But you needed some cuffing when I found you, didn't you?"

Hart said, "Yes ma'am, I guess I did. Probably still do."

She said, "Well, I'm not out yet. I'll be here a little while longer. Here's a message, from that devil defense lawyer in your wrongful death suits." She slapped the phone message down in front of him, and waddled back to her desk.

After he got off the phone with the defense lawyer, he took a deep breath, blew it out. He leaned back in his sunken chair, and put his feet up on the desk and felt his blood pressure lower some. Well, a lot. Looking out over the calm gulf, he thought, *what is a person's life really worth*? Attorneys have to make these decisions all the time. He had been doing it for years, handling other people's business. People get injured, and sometimes killed, by stupidity. Judges or juries have to determine an amount of money the stupid owe the injured, or the survivors of the dead.

And that was the crux of it. Society had long ago decided that resolving disputes between people did not have to include revenge, or vendettas, or duels in the street at high noon. Courts reduce all the hurt, and anger, and depression, and rage for revenge to an amount of money, plain and simple. Nobody is ever really satisfied without revenge, it's human nature. But it's just no longer an option.

The defense attorney had just offered him five million dollars to settle, take it or leave it. Hart said he had to think about it. The attorney had said to let him know by Monday, no negotiations. Hart just stared out at Cat Island. All the suffering, and nightmares, and guilt, and the God forsaken never ending loneliness. Maybe it was finally time to quit just existing, and actually try to live.

On Friday, the court clerk called and said

that the judge would hold a hearing Monday morning to assess progress. Meanwhile, John Hart had another date with Lisette in New Orleans. They ordered drinks, and Hart said, "You're not going to believe this. Yesterday I got an offer to settle the civil case, out of the blue. It's crazy. Here it is, not far from the deadline to produce this driver, and I have no idea where he is. Well, my investigator apparently heard some rumor that the guy had been down around Venice, probably running his mouth. I mentioned in court last time that we may have a lead on him, but I was just screwing with them. It was the remotest of leads. I can't believe they bit, but here it is, the case is about to be dismissed, and they offer to settle. It's crazy."

"What else could it be?"

"That's the question of a legal career. There has to be some kind of underlying reason, something compelling. After all this tort reform nonsense, they would rather sell their own children than pay out any big claim, regardless of the proof. And they know jurors believe that any significant verdict will make their own insurance rates go up, which is nonsense. It costs the insurance industry a hell of a lot more in the long run to defend legitimate cases than to pay for them, because they force so many to trial, or appeal, regardless of the facts. And they win a lot of them because of jury bias, or bad plaintiff lawyers, or both. So this kind of offer, at this stage of the game, is just bizarre."

"What are you going to do?"

"What would you do?"

Lisette said, "What's the best you could do at trial, if you won?

"Who knows. That's probably about as good as it could get, money wise."

"What else is there?"

"I don't know. Revenge, I guess?"

"Okay, and if you win at trial, are they going to apologize?"

"Ha. Hell no. They'll appeal, and tie it up for at least the next couple of years."

"And can you lose?"

"Absolutely. They already claimed in their pleadings that my wife caused the accident. They actually countersued her estate for totaling the truck that killed her. That's the mentality."

Lisette took a sip of wine, and looked away. She looked back at him, right in his eyes, and said, "I don't see what the question is. Of course you take it."

Monday, Hart didn't have to be in court until nine o'clock. It was also the deadline for his answer to the settlement offer. As Lisette had said, there really was no choice. Oddly, the actions that made John Hart rich were as mundane as anything he had ever done as an attorney. He called the defense counsel and accepted the offer. The other lawyer said he had a release and dismissal order already drafted, and emailed them. John Hart signed both, and emailed them back. They would wire the money the next day. One minute, he had been a sustenance level general practice attorney, scrambling, trying to eke out a living in a business environment that had steadily undermined and devalued his profession for years. The next minute he was, by any local standard, rich.

That phone call should have been revelatory. There should have been trumpets, or fireworks, or some kind of second line parade. But there wasn't. There was nothing to celebrate. He didn't even berate himself that his family's lives were, after all this time, being purchased. There was no other way to look at it. There was also no changing the fact that they were all gone, and weren't coming back. There was nothing left to give to suffering. He had suffered out. He was depleted.

He also knew that his time hanging around the relative anonymity of Cedar Point with the Raccoon Queen was over. He just had a subpoena issued for the real boss of the New Orleans Mafia, and was now fully engaged in a completely different war, one that could actually kill him. So he made a few calls. He cancelled his house lease, rented a storage unit, and found a mover who would pack up his belongings too, and told them to start in the morning. Until this trial was over, he'd have to stay anywhere but Cedar Point, where he was too easy to find.

Back in court, the judge had excluded the gallery, and the jury had been told not to attend. The judge said, "OK, we're on the record, outside the presence of the jury. After the trial of this case commenced, I was informed by the prosecution that some new, material evidence may be available. I instructed both Parties that this case would be continued until the new evidence, if any, could be produced. This is an unusual set of circumstances, to say the least. I signed a warrant, and new evidence was apparently collected. Today, I am going to decide if that evidence, whatever it is, is admissible, or not. OK, State, what do you have?"

Jones said, "Judge, we have found the victim's blood in the Defendant's boat, or yacht, if you like, in the Master State Room head. "Head" is what a bathroom in a boat is called. The blood has been verified by the crime lab as the victim's."

"How is it you all are just finding out about this?"

"Like I said before, Judge, the city received an anonymous phone tip."

The judge said, "How the hell can anything be anonymous these days? Can't everything be traced by a computer, or something?"

"No sir. We've been told the crime tip line set up at the police department is literally untraceable. It's to encourage people to report crime without having to worry about retaliation."

"Untraceable, huh? Hmm. Well, that makes a certain amount of sense. But how do you get around probable cause, assuming the previous permission has been withdrawn?"

Hart said, "It has, Judge."

Jones said, "Indicia of reliability, Judge. What's the motivation to lie? Besides, there's the salient fact that blood was indeed found on the boat, as stated by the anonymous tipster."

The judge said, "Well, that's the cart pulling the horse, isn't it?"

"We think indicia of reliability is enough, Judge."

The judge said, "Defense?"

"Hart stood and said, "Judge, the anonymous caller probably planted the blood, we have no way of knowing. Obviously, admitting this kind of evidence at this stage of the trial would make our defense of it almost impossible. How can we examine the veracity of the source, and efficacy of the state's investigation if their confidential, or in this case, anonymous informant can't be questioned?"

The judge said, "State, you had to see that coming."

Jones said, "Judge, the best test of efficacy in any investigation is the evidence it produces. Here, you have a dead man who we are going to irrefutably prove was on the Defendant's boat, or yacht. He was killed, and chopped up, at least partially, and his blood was subsequently found on the yacht. So the integrity of the process is irrefutable. As far as the tipster's veracity? Based on results, they were obviously telling the truth. Without motivation for the tipster to get credit, or rewarded, we get the best evidence possible. It's a product of a perfected system of information gathering."

The judge said, "Are you telling this Court that merely finding evidence is proof of its admissibility in a criminal trial? If that's how this all works, why worry with all these trouble making Constitutional rights?"

Jones said, "No, Judge, but the blood evidence we will present is part of the res gestae in this case. We..."

"The what? Don't make me try to remember law school, State, talk to me in language used in this century."

"The *res gestae*, Judge. All the surrounding circumstances of the death of Rilo Marshall. We believe that this is a matter of there being significant indications of reliability to overcome any questions of compliance with the Rules of Evidence, or procedural due process."

The judge said, "Defense?"

Hart stood and said, "Judge, this system necessitates that any anonymous tipster also has to be assumed to be the source of the evidence itself. How in the world would anyone know the blood was there, unless they put it there? And obviously, Mr. Vacarro isn't going to be the caller, so if anything, this should exonerate him."

The judge said, "Sounds like a good jury argument. State, where do you propose this witness got their information from?"

"Well, it's just speculation, Judge."

"I asked you, so speculate away."

"Judge, we think it could only have been the person who cleaned the boat, or someone she told. We know she is a young, single mother, who hires out to clean boats in the harbor, and charges cash. She apparently performs this service for several boat owners in the harbor, and does an excellent job."

The judge said, "And you can't find her?"

"We're not really sure who she is, Judge. We got different names from different people. We think she was probably in the United States illegally."

"Was?"

"She apparently left the area right after the victim's head was found, Judge. Nobody's seen her."

"What? How do the boat owners know how to get in touch with her when she is needed?"

"They don't, Judge. She's just down there. When they see her, they pay her cash and tell her what they want done."

"She can just get on people's boats? What about unlocking them?"

"It's the Bay Saint Louis Harbor, Judge. The owners just leave them open at an arranged time. I think most of them never lock up their boats, anyway. There's hasn't been any serious crime down there, to speak of. Kids snatching a few fishing rods here and there off the docks, that's about it."

"No serious crime, huh? So the first one is a murder? Pretty impressive start. I don't guess there are any security cameras?"

"Nothing useful. Just wasn't in the budget, Judge. And like I said, really not needed, until now."

The judge said, "Defense?"

Hart said, "Judge, this is the most unreliable potential evidence that can be presented. We would need a mistrial and a group of experts just to examine the issues involving an anonymous Confidential Informant. Assuming the tipster is untraceable, the evidence can't possibly be admissible."

"State, you got any good case law?"

"Not much from our appellate courts, Judge, and what there is just hits around the edges. It's all about indicia of reliability."

Hart said, "Judge, we are going to need probably thirty days to examine the evidence. I'm moving for a mistrial."

The judge said, "Okay. Well, I've heard both of you, and here's what I think. You two lawyers are pretty astute in this court, and I'm satisfied from what I know about both of you that you can handle this analysis on the fly, so to speak. So can I. This is an unusual evidentiary question, but I don't think there has been a Supreme Court criminal case, state or federal, that's come out in the last forty years that I haven't read. Hell, a lot of them from our district I participated in, either as a judge, or when I was an Assistant D.A. myself an eon ago.

"I do not want this case to drag on forever. I'm denying the Defense's motion for mistrial, and giving both sides the rest of the week to get ready. State, your investigators are to cooperate fully with the defense, regarding the whole blood evidence issue. I'm going to tell the jury to be back here next Monday, and we are going forward. By noon this Friday I want both of you to brief me on your positions. Let's keep the length down, say three to five pages. That should be enough. I'll rule on the admissibility of the blood next Monday morning, based on the briefs. If I'm wrong, or you don't like it, you can appeal after the case. I won't be granting any interlocutory appeals, or further delays, not even for me. If you need me, I'll be here catching up on other case hearings. That's the ruling of the Court."

That afternoon, Hart and Vacarro met at the law office on Main Street. Vacarro had gotten there before Hart returned from lunch, and Miss Filomena was busy haranguing him in the conference room when Hart came up the stairs.

Hart said, "We're back to trial next Monday. The judge is going to let the blood in, unless the state manages to screw up the chain of custody, or some similar error. But they're not going to screw it up."

Vacarro said, "What does that do to our case?"

"It doesn't help, obviously."

Vacarro reflexively slapped the table, said, " Dammit, I did not kill that man! Somebody put that blood on the boat. What are we going to do about it?"

"Up until this point, their case was going to be entirely circumstantial inference. You've been seen with the dead guy, he was on your boat, there's some kind of disagreement, he ends up dead. Now this. It's still circumstantial, but a lot more damning. Before, we had the luxury of just picking their case apart. Now we need to blame somebody."

"My uncle?"

"The Raven. We have to make it plausible to the jury that he killed this man, or had him killed."

"Well, he did. Listen, there are some

things I haven't told you."

"Such as?"

"Well, it has to do with the whole New Orleans Mafia thing. I said at the beginning of all this that the Mafia doesn't exist any more. And in a traditional sense, that's true. I mean, my crazy uncle still runs a half-assed crew, as far as I know, which is very little. I have always deliberately stayed away from him, and knowing anything about him. I think, well I've heard, he always has some kinds of rackets going on, drugs mainly. I heard a rumor about them getting fentanyl out of China, from a buddy of mine in the police department. But for some reason, he never gets caught. I've also heard that's because he has some kind of lifetime immunity from being prosecuted, at least by the feds, going back to Castro, and the JFK assassination, and some other things. I don't know any details."

"We've all heard the stories."

Vacarro said, "Well, the assassination part I believe is true. The Bardinos really did scrounge up that idiot Oswald, and it was The Raven who actually set him up in Dallas. Oswald was supposed to try to take a shot, and get killed by the cops in the process. It didn't go as planned, obviously. Anyway, that's the story."

"Okay, so what have you not told me?"

"The dead guy, Mr. Marshall. It's something he said to me on the boat that day. After he got a few beers in him, he kept telling me he wanted out, that his duty was done, stuff like that. He asked me what he could do. I told him I didn't know what the hell he was talking about, which is true. He got pretty worked up about it. That's what that girl saw, or heard, him being irritated with me because I didn't know what he was talking about."

"You really have no idea what he was talking about?"

"Well, I think we can assume he was in some kind of arrangement with my uncle, and whatever is left of the Mafia, and it was my uncle that set up the meeting."

"Which we now know was designed to set you up for the murder."

"Evidently."

"So how does getting rid of you help anyone? Don't you make a bunch of money for your investors?"

"A bunch. We've outperformed the market for years."

"And your work benefits your business partner, The Raven."

"Everyone in the family. Not the Mafia family, but the real blood kin of the Bardinos. There's a second irrevocable trust that the company continually funds. It pays everybody in the extended family, and there are a lot of them. High school and college kids' parents get monthly expense stipends, and their tuitions paid. Adults get mortgages paid, 401Ks funded, even vacation use of several properties the trust owns, one in Hawaii, one in Colorado, one in Key West. The whole thing is administered by a rotating board of directors, which I've served a couple of tours on. Lisette's been on it too."

"So getting rid of you actually hurts The Raven's bottom line?"

"Well, other than inheriting my piece of the company. I'm not saying that nobody else can do my job. It's just that I'm damn good at it. Setting me up doesn't make sense. Besides, if he wanted to kill the guy, why make it public? Why not just whack him, and be done with it?"

Hart said, "I've been wondering that myself."

"So how do we deal with the blood?"

"We point out that it could have been any number of other people who put it there. Reasonable doubt is our friend. Whoever called it in is in on it. The problem is, the damn call is untraceable. Here we go again."

"How do you know?"

"That's what the case investigator tells me. I know the guy, we're friends outside court. He's telling the truth."

"Do you have the information?"

"No, but the judge is making them cooperate. What good is it? It's a dead end."

"Vacarro said, "Actually, maybe not."

"How's that?"

"Anything I tell you is a secret, right? Attorney-client privilege, and all that?"

"Well, not literally everything. Prospective crimes, for example, aren't."

"Ok. I'm going to take a chance here that you won't repeat this. In my business, it helps to be able to get your hands on certain types of information that is not necessarily, you know, accessible to everyone."

"Like insider trading?"

"Some of it falls under those rules, which are ridiculously vague, by the way. But any kind of information that helps us predict stock markets is good. The U.S. stock market is really just an elaborate casino, only, instead of fixed odds on table games the house can analyze, like in a real casino, the odds are always moving, driven by trends, more like sports betting. It's all motivated by fear, basically."

"Fear?"

"The fear of losing money. In my company's case, fear of losing other people's money."

Hart said, "What happened to investing in healthy, growing businesses? Isn't that the whole point of stocks? So a company can raise capital for reinvestment in the business itself?"

"That's a quaint notion that went out the window decades ago. If you liquidated some of the biggest companies in the world, you could never come close to justifying the amount of capital invested in them. It is an illusion based on the principle that the market will always, on average, grow. It's sort of the byproduct of the whole notion that the U.S. economy, and now the world economy, is always on the way up, on average.

"The fact is, the market is not a homogeneous mass, but a moving, three dimensional puzzle of big and little pieces that change in size and position based on trends, whether they are economic, or perceptive, or superstitious. We don't know, and there is no effective comparison model. It's conceptually a lot like your Flogic theory. Our business is about anticipating those trends, and their durations, and investing accordingly."

"So whoever sees the future best wins the most."

"That's it. And some of these movements take months, or even years to develop. But increasingly, some of them are day by day, or even minute by minute."

"What makes you so good at it?"

"Everybody picks the easy winners. It's the marginal securities that make the difference between good players and superstars. There are experts, services we hire around the world, who scrounge everything on the internet to help us find the right issues, and predict future trends."

"And some of their methods might be illegal?"

"I don't know. We don't have access to any of their sources of information, or their techniques, which are their trade secrets. They claim it's all computer algorhythms. Whether or not that's true, I don't know. They provide a service, and we subscribe to it, and I decide whether to follow their advice. It's just like handicapping horse races. Sometimes they're right, sometimes wrong."

Hart said, "How much do you really think is science, and how much guesswork, or decryption, or just plain old spying?"

Vacarro thought for a second, and said, "Have you ever been to thoroughbred horse racing at the Fair Grounds? You go down by the paddock, that's where they walk the horses around before races, for the spectators to see. Anyway, you see some of the greatest characters there. The owners, they like to get out and strut around with their horses. Typically, it's an old guy with Elvis sideburns, dyed hair, fake tan, big gold watch, silk suit and brand new Italian leather boots he squeaks around in. He's with his fourth or fifth wife, or an escort who's decades younger than him, skinny as a straw, and has five pounds of gaudy jewelry hanging all over her like she's at Mardi Gras. I swear, it's a living theater of absurdity.

"There's one stakes race every year, where the winner typically gets invited to bigger and better things, like the Kentucky Derby. Now, there's an old gambler that's always at the track, been there for as long as I can remember. This guy is a horse savant. He almost always picks the stakes winner, which is usually not the favorite. I've seen it happen several times, and he has way better a record than all the so-called experts. Last year, he did it again, and I finally asked him what his secret was. You know what he said? He bets big on the horse whose owner is with the youngest looking woman."

Hart laughed. He said, "How do you know he's not lying to you?"

Vacarro said, "I don't, but that's what he said."

"What about the horses owned by women?"

"He didn't say."

"Well, let's hope your consultants lean more toward science. You think these people can crack this encryption, and tell us who made that call?"

"I don't know. If it can be done, these people would be the ones to do it. We turn over whatever we have, have it analyzed."

"As long as I don't believe anything illegal is being done, we can hire any qualified expert we want."

"Do we have to tell the D.A. about it?"

"Not unless we have information we need to get in evidence, then we have to tell the judge and the prosecution."

Vacarro said, "OK, it's worth a shot. When can you get the system and call information?"

"I have a meeting with the head investigator tomorrow morning. How long do you think your people would take?"

"Could be a day, a week, or never. I'll just run it through the pipeline, and see what comes out."

"OK. Well, I was hoping it wouldn't be necessary, but the blood has changed things. We no longer have any choice. I'm going to have a subpoena issued for The Raven."

Chapter 9

Tuesday Morning, John Hart sat in a grey metal and tan Naugahide chair in front of Larue's desk in his office in the Bay Saint Louis Police Department. Larue was kicked back in his chair, with his feet crossed on his desk. The door was open, and he knew they could hear him out front. He said, "I can't believe this, Counselor. You're working for this murdering Mafia character, and want my help? Hell, I shouldn't even be seen in the same room with anybody that would defend that trash."

John Hart grinned, said, "Well, I appreciate the party line, Larue, but we both know the judge is requiring you to cooperate about this blood evidence."

The investigator looked around, winked at Hart, lowered his voice, and said, "Thanks, Counselor. Just keeping up appearances." He got up and shut the door.

Hart said, "OK, but I don't know if anybody's buying it. If I was you, I'd stick to police work, and avoid acting."

Larue said, "Thanks for that crucial insight, Counselor, now what can I do for you?"

Hart said, "Tell me about this call. I can't believe the judge actually signed a search warrant."

Larue held up his hands, and said, "You're the Officer of the Court, not me. I am merely an Officer of the Law, not an advocate of it. He played the recording, a metallic, computer generated voice that said, "You can find blood on Vaccaro's boat, if you look."

John Hart said, "You got any idea who this is?"

"Probably the cleaning lady, or some acquaintance of hers."

"Any way to verify that?"

"Nope."

"Why does the voice sound like that? Did the caller use a voice modulator?"

"No, the system does that to any caller's voice. We can't even tell if it is a male or female. The whole thing is designed to guarantee that people can report crimes anonymously."

"And you don't have any idea where this cleaning lady is?"

"Depends on who you talk to. Looks like she's a migrant, but that's not confirmed. Some of these boat owners think she is Mexican. Others think she is from Costa Rica, or Honduras. One said El Salvador. All we know is, she ain't here."

"So how did you find the blood?"

"Got the warrant, went in and swabbed every surface."

"Where was it?"

"What was there was in the bathroom in the master suite, or stateroom, or whatever rich people call the biggest bedroom in a boat." He

pointed at a decent rendering of the boat interior his assistant had drawn on the investigative
report. It had been cleaned up pretty well, but
there were traces of it here, and here, and these
other places."

Hart said, "Was there enough of it to tell
what happened?"

"No spray patterns, or anything like that.
Like I said, somebody had cleaned it up pretty
well. Just enough here and there to collect and
identify. We're not talking blood pools. We're
talking molecules. But enough to test."

"So nowhere else in the yacht?"

"Nope."

"You think he was killed in that bathroom, there on the boat?"

"It's not my job to speculate, Counselor. I
just collect evidence."

"Bullshit. You speculate all the time. You
didn't find any blood anywhere else. Isn't that
odd?"

"How's that?"

"Because if he was killed down there,
wouldn't there be at least some blood between
the stateroom and the back deck? I mean, somebody had to get his body off the boat, right?"

"I can see where that might be a curious
circumstance to a criminal defense attorney.
However, an intelligent killer may have made
arrangements to prevent it."

John Hart thought for a minute. He said,

"I need to know how this tip line works, the software, everything. There has got to be some way to trace these calls."

"Like I said, the idea is to make sure these calls are untraceable. It has some kind of system they say is unsolvable."

"I'm going to need all the information you have on the system, and the call itself."

"I'm going to need a subpoena."

"You'll have it this morning."

Larue said, "Then you will, too."

Hart got up to leave.

Larue said, "Hey, John. No shit, be careful. Your guy, maybe he did it, maybe not. Off the record, he seems more like a frat boy than a killer to me. But one way or another, he or somebody around him is dangerous. Watch your back."

Hart ran by the courthouse and got the judge to sign a *subpoena duces tecum* for the hotline information. He dropped the subpoena off, and went back to the office. By the close of business that day, Hart had given all the hotline information to Tony Vacarro.

Monday morning before court, the judge had the lawyers in his chambers. He said, "State, how many witnesses do you still have?"

Laura Jones said, "Eight more, I believe, from the restaurant, five from the island, three boat owners, plus the Captain, the Coroner, lead investigator, forensic accounting and lab. That's about it, unless we have rebuttals."

The judge said, "Well, I admire your strident regard for detail, but unless they've got something to add to the case other than placing the Defendant inside Tracy's in the presence of the victim, I'm going to instruct the jury, if we get that far, to find they were there together. I want to move this along."

Jones said, "Judge, doesn't there have to be a motion, or ..."

The judge said, "Defense, is there an oral motion before the court to stipulate the presence of the Defendant and the victim in the restaurant Tracy's on the date previously presented to the jury, and are you asking the court to instruct the jury as to that stipulation?"

"So moved, judge," said John Hart.

The judge said, "Granted. State, we'll let you have enough time to get your island witnesses rounded up, then let's go. I want your side to finish this week, if possible."

Jones said, "I understand, Judge, but I just don't see how."

Ths judge said, "That's why I said 'if possible.' Defense, what, if any, witnesses do you anticipate, if you are required to put on a case?"

Hart said, "Judge, I need to see how this so-called blood evidence goes, but I had a subpoena issued this morning for a gentleman named Marco Puglisi, whose street name is "The

Raven."

The judge said, "I'm sure we've all heard that name. I think I saw a documentary or some kind of thing about him on TV a few years ago. Does that fact create concerns for either party?" They both shook their heads.

Jones said, "Judge, I understand we can argue relevance at the time, but I'd like to know what this witness would be testifying about?"

Hart said, "Judge, I plan on asking him to explain to the jury why he killed Rilo Marshall."

That day and the next were spent going through the details of Vacarro and the victim's day at Ship Island. It was the first weekend of the year that a lot of boats had gone out to the island. Vacarro had guided the sixty foot vessel close to the old Civil War era fort, on the western tip of the east-west laying island, until they came upon a group of regulars from the area, in a flotilla just off the beach.

Eight or ten boats were anchored in a group that was steadily getting larger, some hanked together with lines and bumpers, forming a temporary boat barge that people could climb and walk over, boat to boat. It was still too early for most people to get in the relatively cold springtime water.

Vacarro had been on one edge of the boat barge, and a good number of the group had migrated to his vessel, with its loaded bar and sound system, and excess area. There were plenty of witnesses to the presence of the defendant and deceased on his boat. There had been a decent amount of drinking, and Tony Vacarro could very well have been legally intoxicated, some said. On the upper bridge some dancing redheaded tourist from Nashville apparently took her top off.

Cross examining one of these witnesses, John Hart said, "Sir, did you see Tony threatening Rilo Marshall at any time?"

The witness said, "No."

"Did they argue?"

"No sir, not that I saw. I don't think I ever saw them even talking to each other."

Did you see or hear any arguments, or threats at all?"

"None. Well, that one girl, the one that kept pulling off her top, her boyfriend threatened to leave her on the boat." The courtroom chuckled.

"I mean anything that might be considered dangerous."

"No sir."

By the time Wednesday rolled around, the gallery had gotten bored again, and half of them had gone back to their jobs or TVs or social media addictions at home. There were still people milling around out on the lawn, and plenty of official and amateur news and gossip people, but the casual bandwagon jumpers had faded considerably.

For most of the day, the state's droning witnesses narrated Vacarro and the deceased leaving the island, headed in with no one else aboard. A couple of other boat owners saw Vacarro's *Negotiable* positioned back in its slip at the Bay Saint Louis Harbor. Nobody saw him or the deceased get off the boat. Nobody saw or heard anything unusual.

So when the judge called for the state's last witness for the day, it was before a jury on the verge of a collective nap. Bailiff Fitts opened the back door of the courtroom, and called down the back stairs, "Arthur Fleming!" Presently old Captain Fleming trundled in the court, a little hesitant, and not perfectly steady.

The clerk swore him in with no difficulty. Just his appearance, a skinny old brown leather Santa in shorts and sandals, was enough to nudge the jury and gallery back into paying attention. Laura Jones asked him his name and address, and was about to get into how he found the dead man's head when the judge said, "Counsel, approach the bench." They did, and he remembered to turn his microphone off.

The judge whispered, "Looks to me like old Fleming here has been in the cups. Anybody think he's sober?"

John Hart said, "Not a chance, Judge. I can smell the rum from our table."

Laura Jones said, "Sorry, Judge. We were trying to keep an eye on him, but...",

The judge said, "It ain't your fault. I doubt if anybody can keep that old pirate from drinking his rum if he wants to. I think we're going to stop here for the day, and I'm going to invite the Captain to spend the night in the county jail so he's fresh tomorrow. I'll have the deputies deliver him for 9:00 sharp."

The word about Captain Fleming testifying got out, and the next morning the gallery was back, and the crowd was bigger outside. The Captain took the stand, and got sworn in again. Jones reminded him of the date and place he had found a head on the beach, then said, "Mr. Fleming, tell the jury how you accidentally came in contact with the deceased victim's head."

The Captain cocked his own head, squinting, and said, "I didn't accidentally come in contact with anything, ma'am. I saw it rolling around down there in the water way before I picked it up. It ain't like I tripped over it." The gallery sniggered.

Jones said, "OK, so just tell us what happened."

Captain Fleming said, "Well, it was just like any day for me. I got up early, which I always do at daylight, and I get some coffee and eat a banana, you know, for breakfast, then I head off down to the waterfront in my cart, where I go most days, huntin' around for doodads that I fix up and sell to the tourists downtown."

"Doodads like shells, and such?"

"Mainly, and pieces of wood, and sand dollars sometimes, stuff like that. I got a little shed out back of my cabin, and got some tools in there, you know, and I make what the tourists call "Mobiles," which are really just shells and little pieces of wood I clean up, and drill holes in, and slick up, and string up on cotton line. They hang up, like decorations. You can find things people lost too, like earrings, or necklaces. And sunglasses, some of them are good ones. People will give you twenty dollars for good ones if they ain't too scratched up."

"And this is how you make your living?"

"Well, I wouldn't call it a living. It's more like picking up a little pocket jack. I get a check, you know, from the Social Security, that I live off of. I just got a little rented cabin out back of town, and I ain't got many bills. And I don't eat a lot, neither." The jury all smiled at him, skinny as he was.

"So tell us what happened that day." The entire gallery actually leaned a little forward at the same time.

The Captain said, "Well, I seen that poor bast-, uh, gentleman's head down the beach a ways, and I knew right off what it was. I mean, I guess there ain't no mistaking a man's head when it's right out there in front of you. So naturally, I halt in place, and eyeball out in the water all around to see if there's any more, you know, pieces of him in the vicinity, and also up and down the beach, and out on the road, and the big houses across Beach Boulevard there, in case anybody's glassing me."

"A normal reaction to stumbling upon a human head, right?" said Jones.

Captain Fleming said, "Hell, I don't know what's normal when you find a head. That was my first one." The gallery laughed out loud, and the Captain shot a glance at the judge, who wasn't looking at him. He continued, "Once I figured that there wasn't anybody else around, this is just after daylight, you know, so once I was pretty sure I wasn't about to get bushwhacked, I figured I better bring it along, because there's liable to be some tourists go down through there soon, or kids, or crabs, and none of them selections would be good. So I found a good stick and stuck it in the sand away from the high tide line, you know, to mark the place I seen it, and picked up the head by the hair, and put it in my bag that I carry." The jury all made sour faces.

"Were there any other footprints in the area, other than yours?"

"No. I was the first one down that stretch of beach that morning. That head came in from the water."

"And how do you know that?"

"Because it was just high tide. If the tide

had been going out, it would have either been stuck on the sand, or out in the sound, where we never would have seen it."

Jones said, "May I approach the witness, Judge?," and grabbed one of numerous photographs off the table. The judge waived her on, and she held up the picture, walking toward the Captain. She said, "For the record, I'm handing you a photograph. Can you tell me what it portrays?"

The Captain looked at the picture, but didn't take it from the prosecutor's outstretched hand. He looked up at Jones, and scowled. He said, "You know damn well what that is. It's that poor bastard's head I found."

The judge said, "Keep it clean, Captain."

He said, "Yes sir, Judge. Sorry about that."

Jones said, "Does this picture accurately portray the condition of the deceased's head at the time you found it?"

Fleming squinted at her a little, and said, "Yes ma'am, it's just as dead as it was when I found it."

The courtroom rustled, but the judge leered, and nobody said anything.

Jones said, "Judge, I move to enter this photograph into evidence."

Hart stood up and said, "Judge, no objection, and we will stipulate that is one of, I believe, some forty different pictures of the deceased's head the state intends to introduce which, while they have nothing to do with my client, are obviously cumulative, and repetitive, and can only be offered in an attempt to prejudice the jury. We suggest that only one picture is necessary to ID the victim's head, and I am making that ore tenus motion."

The judge said, "Ore tenus. For the jury, that means a verbal motion, rather than a written one. State?"

Laura Jones had indeed meant to upset the jury with several gruesome photos. However, having been upbraided enough for dragging out the procedures, she said, "We agree to the one photo, Judge."

The judge said, "Good. It's entered into evidence. State, go ahead and publish it to the jury."

Jones handed the picture, which the Captain had never touched, to the closest juror, and they passed it around, wincing. One juror actually gagged. Jones said, "Sir, how did the victim's head come to be in possession of the police?"

The Captain said, "I knew there wasn't any reason to panic, and it was still real early in the morning, and there wasn't anybody open in town anyway, so I kept on with my beach combing, until later on that morning, and put all my traps in this old golf cart that I drive, and I head downtown to that place Canecutter's, which I knew was about to be open for the day, because I knew if I went down to the police station, well,

I didn't want to get stuck down there. I was intending to have somebody in there at Canecutter's to call the cops for me, but they wouldn't listen to me about the head."

"Why wouldn't they listen?"

"All them smartasses that work there, they ain't nothing but a bunch of college kids, except a couple of the cooks. They may have heard me in a yarn or two in the past, you know, when I was drinking rum, and wasn't maybe distinguishing what I was trying to tell them about the head from, I guess, me having bullshitted them a little in the past. You know, for storytelling sake."

The judge said, "Language, you."

The Captain said, "Shit. Sorry, Judge." He clapped his hand over his mouth. The whole gallery compressed a group chuckle, and somebody way in the back snorted. The judge almost smiled.

Jones quickly said, "What happened next?"

The Captain said, "Well, I'm a little dim on that, Ma'am. I probably shouldn't have, that being way out of normal drinking times for me, you know, but I posted up there at the bar, and got in the rum. By the time I reckon the cops showed up, my lawyer friend over there," he pointed at John Hart, "my old buddy, he saved me from gettin' regulated, they told me later, and them constables, they let me go sleep in my cart out back, and not at the jail. Somebody obviously found the head in my cart, but I got no recollection of it."

On cross examination, Hart wanted to know what the Captain knew about the tide and currents along that stretch of beach. The state objected to speculation, since the old Captain was not an expert on tides or currents, but the judge said he could testify to anything he had personally witnessed, or knew, and the state had opened the door on it anyway. Hart said, "You testified that you believed the head came to the beach in the tide? Please explain to the jury what you mean."

"I been up and down that stretch of beach, on the other side of the Washington Street pier and boat launch, for years," he said.

Judge Donahue said, "Fleming, do you mean the west side or the east side of the pier?"

"The west side, Judge. The east side right in there is just rip-rap. Anyway, that beach where the gentleman's head was is affected by the tide and the outflow from the Saint Louis Bay, which is made up by the Jourdan River and the Wolf River. The current from the bay goes past the city harbor, underneath the railroad bridge and past that city pier, which is on a manmade peninsula that sticks way out from the beach, and makes an eddy right there to the west. And it ain't very deep. In high tide, things from up around the pier direction wash up on the beach. That's where most of the little pieces of wood I use come from. There's cypress from up the Jordan there. Of course there's beer cans and boat trash too. Some boaters are just sloppy, you know."

"Okay, just to clarify, you said you found the head at peak high tide?"

The Captain said, "Yes, and that's why it probably washed up to the beach from that public pier."

Laura Jones almost turned her chair over jumping up to object, but the judge cut her off, saying "Sustained. The jury will disregard the witness' last statement. Allowing him to explain the tides he sees every day does not mean this Court will entertain wholesale speculation."

Hart nodded, but no matter what the judge had ruled, the jury had already heard it. It's an ancient trial lawyer's tactic, asking a vague question about some possibly inadmissible subject, and getting the answer you want. Even if the other side's objection is sustained, and the judge tells the jury to disregard what they just heard, they won't, because human beings don't just un-remember things.

On re-direct, expecting an objection, Jones asked the Captain if he thought that the head could have been dropped off a boat, like the one Vacarro owned. Anticipating this, Hart didn't object. The Captain said, "Sure, it could've, but what kind of a fool would kill somebody on a boat, then throw his head off by the end of the main public pier, right at the busiest beach in town? Mr. Vacarro there don't look like that stupid of a fella, to me. That gentleman's head was like as not dropped off that pier."

It was an error, and totally unnecessary, and Jones knew it. Now, the jury would have an indelible impression that the head had been thrown off the pier, whether that was true or not. But this day was over, and the next couple of days should seal the deal, when she presented absolute proof that the victim's blood was found on Vacarro's boat.

When The Captain emerged from the big front door of the courthouse, he was the star interviewee for every professional and amateur reporter in town. It took him an hour to make it down Main Street to Canecutter's, where he had parked his cart earlier. Walking, he answered questions, and told and recounted the story of the head, and the trial, and some of the parts of his own crazy life he felt like remembering. This continued at the inside bar, in the air conditioning, and he was on the open tab and graces of the general public for the evening. He had some top shelf rum, for sure, but he seemed aware that this crowd of tourists was more crucial than the little pods he normally entertained, and he was careful to stick to the facts. That evening, he told just about everything he had seen and knew.

Hart wasn't there. He had gone home and called Lisette, and told her about the day. How the old Captain had livened up the proceedings, and that he had a subpoena issued for The Raven, if he could be found. He hung up, then looked over the blood evidence discovery once more, then gone to an early bed.

By the time the Captain wrapped up this latest version of The Last Great Drunk, he was not even all that hammered, or irritated. He announced he was done, and said he appreciated all the rum drinks they had bought him, but he could've bought all their drinks, and this whole damn place already, if he had wanted to, but he just never had wanted to, and they all laughed. For once, he made it out under his own power before they all started making fun of him, or kicked him out. In all, it was the craziest day for the old man since he had gone through the hell of losing his wife and kids in that damned hurricane, all those years ago, but for opposite reasons. Today, for once, he wasn't a figure of humor, or pity, or ridicule, but of importance. For one day in his tragic life, he had been important.

His cart was down in the parking lot of the harbor, and he stretched out on the seat where he could keep an eye on the universe. People had always made fun of him since he showed up in town, because they only ever saw him when he was drunk. But he knew most of them couldn't handle what he had been through in his life, and be so lonely, and still keep any kind of sanity. So he had let himself get drunk every once in a while. Not every day, or even every week now, but sometimes. He looked out past the stars. He thought about the locals and tourists back there in the bar, always laughing at him, always making fun, like he was a clown or a jester. They didn't know anything, and he couldn't hear them anyway. They were just company, that's all. He wasn't entertaining them, they were entertaining him. It was worth getting made fun of sometimes, because he could take about anything the damn universe could throw at him, except being lonely all the time. Nobody could take that. And even though the universe had the power to make him be alone, he could defy it every once in a while. And when the universe had tried to relieve its guilt for the cruelty he had suffered, he had defied that, too.

Friday morning was glowing bright outside, in the full bloom of summer. The air smelled green, and people were back excited about the trial. On the courthouse grounds, certain areas of the lawn had taken on a camp aspect, with lawn chairs, and big sun umbrellas, and coolers. Inside, the courtroom was packed. The state's first witness of the day was the Coroner. This had been one of his easiest cases, he said, because there was little to examine, and no doubt that the deceased had been murdered, ten to fourteen days before the head was found. The prosecutor wanted to know if it had been in the water the whole time, but he couldn't say for sure. There was no way to tell any information about the killer, the man just died from a blow to the back of his head. Hart didn't even bother to cross examine him.

Next, the state called Investigator Larue. Jones asked him how he first came to be on Vacarro's boat in the Bay harbor. He said he had actually visited the Defendant's boat on three occasions. "The deceased's secretary had contacted us and filed a report, said he was missing. This is a day after the deceased and the Defendant were out at Ship Island. As far as she knew, he had been in Bay Saint Louis on Sunday, meeting with Vacarro about some business matter. That's all she knew. I located and called the Defendant, and told him I needed to do what is called a 'safety check,' which is visiting a property without a warrant out of concern for someone's well being. He agreed, and that was the first time I went to the boat."

Laura Jones said, "So you got permission to search it?"

"Yes. If I'd seen anything suspicious, I would probably have gotten a warrant, since defense attorneys tend to raise questions about search and seizure if anything significant is found. But he gave me permission for a safety search. When I got down there to the boat, the sliding back door was a little open, and it didn't look like anyone was on board. I went on the back deck, and announced my presence. Nobody responded, so I went through the open door, did a quick walk through, didn't see anything, and left."

"You weren't looking for trace evidence of blood at that time?"

"Objection," said John Hart. "Leading, Judge."

The judge said, "Sustained. You know better, State."

Jones said, "Investigator Larue, did you find anything suspicious at the time?"

Larue said, "Not anything criminal. I thought it was odd that an expensive boat would be left open like that, but I understand that's not unusual around here."

Jones said, "How did you come to search it a second time?"

"That old gentleman they call Captain Fleming showed up downtown at Canecutter's with the deceased's head. We knew by then that he was last seen on Mr. Vacarro's boat, so I went back down to the harbor to look around that boat and dock again. I already had permission to search from the owner, so I did."

"Did you find anything?"
"No I didn't."

"I am sure the defense will be very curious about that fact. Can you explain it to the jury?"

"Yes ma'am. When we did eventually find the victim's blood on that boat, it was all in the downstairs bathroom, in trace amounts, because it had been cleaned pretty well. That second time, I went through the boat and took some random swabs, mainly of different floor surfaces, but not many, maybe a couple dozen. Usually, that's way more than needed to indicate the presence of any blood, especially in a confined space. Besides, I knew I could probably get a warrant at any time since that body part was found. Nothing was indicated, and I didn't see any evidence of a crime, just like before."

"Why didn't you check for hair samples or other forensics?"

"There was no need to. We already knew the deceased had been on the boat, we were just looking for evidence of a crime at that point. And like I said, I knew I could go back on the boat at any time."

Jones asked him how he had come to request a warrant to enter the defendant's boat for a third time. Larue said, "It was an anonymous tip. Somebody called in and left us a voice message claiming there was blood evidence on the boat. We figured it was the cleaning lady, but there's no way to tell."

Hart objected to the speculation, and the

judge sustained it, and instructed the jury to disregard what they had just heard. Jones glanced at Hart, and caught his eye for a second, and just barely winked.

The investigator then meticulously walked the jury through how he and Investigator Angel Williams had this time taken swabs of the interior surfaces, and vacuum samples, and fingerprints, and checked to see if there were any video recording devices, but there weren't. They examined the entire interior with ultraviolet lighting, he said, because it makes phosphorus in blood glow, and what was found, and where. This testimony took all morning, but was moving, by the state's previous standards, incredibly fast.

"Did you conclude anything from that examination?"

"Whether he was killed in that bathroom or not, I don't know. But his blood was in there, and somebody had tried to clean it up, so it is a reasonable suspicion that he sustained some type of injury in that location."

After a short lunch break, John Hart began his cross examination, asking, "Investigator Larue, the blood evidence we're talking about today, it was all found in the toilet, 'the head' as it's known, right?"

"Yes sir."

"And nowhere else?"

"That's correct."

"And none on the walls, like splatter?"

"No sir."

"And none on the stairs connecting the salon and stateroom?"

"None."

"And none in the kitchen, excuse me, I mean galley, or on the back deck of the boat?"

"No sir, none."

"You think there really was some, but you just missed it?"

"No sir. I wouldn't miss that."

"Don't you mean, you wouldn't miss it a third time?" He glanced at the jury.

Larue scowled. He said, "No, I wouldn't."

"So you are sure that there was only blood in that one area. "And you swabbed that area, the head, on your second visit to the boat?"

"A couple places on the floor."

"And found nothing, you said?"

"No, but I didn't use the ultraviolet at the time, and there wasn't a lot of it left, so I obviously just swiped the wrong area."

"You say 'obviously', but that's not the only conclusion, is it?"

"How so, Counselor?"

"Isn't it possible that you didn't find the blood the first two times because it wasn't there?"

Jones objected to the speculation, and the judge overruled it. Larue said, "That is a possibility. Look, we can't check every square inch of the place, we just don't have the resources. So we spot check, swabbing here and there, checking for the presence of blood evidence. If we find something, we bring the whole process in. If we don't, we don't. So either that blood was there, and I didn't find it, or it wasn't there at the time. I just don't know."

Hart took some time looking at the jury. He then said, "Mr. Larue, you've been an investigator in this city for what, about four years?"

"That's right, Counselor. I was hired as an Investigator, what we used to call 'Detective.' I was formerly a uniform cop, over in Lafayette, Louisiana."

"And in your time as a Detective, you've investigated what, dozens of felonies?"

"At least that, yes sir."

"And how many homicides?"

"We don't have that many here. I guess this is the third."

"But plenty of crimes where a search warrant was issued?"

"Plenty. A couple hundred I would say, more or less."

"And you have to demonstrate probable cause to a judge to get a search warrant, right?"

"Well, the prosecutor does, but I have to swear the affidavit, and testify."

"And these cases, where probable cause has been demonstrated, and a warrant issued, usually end up in an arrest, don't they?"

"Well, yes. Where's there's smoke, there's usually fire."

"And when a person is arrested and charged with a felony, in the cases you've worked, they usually end up pleading guilty to some crime, or getting convicted at trial, right?"

"The vast majority of the time. Unless somebody like you can get them off on some technicality."

Hart said, "Everything in the law is a technicality, Detective, that's why we bother to write it all down. Now, do you usually ask a suspect for permission to search a criminal suspect's property, before you get a warrant?"

"Not in every case, but that's not unusual."

"And you don't need a search warrant if you have permission to search property, right?"

"No sir."

"And you've had to obtain a couple hundred warrants."

"That's right, give or take."

"So you get denied permission to search most of the time, is that fair to say?"

Jones stood and said, "Judge, I object on the bases of speculation and relevance. What does any of this have to do with this case?"

The judge said, "Defense, that's a valid question. Now, do you have one for this witness?"

Hart said, "I do, Judge." Turning to Larue,

he said, "Based on your testimony here today, it's fair to say that guilty people hardly ever just give you permission to search their property, do they?"

Jones popped up and said, "Objection!" The judge sustained it, but John Hart had already sat back down, and was looking at each juror, one by one.

The judge could tell the jury was getting tired, and decided to release them for the rest of the afternoon. Afterwards, the attorneys were in his chambers, and he said, "State, I knew we were never going to finish this week, but I commend you moving forward the way you have, after that slow start. What's next?"

Jones said, "Judge, we will call the crime lab expert to positively ID the blood found on the boat, then we have an expert to prove the Defendant's company handled all the victim's finances, which were fairly extensive."

The judge said, "And that is relevant because?"

Jones said, "It certainly is fraught with possibilities for motive, Judge."

The judge said, "Fraught, huh? Well, I guess we'll see."

Hart said, "Judge, apparently they can't determine one way or another when or how the blood got on the boat. Because of that, we will stipulate the blood being that of the victim, and they can get on with their last witness."

"Stipulated, and instructed," said the judge. "State, looks like you can wrap it up on your case in chief, maybe Monday."

Jones said, "Maybe so, Judge."

The judge said, "Defense, what do you think, witness wise? I know you listed just about everyone they did, but who do you expect to actually call?"

Hart said, "Don't know yet, Judge. I don't know if we need to call anybody, since I haven't seen anything that comes close to proof beyond a reasonable doubt."

Jones said, "We think the murdered man's blood in the Defendant's boat is pretty good evidence of what happened, Judge, but I guess we'll soon see what the jury thinks."

That day was Miss Filomena's last in the office. John Hart had been dreading it, not because he knew she was going to be upset, but because he was going to miss her, and he didn't want to be upset too. He took his time getting back to the office, having expected to be in court most of the afternoon.

She had spent all day going through every file he had, which weren't that many, and hammering out every possible detail of information needed, or activity to perform, or money owed from this or that fookin' client, who were all taking advantage of him, because he was weak. She had it all in her notes, which she had copied to every file, in electronic documents and printed ones. Consequently, though he didn't have a great book of business, Hart was as profession- ally prepared as he had ever been in his career.

When she had finally gone through every- thing, and straightened the office, and warned him about drinking too much beer, and shady women, and all his miscreant friends, she made him stand up, and hugged him, her face buried in his belly, and blubbering.

She said, "I'm sorry I have to go, Johnny, because you can't do anything right without being told first. But I'm going to miss you any- way."

He said, "I'm going to miss you too, Miss Filomena, but not because I like being bossed around all the time. I guess maybe I needed it when you got here, though. I'll come see you over there, I promise."

She held him away at arms length, look- ing almost straight up, and said, "Now don't you lie to me the last time I see you, I won't have it. And quit calling me Miss Filomena. From now on, you call me Fefe, which is what a battalion of rattling little Welsh grand-nieces and grand- nephews and whatnot call me over there. You're to call me that."

Hart got an envelope off the desk, and handed it to her. He said, "This will take care of you, so don't worry about money. And don't give me any grief about it. For once, you have to do what I say."

She took it, and said, "Bend down here." He did, and she kissed him on the cheek, and hugged him around the neck. "Goodbye, son," she whispered, crying, and patted the top of his head.

"Goodbye, Fefe," said John Hart, as he fought back tears.

Chapter 10

King Irving knew he was famous, but he didn't know why. He had suffered many indignities in his younger life, not least his name, when it was only Irving, declared so by a young girl who was a member of the family who adopted him as a puppy from a New Orleans animal shelter. That was well before he became famous, and the master of his street corner in front of the Moon Mart, in the New Orleans French Quarter.

The origin of his fame was an incident during a festival some years ago. This was before his human family realized he was mostly a Great Dane, and always hungry, and destined to be the size of a Shetland pony. At the time, he was still a gangly six-month-old, and liked to occasionally escape his humans, and barrel up and down Royal street, violating leash laws and trash cans, looking for something to eat. Around the Quarter in those days, he was not famous, or even popular.

During the festival he escaped. After scattering and wallowing in the cornucopia of festival garbage, and consuming a decent amount of it, he ambled upon a fairly good sized crowd of tourists and local condo owners clogging Ursulines Street, cheering a balcony full of titty dancers who were off work and stripping for free. Into the excitement Irving lumbered. At the same time, a young New Orleans police officer trotted up on a horse. The officer was fairly new, and eager, and grinding his teeth from the steroids he had injected that morning.

He decided the street was being illegally blocked. When the crowd failed to immediately respond to his dispersal orders, he whipped out his black baton and started cracking people over their heads, starting a drunken stampede. Part of the stampede went over Irving, rolling him out on the sidewalk. Somebody stomped on his tail. Caterwauling like a wild coyote, Irving got up and charged in any available direction to evade the madness. He happened to run under the officer's horse, which then reared its rider off onto the pavement. Somehow, the horse's tail mane got hung in the huge group of crime fighting accoutrements on the cop's wide belt, and the horse bolted in the same direction as the howling Irving, who he quickly overtook, yanking his rider behind.

The cop temporarily regained his footing, and gamely sprinted it out a few steps before the horse got up to full speed, galloping down the street with his rider bouncing and skipping behind, just ahead of Irving. In the chaos, it looked like Irving was actually chasing the officer and his beast away, which made him an instant hero. The stampede picked up momentum for a little while, and the cop eventually got knocked off his horse's tail by the iron base of a corner street sign. The sprinting mob eventually ran out of panic, and breath, and dissipated a block or so away.

Irving knew several good hiding places in that part of the Quarter, and was in one for a good while, under a short porch on Dauphine Street, until he got hungry again. Wandering back, he was greeted as a liberator, and christened King Irving, and never had to search for food in trash cans again. The cops made a sheepish attempt to find him, but the sore horse officer had never gotten a clear view, clattering down the road as he was, and the locals didn't want him caught, so they wouldn't help. The matter was eventually dropped.

Later on his humans, for professional reasons, had to move out of New Orleans. King Irving was just too big to go. The young girl who had named him was in high school by then, and tearfully begged the neighbors to take him in, so he wouldn't be sent back to the shelter of his youth. A group of them decided to keep him as sort of a community dog, whereupon King Irving had taken his place at the corner in front of the Moon Mart, a little neighborhood grocery store with takeout homemade Creole food, where he had reigned ever since.

Beyond Jackson Square, trees are a rarity in the French Quarter. Fortunately, a big old Mimosa tree lived next to the Moon Mart, providing shade to King Irving and his minions. Unfortunately, a set of Mockingbirds had recently moved into the tree, set up a nest, and produced some babies. Like all Southerners, Irving knew about Mockingbirds. While pretty, they are by nature irascible, and regularly offset whatever goodwill their incessant and genuinely impressive song portfolio generates with an irritated, paranoid nastiness. They habitually attack any other creature in the area, ostensibly to protect their homes and babies, but in reality for no good reason at all.

Possessing impressive aerial skills, their modus operandi is to dive in, claw or peck their target on or around the head, then rocket away before the victim has adequate time to retaliate. This causes no great damage. The Mockingbird, while loud, quick, and perpetually angry, is not particularly strong, or dangerously armed, and therefore no serious physical threat. But nobody likes getting pecked, so the Mockingbird attacking every living creature on King Irving's corner had recently soured the normally festive atmosphere. The way Irving saw it, he had lived there way before the birds moved in, and was not about to give up his realm, or his shade. Besides, he didn't really have anywhere else to go. So day after day, he lay there taking abuse, plotting. He decided that if he didn't react to the attacks, and just ignored the birds, they would eventually get lazy, and slow.

So were Irving's plans when just before dark, a Mockingbird swooped in, flapping, hovering, mauling his ear, and taking too much time doing it. King Irving sprung, and made contact. The startled bird hit the sidewalk, quickly recovered, scrambled, and regaining low altitude, streaked across the street, with Irving in close lumbering pursuit. The Raven was walking down the opposite sidewalk, under his dark umbrella. First the Mockingbird streaked by, then Irving took The Raven down with a perfect, galloping, leg-sweeping tackle.

The next instant, an ancient brick in the adjacent wall exploded. The Raven, who had fired many bullets in his life, recognized the impact of one. He jumped up and scooted out of the area with amazing speed for a creature of his many decades. Down the street, the traumatized Mockingbird finally gained sufficient altitude, and escaped. Irving barked at it, plopped down, and caught his breath for a few minutes. Then he got up and trotted back to the Moon Mart, wagging.

On Monday, the state called its last witness. Steven Reynolds was a forensic accountant, and also an attorney, and had been testifying as an expert, he said, for over twenty years, in cases of all types. He spent most of the day meticulously going through all Rilo Marshall's business and personal accounts and investments, which amounted to around five million dollars, and the jury was nearly bored to sleep by the time Jones said, "Mr. Reynolds, can you tell us what a Paid On Death assignment is?

Accountant said, "It's a declaration by the owner of an account, like checking or savings, which most people have, stating where the assets in the account go after the death or incapacitation of the owner. The same goes for stock accounts, or any type of assignable security, or liquid asset."

"And did you come across any of these such statements when examining the estate assets of the victim?"

"Yes, I did."

"And what did they say?"

"Every asset that could be assigned in such a manner named Puglisi and Navarro, Ltd. as the beneficiary."

"And not to his wife and children?"

"He was divorced. He had a grown son, but children can be left out of estates in Mississippi, so that's not unusual."

"And who is the owner and the manager of Puglisi and Navarro, Ltd.?"

He pointed at Tony Vacarro. "The Defendant." The jury snapped awake. The courtroom came alive. The packed gallery started chattering, and the whole room got loud.

"What about land, or chattels?"

"He had a house up in north Gulfport, and some land and a cabin up around Picayune. They were in life estates, with the remainder, the beneficiary being Puglisi and Navarro, Ltd."

"What exactly does that mean?"

"He got to live there, and when he died, it all went to the Defendant's company."

How much was the house and cabin, and land worth?"

"A million, give or take."

"So when the victim got murdered, the Defendant's company got six million dollars?"

He said, "Yes. The Defendant and the victim had economic and business ties to that amounted to financial marriage."

John Hart said, "Objection!"

The judge said, "Sustained. State, you've made your point. Jury, you are to disregard the witness's statement about financial marriage."

Laura Jones said, "Judge, just a minute, please." She walked over to her table, leaned down, whispered to her assistant. She took as long as she thought the judge would let her, to let Vacarro marinate in the implications. She said, "Mr. Reynolds, I have just two more questions. Did the deceased inherit any of his six million dollar fortune?"

"No sir. He came from a poor background, actually. He spent his whole life working his way up through the system on the harbor docks."

Jones said, "Okay, one last thing. Six million dollars. There's no way all that wealth was accumulated by a man just using his income as a shipyard manager, right?"

Hart said, "Objection!"

The judge said, "Sustained. Jury, you are to disregard that last question."

Jones walked back to her seat. On the way, she looked over at Hart and grinned a little, where the jury couldn't see. She turned to the judge and said, "We tender the witness, Judge."

The judge said, "It's getting late in the day, Defense. You can go ahead and start your cross examination if you want, and we can break, and pick it back up tomorrow. Or you can just save it all for tomorrow."

Hart said, "Judge, I just have a couple of questions, then we can break, if that's ok." Addressing the witness, he said, "Mr. Reynolds, based upon your research in this case, do you know the ownership structure of the company Puglisi and Vacarro, Ltd.?"

"No sir. It's a closely held company, which means its not publicly traded. So their stock distribution is not a matter for public disclosure. All we can see are the Members."

And do you know who they are?"

"Yes sir. You're client, there, is one. Someone named Lisette Vacarro is the second, and Marco Puglisi is the third."

This Lisette Vacarro, she is Mr. Tony Vacarro's sister, isn't she?"

"That's my understanding."

"And Marco Puglisi is those siblings' great uncle, right?

"I believe that is true, yes."

"Do you know any details of their great uncle?"

Jones stood up and said, "Judge, I object. What's the relevance?"

The judge said, "I'll allow it, but not indefinitely, Defense."

The witness said, "I checked him out, but there's not a lot to know. They call him 'The Raven' and he is supposedly the last of the old New Orleans Mafia."

The courtroom got loud. Jones screamed, "Objection, Judge!"

Hart shot a hard glance at Laura Jones. Over the din, he said, "Withdrawn, Judge. I think we can break here for the day."

Tony Vacarro had been staying at the family compound, down on South Beach Boulevard, with security guards all around. It was on the western edge of the hill that forms Bay Saint Louis, and had been in some tendril of his family for a century or more. Ironically, it was within distant view of the place old Fleming had found the head. The property had a main house, and several other structures, including cabins, an entertainment pavilion, and a chapel. It was part of the sprawling family trust properties administered by Vacarro's firm. Since the start of the trial it had become a tourist attraction. There was a constant flow of slow traffic, people gawking through the gate.

Since he moved out of the Cedar Point rental, most evenings John Hart had been staying in one of the cabins on the property. He and Vacarro were eating dinner in the living room of the main house, the television droning, when Vacarro said, "I just got an email from those investigators we hired."

Hart said, "What does it say, 'Tough luck, couldn't help you.'?"

Vacarro opened it, and said, "Not at all. It says, 'The following results have been obtained regarding the subject matter examined:

1. The anonymous call was made from a prepaid cellular device.

2. We were able to obtain footage of the purchaser of the device. Find attached a single frame photograph of the purchaser.' "

Hart said, "What the hell? They were able to hack not only the police system, but a security video from some store?"

Vacarro said, "I told you these people are good. He pulled up the picture on his device, looked at it, and slowly laid it on the coffee table.

Hart stared at it , picked it up, and said, "Is this supposed to be some kind of joke?"

Vacarro said, "Nope. There it is, clear as can be."

John Hart just said, "Holy shit." On the screen was the unmistakable image of Lisette.

The next morning, the judge had all the attorneys in chambers. Jones and her assistant were there, and the actual D.A. had made an appearance. The judge said, "District Attorney, glad to see you show up for the ribbon cutting. Assistant District Attorney, it looks like you're about to wrap up your case. You have any more evidence after this expert?"

Jones said, "No, Judge, we'll be resting after the defense's cross is over."

The judge said, "Defense, who have you got? Did you ever find this Raven character, and get him served?"

Hart said, "No, Judge. We're still looking. My process servers have been all over New Orleans, but so far he can't be found. However, based on some recently obtained information, I may have a witness who was not disclosed. That is, assuming you deny our motion for a directed verdict."

"You may make that assumption. This is definitely going to the jury."

"In that case, we have asked Lisette Vacarro to appear, although no subpoena has been issued, and I did not actually talk to her. I don't know if she'll be here."

The young D.A. said, "Judge, the state has to have some kind of opportunity to prepare for what amounts to a surprise witness..."

The judge cut him off, saying, "Mr. District Attorney, if you had been present during this trial, you would have noticed that your side has had some surprises itself, related to the victim's blood being discovered on the Defendant's boat halfway through the proceedings. If this Lisette whoever shows up, she'll be testifying, and your assistant, who's done a great job, as she always does, can make the proper objections at the time."

Hart resumed his cross examination of Steven Reynolds, trying to drag out the proceedings to give Lisette time to show up, if she would. According to the expert, Rilo Marshall's wealth had been largely accumulated through a series of what amounted to be brilliantly successful, risky investments managed by Puglisi and Navarro, Ltd. Initially, he had cashed out his retirement, and doubled it, and reinvested his capital gains several times in succession. It was tantamount to, he said, a gambler rolling seven at a craps game several times in a row, and letting it all ride every time. Unusual, but obviously not impossible.

John Hart was running out of time, and this part was not going well for Tony Vacarro. For the first time since he met her, Lisette had not returned his phone calls or messages. He avoided eliciting any other testimony about The Raven, who had been sufficiently planted in the minds of the jury by now, and may be getting too closely associated to his client. In retrospect, Hart wished he had not left Lisette a voice message saying her name had come up in connection with the murder investigation. His last text message simply asked her to be in court this morning if she was interested in helping her brother. It was the absolute worst position for a courtroom attorney, not knowing if a witness would appear, or what they would say if they did.

As his cross examination trudged along, Hart emphasized and re-emphasized the remoteness of personal connections between Vacarro and the deceased to the point that he could tell the judge was getting impatient. Worse, the jury was not paying attention, and getting restless. That usually meant they had their minds made up, and were ready to render a verdict and get out of there. After an hour and a half, Hart was about out of questions, the judge was out of patience, and half the jury was staring at the pretty scalloped molding in the ceiling.

Suddenly the courtroom door swung open, and in walked Lisette. The gallery chattered and squirmed like they were at a concert as she strutted like a star across their view. She didn't look at John Hart. Since she was now on the witness list, the Bailiff intercepted and deposited her in the unoccupied jury room off the back hall, to await being called.

The room settled down, and Hart quickly wrapped up the cross examination. Laura Jones wisely recognized the jury was restless, and had no re-direct. The State of Mississippi rested. The judge had already indicated his intent to deny the defense's motion for directed verdict. That procedure always took place outside the presence of the jury, so Hart knew the judge would handle it after the jury was dismissed for the day, or sent out to deliberate. Once the state had rested, Hart had to declare whether he was putting on any witnesses, or resting too. And he still had not talked to Lisette. He said, "Judge, can I have a short recess?"

The judge said, "Fifteen minutes. Gallery, if you got 'em, smoke 'em."

Hart visited Lisette in the jury room. He tried to quick-kiss her, but she recoiled. He said, "We only have a few minutes. I can't tell you how, but I know you purchased the burner phone that made the anonymous call to the Bay police about the blood on your brother's boat. Please tell me there is some reasonable explanation."

"There is. I bought that phone for my uncle."

"Thank God. Why haven't you told me this before?"

"I didn't know it mattered. I've bought that old man lots of disposable phones over the years. He doesn't like going out in public, and

I'm the only one who still visits with him."

"Don't you think that's suspicious, him needing so many disposable phones?"

"Really John, what do I know, or care? What my great uncle does is none of my business. And buying cheap cell phones is still legal, isn't it?"

"Yes it is. I need to prove you bought that phone for the Raven. The problem is, I can't get it into evidence, because our information may have been obtained illegally."

"Then why don't you ask me what you really want to hear?"

"I'm not sure what you mean."

"Ask me who killed that man."

"Okay, who did it?"

"My great uncle, The Raven."

"How do you know?"

"Because he told me, just yesterday."

"What the hell? Where is he?"

"He was in Venice when I saw him. That's where I was when you left those messages. There's usually no reliable phone signal down there. I just got back to New Orleans this morning."

"What were you doing in Venice?"

Lisette stopped smiling. She said, "Really, Counselor, I don't think that's any of your business. Just because we've been socializing doesn't mean I have to account for myself to you, or any man."

Hart had never seen her indignant. He said, "Socializing? That's about as generic a word for it as possible. But we'll have to cover that later. Obviously, I didn't mean it that way. It's just, they are about to knock on that door, and since you're here, I assume you are about to testify, and I don't know what you're going to say."

She said, "I was down there because he sent for me. When a man like my uncle says to be somewhere, you go. I drove down there yesterday. He knows you have a subpoena out for him, and he's making himself unfindable. He knows you and I are dating, which is probably the only reason you are still alive, after that subpoena was issued. The dead guy was involved in some kind of business deal with my uncle, and wanted out. My uncle had him killed, and set up my brother, it's that simple. Your subpoena has him avoiding the area, for now. After this trial is over, it wouldn't be a bad idea for you to avoid it too, since he's not very happy with you."

"Where is he going?"

"I don't know, and you will never find him. Believe me, you don't want to."

"But why would he set up your brother, who runs an apparently legitimate company that makes everybody involved rich?"

"Who knows what that old man thinks? My brother was never part of the old Mafia and as far as I know, is as naive as he appears. Maybe The

Raven wanted him put away so he could replace him with his own person. I really don't know."

"And we can assume The Raven really was behind getting me hired? That's what Tony thinks."

"I would say so. We can only speculate that he thought you couldn't handle the job, and my brother would be convicted."

"Well, why the hell didn't he just kill your brother, too?"

Lisette looked him straight in th eyes, and narrowed hers a little. She said, "That's a little surprising, Counselor. Then who would be left to blame for the murder? This Marshall wasn't just some street punk that no one would miss. The law would be looking for someone to blame."

The Bailiff knocked on the door, and said, "Mr. Hart, Judge says it's time."

After the Bailiff called the court to order, and the judge told everyone to sit down, John Hart announced Lisette as his next witness. The gallery had been chattering, but her regal stride to the witness stand quickly settled them down. Gazing upon her, one middle aged man at the end of the front pew could not restrain a barely audible, long whistle. Being suddenly conscious of it, he got up and quietly excused himself from the courtroom, under the damning glare of the judge. The clerk swore Lisette in.

The jury was once again paying attention. Lisette was dressed in a light colored pencil skirted business suit, and smiling. After Hart had established her identity, and where she lived and worked, and her connection to the Defendant, he said, "Miss Vacarro, do you understand that we are here because your brother has been charged with the murder of a man named Rilo Marshall?"

"My half brother. We have different fathers," she said, looking at Vacarro. "But to answer your question, I do."

"OK, do you have any knowledge of, or about, who may have killed Mr. Marshall?"

She said, "I do."

"And what is that opinion?"

"My Great Uncle Marco Puglisi, the man known to the public as The Raven. He killed him."

The gallery exploded, and it took the Bailiff a solid minute to settle everyone down. The judge was variously eyeballing the witness and the two counsel tables, and deliberately letting the crowd burn off some energy.

When the room was finally quiet, Hart said, "And how do you know this?"

She said, "Because yesterday he told me so."

The gallery busted again, and Laura Jones and the D.A. sprung up simultaneously, yelling objections to hearsay. Bailiff Fitts screamed for quiet. The judge just sat in silence. Soon, so did everyone else. The judge calmly said, "The jury will disregard this witness' last statement, which will also be stricken from the record."

Hart told the judge he had no further questions for Lisette, and tendered the witness. The State wisely chose not to ask her any, since nothing she could say would help, and every-thing she could say would probably further hurt their case. The judge excused her, and after a long look at John Hart, she left.

The judge said, "Defense, call your next witness."

The courtroom was completely silent as Tony Vacarro took the stand. After he got sworn in, Hart said, "Tony, you've seen and heard everything in this trial. Tell the jury, did you kill Rilo Marshall?"

Vacarro turned to the jury, said, "I did not kill that man. I've never killed anyone, and I never would."

Hart said, "The State of Mississippi says you did. You were with him right before he died. How do you explain that?"

Vacarro said, "I got a note in my office, telling me to be there."

"Where is this note?"

"I burned it."

"Why did you do that?"

"Because the note said to."

"It was a paper note?"

"Yes."

"Handwritten?"

"No. Typed."

"What did it say, exactly?"

Jones said, "Objection, hearsay."

Hart said, "Judge, it's not being offered to prove the truth of the matter or matters asserted, but to explain the witness' subsequent actions. This goes to the heart of the issue before the court, which is specific intent to commit murder. My client's Constitutional rights to put on a defense, to procedural and substantive due process, supersede any rule of evidence if in direct conflict."

Jones said, "That's nonsense, Judge, it's rank hearsay, and furthermore an attempt to end run the necessity of authenticating a document which the witness just stated under oath that he destroyed. That information can't be admissible under any scenario."

The judge leaned back in the big wooden chair. Addressing the jury, he said, "Jurors, this is the kind of conundrum that sometimes makes people get frustrated with lawyers. You see, without trying to go into the whole history of the court's rules, and the defendant's due process rights, and what the state and federal Constitutions say or mean, the bare fact is these two lawyers are probably *both* right. Judges make decisions in every trial that can go one way or another. That's why we have appellate courts, and keep them pretty busy.

"Now, I am going to allow this Defendant, Mr. Vacarro, to tell his story up to a point - he - glanced at John Hart, and then back to the jury - and count on you people to use your good judgement and common sense, and apply the facts as you see them, and the law as I instruct it, when I send you out to deliberate. Anyway, lawyers, I am overruling the objection. Mr. Vacarro, answer the question."

Vacarro said, "It just said 'Meet Rilo Marshall at Tracy's in Bay Saint Louis at noon on whatever day that was. And that he had some information for me. And to burn the note. That's it."

Hart said, "Who sent the note?"

"I can't swear that I actually know."

"At the time, who did you think sent it?"

Jones said, "Objection, Judge. Speculation."

Hart said, "I'm asking what he thought at the time, Judge. Recalling his own thoughts is not speculative."

The judge said, "The objection is overruled. The witness may answer."

Vacarro said, "I thought it came from my great uncle, the man they call "The Raven."

Hart said, "So you just did what you were told?"

Vacarro said, "Yes sir."

Hart said, "Well, why? Is your uncle your boss, somehow?"

Vacarro said, "No sir. It's just, I wouldn't ever want to disappoint him."

"Why? Because you're scared?"

Jones said, "Objection! He's leading the witness, Judge."

The judge said, "Sustained. You need to be headed in some particular direction, Defense."

Hart said, "Mr. Vacarro, are you a member of an organization known as the New Orleans Mafia?"

Jones jumped out of her chair and literally yelled "Objection!" The gallery was curiously quiet.

The judge said, "All lawyers approach the bench."

When they got there, he growled, "Hart, tell me you aren't trying to make me declare a fucking mistrial."

Bailiff Fitts said, "Uh, Judge, your mike's still on." The judge flipped it off and swatted it out of the way.

Hart said, "No sir, Judge. Why would I? This case is shot through with reasonable doubt."

The young D.A. wisely remained silent. Jones said, "Judge, he has obviously irreparably tainted the jury with that question."

Hart said, "Judge, it needs to be asked, because everyone in the jury probably thinks it's true. In the first place, if he says he's in the Mafia, how does that help? And if he says he isn't, he's just addressing what is implicit in the state's own case, whether this Defendant was acting in concert with someone else in the murder he has been charged with. They haven't even suggested to the jury that he actually physically killed the man. Therefore, they have either by design or by implication left open the question of the involvement of one or more other people. In other words, an organization. If there is an organization, it might or might not have a name."

The D.A. jumped in, and said, "Judge, that's crazy. There is no way the term 'Mafia' can pass any evidentiary smell test, and the jury can't un-hear it. We're demanding a mistrial, and we think you'd better grant it."

The judge squinted at the D.A., but before his nose opened all the way up, Hart said, "Judge, if I may, we think the question *is* relevant, but there is one more consideration."

The judge said, "Go on."

Hart said, "Judge, there is not one person on that jury who hasn't grown up around here hearing about the New Orleans Mafia, or the so-called Dixie Mafia, or the Mafia in general. The same thing applies to the gallery, which is the community, and the prosecution here, and you and me. We think it's a fair question, and one we weren't allowed to explore in voir dire, although that's what everybody was thinking, and is one this whole county wants to know the answer to. Stopping me from asking it is practically conceding that he is a Mafioso, with all the attendant prejudicial conclusions. That's what this jury is going to think, regardless of what the rules of evidence say."

The judge sat back, and looked out the window. There was a group of what looked like 1960s hippies sitting and laying on a couple of Mexican blankets on a lawn across the street. Two of them were playing acoustic guitars, and another was lighting up something that had to be a big joint. He smirked. Looking back, he said, "State, in the first place, don't tell me I'd 'better' do anything. He blew out a long breath, and said, "Nobody knows this yet, but I'm not running again. I'm about to announce my retirement. This will be my last trial. In fact, I have apparently come down with the damned cancer, according to the doctors, so I might not even be around to see how any appeal that may be filed comes out.

"But I do care about my legacy, and for good or ill, I have always tried to abide by the rules of procedure and evidence. Now, one of you may fill this chair when I leave it. If so, you will immediately realize that the hardest thing we trial judges do every day is make calls about evidence. The rules are not perfectly clear, and not meant to be, since in real life there are an unlimited amount of scenarios which no rule can anticipate. That's why we trial judges have so much discretion, because we always have to keep one eye on the rules, and one on this quaint old notion called 'justice.' Now, that might not be perfectly enunciated in those rules, but it is sometimes clear as day sitting up here in front of the courtroom.

"Defense, I don't agree that it is necessarily relevant whether your client is a member of any New Orleans Mafia, or even whether that organization still exists, if it ever did. But I do agree that question has been hanging in the air of these proceedings the entire time. So I am going to let him answer it. If that's an error, and he gets convicted anyway, it won't matter, because his own lawyer asked the question. If he gets acquitted, it won't matter either. State, you can cross examine him about it if you want to. That will be my ruling. And by the way, keep the part about the cancer to yourselves." Of course, he knew they wouldn't.

Back in session, the judge said, "The Court Reporter will read the question, and the witness will answer it."

The Court reporter intoned, "Mr. Vacarro, are you a member of an organization known as the New Orleans Mafia?"

Vacarro said, "No, I am not."

Hart said, "Are you a member of any criminal group or organization that goes by any name?"

Vacarro said, "I'm not."

Hart said, "To your knowledge, is your

great uncle 'The Raven' a member of any such organization?"

Jones said, "Objection, Judge!"

The judge said, "Sustained. Move along, defense."

Hart said, "OK, Tony, have you ever before received what you considered to be directions from your great uncle?"

"A few times over the years."

"How so?"

"Well, we are business partners, although I never see him. I don't want to see him, and I made that clear a long time ago. He occasionally sends me notes, has them delivered to the office. They are about certain business investments he wants to make."

"And you do as you're told?"

"Well, I always have."

"When is the last time you got one of these notes?"

"I got one saying to meet you at Gabriella's in New Orleans and hire you. I believe it was back in March."

Hart said, "Tony, one more question. You testified earlier that you did not kill the deceased. Do you know who did?"

Vacarro said, "Well, I have my suspicions, but no sir, I don't actually know for sure."

Hart said, "Tender the witness, Judge."

Jones strode to the podium hastily. She said, "Mr. Vacarro, do you deny that your company was the beneficiary of the deceased's entire six million dollar estate?"

"No, but I didn't know that until this case was filed. I saw it in the discovery, in a synopsis of your expert witness's testimony."

"Is it true?"

"Apparently. I had our in-house legal team look into it. But I didn't know it before."

"You don't seem to know a lot of things about the business you run."

Hart said, "Objection!"

The judge said, "Sustained. Ask questions, State, do not make statements."

Jones said, "Yes, Judge." Turning to the witness, she said, "And you now know that your company is the sole, exclusive beneficiary of the deceased's estate?"

"It appears that way."

"You got into a loud argument with the deceased on your boat that day, didn't you?"

"No, there wasn't any argument. He was drunk, and got mad, and started yelling."

"About what?"

"I'm not really sure. Like I said, I had never met him before, so maybe he just couldn't handle his liquor."

"You must have some idea."

"He just said he wanted out. I didn't know what he was talking about, so he got more in-sistent, kept saying he was done, that he wanted out."

"That he wanted out of his investment arrangement with your company, right?"

"That's not what he said. He just said he wanted out. I didn't understand it then, but now I think he meant the Mafia."

Jones turned to the judge, and said, "Judge, I object to the witness's non-responsive speculation, and ask that it be stricken from the record."

The judge said, "State, it's your cross examination, and that door has been opened already. Overruled."

Flustered, Jones said, "So by your own assessment, the murder victim in this case apparently thought you were in the Mafia?"

"Yes ma'am. That's what it looks like to me now. But if that's what he meant, he was wrong. And if you think I'm in it, you're wrong too."

Laura Jones said, "One more question. You testified earlier that you hired Mr. Hart here after you were told to. Is that correct?"

"Yes."

"OK, was this before or after the head of Rilo Marshall, the man who was last seen on your boat, was found on the beach?" The gallery shifted and craned.

"It was before." The gallery chattered loudly.

Over the noise, she said, "That's because you knew that Mr. Marshall was dead, and it was just a matter of time before somebody found his body, isn't that right?"

Hart jumped up and said, "Objection!" The gallery got louder.

Bailiff Fitts yelled, "Settle down!" The noise trailed off.

The judge said, "Answer the question, Mr. Vacarro."

Vacarro said, "No, I didn't know he was dead. The guy was missing, the investigator had called me, and I called a lawyer, which is normal. I didn't do it."

Jones said, "Sure you didn't. No more questions, Judge. She stared at the jury as she picked up her note pad, scanning each one in turn. Hart decided not to ask any questions on redirect, and rested the defense.

It only took the judge twenty minutes to instruct the jury. The attorneys and Defendant sat quietly as he read the written Jury Instructions. At the conclusion, he said, "It's pretty simple. What the lawyers say is opinion, and doesn't count as fact. They are trying to talk you into something, so you can listen to them, or not. That's up to you. The rest of it, I'm satisfied I've made clear."

Afterward, the attorneys had to do closing arguments. Laura Jones knew better than to overly belabor the points of her case, since the whole jury looked tired, and ready to get done. She simply pointed out how the dead man was in town only to meet Vacarro, was later on his boat, that they were both drinking, and there was some type of confrontation, as Vacarro had testified, and the man wound up dead. The dead man's blood was found on the boat.

She said, "The defense is going to want you to believe that we should produce an eye-witness to the murder for you to believe Vacarro is guilty. But that is a common, specious criminal defense attorney tactic. There's an old story about chickens, a bit of country wisdom you may have heard. If you walk into a chicken coop, and it's full of chickens and chicken houses, and there are a bunch of eggs in the chicken houses, you can conclude with a certainty beyond a reasonable doubt that those chickens laid those eggs. This is without having seen it happen, or someone telling you it happened. Here, the evidence all points to one inescapable conclusion, and that is, Tony Vacarro," she walked over in front of the defense table, and pointed at Vacarro, "killed Rilo Marshall. It's that simple. And it is now your sworn duty to find him guilty." She sat down.

Hart took his time getting to the podium. He didn't have any notes. He looked around the jury, to each member, until he was satisfied they were all looking at him. He said, "I'd like you all to recall when we were going through *voir dire* together at the beginning of this process. I asked you, as a group, whether you believed that it was unfair for the state to have to prove a criminal case beyond a reasonable doubt, and why that is the standard.

"Well, let me tell you why I believe that rule is in place. I have been doing this for a long time. I have tried many cases in this very courtroom, most of them criminal ones. And here's the thing: when a person is truly guilty of a crime, the evidence *screams* guilt. The conclusion of guilt is inescapable. I want you to think about that. When a person is actually guilty, he is *obviously* guilty. So proof beyond a reasonable doubt is an easy threshold for the prosecution to overcome, not a hard one. It's when the evidence is dubious that reasonable doubt arises.

"The state's case is, as I said at the beginning, reliant on you connecting some dots for them. Old Captain Arthur Fleming told you that the poor deceased man's head was right there in the shallow water on the beach next to the public pier and boat launch at Washington Street. Now, are we to believe that Tony Vacarro, after a day of partying at Ship Island with dozens of other people, killed that man, cut him up, and threw his head out of the boat right by one of the busiest spots on the waterfront in Bay Saint Louis? Does that make any sense? No, it doesn't. It's doubtful that an educated person would do such a stupid thing. That is the very definition of reasonable doubt.

"What about the blood? The police were

on the boat twice, looking for evidence of wrongdoing, before the blood was mysteriously, anonymously reported to the police. Why did they miss it? Because it wasn't there before. It was most likely planted there by the guilty party, to frame Mr. Vacarro. Do we have to prove that to you? No, because we don't have any burden of proof, and they do. That's the very definition of reasonable doubt.

"My client was only there because someone, most likely his uncle, asked him to be there. My client believes he was set up. His sister thinks their uncle did it, and so do I. You should too, but whether or not that's true, the state simply has not proved their case beyond a reasonable doubt. The evidence doesn't scream guilt. Do you know why? Because he didn't do it. Somebody else did, and you probably all know who that is.

"We all have sympathy for the dead man, no matter what his motives for meeting Vacarro were. We will probably never know. He was someone's victim. But the victim in this room today is Tony Vacarro." He pointed at Vacarro. "He has been dragged through the nightmare of being accused of something he didn't do, and all he has is me, and now you, to end it. You should acquit him, and quickly, so the police can get back out there and find Mr. Marshall's killer."

After making sure they had written instructions, and all the tangible evidence, and their notes, the judge sent the jury back to the jury room, and told the Bailiff to order out for an early lunch of pizzas and salads. He wasn't about to let them take a needed break, sending them out in public now, expecting them not to discuss the case. Outside, the front of the courthouse was inundated. The normal tail-gaters, tourists, media people and Woodstock-ian stoners had been supplemented by the entire gallery, over a hundred in number. Media people scattered to interview them, and suddenly everybody was a celebrity. Hart and Vacarro snuck out the back door, and slipped around the side of the old jail, and down the sidewalk on Court Street, before any of the crowd out front noticed.

When she had left the courthouse, Lis-ette was escorted to her vehicle, shielded by a couple of extra deputies. They had been brought in after two tourists from Florida posted some pictures of themselves screwing with the court-house in the background.

Later, Lisette finally answered her cell phone after several calls. John Hart said, "The jury's out. Where are you? Can you meet me?" There was an uncomfortably long silence. Hart said, "Are you still there? Can you hear me?"

Lisette said, "I've left Bay Saint Louis. I can't tell you where I am, or where I'm going."

Hart said, "What are you talking about?

We're about to be finished here, and I was hoping you and I could get away for a while, maybe go to an island. I sure can use a break, and I bet you can too."

She said, "John, I knew my brother was naive in certain ways, but you surprise me. I just testified under oath in open court that The Raven, the last standing member of the old New Orleans Mafia, murdered a man. There's no telling how many people he has killed in his life, and killing me or you wouldn't matter to him one bit. Regardless of what I have done for him in the past, or how many times I have visited him, or helped him out, he won't let this go. From now on, he will be trying to kill me for betraying him to save my stupid brother."

"Are you saying we're done? That I can't see you now?"

"I'm saying that you need to leave, too. My uncle can't live forever, but as long as he is alive, your life is in danger, along with mine."

"You didn't answer me. Is this it for us?"

"I didn't make that decision, Counselor. You did, when you put me on the witness stand. You're a trial attorney. You had to have known that."

Hart said, "What the hell was I supposed to do? Your brother may get convicted for a murder he obviously didn't commit. Listen, let's slow down for a second. I've never... I haven't told you this before, but I think I love you. I didn't think that was possible anymore. You have to feel the same way about me, don't you?"

Lisette said, "John, I'm not trying to be coy with you, but you have to put aside your feelings, and see this clearly, like a lawyer. Whether or not we are in love is, as you all say, irrelevant. The only thing we could share now is danger. Because we do care about each other, we have to let go. Please take care of yourself. Goodbye." She hung up.

Hart was shellshocked. What happened? Had he just saved his client, and lost his girlfriend in the process? How had he not anticipated that? Even if he had, did he have any choice?

By Friday, it was apparent that the jury was struggling. They had sent out several questions for the judge, some about the evidence presented, some about what they were expected to forget, or remember. At one point, they wanted a legal dictionary definition of "beyond a reasonable doubt." The judge decided to sequester them, and sent them for the weekend to a little hotel out on the highway, along with deputy escorts.

Hart had decided that, no matter the outcome, he was leaving Bay Saint Louis after the trial, for safety sake. He had kept himself busy getting the few cases he still had referred out to other attorneys. He had originally just wanted to go on a long vacation with Lisette, but now it was about survival. He figured The Raven would leave him alone at least until the trial was over, since the plan all along was to frame Vacarro for the murder. If Vacarro got convicted, it was an accomplished mission, and killing his lawyer before the verdict was in might actually prevent that result.

He had tried calling and texting Lisette up until last night, but she was apparently just gone. He refused to let himself get upset, or maybe he didn't even have the capacity. If he had to, he'd go on without her, but more grief would be a reversal of progress, he told himself. He was never going backward again. If she was truly gone, then at least she had shown him the way out of the Godforsaken death hall of his nightmares. He was once again free to move forward. His phone rang, it was Larue.

After he hung up, he slid open his desk drawer, and pulled out Captain Fleming's envelope. He found a letter opener, and sliced it along the seam. Larue had told him old Arthur Fleming was dead, that the postman could see him through the dingy window in his front door, sprawled out there by his little breakfast table. The coroner was on the way over there now.

He slowly unfolded the Captain's letter. It read:

Lawyer,

Since you're reading this, I guess they finally killed me. They sure took their time. Anyway, I hope I got that will right. I was following your directions, so if it ain't right, it's your fault, and you got to fix it. Do what the will says, and get rid of this letter when you're done reading it. You'll see why in a minute.

Like I told you before, I lost my whole family too, in that damn Hurricane Camille. That storm killed me, even if it took me all this time to die. I even tried to get killed afterwards, which you'll see for yourself in my cabin, I guess. I was still barely young enough to sign up and go over there to Vietnam. I didn't know what else to do. I killed a barge load of strangers who just had the bad luck to get in the vicinity of a pissed off coonass from Pearlington. I wasn't mad at anybody but the universe. Which I guess included all those dead strangers, if you think about it.

That's why the first point of this letter is to tell you to not let what happened to me happen to you. I never could be happy again after my family died, unless I was drunk. It felt guilty. But I was wrong thinking that way, because it's a bad thing to waste your life hurting. I know people around here have always laughed at me. I'm ashamed about it a little, but for me it's too late. When I lost my family, I lost my compass, and I never could figure out a good heading after that. You ain't doing your dead family any good drag-assing around Bay Saint Louis. You need to get out and do something important while you're still able to.

Which brings me to the second point of this letter. You remember when we first met, after Hurricane Katrina finally ran me out of Pearlington? We were talking about the treasure them pirates had supposedly left down the beach somewhere around that old Pirate House. Anyway, we never got to finish talking about it.

A lot of pirate stories around here are just bullshit the locals tell the tourists to sell stuff. I know you know that, but there really were a lot of actual pirates around here way back when. Most of them got killed, or hung, or run off by the government, but some of that sorry bunch just quit pirating, and got up in the marsh, and the swamps, and the rivers, and got away from the law.   I grew up in the Pearl River swamp around some of the line left over by that kind, their great great great grand-bastards and what-not, who ain't much better improved by generations, I can tell you, and are just as shifty and lazy and greedy as their sorry great-whatever grandaddies were. The ones I grew up around, they damn sure all believed that pirate treasure was out there somewhere, and went on about it all the time. They all said the same thing, they heard the treasure was in a whiskey barrel the pirates buried some time in the late 1700's or early 1800's, when the English and the French and American Navies were all after them, and a hurricane was on the way to boot.

They buried it down there by where that Pirate House used to be, the story goes, and a big blow came through, and the pirates that didn't get drowned, and didn't get killed or hung by them navies, they all lost track of where the treasure was, or didn't know to begin with, and never could find it again. Supposedly over the years, and decades, a lot of people got killed trying to find it, and of course it was bound to have some kind of a curse on it, which is exactly what you'd expect to hear in this roll of yarn.

Anyway, I'd kind of put all that out of my mind as being swamp stories told by layabouts always looking for a way to get out of honest work. But after me and you talked, I got to thinking about it again, and I figured maybe that's exactly what them backstabbing scoundrels would want people to think, that it had a curse on it, so nobody else would try to find it. So, I start thinking that maybe there really was something buried down there somewhere, and them pirates would want people to think they put all that loot right there at that house site, so they could lie about it and hide the real spot.

Anyway, I didn't have nothing else to do in those days, and there wasn't any houses down that stretch of the beach, because Hurricane Katrina had wiped them all out. I found another old coot who showed me where that property was, and that pirate house used to be, and I went out there and walked around it trying to figure how them skunks would be thinking, if they really did bury treasure.

Well, that property is right on the road, and that old pirate house was too, before it got blowed away, and that means it was right on the beach way back when. I figured if they buried anything, they would want to bury it somewhere off of that main piece of property, way back from the water, but where they could find it again easy enough, since you know, hurricanes can change the whole beachfront if they want to. So I figured they would want to put something in the ground, some kind of marker that a hurricane couldn't move, and could be lined up with something else.

And not wanting to get the house in the way, if it was there at the time. I figured it would have to be somewhere out along the edge of that property. So I went out there many a night digging around in the dark, when nobody could see me. Sure enough, after a while I found what I thought was a piece of buried granite, or some kind of rock, right about where the back corner of that property should of been. And of course, Mississippi ain't got any granite in the ground, or leastways not around here. So in a while I had this thing dug out enough to see it was really a big old buried petrified log, near to standing perfectly straight up and down.

Now, we got a shitload of petrified logs in Mississippi, but this one looked like it was put there on purpose. So I figured the pirates did it, and they would have to have something to line that marker up with, something that was bound to survive a hurricane, and the only thing for sure like that around here is Cat Island, out on the horizon. Now you can hardly see it from there, unless it's low tide, but I did, and lined them up, that marker and the middle of the island, and give it a little leeway in wideness, and headed off away from the beach, and I took a compass reading, and got a cheap metal detector, just in case, and I start detecting and digging down that line, behind that Pirate House property, most nights.

I can tell you, there's a lot of crap in the ground that a metal detector finds. I had to refill a bunch of holes, you better believe, to hide what I was up to. I must have dug up enough rusty bed springs, and car wheels, and goddamn metal buckets and angle iron and tin roof pieces to start my own dump. Hurricanes bury a lot of stuff over time. I done this for several weeks until it was finally clear I was on the wrong trail. I figured that pirate treasure talk was all just lies, and somehow that petrified wood just got stuck there by some old hurricane by chance. So I went home.

Then one night, I was down at the beach sticking flounders, you know, when there ain't no moon, and looking up into the universe, when it occurs to me, what if them scoundrels figured they couldn't count on Cat Island being there, either? It made sense, the more I chewed on it, because them islands can get cut up, and moved around, and done away with if that gulf wants to, or hurricanes. The only thing that's always there no matter what, that the pirates, or any sailor could always count on, was the North Star. So I went back down there and dug up that petrified log, and lined it up with that star, and headed off on another line of holes.

Now Lawyer, you might not believe it just now, but one of those nights I found that pirate treasure. The metal detector picked up the old iron rings around some barrels, buried in some pretty good clay, and not real deep, or all rusted away, even after all this time. And it was way more than one little whiskey barrel. Believe me, it took a bunch of bucket trips, I'm saying, to get all of it out of there. And you know what it was? It wasn't gold and silver coins or jewelry like the pirate treasures in the movies. It was all pearls.

There's thousands of them, but I ain't ever counted how many. I don't know about pearls, but they are every size, and all perfect shaped, with no flaws. There ain't no telling what they're worth. They're in a couple of big steel barrels in that little storage shed out back of my cabin, by my tools, and I am giving all of them to you. There's a pad lock on the door, and the key is around the right side there under a perfect white nautilus shell I found a few years ago down on the beach right about where that poor man's head was.

I guess you want to know why I didn't cash it all in, and live it up. Well, that's between me and the universe, or God, if there is one, which I reckon I'll know something about by the time you read this. Like I said, some of these fools claim that old pirate treasure has a curse on it, but I don't believe it. I did sometimes wonder who else might claim to own them pearls, like maybe whoever owned that property where it was buried where I found it.

But I also got to thinking, who could they really belong to? The pirates that buried them pearls probably stole them way earlier from the French, who used to go through oysters around here by the millions. That's how the Pearl River and my hometown Pearlington got named, you know. I looked up all this business down at the library. The French, the ones that done it, claimed there weren't any pearls around here to amount to much, not good ones anyway, but I figure maybe they were lying to their investors, or their kings, or whatever, and keeping everything for themselves. Or maybe all those pearls aren't even from around here anyway, pirates being pirates. Maybe they got robbed from some ship out there in the gulf.

Who knows where they came from? Also, they were buried a long ways off the beach, behind that house site, and I wasn't measuring anything, just following that line off the North Star and that log marker, and it was always dark, too. I don't have any idea where they were actually buried, or whose property it was on.

Anyway, those pearls don't have any curse, I don't believe. They never did me any harm, or any good either, except making me grin a little inside when some of these rich people in town looked down at me, and the tourists made fun of me, me knowing I was probably richer than all of them, if I wanted to be.

I told you I'd be paying you one day. I bet you ain't ever had a client that ran up a bill then paid it all off with pirate treasure, with a big bonus to boot. Ha ha ha. Well, it's all yours now, and I want you to use it for whatever you decide, but mainly to get the hell away from being sad. Burn this letter after reading it, like I said, because I don't want anybody else like them landowners or any other pirates trying to claim those pearls. There's a will in this same envelope, like I said, and it gives everything to you.

Well, that's it. I told you all my stories were true. Thanks, Johnny Hart, for being my only friend. See, I knew your name the whole time.

Captain Arthur Fleming

Hart parked in front of the small World War Two era shotgun house by the tracks behind the Depot District in Bay Saint Louis. The coroner had already come and gone. There was a single, short strand of yellow police tape across the front door. The handle was unlocked, and Hart opened the door. He ducked under the tape and went in.

The dingy little building smelled like it looked. There was a tiny kitchen area with a two person table where Captain Fleming had been found. There was one bedroom with a single bed and a short chest of drawers standing in an open closet with no hangars. The kitchen had an antique porcelain sink with a bunch of dark dings and rust stains in its faded white surface. The refrigerator contained a can of chicory coffee, and an open tin of mustard sardines, half empty. Hart said, "Well, Captain, I guess we finally know what it takes to kill you."

The tiny living room was empty, with no TV or radio, just a small lamp table with one chair, and one picture hung above on the peeling papered wall. It was a fading black and white photo of the Captain, his wife, and their small kids on the back deck of a wooden diesel trawler that had the name *The Lord's Bounty* painted in big cursive across the transom. There was a drawer in the table, and Hart slid it open. Inside were a pile of military medals and citations, including a silver star and enough purple hearts for a collection. Maybe Arthur Fleming really couldn't be killed. He took the medals, and the thin gold plated frame from the wall, and went back out the front door, closing it.

Around back, Hart found the key where it was supposed to be, and the barrels. He found a hammer among the tools on a work bench, popped the top off one, then the other, and they were indeed full of pearls, thousands of them. He reattached the metal lids, locked the door to the shed, and took the key.

Chapter 11

Monday morning, the judge's staff attorney called John Hart, saying the jury had sent a note to the judge. They were hopelessly deadlocked, and there was going to be a mistrial. The attorneys needed to be at court, and be prepared to set a new trial date. The word had gotten out, and Judge Donahue sealed the entire courthouse from the annoyed public, and called the jury in. He asked the jury if it had any announcements to make. Up popped a lady with thick glasses and said, "Judge, I was asked to speak on our behalf, since I was elected the foreperson. The only thing we can all agree upon is that it is impossible to reach a unanimous verdict in this case."

The judge said, "Impossible, huh? What's the percentages?"

She said, "Judge, we've taken several votes. It was six to six every time. And I've got to say, I can not fathom how anybody with any common sense could believe that pretty lady when she swooped in here at the last second and blamed this all on somebody other than her brother. It seems perfectly clear to me that the Defendant is guilty as hell, if you'll excuse my expression."

A man on the other end of the jury box said, "That's crazy, Judge. They want you to believe that man's guilty just because he's kin to some bad people, since we all know about the

New Orleans Mafia. The state ain't proved a damn thing beyond a reasonable doubt. That's the basic facts." The whole jury started talking at the same time.

The judge held his hand up, and said, "Alright, alright, everybody settle down. This is why we have trials, and juries. Ladies and gentlemen, it appears to the Court that you are, as we say, 'hopelessly deadlocked.'" The jurors all nodded. "So I am declaring this a mistrial. Check with the clerk in a couple of days about getting your checks, which aren't going to be much, so don't get excited. Thank you all for your service. By the way, you are all free to speak about the case now. You're released."

He waited for the jurors to shuffle out and head down the stairs.

He looked back and forth between the counsel tables. The young D.A. was not in attendance. Judge Donahue said, "State, let's pick a trial date while we're here. I'll clear another couple week segment on my calendar, and we need to make it real soon."

A cheer went up outside like somebody just scored a touchdown. Laura Jones said, "Judge, I have been instructed to inform the Court that, owing to the dramatically split vote, and certain matters that were revealed in trial, the State of Mississippi will not be pursuing this case against this Defendant any further.

The judge said, "Well, Mr. Vacarro, that

means you're released from your bond, too. You are free to go."

Vacarro put his head in his hands, then clasped them like he was praying, then jumped up and hugged John Hart. Hart walked over to Laura Jones, who was closing her box of case files. He stuck out his hand, and said, "Good job as always, Counselor."

She shook it, and said, "You too, John, but I want you to know, I didn't make this decision. I still think he did it."

John Hart and Tony Vacarro spent the next couple of days partying downtown, and on Vacarro's boat, and at the family compound. Hart figured that if The Raven wanted to take a shot at him, it wouldn't be right in the middle of town, right after the biggest trial in the county's history. There was just too much attention on the case. On Thursday, Hart went to his office and drafted the initial pleadings for probating the testate estate of Arthur Fleming, and filed them at the courthouse. Since he was its sole beneficiary, he asked the Chancery Clerk to serve as the executor, who agreed. When she saw the initial inventory, she understood why.

The Raccoon Queen had never taught any other raccoon how she knew what she knew, and none had ever inquired. She was the tribe's unchallenged leader. She was now the oldest, and the rest were either her younger siblings, or cousins, or nieces and nephews, and all each other's, and with no clear breeding rules, odd combinations of each. There were forty or fifty of them, depending on the night, and for most of her life, their country had been the general area around John Hart's former rent house on Cedar Point.

Even before he arrived, it had always been full of natural raccoon food, but was also dense with snakes, and scattered with alligators, and patrolled by hawks and owls, and at least one gigantic white headed Bald Eagle, all of whom considered baby raccoons delicious. Since there was a fairly constant supply of raccoon babies, safety was her second concern, after food. The tribe maintained good escape trails, but no permanent housing. Mobility was crucial for survival, but the presence of the big hairless raccoon around here had always made the risk worthwhile.

One evening, the Queen woke up, climbed down out of her favorite tree, and waddled across the hard trail. There were no more vines, or hanging cocoons of food, or hard shells, or anything left of the big hairless raccoon. It was gone, and it had been for a while, and apparently wasn't coming back. She padded back out to the hard trail, looking down one way, then the other. She had seen other empty trees in their country, and they were probably full of big, hairless raccoons too, with cocoons of food. It was time to relocate the tribe.

The Raven's big Sportfisher *Tit for Tat* headed out of Venice Marina, through Tiger Pass, and opened up to its top speed of twenty knots. A while later, she emerged from a canal west of Southwest Pass, the long main commercial shipping channel of the Mississippi River where it dumps into the vast Gulf of Mexico. Ocean going vessels lined up to enter the channel, and outgoing ones paraded into the blue water horizon.

The fishy smelling air was full of seagulls and terns, flitting around, plucking herring off the rocking water surface. Huge brown pelicans cruised overhead, periodically bowing into graceful dives, plunging deep for the bigger ones. After a while, *Tit for Tat* reached the descending edge of the continental shelf, where the water eventually gets a couple of miles or more deep.

Lisette Vacarro walked out of the salon and onto the back deck. She was wearing a cotton smock, and had a canvas bag slung over her shoulder. She made her way around the outside of the cabin, holding on and carefully negotiating the narrow flange of the boat's gunnels, to the covered bow. She spread out a thick white beach towel, took off her smock, now wearing only a tiny bikini, and sat down. She got a chilled bottle of sparkling wine out of the bag, and a wide, laminated metal cup, and filled it up.

On the bridge, the Raven's full time captain tried to focus on his job, and not on Lisette, who had now stretched out on the foredeck, her feet toward the front of the boat, and was practically naked. He was sure he could see under the front edge of her bikini bottom, stretched as it was between her protruding hip bones, and that she knew it. Her body was perfect. He sent his first mate down the ladder to keep him from gawking too, and interrupting his view.

On the back deck, the missing driver who had killed John Hart's family was busy fooling with a tuna fishing rod. He was tying a heavy plastic monofilament leader, about to bait it with a ballyhoo rig. The mate went into the salon and re-emerged with a fish whopping stick, a hollow metal implement that looked like a half sized baseball bat, made for killing pelagic game fish like tuna, Dorado, Ling, or even swordfish, which can be very dangerous flopping around on a boat deck.

The hand eased up behind the driver, and stroked him over the head. The driver fell unconscious. The mate went back inside and came out with a forty pound weightlifter's dumbbell, which he set down. There was a small door in the transom, designed for getting big fish up on the back deck of the boat. He brought out three more of the weights, and retrieved a spool of heavy nylon line. After a while, he had the weights all separately tethered to the driver, who was still breathing, but unconscious, and bleeding from a vicious cut in the top of his head. The deck hand whistled up toward the fly bridge.

The Captain had developed a stress headache from gawking at Lisette. Now she was spraying on tanning oil, and he was having a hard time concentrating on driving. Annoyed at being interrupted, he checked the depth meter, which indicated over a thousand feet. He whistled back down toward the mate, who swung open the transom door, and slid the first two weights off the back. They were connected to the driver with ten feet or so of line, and he was wrapped up in a spider web of it. Their weight, along with the boat's forward motion, dragged the driver over to the door's opening, but not immediately out of it.

He suddenly regained consciousness just long enough to stare up into the hot blue sky and say, "What the fuck?" The mate slid the other two weights out the transom door, and the trundled driver shot out the opening. The mate unwound a hose from underneath one of the gunnels, turned on the salt water pump, and rinsed out the blood. He went back inside, brought out a gallon of bleach, and used it all to scrub down the deck. He rinsed everything again, and closed the transom door.

Lisette knew the captain was trying to see her crotch, and she was doing her best to give him a good angle. She smirked to herself. Men.

They're so simple, and predictable, and easy to manipulate. Just like the rest, the boat captain could gawk at it all he wanted, but he could never have it. It made her surge with power. She reached and slid her bikini bottom down a little more, where it barely covered anything.

She closed her eyes, and let the warm sunlight seep in, and remembered how everything had led to this moment. It started with the death of her mother, who she never knew, and how her brother had acted about it. He had threatened her, told her he would have her disinherited if she ever mentioned their mother again. *Their* mother. His mother. In the patriarchal tradition of their family, and also because of her youth, he could have done it. By the mere fact of being male, and firstborn, he could have ruined her life. So she took his abuse, and consumed it, and let it fester in her.

His insistence on banishing the memory of his own mother was a sick symptom of the same old stupid patriarchy. There was nothing she could do, back then. So she hid her anger, layered and hardened it, and made it her pearl. And just like a pearl's cool exterior luminescence, she had become physically polished. She had hidden the hatred in her heart, and turned it into perfect, beautiful vengeance.

Her mother had gotten pregnant by another man, and even though their father regularly had extramarital affairs, that fact had doomed her. Being Catholic, her mother had no choice but to give birth to Lisette, and being a suspected harlot meant she had no other real choice but to kill herself, to save Lisette from being thrown out in the streets with her. And she had to make it plausible that her death might have been an accident. So she did what had to be done. And in doing so, she set the example Lisette would follow in her life: doing what had to be done.

When Lisette had gotten groped by the drunk on the river front all those years ago, she had decided she would never again be defenseless. So when she saw the same cretin again, several months later, she was ready. She had purchased an ancient, long, narrow knife in a Royal Street antiques shop. It probably came into existence as a steel letter opener, but after she had it razor sharpened, it was an elegantly deadly weapon.

She was again handing out food and water to the homeless down the levee, toward the French Market, away from the normal mixture of homeless and regular tourists. The same crude man who had touched her before appeared. He evidently did not recognize her, or at least didn't say so, but he was drunk again, and pawing, and stupidly arrogant. She had motioned for him to head further away, down the levee, behind the flood wall, and the fool had followed her.

It was getting dark, and she made sure no one was watching. She didn't stop him from touching her, aggressively grabbing her breasts and ass, and groping between her legs, just to make sure he deserved the blade she easily slipped into his beleaguered liver. She popped it out and wiped it off on him and wrenched out of his disgusting grip. She was walking away before he realized what had happened. Where he was, nobody heard his cries.

By the time she got back to her car in the public parking lot next to the old Jax brewery, he was dead. As she lay in her bed that night reading, she found it curious that she killed a person, and had no regret at all. The dead man had simply gone beyond what is allowed in this life, or should be. He had lived beyond any ability or desire to contribute anything useful to society, and was obviously not even able to help himself. So she had relieved him of that burden, and his burden on society, which without him was better. It was no more or less than killing a roach. She had gone to peaceful sleep, satisfied that the whole scenario had done all concerned some real good.

Even though she was also an owner, her brother had given her what was meant to be a token Vice President position in the family business. She had an expense account, and a Mercedes sedan, and a penthouse condo in New Orleans' Central Business District. She had charge accounts at every major restaurant in the city, and never saw the bills, which were paid by company accountants. He had made it clear that she was not expected to work, or accomplish anything.

For an educated woman, being underestimated was the worst insult she was capable of silently enduring. But it had gradually occurred to her that she may actually be in the best possible position to achieve what she wanted most, which was simple revenge on her brother. It took her a while. She came to realize that her great uncle The Raven was the key to gaining the power she needed. Her brother wanted nothing to do with the old man or, as far as she could tell, the New Orleans Mafia, if there was anything left of it then.

So she had started visiting The Raven in his mausoleum of a building in the French Quarter, where he had become ensconced like a vampire. She brought him wine and fresh meat, although he didn't appear to need or use much of either. He was still in remarkably good physical shape, but was almost completely insane by that time. In his spookily high pitched voice, he told her everything he remembered, or maybe just thought had happened in his life. She wasn't sure if he always knew who he was talking to, or if he was talking to anybody at all, but she culled out the useful parts of his ramblings about government ties and mutually destructive secrets.

CHRIS JOHNSON

She ignored the gory details of shootings, and stabbings, and mutilations. He once told her he lived off the blood of his victims, but she dismissed that as simply too impractical. She had several doctor friends in town, and eventually got antipsychotics prescribed that made him relatively mentally stable. Meanwhile, on the deep internet, she contacted some of the government spooks he had told her about, always under the guise of being The Raven himself. Doing so, she created a mythos about the old man's competence, durability and danger among the handful of governmental decision makers who could have, and should have had him destroyed.

But they gave in, and she had made the arrangement he now enjoyed, the systematic elimination of rats under federal witness protection. It served a useful purpose to the government, because these people, in addition to being lowlifes themselves, were expensive pains in the ass who knew too much about everything. Plus, it gave her old uncle something to do that he enjoyed. And it gave her family a new grip on the collective balls of the government of the United States. Thus, the new New Orleans Mafia was born.

She spoke with her half brother at the office when necessary, always under the ruse that she was relaying messages from the Raven, and trying to protect Vacarro from any culpability in connection with the old man. She communicated financial instructions to him through notes at the office supposedly from the Raven. In this way, she had set up and funded accounts through the business which she used to finance certain operations, and business was booming. Her brother delivered whatever she asked for, always thinking he was acting on the orders of The Raven, but never wanting to know any details.

This only increased her contempt for him, and men like him. He had spent his whole life being handed things because it was always assumed he was in the Mafia. He never claimed any connections, but he didn't publicly deny them, either. He enjoyed the perks, but damn sure didn't want to have any resulting responsibilities. He was happy to get the best seats in restaurants, but he never wanted to get his hands dirty, and seemed genuinely repelled by the whole idea of committing any significant crimes. Fortunately, when dealing with real criminals, she had no such compunctions.

Both her family businesses, Puglisi and Vacarro, Ltd. and the New Orleans Mafia, had long been involved with the shipping industry. The Mafia had been first, in the old days extracting payments from shippers who needed access to the docks and facilities in the port of New Orleans. Later on, Tony Vacarro had established a substantial presence in re-insurance, underwriting the myriad risks involved in port operations for international shipping, a legitimate and highly profitable business. She had convinced her brother to let her get involved in that aspect of the company, and he reluctantly agreed, on the basis that her good looks would keep the clients entertained.

This afforded Lisette opportunities to visit and inspect their insured clients all along the Gulf of Mexico, where the business was concentrated. And it worked. Clients from Texas to Florida, all men, wanted Lisette's attention. This required her to be in ports and harbors all the time.

An old college friend from China, whose family was in the shipping business, had once told her about the huge black market for counterfeit pain meds made with Chinese manufactured fentanyl. Legitimate pharmaceutical companies had made fortunes while substantial numbers of people in the U.S. had gotten legally addicted to pain killers. Then the U.S. Drug Enforcement Administration decided to start arresting doctors for writing too many pain prescriptions. Thus the DEA had practically created the market for fake pain killers itself when, after decades of allowing the treatment of pain as a primary medical condition, they reversed course and decided to squeeze off the supply.

She had recognized the incredible profit potential. Her Chinese friend was in shipping, and she was in shipping insurance, so it was a perfect economic marriage. She had anonymously recruited key port facility managers along the gulf, in Tampa, Pensacola, Mobile, Gulfport, and of course, New Orleans. Her Chinese partner shipped fake pain pills, and her underlings unloaded them all along the gulf.

Recruiting key port managers was fairly easy. In cases of married men, she arranged for high end escorts to seduce them, then retained them by extortion. They were offered incredible wealth for their cooperation, and death if they refused. Of course, she did none of this personally. All initial communications were by courier, and in each case her target was led to assume he was dealing with the old New Orleans Mafia. Everyone involved in her business naturally assumed The Raven was behind everything, even though he wasn't aware of any of it. And all the individuals involved were unaware of anyone else in her operations.

She sometimes used burner phones for messaging. She had done it for Tony's meeting with Rilo Marshall. When it was necessary for Tony to approve some particular action, or be somewhere she needed him, she would have notes delivered. He always assumed they came from The Raven, and he always did was he was told. When she needed The Raven involved in the initial meeting between Tony and John Hart, she just told him. Her uncle always did what he was told, too.

The street network for illegal pain killer distribution was not traditional. Lisette was constantly in attendance at social events where middle aged ladies with the need and means for pain killers were willing to get them however they could. Traditional drug consumers could adjust to the lack of painkillers by moving on to other highs. But legions of middle aged people with backaches weren't interested in tripping, they just didn't want to hurt.

So she recruited pharmacists and doctors, using the same hooker techniques, who provided her secret organization with bullet proof legitimacy, even while distributing illegitimate pills. In yacht clubs, and country clubs, and business groups, and historical societies, and civic associations all across the Gulf South, a new black market was born. The Chinese pills were indistinguishable from real ones, and they could not be made fast enough. If well-heeled consumers thought they were purchasing illegal pain pills, they would do it anyway, taking the risk to avoid pain. However, if they thought they could buy legal pills at a premium, they would buy unlimited supplies. And they did.

She had eventually concocted a system that allowed the patient to conduct the whole transaction by phone. While on the road, Lisette would attend some social function and casually mention the subject of doctors cutting off people with legitimate needs for pain killers. She would give the phone number of a doctor she knew to an important member of that social circle, who would eventually bring her friends into the scheme. Of course, she had other means of bulk distribution, pills that left the ports and went to the rest of the country. Where they went, and to whom, she did not know herself. She had captured and detained a small number of underlings in her secret new organization, like the crew of *Tit for Tat*, all of whom were compromised in some potentially fatal way. They saw her around but were always under the impression that they were working for The Raven, not her.

Gulfport was the crux of the whole thing, since that's where most of the country's bananas came in. Fentanyl that made it from China to Panama was transferred to banana shipments from all across Central America, and sent north. The whole fentanyl operation was seriously threatened when, six years earlier, an unfortunate longshoreman in Gulfport had gotten crushed by a container full of bananas and fentanyl-laced pain killers. The pills had been successfully removed, and weren't discovered by the police. Still, this attracted considerable uncomfortable attention from the authorities, who concluded the tragic death was a civil matter, and moved on. So it looked like she had dodged a potential disaster.

Then an overly curious New Orleans attorney named John Hart had gotten assigned to defend the insurance carrier. The underwriter was reinsured up the line by Puglisi and Vacarro, Ltd., through an offshore company that her brother had set up. Hart's firm had done much work for Puglisi over the years, so she knew most of the senior partners there. They certainly knew who she was. Lisette made sure they knew to settle the matter immediately, and that the word had come from her brother, the boss. The partners did as they were told.

But Hart had insisted on visiting the site in Gulfport, unnecessarily extending the danger. Then he had planned a second trip, and she just couldn't take any more chances. She couldn't have him killed, that would draw more unwanted attention. She had to put him out of commission, and make it look like an accident. So she had anonymously hired the idiot driver along with a couple others like him from a New Orleans trucking company Puglisi reinsured. They were to fan out along the coast, locate Hart's car and run into it that day. The aim was not necessarily to kill, but to incapacitate and neutralize the lawyer. If he got killed, so be it. It was not her normal practice to harm innocent people, but he had not followed orders, and therefore put himself in danger. Besides, he was a lawyer, and therefore by definition not innocent.

Of course, the damned driver had gotten drunk, and let his phone go dead, and missed the order to stand down, and overdid the job. He killed Hart's family, who weren't even supposed to be there. To make matters worse, he had taken off and disappeared for a while, and caused more unnecessary media scrutiny, which threatened to upset her empire. On top of it all, her guy in the Gulfport Harbor, who had been the boss on the docks, got cold feet. When he found out this bigshot New Orleans lawyer was wanting to talk to him, he feigned having the flu. Then, when he found out the same attorney was coming back to find him, and that the lawyer's family got killed that day, he recognized it as a hit. He lost his nerve, had a full blown freakout, and had to be removed entirely. That's where Rilo Marshall came from, a battlefield promotion.

She had located and kept tabs on the missing driver for all these years, until he had outlived his usefulness just a few minutes ago. She had kept him alive, not knowing whether she might need him in her ongoing manipulations of attorney John Hart. You just never know. But she had found another disposable man down around Venice, one who ultimately made the driver less valuable. This guy was one of the rats that her uncle took for one-way boat rides every once in a while, who had somehow escaped. A local commercial catfishermen, running droplines in the lower river, found him starving and delirious, and half dead from mosquitos and horseflies, and got him back to Venice. Luckily, she had gotten wind of this before The Raven, and she soon had him stashed away in case she ever needed him. It was now pretty obvious she was going to need him, and soon.

John Hart had eventually filed the wrongful death lawsuits, and Puglisi and Vacarro, Ltd., the reinsurer for the trucking company, also controlled the handling of the defense of those cases. Their presence in the chain of command was not obvious, or even relevant, and hidden by a couple of layers of holding companies, and ultimately an investment trust. Of course, Puglisi had always reinsured the bulk of their reinsurance holdings, so the amount of any payouts were ultimately inconsequential. Lisette had arranged for there to be a two million dollar settlement offer to the hapless Hart. He was broke and washed up, and she was positive that he would have no choice but to take the money, and finally end the series of attention grabbing events in Gulfport. That was three years ago. Hart had shocked her by turning it down.

Then, to keep up the annoying trend, Rilo Marshall had gotten antsy and wanted out. What was it with these fools up in Gulfport? It had cost a minor fortune to keep Marshall in line up to this point. Over time, she had arranged for his investments to grow to something like five million dollars, which the company would eventually recoup. That was possibly her one big error in managing the whole multi-year crisis. She had to make Puglisi the beneficiary of his holdings, because otherwise strangers would eventually come to know about Marshall's wealth, and probably want to know how it happened. It was just a choice between two bad options, and a call that had to be made. Then one day recently, Marshall had discovered what Paid on Death designations meant, and that his POD made Puglisi his sole heir.

Marshall had attained his station by usefulness to Lisette, not by brains. She was therefore shocked that he was smart enough to figure out PODs, but not surprised at all that he was stupid enough to want to meet the boss, which he probably understood to be The Raven, and had called Puglisi and Vacarro demanding it. Lisette had long ago purchased the loyalty of Tony's executive assistant, who was under several strict instructions, but especially to refer any matters concerning her uncle to her. She sold this arrangement as a way to keep Tony out of any inadvertent trouble.

By this time, Lisette had had enough of Rilo Marshall, who was way more trouble than he was worth. She wasn't about to let her painkiller empire be brought down by a redneck who couldn't appreciate what he had been given. So she decided to remove him, and go ahead and set up Tony to take the fall in the process. He had made them all plenty of money, and she would end up with half his shares in Puglisi. She would finally get her revenge, and her brother would never even know how it all happened. It was perfect.

The Raven was, as usual, oblivious to the whole operation. Who knew what that old creature thought about, if anything at all. That Sunday in New Orleans, after Vacarro came out of Gabriella's, The Raven was to either kill John Hart, or the kid he shot over in the Marigny, depending on whether Vacarro held up two fingers, or none. She had found the Creole kid down on the river front, jacking tourists with his own homemade shank. He tried to rob her, but she surprised him with her weapon, disarmed and then recruited him. She didn't let most of her criminal recruits actually see her, but this one didn't matter. He was not going to survive his unfortunate decision to try rolling Lisette Vacarro.

When Rilo Marshall got off Vacarro's boat back at the Bay harbor that night, she had him picked up and killed. Her crew, which included the same deck hand who just dispatched the driver, and the slobbering Captain upstairs, had squirted some of his blood in Tony's boat. But apparently not very much, and the mysterious, unanticipated cleaning lady had cleaned it all up. She probably thought the blood was from a cut foot. She had done too good of a job, and the cops had just done a sloppy one.

The crew had kept some of Marshall in an icy cooler of gulf salt water, just in case. The rest of him wound up in the deep gulf trench presently under the *Tit for Tat,* where the worthless driver was now headed. Since the blood on the boat had not implicated Tony, they had periodically dropped pieces of Marshall out in front of the Washington Street pier, but they kept floating away, or getting eaten. Either way, they were down to the head, which was getting in bad shape, when she made sure they dropped the damn thing right on the beach, which required one wading up from the waterside. If that old drunk hadn't found the head, then the whole scheme for setting up Tony may have been pointless, other than just eliminating Rilo Marshall, which she could have done at any time, with a lot less headache.

Then the prosecution looked like they may screw up the murder case, so she had to make the anonymous call about the blood. Then John Hart had The Raven subpoenaed, and she made the reluctant decision to have him killed. Her uncle was just too much of a wildcard to possibly end up on TV. She had been keeping the stupid driver under tabs all this time, so she brought him back to New Orleans, where he staked out The Raven's area and took the shot. The incompetent fool missed, and wound up blaming the whole incident on some big dog. Her uncle had taken to his house fortress in the Quarter, and he might not ever come back out. He wasn't in Venice, as she had told Hart. She hadn't seen or talked to him since he got shot at. To the extent he understood anything, she was pretty sure her uncle didn't suspect her.

Then Hart almost found her out because of the picture of her buying the burner phone. She was forced to testify, implicating her uncle and actually saving her brother to cover her own ass. She had blamed him for murder, because otherwise she might be blamed. That testimony would be tough to explain to The Raven, if he ever asked. She would just have to deal with it then.

From the beginning, John Hart was involved in something he never understood. His own desire to do a good job in the original Gulfport case had gotten his family mistakenly killed. Then, when Marshall wanted out, and she wanted to sacrifice her half brother in the process, she figured he was the best candidate for the job of losing the case. After all, he had been devastated by what had happened to his family, had moved back to the Bay and spent the last few years doing basically nothing. He was, from all appearances, just the type of burnout she needed to fix her brother's fate.

Then she met him. She had arranged it, intervening when he thought he was meeting her brother at the company offices. At the time, she figured he was getting cold feet, and he was. She wanted to keep him on the team, and avoid having to kill him yet. The bodies around the whole sordid mess on the Mississippi Gulf Coast had been piling up, and that was never good for business. So when he had asked her out on a lunch date, she agreed.

As it turned out, she actually kind of liked the guy. She had also miscalculated his legal skills. He proved to be a decent lawyer, even a good one. He also had a real chance to cause more problems with his wrongful death civil case, if he could ever find the damned driver, who was at the time more valuable to her alive than dead. Of course, the driver always assumed he had been working for her uncle, or her brother. Nearly all men in her employ were unaware of being under her control, and doing her bidding.

Attorney John Hart had been a pain in the ass for Lisette ever since she first heard of him. He was probably never going to give up looking for the man who killed his wife and mother. It was like a repeating nightmare with this guy. She had gotten to know him pretty well, and she knew he would never quit, especially if the case was dismissed and he got nothing. She just didn't need the prolonged scrutiny. So she had arranged to have his case settled, for the second tier policy limit of five million dollars. That the underwriter was a company primarily owned by Puglisi and Vacarro was a fact Hart never realized, because he had no reason to suspect such a connection. She had to make sure he never did.

In retrospect, she probably should have arranged that result years earlier. But now, she had the benefit of the experience, and would not make a similar mistake again. She almost dozed off, thinking of Johnny Hart. She had unaccountably gotten fond of him, or was at least well entertained. So she had dated him, watching, listening, making sure he never got too close to what was really going on. Then he started getting too close to her. It even looked like he was falling in love, the poor guy.

She figured the *Tit for Tat* had headed out long enough. Knowing the captain would still be ogling her, she stuck her hand up, raised one finger, and twirled it. He turned the boat around. Once they were headed back north, she flipped over on her stomach, her head pointed toward the bow, her t-backed bottoms covering nothing. She sprayed tanning oil all over, untied her top, and stretched out, letting the captain gawk at her glistening ass for the ride in.

She thought about it all. The panting captain up there, and the man she had dated for a while, and the public, the press, the deep spooks in the federal government, they all saw her, if they thought about her at all, only as the hot single niece of the last significant figure in the old

New Orleans Mafia. And of course, the sister of the preppy guy who was maybe its new boss.

In New Orleans, there were always questions, whispers about the Mafia. What had happened to the Bardinos? For a century, they had run New Orleans. They controlled shipping, and banks, and insurance, and Mardi Gras. They owned casinos, and elected governors and senators, and Congressmen. They had legions of men killed, including an American president. Everyone had questions, and not one of them would be able to divine the true answer. Not only had the New Orleans Mafia not gone away, it had been resurrected and transformed into a modern, efficient, worldwide money making organization that truly only existed in one person, Lisette Vacarro.

It was new and perfect, and made completely secret by the profound ignorance of the male gender. In her Mafia, it was no longer necessary to initiate men into a known organization that demanded fealty with the mere threat of death. Fealty was the weak part, because it was based on knowledge. That old arrangement had brought down the whole Mafia house, nationwide. Of course, the threat of death was still useful, but Lisette had figured out that the best secret organization is one that is kept a secret from its own members.

She not only entrapped her recruits with sex, and held their loyalty with incredible payouts, but they never even contemplated that she might be the Boss, because men simply can't conceive of being outsmarted by a good looking woman. The only people on Earth outside China who knew she was involved in anything illegal were the small crew on this boat. And when she gave them orders, they always thought she was relaying them from The Raven. She was, as the old saying goes, hiding in plain sight.

Lisette sat up, dropped her bikini top aside, and poured another glass of wine. She thought about it all, and smiled. The fentanyl business alone was generating millions of dollars a year. The Raven was busy cleaning out the feds' witness protection program, and was making another fortune doing it. And she was looking at new opportunities, considering expanding dramatically into the Caribbean. The Mexican cartels were getting to be a problem in the fentanyl business, and they weren't just supplying old ladies. They were slaughtering people, and she wasn't sure if the cost of doing business in counterfeit pharmaceuticals was going to be worth it much longer. She just didn't know.

In this moment she realized she no longer really hated her brother, or any man, for what happened to her mother. Hatred makes people too important. If anything, she was completely indifferent now. Let the men she controlled continue to believe they were gender superior. Let that ignorance blind them to their own inferiority, one so profound that it prevented them from seeing the most important truth that permeated their lives: that the New Orleans Mafia is alive and well, and better than it was. Its new members don't know each other, and don't even know what they are a part of. And everyone still thinks The Raven or Tony are in charge. She couldn't help but laugh a little.

She took a long sip of sparkling wine. There was the remaining problem of John Hart. He had been a far better attorney than she anticipated. He had done his job well, and in doing so, forced her into the position of exposing herself to danger, and more than once. Her brother was probably going to be hiding out from the Raven for a while, but at least he could be controlled. She was tired of having to clean up Hart's messes. He was just too smart and durable for his own good, and hers. No matter how much she had grown fond of him, one thing had become apparent. The lawyer had to go.

It was Saturday afternoon, and Sid was on the second story deck of the rustic restaurant and bar overlooking the Venice marina. A big floor fan at one end of the deck slowly moved the hot, heavy, fishy air, and beat out rhythmic background noise. He and Angel were down fishing for the weekend, and she was getting changed in the head under the center console in his boat. He was retrieving a couple of to-go frozen drinks,

"Bushwhackers," for the twenty mile ride out to meet Tony Vacarro and John Hart around Breton Island. They were staying on the *Negotiable*. The plan was to cruise around for a couple of days, fishing in Sid's fast fishing boat, and spending the nights on Vacarro's luxury one, before everybody decided what they were going to do.

Down along the bulkhead, boats were tying up, or pushing off. A few kids were cleaning fish. For the last several minutes he had been watching a contest between seagulls and terns for scraps. The gulls were bigger and stronger, but slow and gangly in close quarters, and no contest for the lightning quick terns, who occasionally left the gulls an opening by breaking into fights among themselves.

At a nearby table, a couple of guys were hunched over their beers, talking over the noise of the fan and the marina. Sid thought he heard the older one say the name "Vacarro," as the bartender arrived with his drinks. Paying, he had his back toward them, and tried to focus on what they were saying. They got up and walked around the corner. Sid got his drinks and followed. They stopped out on the parking lot side, by the dumpster. Sid stood around the corner, and could hear them clearly.

The older one said, "I need some help, and it's going to be dangerous. There's a boat owned by this guy Tony Vacarro right now out in the gulf, around Breton Island. You know who that is?"

"That's the dude everybody says runs the New Orleans Mafia, right?"

"That's him, but he don't run a damn thing. It's this old man... anyway, that doesn't matter. The thing is, I need a favor, and I just wanted you to know who we're dealing with."

The younger one said, "Hell I'll do anything for you, bud. Especially if it's dangerous, I'm in."

The older one said, "Remember me telling you when we got drunk that time how I got in some trouble a while back?"

"Yeah, somebody tried to kill you out in the river?"

"Yeah. Well, I found out a way I can get all that taken care of. It involves some dirty business, and I can't do it alone."

The younger guy said, "I'm in, let's go."

"I need you to drive me out there right now. I have to get on that boat, and get right back off, and get away. You have to drive."

"What are you going to do?"

"You don't worry about it. You're just driving. Let's go."

They headed straight to the docks. Sid followed long enough to see what boat they got on, and saw it quickly pull away. He ran around to his pier, and untied the lines, and jumped on. He yelled for Angel to hang on, and headed out, causing too big of a wake, which caused some cussing along the edge of the marina. As soon as he cleared the no wake zone, he slammed the throttles down, and shot out toward the main channel of the Mississippi River. The other boat was fast, but his was faster, and Sid knew he'd catch them soon enough. They had to go out of the river at Baptiste Collete Bayou and head east to get to Breton Island.

Meanwhile, he was on the VHF radio, trying to hail the *Negotiable*. Cell phones didn't work where they were, and he knew the bad guys were probably on the same universal marine channel, so he tried not to sound urgent. It would not be unusual for any vessel out there to be receiving radio contact, especially one with bigshots aboard. He also knew that Tony and John, and whoever else might be there, were probably out on the back deck having drinks, and not listening for the VHF radio.

Ahead, the smaller boat sped toward Breton. The older one, the former Hoyt McGinnis, had gotten a written message that afternoon that was very clear: *The Negotiable is in Breton Sound. Tony Vacarro and an attorney named John Hart are aboard, and maybe others. Get on board however you have to. Kill the attorney. Kill everybody else if absolutely necessary. Do it this afternoon.* There was a paper picture of the lawyer. He had burned the note and picture, as instructed.

Pretty soon, Sid got within a couple miles

of the smaller boat, which he could see headed into the late afternoon red sky. They were rapidly approaching Breton, and he had not mentioned anything to Angel about what was going on. She was happily sipping her Bushwhacker, bouncing on the wide seat to the music blaring on the stereo, thinking they were zipping out to party on Vacarro's yacht.

Sid eventually realized he wasn't going to be able to warn Tony Vacarro and John in time. If he called the Coast Guard, they would be too late. If he tried to get to the *Negotiable* first, the bad guys would see it and kill them all. If he tried to overtake the bad guys, they would kill him and Angel, then everybody else. Breton would soon be in sight. There was only one thing to do. He slowed down, reached in his overhead storage and grabbed a ditty bag with a waterproof satellite phone in it. He turned the phone on through the heavy plastic. He turned off the music, and handed Angel the phone. "Hold this," he said, and reached under their padded seat, and pulled out a life jacket.

"Put this on, please," he said.

"Angel said, "What's wrong, are we sinking?"

"He said, "No. Listen, I don't have time to explain. Call the Coast Guard. It's speed dial number one. Then call the Plaquemines Parish sheriff, it's number two. I'll see you soon." He scooped her up and threw her overboard before she could say anything. He circled her once, making sure she was floating, and had the phone. She screamed, "What the hell is going on?!"

He yelled back, "I love you, lady! I'll explain later!" He roared away, hoping he had enough time to overtake the bad guys. After a couple minutes, he saw them, and began rapidly gaining. He was nearly on top of the killers, intending to ram their boat with his, when they saw him, and veered. Sid sped by and one of them started shooting at him. Sid whipped his boat around and they headed south, for some reason. He had the angle and the speed, and sped directly toward the driver's side. He could clearly see the older one firing away, the gun flashing in the waning light, bullets pinging off his metal flybridge supports.

At the last second, the young boat driver cut back to the right, and Sid's bigger vessel went right over theirs, stem to stern, then flipped several times, stopping upside down, where it stayed. The smaller boat, gutted of its transom, outboards, and passengers, briefly caught on fire, then gulped a ton of seawater, and sank. Sid's broken engines, sticking straight up, sputtered and smoked, then choked and stopped. Then it was quiet, except for a squad of squawking seagulls that flew over from Breton Island to see if there was anything fit to eat.

Vacarro and Hart, and Vacarro's date, a young lady from Gulf Shores, Alabama he had met the day before at Canecutter's, had not been on the back deck. They were inside, where they had the music blaring, and were waiting on Sid and Angel. They hadn't seen or heard anything, and when their guests never showed up, they grilled shrimp out back, drank all Vacarro's good wine, and went to sleep. John Hart did, anyway.

It was the next morning before they discovered that there had been some kind of accident. By then, Angel had been rescued by the Coast Guard, and Sidney Fortenberry was declared officially missing in the Gulf of Mexico.

The judge in Captain Fleming's will probate had listened to, and ultimately rejected a few attempts to claim the pirate treasure, which had first been revealed in the inventory filed by John Hart. A matter of public record, it had been discovered by the whole town, then the whole internet. Five people from Pearlington had filed sworn affidavits, claiming to be heirs of the Captain, but couldn't prove it. One man from up the Pearl River claimed to be his son by "common law adoption" which the judge said did not exist in the law.

Nobody could prove a blood connection to the pearls, and it didn't matter anyway. The judge ruled that Arthur Fleming had left a handwritten, holistic will. That meant since nobody with standing could prove the old man was under duress, or undue influence, or impaired at the time to the point of not understanding his actions, then all those pearls belonged to Attorney John Hart. And that was it.

The Bay Saint Louis law office of Hart Law Firm, PLLC, was open for one last day of business. Sammy Ward hobbled up to the front door and knocked. A temporary employee answered, and led him upstairs. It took him some effort to get up to the conference room, where they both sat, along with a Mrs. Jennifer Shannon, who was an attorney and a vice president of the bank downstairs. She had been appointed Trustee of a trust fund set up by John Hart, she said. She was there to explain to Sammy Ward what her business had to do with his.

The testate estate of Arthur Fleming had finally been closed, she told him, after several hearings. Its proceeds had been passed to John Hart, who had set up an irrevocable trust, and gotten her appointed Trustee. Those pearls were in the trust, and were to be auctioned off over time. It was a *lot* of money, she emphasized, because natural pearls are rare, and crazily expensive, and there were thousands of them, so the trust fund's assets would be in the multi-millions.

Sammy said, "Mrs. Shannon, this is all real interesting, but why in the world did you call me? And where is Johnny? I got a letter from him saying he was moving, but it didn't say where."

"Mr. Hart has taken an extended leave of absence. He set all this up before he left, and it has something to do with you."

"But where is he?"

"I couldn't tell you, even if I knew."

"So why am I here?"

"Because, although the trust has many beneficiaries, the public school district, for example, and many local charities, you are the first one named."

"I don't understand," he said.

"It means you, as a beneficiary, get paid a certain amount of money from the trust, every month, for the rest of your life. And when you pass, your daughter, the disabled one who lives with you, will also be supported for the rest of her life. Mr. Hart wanted to make sure that you never have to worry about money again, Mr. Ward. Congratulations."

For the second time in his life, Sammy Ward, the tough kid who had once gotten famous making The Jump, sat in attorney John Hart's office and cried.

The Coast Guard finally gave up looking for Sid Fortenberry. It was a mystery. His boat had some signs of receiving gunfire, and the other one was just too damaged to tell what happened. It looked like the men in the two boats had just gotten into some kind of a pissing match, and the two dead guys shot at Sid, and he ran them over. What happened to Sid, nobody figured out. Angel's version, even though she was a cop, just sounded fishy. How the hell did she wind up floating around with a satellite phone while everybody else was dead? In Venice, everybody just assumed that it was some kind of drug thing, that old Sidney Fortenberry had finally just partied too hard, and went way too far over the line. News that he last had a Bushwhacker before going kamikaze on his assailants touched off an historic run on sales of the drink, which all around the gulf was renamed a "Sid Vishus."

Sitting at a bar in the shady slated courtyard of a converted old townhouse in the Bahama Village area of Key West, John Hart ordered a beer. Nearby, under a giant avacado tree, three ladies at a table were drinking something that had to do with mangoes. One of them kept glancing at him, and he was either going to have to go talk to her, or retreat. He knew it was probably going to be the latter.

Tony Vacarro spun around in his barstool and said, "Hey Bud, you're gonna have to brighten up. Forget about my crazy sister. She'll come back around someday, and if she doesn't, too bad for her. There are many, many more fish in the sea, especially in Key West, baby. For instance, that lady right over there has been wanting you to come to her table for a while now." He had been engaged in some lively conversation with his half of the bar, and spun back around and ordered a round of drinks for all of them, who had no idea who he was.

It had been several months since he last saw Lisette. Thinking of her still made him smile. Before he met her he had been down, as low and depressed as a man could be. Afterwards, he started getting better, and she had been the reason. But then she was gone. He'd been around and around the scenario in his head, and there was no good answer. She was just gone.

So much had happened in the short time they were together. It was luck they had even met. He had intended to give the money back to Vacarro, but he was out of the office that day in New Orleans, and Lisette was there. Otherwise, he would never have known her. Later, the wrongful death case had been in the ditch, and then the insurance company settled it. She was like his good luck charm.

But the part about her testifying, was he really to blame? He didn't even know what she was going to say, because of the circumstances of the case, the timing. If she was in trouble, why couldn't she just come with him? They could have avoided The Raven together indefinitely with the money he had gotten from the settlement. And she had her own money, anyway, a lot more than him. Besides, The Raven couldn't actually live forever, could he? Her just disappearing from his life made no sense.

Unless... there was this faint inkling of a

possibility. He had told her the state's case was shot when they couldn't locate their witness, the one that saw and heard an argument between Vacarro and the dead guy. Right after that, the anonymous call came in, and then the video of her buying the phone. And then there was her testimony, which probably saved the case for him. Half the jury obviously believed The Raven was behind everything, and that information came from one source, Lisette. Testifying took the heat off her, too. So... was it even remotely possible that she was somehow in on it all?

But that would have made her complicit in the murder of Rilo Marshall, and her brother's arrest, and his own hiring, and maybe settling the civil case, and the blood evidence on the boat, and pinning the murder on The Raven, then leaving him all alone again and cutting off communications. It was all too much. It couldn't be true, because that would make her some kind of a criminal mastermind, and a pathologically cold, calculating liar. She was just too good of a person, and he felt like a guilty ass even thinking about it.

He checked out the lady across the courtyard, and knew he was going to have to make a move someday soon. It was time for him to learn, once again, to get on with his life. He had spent so much of it suffering over the past. But no more. Like Captain Fleming said, it was time to get the hell away from being sad. He decided to wait until next time to make that walk, meet that new lady. He paid the bartender, and waived at Tony, and strolled over toward Duval Street, and Mallory Square, and the sunset.

Walking, he thought of the father he never knew, of the sister he never really knew, of his wife and mother, and the child he never had. Maybe he was just not allowed to love. Maybe his life was just some experiment for the amusement of some greater being. Or maybe he was just unlucky that way, and it didn't matter to anyone but himself. He thought about Sid. They were supposed to meet at the boat that evening. What the hell happened? Did Sid go crazy, and get in a fight with those guys, and get himself killed? That just didn't sound like Sid. He was always too happy for it to end that way. Still, he was gone. He thought of Captain Fleming, who had lost everything, and in doing so, learned how to be truly free. The Captain would not compromise his bitter freedom, even for all the riches the damned universe could offer. So it finally killed him, and in doing so, released a fortune that would help innumerable other people who needed it. And he thought about Sammy Ward. Maybe in the end God really did love bravery.

Walking down the sidewalk, dodging the cruise ship tourists, and the traffic, and drunks on scooters, he thought of his own life, about how that movie had turned out, so far. First he hadn't cared at all, then he had cared too much. Then fate tried to destroy him, and almost did. Then Lisette came along, and made it all okay, for a little while. He got to Mallory Square just before sunset and the daily swivel cannon blast. He moved among the throngs of tourists, and hustlers, and locals, and kids laughing and running, and passed a clever dog named Beauregard who was always down there, and would eat the pulp out of a whole coconut if you cracked it open for him first.

John Hart stopped at the edge of the square, at the end of the continent, and of the world as far as he was concerned. He squinted at the blazing red western horizon. The sun just barely touched the Caribbean, and the swivel cannon boomed, and the crowd cheered, and he thought of Lisette.

Always, Lisette.

THANKS TO:

Jacob Johnson, Laura Haas, David Buck, Lynn Hightower, Steve Haas, and Hayes Johnson for their assistance in editing and formatting this book. A special thanks to Laura for reminding the author that just one is all it takes.

Made in the USA
Columbia, SC
20 June 2020